Myths, Gods & Immortals

Circe

New & Ancient Greek Tales

FLAME TREE PUBLISHING

Contents

FOREWORD

Dr Ellie Mackin Roberts 6

ANCIENT & MODERN: INTRODUCING CIRCE

by Imogen Dalton 10

1. A Multifaceted Goddess.. 11

2. The Real World around Circe's Myths 43

3. Impact and Influence: Circe's Far Reach in
Cultures Through the Centuries................................... 57

4. Conflicts, Controversies and Misuses..................... 75

MODERN SHORT STORIES OF CIRCE

Rise of the Witches

L.D. Burke 121

Darkness

Z.D. Campbell 138

A Mother's Blessing

C.B. Channell.. 152

No Good Curse

Mason Graham 170

CONTENTS

The Island of Pigs
Kay Hanifen 188

Something New
M.J. Harris.. 204

This Slow Death
Elena Kotsile... 219

Shifting Destinies
Claire L. Marsh... 234

Pork
Erin Murphy 252

A Friend Made of Clay
Lourdes Ureña Pérez... 267

Prove Them All Right
Elizabeth Roberts 279

From Darkness, Awake
Zach Shephard 292

The Circead
Jamie Simpher... 315

The Perfect Distance
Theresa Tyree.. 328

Blood Stains the Golden Fleece
Mathieu W.R. Wallis 347

BIOGRAPHIES **362**

MYTHS, GODS & IMMORTALS...................................**367**

FLAME TREE FICTION **368**

Foreword

Dr Ellie Mackin Roberts

Few figures in Greek mythology are as enigmatic as Circe, the daughter of Helios, the sun god, and the Ocean nymph Perse, with famous siblings Aeëtes (keeper of the Golden Fleece) and Pasiphaë, who marries King Minos to become Queen of Crete and later mother of the Minotaur. So Circe is both divine, and a part of a network of other powerful mythological figures whose stories are foundational in the mythic landscape of ancient Greece.

Homer's 7th-century BCE epic poem, *The Odyssey*, is one of her earliest mentions in literature. She lives alone on the island of Aiaie, although Homer does not tell us where it is located. When Odysseus lands there, she transforms many of his dwindling crew into pigs, immediately placing her into the role of antagonist. Yet, as the story moves on, the impression the audience is given of Circe transforms, and she becomes an invaluable ally to Odysseus. This duality is central to her representation; she is both dangerous and helpful, a powerful magician, and a source of wisdom. Her relationship with Odysseus is characterized by both intimacy and respect and subverts the expected power dynamics and gender roles of the time – and which we see in the rest of the poem.

A second major source for Circe is Apollonius of Rhodes's epic *Argonautica*, written in the middle of the 3rd century BCE, where Jason and Medea visit Circe to seek out purification for the murder of Medea's brother. Here, she is not simply a caster of magic but a healer and purifier. This episode in Circe's mythos is a key example of the complex role of the witch in ancient contexts. Witches like Circes do not just practise magic, but have knowledge of herbs and other natural remedies that we would now consider the realm of traditional medicine. This complicated role demonstrates how they can serve as intermediaries between the divine and mortal worlds – this is why Circe is able to purify the pair. The act of purification is deeply symbolic, representing the restoration of balance and the lifting of miasma ('pollution'), from the individual and – by extension – the community. Circe's ability to purify the pair underscores her importance within the narrative as a figure of authority and knowledge, as someone who transcends the typical boundaries of mortal and divine law.

The portrayal of Circe across various ancient sources further illustrates the elasticity of her myths. In Roman poet Ovid's *Metamorphoses*, written in the early 1st century CE, her story is deeply tragic: here, she is a sorceress driven by love and rejection. This is where we hear that it was Circe – driven by jealousy – who turned Skylla from a nymph into a monster, and transformed King Picus into a woodpecker after he rejected her advances. That such variation can occur even within the ancient world shows that Circe is a character filled with adaptability, but this also reflects the preoccupation of ancient authors with themes of transformation, the interplay between the mortal and divine worlds, and the way women are driven by the male protagonists of their stories. Circe's dual identity as both a divine and magical figure encapsulates the ancient world's ambivalence towards women who wield power and independence. After all, Circe not only lives alone, but turns the men who arrive on her shores into animals.

Beyond the ancient world, Circes's story has been manipulated by countless writers and artists, each breathing a new life into her. In the Middle Ages, she was often interpreted as a cautionary figure, embodying the perils of enchantment and the subversion of the natural order. The revival of classical antiquity in the Renaissance renewed interest in Greek and Roman mythology, with Circe playing the part of cautionary tale as the archetypical 'predatory woman'. More recently, we have witnessed new reimaginings of Circe's story, with fictional works such as Madeline Miller's *Circe* offering a portrayal of a woman charting her own destiny, a stark contrast to her traditional depiction as a character defined by her interactions with male heroes.

Circe's transformation into a feminist icon is a striking testament to her narrative's adaptability. She has transcended her role as a frustrator of male protagonists, emerging as a beacon of female empowerment and resistance. Her evolution from a character whose identity is shaped by the desires and actions of men to one who forges her own path and asserts her autonomy resonates with many contemporary audiences. This shift not only mirrors the changing societal attitudes towards

FOREWORD

gender, but also highlights the enduring relevance of her story in the ongoing discourse of female agency and power.

In the broader context of Greek mythology, the many ways Circe's story has been told are a powerful reminder of the capacity of myths to reflect and shape the human experience. Her story, rich in the themes of transformation, power and identity, continues to inspire and provoke thought. As we – and the authors in this volume – delve deeper into the ancient world's narratives, Circe stands as a symbol of the intricate relationship between myth and society and the unceasing dialogue between our past and our present.

Circe and the mythology that surrounds it is a clear demonstration of the enduring power and adaptability of ancient stories. From the ancient world, and throughout time, she is a figure of remarkable complexity and transformation. She challenges us to reconsider what power, autonomy and femininity are, both then and now. She is a reminder of the expanse of human imagination and the enduring dialogue between the past and the present.

Dr Ellie Mackin Roberts

Ancient & Modern: Introducing Circe

by Imogen Dalton

1.
A Multifaceted Goddess

'We received the cups presented by her sacred right hand. Soon as, in our thirst, we quaffed them with parching mouth, and the ruthless Goddess, with her wand, touched the extremity of our hair (I am both ashamed, and yet I will tell of it), I began to grow rough with bristles, and no longer to be able to speak; and, instead of words, to utter a harsh noise, and to grovel on the ground with all my face.'
– Ovid, *Metamorphoses*

CIRCE: THE EVER-CHANGING ICON

The myth of Circe, as well as many others, takes on multiple forms. It morphs and changes, as any good myth should, within the cultural context to which it belongs. Circe is now not only a plot device in the stories of other, 'more famous' mythological characters; she also takes on a life of her own, giving new and important meaning to being a seductress, a sorceress, a witch and a woman.

HOMER'S ODYSSEY

Circe's main mythological story comes from the famous epic poem attributed to the ancient Greek writer Homer. This poem tells the tale of the classic Greek hero Odysseus, and of his long journey home following the infamous Trojan War. Odysseus comes across our heroine, Circe, as he travels home to Ithaca from Troy after he and his men have just encountered the Laestrygonians, a race of man-eating giants. Odysseus's ship was the only one to escape.

Having reached the island of Aeaea, Odysseus stays behind while his men go in search of help. The men are understandably feeling disheartened at this point; they are seeking shelter and then find it with Circe – well, sort of… Circe is in fact a powerful enchantress with a knack for turning humans into animals. The men find Circe's home surrounded by tame lions and wolves who greet them happily. From outside they can hear Circe's enchanting singing and so they enter – except for Eurylochus, Odysseus's brother-in-law, who is wary and suspicious. Circe gives the men a potion mixed into their wine and turns them physically into pigs, although emotionally and mentally they are still human. Eurylochus escapes and runs back to Odysseus to tell him the news.

On the way to confront Circe Odysseus comes across Hermes, the messenger god, who gives him a magical plant called moly to protect him against Circe's sorcery. When Odysseus drinks the wine he does not change into a pig as his comrades have done; instead, he attempts to kill the enchantress with his sword. Defeated on this occasion, Circe suggests that they take to the bed instead and make love. She then vows to never harm Odysseus, before turning his men back into their original human form.

Odysseus and his men remain with Circe for a year, during which time he and Circe enjoy the pleasure of being lovers and his men relax with much merriment and feasting. When it is time for him to leave, Circe gives Odysseus important advice. She tells him to visit Hades in order to consult the spirits of the dead and to gather warnings about more dangers that await him on his journey home to Ithaca.

DIFFERENT STORIES IN DIFFERENT MYTHS

Circe is said in some myths to have had three sons by Odysseus as a result of this relationship; Agrius, Latinus and Telegonus. The last of these goes on to mistakenly murder his father as an adult. In other versions of her story Telegonus is Circe's only child by Odysseus; he again mistakenly becomes the murderer of his father. Circe plays a part in some other myths too. She is the aunt of the powerful witch Medea, famous for murdering her own sons to revenge herself on her cheating husband Jason (of Argonaut fame). Prior to this, when Medea and Jason are returning home with the Golden Fleece that Jason was challenged to acquire, Circe assists them in rituals of purification – until she learns that the couple's need of purification is caused by their murder of Apsyrtus, Medea's younger brother. In Madeline Miller's version Circe regrets assisting the couple with this.

In his *Metamorphoses,* the Roman poet Ovid describes how when Picus, the son of Saturn, rejects Circe romantically she turns him into a woodpecker for revenge. Another instance of

Circe's anger occurs in her treatment of the nymph Scylla. In Ovid's tale the sea-god Glaucus goes to Circe for a potion to make the nymph Scylla fall in love with him, only for Circe to fall in love with Glaucus herself. She then turns Scylla into a hideous monster, doomed to prey on sailors.

Circe features several times in Homer's *Odyssey*, her influence providing a necessary plot line to Odysseus's own story. She is first mentioned in Book 9 of the *Odyssey*, which tells of his encounter with the Cyclops. Here Odysseus speaks of how both Calypso and Circe had wanted him for a husband. He mentions Circe in passing, describing the time he spent with her and the way that she managed to 'detain' him. This introduction to Circe tells us much about her, or rather about Odysseus's interpretation of the enchantress, before we even meet her. She comes across as desperate and manipulative for holding Odysseus against his will when he was on an important journey.

Circe as a Lover

The next time we see Circe mentioned in the *Odyssey* is in Book 10, which recounts the story of Odysseus and Circe in detail. Odysseus describes how they found Circe's island of Aeaea, referring to her as a beautiful goddess with a woman's voice. The daughter of the sun god Helios and Perse, the daughter of the ocean, this description is not without affection; the notion of Circe being someone whom Odysseus would reject and think poorly of does not necessarily ring true.

In the first passage of course, Odysseus is speaking to a king; in telling him the story of his adventures, he is quite likely trying to present a certain impression of himself. Upon seeing red smoke coming from the chimney to Circe's house, Odysseus dispatches an exploring party to investigate for him rather than going himself – ultimately sacrificing the men he sends, as he probably assumes the house to be unsafe or at least suspicious. Eurylochus goes to explore with 22 men and they come across Circe's house. Outside, in alignment with other depictions of Circe, are many prowling beasts, including lions and wolves. Within the house they can hear Circe singing in a beautiful female voice. For men, women's singing can be a dangerous lure in the mythological world, suggesting a possible sign of danger. However, as Circe is found singing and weaving on a loom, it suggests that she is content and calm in her own world, not expecting a party of men to arrive at her home. Once she is aware of them, Circe's voice calls to the men to enter.

Lovely and Evil?

Odysseus comes across Circe's house and he finds her the same as ever, singing and lovely. She welcomes him into her home, where she shows Odysseus hospitality. He describes her as a 'lovely goddess', yet claims that when she gives him the poison, it is with evil in her heart. Certainly this seems a contradictory way of describing someone. In this context, however, 'lovely' means beautiful and attractive to him.

The events unfold exactly as Hermes had warned Odysseus they would before he entered Circe's house; first the poison, then Odysseus's attempt to attack Circe with his sword, then the subjugation. She in turn vocalizes her surprise, realizing that it is Odysseus that she is facing, then invites him to her bed so they can learn to trust one another. Odysseus resists at first, saying that he has concern for his manhood, but Circe swears that she meant him no further harm. And so Odysseus agrees to accompany Circe to her 'beautiful bed'. She and her maids set about making Odysseus as comfortable as possible, bathing him, covering him in oils and setting out a feast for him. When Odysseus is unable to eat, Circe asks him the reason; it is, of course, because his men were not yet free of her spells. Circe then leaps to attend to Odysseus's will and changes back his men, even improving on their original health, age and looks!

After a very emotional reconciliation Circe tells him to bring his boat on to land and then come back and rest with his men. On his return Odysseus finds his men bathed, oiled and eating with Circe. She convinces Odysseus to stay with her; after all his ordeals, it is time for him to learn to enjoy life again. They stay together for a year, and Odysseus would apparently have stayed even longer if his men had not told him it was time to leave. They enjoy one final day of feasting and wine, after which Odysseus goes back to Circe's beautiful bed one more time and explains that it is time for him to leave. Circe does not put up a fight (maybe she's had enough of all the bathing and feeding too?) and she leaves him with a warning about his onward journey. The next morning she dresses Odysseus and herself and then disappears, leaving the party with a black ram and ewe as a blessing.

KINDNESS AND HOSPITALITY

In Book 12 of the *Odyssey*, Odysseus revisits Circe's island to bury his friend Elpenor after the party return from their visit to Hades. Circe welcomes them back and again displays her hospitable side, offering them meat, wine and handmaidens. She tells them to rest until the morning when she herself will guide them onward. As they lie side by side – in a position of affection and trust – Odysseus tells Circe the story of their trip to the underworld. She then again helps Odysseus with his onward journey by warning him about dangers still to come and suggesting how to overcome them. She tells Odysseus to plug his men's ears so they are not enchanted by the music of the Sirens, then tells him of the two difficult routes he faces: one with scary, dangerous birds and the other with a feared and dangerous monster called Scylla, known to devour the crews of entire ships. Odysseus asks if there is an easier way and Circe responds by calling him an 'obstinate fool'. Yet she continues to explain why Scylla is to be feared so much.

Circe reveals to Odysseus that Scylla was brought into the world by her mother to be the bane of mankind (a different story of origin to many). The only way to evade her is for the sailors to call on her mother Cratais and force their way through on their ship; even then they will inevitably lose some men. She then gives her final warning about a flock of sheep that Odysseus needs to be careful not to harm. Once Circe has finished her predictions and warnings, she sends Odysseus's ship on its way with a favourable wind. His final description of her is 'that formidable goddess with the beautiful hair and the woman's voice'.

And so the story of their time together comes to its close. Odysseus certainly needed Circe on his journey, even if what brought him to her in the first place was an act of evil: the horror of having some of the men of his party transformed into pigs. Yet had he not come across Circe's island and experienced her many interventions, Odysseus's story would be quite different.

CIRCE'S OTHER ORIGINS

In Ovid's *Metamorphoses* Circe is described as the daughter of Helios, the sun god, and of Perse, a sea nymph. She is famed for her beauty and her magical ability.

Let us think about Circe's main myth first. She lives a life of peaceful solitude, on an island, without disturbances: a life that many modern women would dream of. We must interpret for ourselves why the men she comes across are turned into beasts. Perhaps it is because they are trying to harm her or disturb her peace. Maybe they reject her romantically (certainly this did not turn out well for Picus). Or she may have feared that they would seek to control her. Whatever her reasons are, Circe is taking no bother from anyone, particularly men.

When Odysseus's party first encounter Circe, she is alone at home, going about her day and singing to herself. I don't know about you, but when I am alone and singing to myself it's because I am happy and content. Yet Circe's immediate reaction is to bewitch the men and turn them into pigs. Perhaps she felt threatened. Yet I wouldn't necessarily see her as a scared or threatened figure – rather one who chooses to exploit her ability to put men in their place, keeping her life and home as they are. In so doing she avoids the trouble of bringing a lot of strange men into her world, when she has been scorned before.

Circe and the Néreïds

In Ovid's version of the tale the party find Circe in her palace; she is directing Néreïds (nymphs) in sorting herbs and flowers, ingredients for magical potions. She greets the party graciously, then instructs the Néreïds to concoct a certain potion which the party gratefully accept, then drink. Circe then casts a spell on the men and they turn into pigs, with Ovid's trademark descriptions of the process of metamorphosis.

Often in Greek myth we are left to interpret for ourselves why people have acted in the way that they do. Just because Odysseus was a Greek hero, he was certainly not perfect or even necessarily a nice person at the best of times. This is particularly true of men in ancient Greece, held to a completely different standard to women in terms of honour and integrity. Odysseus is often described as arrogant, selfish and disrespectful. We may speculate that Circe knew this, so took it upon herself to teach him a lesson. Often the story we know only shows the hero's point of view.

Medea and Jason

Circe features in the *Orphic Argonautica*, an epic Greek poem dating from the fourth century CE. In the voice of Odysseus, it tells the story of Jason, the Argonauts and their quest to find the Golden Fleece. He is sent on the mission by Pelias, the king of Iolcus. As a child Jason had been sent away by his mother to keep him safe; he was raised by the centaur Chiron. Pelias knew that Jason was the rightful king of Iolcus, so when met the adult Jason he sent him away on what he believed to be an impossible mission – to retrieve the Golden Fleece.

Medea is Circe's niece through her brother, and therefore of the same divine lineage of Helios. She is made to fall in love with Jason by Aphrodite, the goddess of love, because Hera (wife of Zeus, the king of the gods) wanted to help Jason; Medea had the skills that would be useful to him. So it comes about that Jason marries Medea. The dramatic and tragic consequences of their liaison are told in different ways in Greek literature, but most famously in Euripides's tragedy *Medea*. Another powerful goddess character, Medea is extremely divisive and controversial, but driven to be so at the hands of a man who exploited her. Jason cheats on his wife when she is no longer useful, replacing her with a princess as his new bride. She then murders their two infant children in an act of revenge.

Of course Medea's skills in cold-blooded murder are what Jason needed her for in the first place; she assisted him in this way on a few occasions. This is what brings her to Circe's island; having killed her brother Absyrtus, she needs Circe's powers to cleanse her of the deed. On their arrival on Circe's island, the couple are surprised to find Circe, not men, as the resident of the island: another example of Circe not adopting the expected behaviour of women in ancient Greece. Described as beautiful and shining, in the *Orphic Argonautica* Circe addresses Medea and agrees to help her atone for the murder of Absyrtus. She will help the couple to cleanse, although she says they may not enter her house until this has been achieved. This is in contrast to Miller's tale where she finds out after the rite what the couple have done and says that had she known what they did she would not have performed the ritual. Yet Circe is a nurturing and caring host who still prepares food and wine for them to have on their ship. She advises them to cleanse themselves on the shores of Maleia, before they return home.

The Telogony

Another great resource we have for discovering more about Circe is the *Telegony*. This is a story of Telegonus, the son of Circe and Odysseus. It is described as a lost poem by scholars in that very little of the original poem remained to be reinterpreted over time. This is the epilogue to Homer's *Odyssey*.

Some literature says that Circe had three sons, one of whom was Telegonus. This is recorded by Hesiod and Dionysius of Halicarnassus. This knowledge introduces another aspect of the character of Circe: the mother. For Circe's sons to survive infancy (unlike Medea's, for example) and to become adults and by some accounts rulers, we must consider Circe to be a loving and nurturing person. It does not seem unusual to think of her as being nurturing and caring now we have seen her hospitable side; she is clearly helpful with people, such as Medea and Odysseus. So the image of her as a cruel and evil witch does not really fit here. Having seen this aspect of her nature, we can imagine even more her kindness and patience as a mother.

Odysseus believed that he would be killed by his son because he was told so by a seer. He did have multiple sons, however, including Telemachus with his wife Penelope, who he believed would be his killer. When Telegonus was an adult, Circe gave him a spear tipped with the barb of a stingray so that his father would recognize him when he went to find him; in some versions of the myth she encouraged him to meet his father and introduce himself. As his guards were aware that a son of Odysseus would be his killer, the more Telegonus insisted that he should see his father the more determinedly they resisted him. At this Telegonus got angry and went on a killing spree with the guards. They believed that it was Telemachus in disguise and warned the king when they could.

Odysseus assumed that Telegonus had been sent by Telemachus and went to attack him first with a spear. Telegonus then threw a spear back and mortally wounded Odysseus, who believed him to be a stranger; he was thus deeply relieved that Telemachus had not committed patricide. At this point Telegonus realized that he had in fact killed his father and lamented dramatically. Telemachus took over

Odysseus's role in the kingdom, giving its far reaches to his brother Telegonus.

CIRCE THE MODERN ICON

A more recent retelling of Circe's tale is *Circe* by Madeline Miller, published in 2018. There are dozens of examples of the stories of mythological characters, retold with modern language and offering more modern and in-depth interpretations for characters such as Circe who have not historically had their own stories. Some stick to the original tales of Homer; others reimagine and reinterpret the story from the point of view of a character not previously given a voice. This is particularly powerful in the cases of mythological women, who may well be as misunderstood or prejudged as real women are today, or of same-sex relationships that have been misinterpreted or trivialized over the years. These characters are now providing powerful and relatable content for the modern reader.

Miller's story begins at the very beginning of Circe's life. It gives her a traumatic backstory and a neglectful childhood that explains her behaviour towards others. It shows her as misunderstood, complex and thoughtful. The changing of Scylla into a monster is something that she will try to reverse; it causes her frequent regret throughout her life because she has a sympathy for humans. She also has a complex relationship with her family, with her mother, father and siblings all adding flavour and motive to Circe's actions.

CIRCE'S SPELLS: JEALOUSY AND REVENGE IN MADELINE MILLER'S CIRCE

Circe's desire is for Glaucus to transform into his truest self – although whether or not this is how her spells work is debatable. Why some would transform into a monster, others into pigs and Glaucus into a sea god is an interesting consideration. However, Glaucus's lifelong job as a fisherman and his special relationship with the sea make it logical for him to be transformed into a god of the sea. When he changes, he becomes so far beyond human that even Circe is shocked and surprised. His skin turns blue, barnacles appear on his skin and he grows a long, green beard. Glaucus feels in himself the power, energy and strength of being immortal. This vitality, and the accompanying lack of pain, fuel his desire to be among the gods and be their equal.

Glaucus quickly becomes obsessed with his life as a god; hungry for power, his attention and devotion to Circe disappear. She has created what she thought she wanted, but in the process she changes him so much so that he would not – and could not – be what she wanted any more. His humanity is ultimately what she fell in love with; his transformation did not simply make Glaucus immortal, but it also made him inhuman. By her action Circe isolated herself from him, just as she was from all of her divine family. Ultimately she was pushed away in favour of them. At this critical point Glaucus noticed Scylla, a beautiful nymph who caught his eye. As a newly powerful sea god, Glaucus could have anyone he chose.

He sought to marry Scylla because of her beauty, a prize to be won by whichever god is deemed most worthy.

THE BEGINNING OF THE END

Circe believes that Scylla's intentions are not kind when she shows attention and affection to Glaucus. She thinks perhaps it is to take something from someone more divine than her, as a story to tell or because she enjoys making fun of Glaucus's form. At this stage Circe cannot believe that Scylla and Glaucus will be a good enough match, and she is convinced that she should be in Scylla's place. This sparks many feelings of injustice and inadequacy that inspire her subsequent actions. These change the course of her life forever, driven by emotions that can be described as self-centred and delusional.

Most people (although not all) appreciate that just because you want something you cannot have, you cannot ruin other people's lives for that reason. Yet this awareness is the difference between the divine world of the gods and the world of humans. For a god it is nothing to strike fear and wrath into the heart of your enemies. Although we may perceive many nurturing, caring and sweet sides to Circe, she is still a divine goddess – her instinct is thus to act in a way that will punish beyond comprehension.

A TERRIFYING MISTAKE

When Circe seeks to harm and to exact revenge on Scylla, she doesn't really know or comprehend what the outcome of her actions will be. When she transformed Glaucus her intention was for him to be immortal and to be hers as a husband and a lover, but she also intended for him to take on his 'truest form'. It is debatable whether or not this is what happens when Circe causes the transformations of those she targets with her sorcery, but her intention with Scylla was the same. She wanted Scylla's true form to be as ugly as she seems to Circe on the inside, revealing to the world that she is not the precious darling they all seem to think she is.

We may all have met people who seem to be treated a certain way because of how they look, yet on a deeper level are ugly inside. Unfairly, such people seem not to be treated as such because of how they look. Yet when we interact with people we often judge them on physical appearance, even if subconsciously; it is an unfortunate fact of the world in which we live. Circe's intention was simply to show Scylla's ugliness on the outside, fairly reflected in her physical appearance. She did not intend to turn Scylla into a monster beyond humanity, nor for her to become the reason and cause of the deaths of hundreds of sailors who crossed her path. When her sorcery went too far, Circe expected some sort of repercussion from her actions almost immediately.

In Miller's book she overhears her aunt discussing what happened to Scylla and decides to pretend that she knows nothing about it. The description she overhears tells of Scylla's transformation in graphic detail. The dramatic story also becomes the gossip of the court; Circe's own family seem to revel in the details of what happened, without considering the horror of what Scylla went through. The only person who seems to comprehend the awful outcome of events is ironically Circe herself. The one person who Circe wanted to discover Scylla's fate was Glaucus. She expected him to run to her when he did, but he inevitably points out that although it is a shame, there are many more beautiful nymphs where she came from. The whole debacle is thus an exercise in futility; it did not have the outcome Circe had hoped for, leaving her to live with the guilt of knowing what she had done.

Running in the Family

Circe bonded with her brother Aeetes over their common ability with sorcery. Aeetes takes the leading role; he has known how to use magic for longer and is therefore more experienced, able to share his knowledge with Circe. He even explains to her that it cannot be taught as such, but must be discovered. Aeetes goes on to admonish Circe for humiliating Helios with her skill; she needs to know how to use her powers if she does not want to be judged. He explains that the gods themselves are fearful of their skills as these are not something that they can influence or control, so to have a skill beyond the power of the gods is potentially very dangerous indeed.

At this point both Aeetes and Circe are unable to leave the residence of their father Helios until he has spoken to Zeus. A decision has to be made about what will happen to them: whether they are deemed dangerous enough to warrant punishment or whether the turmoil that Circe's sorcery has caused is enough. Aeetes's belief is that the spells Circe cast upon Glaucus and Scylla did not make them 'who they are within', but rather that the sorcery made them who Circe wanted them to be. This places more responsibility and guilt upon Circe, who has to come to terms with her part in their transformation.

The Confession

Circe then feels the need to confess her actions to Helios, admitting her responsibility for the terrifying transformation not only of Scylla, but also of Glaucus. In doing this she knows that she will be punished and is bearing in mind what happened to Prometheus when he was punished by Zeus for giving humankind the gift of fire. Yet Circe was ready and willing to take her punishment – perhaps because she had nothing left to lose now, as Glaucus would not choose her regardless of what happened to Scylla, or perhaps she wanted to be absolved of the guilt she carried. Either way, her brave action is not something that many would have done. Circe is a unique case among the gods and nymphs of her world.

When she confesses to Helios, he at first dismisses her. He says that the flowers she used cannot do what she intended them to; they have no power left at all, as he and Zeus had made sure of that. The way in which he dismisses her, even taunting Circe about her confession, aggravates his daughter further. Increasingly angry, she determines to show them that she does have the power to change others using *pharmekeia* (a Greek word meaning witchcraft). The resulting argument with her father caused him to punish her – not for her deeds, but simply for suggesting that she had the power to use the *pharmekeia*.

Helios uses his power as the sun god basically to burn Circe to a crisp. He knows that she will heal relatively quickly and survive as she is immortal, but he seeks to show her his true power and strength through physical punishment in order to make it clear that he is the one with the true power. How could she suggest that she has the power to act in the way that only the gods should act? She is powerless and could not act as she suggests. Helios is cruel in his reparations; he chars Circe's skin and limbs beyond recognition, torturing her to the point where she would probably wish she could die. Helios has no sympathy or softness for her as his daughter. On the contrary, it is likely that this makes him even crueller, conscious that he is being watched and judged for his family's actions.

Pharmakeia

Eventually Circe is healed enough to be almost back to her normality. She then receives a visit from Aeetes, her brother. He points out to both Circe and Helios that it was not the Fates that caused the transformation of Scylla and Glaucus, but Circe's actions with the use of *pharmakeia*. The reason Aeetes knows this to be true and knows the effects *pharmekeia* can have is because he has been practising it himself; he possesses the same abilities and can prove that *pharmekeia* is real, much to Helios's dismay. Aeetes gives Circe the title *'pharmakis'*, or 'witch', to explain her actions.

Circe appreciates that Helios's trepidation derives from fear – probably the realization that a *pharmakis* could become more powerful than even a god, and so something that he, and certainly Zeus, would need to control. Now a grown man and the king of Colchis, the treatment that Aeetes receives because of his skills is different to Circe's. People are more scared of her, but why is this so? The answer is in part that Aeetes is a man, and in the world of ancient Greece men are deemed to be more rational, less volatile and calmer. Yet this is not the only reason. Circe's actions involving Glaucus and Scylla are already well known and widely understood; those around her may well be alarmed that they could end up as monsters like Scylla. Such fears are sufficient to keep Circe isolated even before she is exiled.

Punishment

Zeus and Helios come to agreement regarding the fate of Circe and Aeetes. Helios knows that the most important thing to do is to appease Zeus however he can, while still saving face for his family. The power is held by all of Helios's children with Perse, but the other three are not seen as a threat: Aeetes has done no real harm and can be watched, Pasiphae is married to a son of Zeus and so can be controlled, while Perses lives further away. Circe is a problem to be solved, however. She sought out her powers herself, she disobeyed when Helios had warned her not to find the flowers and she has already caused serious damage.

It is thus deemed that Circe has the most power and is the most dangerous of Helios's four children with Perse. That is why she was then exiled. The others pose less of a threat – they don't understand in the way that Circe does, nor have they had her background of neglect, abuse, trauma and empathy with those who have been mistreated. This constitutes part of her threat to Zeus and the other Olympian gods, as well as Helios and any other Titans. Being exiled is in itself almost a confirmation of how she has been mistreated in general. Had she been cared for and treated well by her family, would they really have had any reason to fear her power? If that had been the case they would be excited and empowered by her skills, with no reason to be afraid.

RELATIONSHIPS WITH MORTALS AND IMMORTALS

Another god with whom Circe interacts is Hermes, the messenger of the gods. He is a mischievous trickster god, however, who chooses not only to cause problems for Circe but also to assist Odysseus. There is no explicit reason in classical mythology why Hermes decides it is his place to help Odysseus with the knowledge that Circe would try to enchant him, especially as many have already succumbed to her spells. Madeline Miller creates a romantic entanglement between Circe and Hermes that ends in irritation, particularly on Circe's part, as a reason for him to take this action.

Hermes is thus the god who in many versions of the myth warns Odysseus about Circe's spells. He may be acting as a messenger for Athena as he is a messenger god. He tells Odysseus that Circe will try to enchant him by giving him a potion; the only way to counteract this is to take a certain plant called moly. He also advises Odysseus that he must go to bed with Circe in order to appease her when she realizes that her spell has not worked. This is a tool used in the story to remove any kind of blame from Odysseus for succumbing to, then staying for some time with, someone considered a troubled woman of poor morals. Of course a hero couldn't make that decision for himself – even though the decision to stay with her for so long is certainly his own choice.

IN LOVE WITH A MORTAL

When Circe meets Glaucus she is already fond of mortals. Being likened to mortals from her family, along with her connection to Prometheus and his affection for and support of mortals, have both had an effect on her and influenced how she feels about mortals. Glaucus is a mortal fisherman whom Circe encounters before she is exiled, as described above. Initially her fascination derives simply from the fact that he is one of very few, or the only, mortal that she has met. Glaucus worships and adores her as a goddess, as any mortal should, and asks her to bless his nets so that he may catch more fish. Having not previously felt the adoration that comes simply from being a god, Circe is spellbound by it; she relishes her first taste of worship.

Gradually Circe becomes more and more attached to Glaucus and he to her. Their relationship is not romantic or sexual until she tells him the story of Prometheus. Glaucus is shocked to realize just how old Circe is, as the story is centuries old. Obviously this is nothing to an immortal, but it startles a mortal who has not considered how old a goddess could be. This gives Circe the impression that she is too human for the world of the gods and too divine for the world of the mortals; poised in between, she cannot fit in either way. Circe's love for Glaucus made her approach Helios and ask if he can make a mortal into a god so that she could marry him. Although her father had not promised her marriage to a god but to a prince or king, a god would certainly be acceptable – and either would be better than a mortal fisherman.

Taking Control

Circe is now beginning to contemplate what it would mean for her to love a mortal, as well as what it means to die and be no longer alive. She approaches her grandmother Tethys, the great sea nymph and goddess, to seek her advice on the matter. She asks about *pharmekeia*, having heard the word from Aeetes, but is chastised for even saying the word. This is when we begin to see how fearful the gods are of this sorcery, and thus to realize just how powerful it must be. It is at this point that Circe begins to scheme and plot how to harness this power for herself. It could be exactly what she needs to make Glaucus into the immortal that she desires, after which they could be together forever.

This is Circe's first experiment with *pharmekeia*. She does it for selfish reasons, without considering whether Glaucus would want to be immortal, or indeed without even asking him. Yet she is also guided by her own trauma and neglect – as well, of course, by her longing to be loved and accepted, and so she creates the spell that will make Glaucus divine and immortal. Madeline Miller beautifully describes how Circe tries to change Glaucus, but is unsuccessful at first, weeping for her loss as it did not work. Then she is visited by a deep 'inner knowing', a voice within that tells her the magic she needs from the flowers is in the sap.

Such inner knowing of how to make the magic work suggests that there is a bigger picture at play. Perhaps the Fates had already worked this story into Circe's life? Or maybe it is because the gods (possibly Athena?) knew that Circe needed to make certain mistakes in order to be exiled and so able to help Odysseus. Often these small actions are simply part of the bigger picture of what the gods or the Fates have planned.

CIRCE AS THE ARCHETYPAL PROTECTIVE MOTHER

Even when he is a child, the goddess Athena's attention is on Telegonus. She visits Circe and tells her that she wants to take Telegonus, even offering her another man and child in his place. At the time Circe is struggling with parenting Telegonus who is a difficult child to manage. However, she declines Athena's offer and spends much of Telegonus's childhood trying to shield him from the goddess. She casts spells all over the island to protect him, continuing to do so throughout his life until the young man decides that he wants to leave to find his father. When Telegonus returns after accidentally killing Odysseus, he brings Penelope, Odysseus's widow, and their son Telemachus with him. Athena returns to the island, offering Telemachus the chance to be her new hero. However, he declines; he is not the same kind of person that Odysseus and is not interested in what she suggests.

This is when Telegonus steps in. Much more inclined to dream of fortune and fame, he offers himself to Athena as her patron. Obviously this is devastating for Circe, who has spent Telegonus's whole life trying to protect him from the goddess. However, she knows that she cannot stop him now and eventually concedes; the will of a goddess is not something to battle, and neither is the will of her adult child. Eventually we all must release our children into the world to make their own mistakes and live their lives, heart wrenching though it may feel at the time. Even as an incredibly powerful sorceress, Circe cannot affect Telegonus's own will and make him stop wanting what Athena could offer. Even if she could, would she want to, knowing that he would not be happy forever living on the island with her? His time is limited in a way that hers is not, so the need for adventure may come from that fact. Telegonus has his own life and he wants to make the most of it while he is able – something that immortals do not need to consider in their own lives.

One final point is that the will of the gods will likely always win out. Athena was determined that Telegonus would be hers and eventually, of course, she will get her way – even if this involves defeating the powerful sorceress Circe.

Telegonus's Search for Odysseus

Circe's priority is to keep Telegonus safe, not only from Athena but also from the other dangers of life on an island. A typical part of motherhood is to try our hardest to keep our children safe until we can do so no longer; then we need to allow them to be free. This release of children into the wider world comes with fear and risks that you have never known before. However, we know from multiple accounts that Circe encourages Telegonus to find his father. She does not know that he will end up committing patricide, but she feels secure enough in her relationship and her ability to raise an independent, well-adjusted man that she can send him to find his father.

Her decision to release Telegonus is a sign that she believes in him and that she recognizes her job as a mother is done. It must be very difficult to send your child away to a foreign land not knowing when you will see them again or whether they will be safe; this must be a very hard decision to make. Yet Circe decided to make it, with what appears to be a very selfless determination to benefit her child rather than herself.

Concerns for Telegonus Finding Odysseus

In contrast to other versions of the story, Madeline Miller's Circe really does not want Telegonus to go and find his father. She has been protecting him until he safely made it to his late teens and then, when they assist some travellers to the island, he asks for help in making a boat, deciding that it is time for him to leave and go and find his father. Circe does not want him to go, but Telegonus declares that he would rather die than stay on the island forever. Again this is a part of parenting that most people will relate to, whether it is the side of Circe, Telegonus or both. When we become adults we want our freedom, and our parents inevitably worry that we may not be safe.

Circe is a normal mother in that regard. However, the difference is that she is battling gods and monsters instead of the monsters we think of in our own daily lives. She has cast spells on Telegonus and on her island in order to keep him safe, doing whatever she can within her own sphere. I'm sure this is something we often wish we could do too as parents, but we have less power to do so and so have to trust that our skills at teaching our children how to be safe and when to be cautious will have to do. Ultimately, whether human or divine, we have to let our children leave and find their own way in the world, figure out how to be safe and risk danger in the same ways we probably did as teenagers. This is what life is about when you are beginning the journey on your own instead of under your parents' watchful eye's.

For Circe, her upset and concern is amplified by the fact that she is a single mother. The relationship and attachment you have to your children as a single mother is different. You become more of each other's world in a way that is not possible if you are sharing parenting and sharing yourself with a partner too. Circe has to face the fact that one day Telegonus will die; unlike her, he is mortal. Eventually she will have to face the fact that he will die and she will not, regardless of how much she tries to protect him by using spells or keeping him on the island. This is a harsh fact of life for immortals who love mortals, unlike in the human world, where we mostly believe that our children will outlive us, and we know that losing a child must be the hardest thing in the world for anyone to experience. In Circe's world, losing her child is inevitable. Any mortal that she loves or gets close to – Odysseus, Daedalus, even her own son – will die, leaving her to live on with her grief eternally.

CIRCE AS A FRIEND AND LOVER

The relationship between Circe and Penelope, Odysseus's wife, within the context of Madeline Miller's retelling of the story is really interesting. Both women are aware of each other but they only come together after Odysseus's death, when Telegonus brings both Penelope and his half-brother Telemachus to Aeaea. Telegonus originally brings them out of guilt for what he mistakenly did in killing his father, and to give mother and son some sort of refuge from their grief and loss.

Inevitably while they are there Circe has significant relationships with both Telemachus, which is unquestionably romantic, and with Penelope. For the latter Circe has a large degree of respect and comes eventually to care for her deeply, in the way she usually does with others, once she is able to gauge whether they are a threat or not. This is, of course, exactly what Circe does first; she decides if she believes that Penelope and Telemachus will hurt her or, more importantly, her son, then learns to trust them and to work together with them. Circe allows Penelope to use the loom that was given to her by Daedalus. She houses and takes care of them both, even helping them to reconnect with one another, and holds off Athena when the goddess comes to claim Telemachus as her next patron hero.

An Unlikely Pairing

The women clearly connect over their love for the same man, with whom they both have deep and meaningful relationships. Circe always knew that her liaison had an expiration date while Penelope had to endure many years of being alone and waiting for her husband, partly because of Circe. Yet they respect each other for the individual ways in which they bonded with Odysseus. Circe also respects Penelope as a parent and as a creator, which is why she allows her to use the precious loom from Daedalus.

Although Circe and Penelope were destined to be opposites and unable to get along, in Madeline Miller's world they rub along together just fine. And why shouldn't they? The world needs harmony and balance. The good and the bad, heroes and villains, yet there's no way we can label either Penelope or Circe as 'good' or 'bad'; as we've already noticed, people (and gods) are rarely that simple. There are aspects of Circe that Penelope will recognize in herself and vice versa.

In fact, I believe that we all are likely to have both a bit of Penelope and a bit of Circe in us. A homebody who wants to nurture and be loyal as well as a fiercely independent woman who can look after herself and is severely protective of her world. As humans we change so regularly that one day we may think we want one thing and then change our minds the next. Women are by nature cyclical, with emotions often ruled by our hormones, so we cannot expect to want the same things or behave in the same way week on week. I think the time has come to acknowledge and accept that about ourselves.

BECOMING MORTAL

In Madeline Miller's tale of Circe, the enchantress makes the decision to sacrifice her immortality; she decides that immortality is not better than being human. The story ends with her living out her days in domestic bliss with Penelope's son (and her own son's half-brother) Telemachus and their two daughters. Penelope is also still on the island and a friend to Circe. They eventually grow old together, with Telemachus as well. Many humans would choose to swap with an immortal and live forever, believing that is what they really want. However, if as an immortal you actually have more connections, friends and family with humans than your divine kin, immortality means that you will inevitably end up outliving everyone you love and care about: your partner, friends or children. As a mortal Circe is able to treasure the time spent with her loved ones and accept that she will grow old with Telemachus.

He emerges as an interesting character in Miller's story. In a lot of ways Telemachus is the anti-Odysseus, because he does not seek fame, fortune and success as his father did. He is happy exploring the world with Circe and enjoying their family. Their relationship is calm and deep, unlike Circe's relationship with Odysseus, which she entered into certainly with the knowledge that it would be temporary – not only because he already had a wife and family, but also because of the way it began, surrounded by mistrust, trickery and spells. When Circe met Odysseus she had already turned his men into pigs. His motivation for wanting a sexual relationship with her was because he was told this would happen, and he needed her assistance to escape alive with his men. Initially Circe attempted to turn Odysseus into a beast as well, seducing him only as a last resort. It does indeed appear that the relationship grows and becomes something special from these uncertain beginnings. Yet in comparison with how the relationship with Telemachus began, slowly and gently, there certainly seem to be more toxic elements.

Circe is, of course, suspicious when she meets Telemachus for the first time, but that is because of her extreme and fierce protection of her son. She expects Telemachus to want to harm Telegonus in revenge for him killing Odysseus, but that is only because she doesn't know his personality yet. As the story continues, it becomes obvious to Circe and the readers that Telemachus is not a person who would seek revenge or glory; he prefers peace and simplicity. Being the hero son of Odysseus is actually, ultimately, much more suited to Telegonus's character, even though he grew up without his father. Perhaps it is a genetic disposition. Or it could be that Circe's recounting of Odysseus's adventures to Telegonus as a child gave the young man a taste for glory and adventure.

A Happy Ending

By the end of Miller's story book we find Circe again settled in the archetype of lover and mother, and happily so. Once again experiencing motherhood, she is making the most of it, enjoying it and actually relishing its challenges. She has a partner in this now in Telemachus, so motherhood is not as scary or difficult as when she was alone. Her two daughters are calmer and easier to raise than Telegonus; they have Telemachus's laid-back disposition, helping to make parenting easier and more enjoyable for Circe. The presence of Penelope, both a friend who she cares about and respects and the grandmother of her children, makes a big difference to raising a difficult child on an island with only the animals for company.

Circe continues to have a good relationship with Telegonus, for whom she has always done her best. Despite the difficulty of his childhood, she protected him at all costs – even against Athena, a powerful Olympian goddess. When Circe is living her settled family life with Telemachus, she visits Telegonus's new realm where he is ruler with her new family. Telegonus becomes the founder of a new city south of Rome called Tusculum, he marries Penelope and they have a son called Italus, who it is said gave his name to the country Italy.

2.

The Real World around Circe's Myths

'The goddess Calypso kept me with her in her cave, and wanted me to marry her, as did also the cunning Aeaean goddess Circe; but they could neither of them persuade me, for there is nothing dearer to a man than his own country and his parents, however splendid a home he may have in a foreign country.'
– Homer, the *Odyssey*

WOMEN'S ROLE IN MYTH: CONTROVERSY OR COMPLIANCE

The Trojan War itself is a mythological story that may even be based on fact. For a very long time there has been scholarly research into the events, and a lot of evidence supports the belief that Troy was real and the war in some form really happened. The circumstances around the war – from its gods and myths to characters and heroes – are another matter. Mythology was a device used to entertain, teach and spread an agenda of what behaviour was good and bad; in sharing stories ancient societies could show examples of intelligence, resilience and skill. The agenda for writing about a woman such as Circe -- independent, powerful, solitary yet ultimately defined by her romantic journey – the rejections, the relationship with Odysseus that happened *after* he had outwitted her – is likely steeped in patriarchy. Ancient Greece was a notoriously patriarchal society in which women were not even classed as citizens, their roles mostly limited to those of wife and mother. In any theatrical adaptation Circe would be played by a man, as would any other female characters; women were not expected or allowed to be a part of this world. This forms part of the background agenda of portraying 'bad' women such as Circe, Medea, Medusa etc.

Let's think of Circe in a different way. When I personally reflect on Circe's story I think of her personal power. She is not a victim of her circumstances, but rather chooses to make the most of them: she creates her world and makes it happen. Whatever it was that brought her to her island she is happy with it, seeking to defend her territory at all costs. Women in Greek mythology generally get a bad rep, even those who are divine! They are characterized as jealous, bitter, cold and angry. One of the few good things they can be is beautiful, but even this is something to be wary of. Helen of Troy, said to be the daughter of Zeus, king of the gods, was the most beautiful woman in the world, yet her beauty caused the death of thousands in a war that lasted 10 years.

Women, and beautiful women in particular, are clearly to be feared – don't forget that, as far as we know, the stories, poems and plays in which they appear are mostly written by men. Many modern interpretations of mythological women seek to level the playing field by telling the stories from the point of view of the character involved, and by giving the character a backstory to explain their actions where none existed before. The contrasting character of Penelope, Odysseus's devoted and patient wife, complements that of Circe, showing what was considered 'good' and 'bad' conduct for a woman in ancient Greece.

THE ANCIENT PATRIARCHY

In ancient Greece there were certain expectations of behaviour for elite women – well, actually for everyone, but the rules were very different for men and women. Men were expected to be fearless, intelligent and powerful warriors. A virtuous woman should be married, loyal to her husband, a good mother and obedient, qualities epitomized by Odysseus's wife Penelope. She waits for him loyally for 20 years, despite the many suitors who wish to marry her. Sometimes you may wonder whether we've really come far enough in the last few thousand years. In mythology particularly, females of divine lineage would be used by male writers as examples of what a woman should *not* be like.

Homer was supposedly a male writer and is credited with writing the epic poems *The Odyssey* and *The Iliad*. Debates over whether Homer was actually one individual person who wrote these poems or whether more than one author was involved are ongoing. It is likely that the myths attributed to Homer existed before he wrote them, as stories told orally for many years. This is why mythological scenarios or characters repeat through different writers with slightly different, or very different, versions of events. It also explains why many tales of myths ripple across the world slightly differently, or with different names. The origins of a story may have come from anywhere that the ancient Greek world had contact with. Myths were tales told to show the difference between good and bad, right and wrong, and what is morally acceptable in society – much as fairytales, folklore and even Disney films do today.

THE FEAR OF SEDUCTION

Another side to Circe's character that would put fear into the heart of men is the assumption that she is a seductress, able to get her own way and manipulate men out of their senses. The fear is that when men are seduced by a woman they lose control, giving her power they don't want her to have. The reason for this is that such men are not as powerful as they want to be; they are thus anxious about what a woman with power could do. The interesting things about men who fear seductive women is firstly that they are so easily seduced, and secondly that they assume women can't have power of their own but must steal it from men.

Obviously this does not apply to all men, nor to all societies. It is a stereotype of a fearful man bred from the stereotype of a seductive woman. Circe, along with many other mythological characters, cannot just be a seductress for its own sake, including the satisfaction of their own sexual desire; there has to be a deeper motive involved. When Circe seduces Odysseus it is because she is trying to protect herself, to prevent him from rushing at her with a sword ready to kill her; in Homer's eyes sexuality is all she has left to protect herself. In the story, the only reason that Odysseus goes along with this is because Hermes instructed him to do so and he needed to save himself and his men. However, there is no need for him to hang around after he has done so. As we know, he chooses to stay with Circe on her island, creating a life and a home with her and her nymphs. Yet as Odysseus is a hero, married with a young son, and Circe is a single, self-sufficient woman, she is often portrayed as evil, dangerous or selfish, deliberately keeping him away from his family.

In actual fact, we know that Circe could not keep Odysseus to herself without his agreement. He is a warrior, a strong and fearsome man who has battled monsters, fought wars and saved lives, so would be no match for Circe's powers unless he wanted to be. Odysseus is the first man that Circe does not need to be angry with and to seek revenge upon because, at least for a time, he chooses her over everything else, including his wife and son.

VARIATIONS ON MYTHS

In classical mythological versions of Circe there is little or no connection between Circe and the goddess Athena (Odysseus's patron goddess in all versions of his myth). The goddess of wisdom, craft and war, Athena protects Odysseus and guides him on many occasions. She also intervenes in his encounter with Circe, telling Odysseus how to overcome

Circe's sorcery (in some versions of the story it is Hermes who helps him here). In mythology Athena and Poseidon compete to see who will be the patron saint of the major Greek city; both deities are expected to offer a gift to the people of Athens in order to choose who it would be. Poseidon produces a well and Athena an olive tree. It was thus she who is chosen and after whom the city is named.

Athena was famously born out of Zeus's head when he swallowed his wife in order to protect himself, having been told that he would have a son who would exceed his own power. A major deity with cults dedicated to her, she is certainly not a goddess to be trifled with, proving fierce and rather determined in all aspects. However, Madeline Miller's story of Circe creates a dramatic dynamic between the enchantress and Athena. Following Odysseus's death at the hands of Telegonus, the goddess shifts her attention onto his son. When Miller expands on these probably impossible connections between Circe and other famous mythological characters, she gives rhyme and reason to Circe's actions – something that the male writers of ancient Greece felt no need to do. Homer, after all, was writing about Odysseus rather than Circe.

PROMETHEUS'S TALE

In traditional mythology Circe would not have encountered the Titan Prometheus, as they were on completely different timelines. However, Madeline Miller uses Prometheus's story, intertwining it with Circe's in a beautiful way that gives an explanation for some of the decisions Circe makes and for much of her story. Prometheus was famously punished by Zeus for giving humans the gift of fire, allowing them to rival the gods in their power and to be more in control of their own destiny. For this he receives from Zeus one of the cruellest punishments, even by the standards of the gods; he is chained to a rock and an eagle comes every day to pluck out his liver, obviously causing immense pain. As Prometheus is immortal his liver grows back nightly, only for him to have to endure the pain again the next day, and so on into eternity. Prometheus's fate is beautifully reproduced in many pieces of art, and told as a story to warn any who dared to defy the gods. In my opinion it is indeed one of the most brutal punishments in classical mythology.

In Madeline Miller's interpretation Circe is extremely worried for Prometheus, her uncle. She has sympathy for him, as well as an understanding of why he wanted to help humankind; this is indeed partly where her fascination with humanity begins as a child. The young Circe is shocked and appalled at the way the Titan has been treated by the other gods, including her father Helios. When she is able to be alone with Prometheus she brings him a drink and tries to soothe him. Circe later confesses her action to her brother Aeetes, but she keeps it to herself for a very long time, conscious that she would be severely punished for defying the will of the gods, particularly Zeus. Circe is also shocked at the enjoyment that some seem to get from it, perceiving the punishment as a sport or entertainment. In her eyes, what Prometheus did was ultimately not that bad; ironically what Circe eventually does is so much worse.

ANCIENT RITUALS AND BELIEFS

There is no documented evidence of cults dedicated solely to Circe in ancient Greece. However, there are many instances of possible cults dedicated to the enchantress, including potential rituals that they may have performed. There were certainly reasons for dedicating a cult to Circe, if the followers of that particular ancient cult were practising *pharmekeia* (the practice of making drugs and sorcery) or using plants for various reasons in a form of herbalism. It would not have been unusual for women to hold rituals and create herbal remedies around these themes, nor to work together with these practices in general. Such practices have been passed on for thousands of years and were one of the reasons for hunting 'sorcerers' during the witch trials in the sixteenth and seventeenth centuries.

An island called Farmakonisi has been suggested as a possible location for a cult dedicated to Circe. Named after the pharmaceutical herbs that grow on it, the island in ancient times was called Pharmakousa, creating an obvious connection to *pharmekeia* and possibly to Circe. On this tiny island of only 21 inhabitants we can also find a church and the ruins of an ancient Roman temple; it is suggested that the tomb of Circe may have been located on this island too. Other sources connect Circe to cults dedicated to Hecate, the ancient Greek goddess of sorcery and witchcraft, as well as other powerful 'witches' such as her niece Medea. Many speculative articles discuss potential sites of cult worship in various locations, among them the island of Naxos and various places in Italy. Regardless of whether these speculations surrounding ancient cults dedicated to Circe are substantiated or not, we can imagine that it is likely that an ancient Greek woman dedicated to the practice of herbalism or *pharmakeia* would probably have had some sort of connection to Circe and her myth.

Even in ancient times a story meant to warn and scare women into behaving in a 'proper' or 'well-behaved' way could also show women how powerful and independent they could be – especially if they dedicated their life to a practice such as *pharmekeia*. The current pagan or Wiccan rituals and rites dedicated to Circe are unlikely to have a direct link to ancient practices of the same sort. Yet as those practices are based upon ancient texts and other ancient cults, there may well be some association, even possibly some replication. We will find out more about these practices later.

THE NYMPHS

Some versions of Circe's story describe her as completely solitary on the island, but in others she is assisted at her home by nymphs. Nymphs vary in their background, but are essentially both part divine and part of nature. There are thousands of nymphs in Greek myths, personifying the natural elements they represent.

Nymphs in Greek myths include:

- **Naiads** (who represent fountains, wells, springs, streams and brooks)

- **Oceanids** such as Perse (who are the daughters of Oceanus and Tethys and represent the oceans)
- **Dryads** (who represent specific trees)
- **Nereids** (who represent the seas)

There are many more besides, representing sunsets, mountains, more trees, glens, groves, gardens, flowers, animals, the underworld, clouds, breezes, fresh water, marshes, swamps, meadows, winds, valleys and others. There are usually thousands of each kind of nymph and they are always female, reflecting the ancient Greek belief in the divine connection of women and nature: they literally personify the earth and all the natural beauty it contains.

The nymphs who end up on Circe's island serve as helpers and handmaidens to her. Whether they are sent there by a regretful Helios to provide company and assistance for his daughter, or whether they were sent to learn from Circe's skills varies between different stories. However, the symbolism of Circe receiving help from these nymphs could represent a multitude of things, for example, the connection of solidarity between women and their ability to learn from and teach each other in ways independent from the patriarchal society and their roles in the lives of men, valued only for child-rearing and wifehood. The nymphs' connection to nature also mirrors and amplifies that of Circe. Women are inherently connected to the natural world around them; when they are aware of that and use it to their benefit magical things can happen. Women learn from a young age that their energy ebbs and flows in response to their menstrual cycle, which echoes that of nature: the changing of the seasons, the rise and fall of the tides, the lunar and solar cycles and so on.

THE TELEGONY: A MEDIEVAL WITCH WARNING

As with most myths, there are many versions of the story of Telegonos, Circe's son by Odysseus, often referred to as The *Telegony*. The version that I want to look at now comes from medieval Britain. It is a great example of how the story of a woman such as Circe can be framed as a warning and be twisted into something quite dark and scary in the hands of those wanting to exert power, especially over women.

Circe is chosen deliberately in the *Telegony* to bear the children of Odysseus. When Circe is pregnant, Odysseus leaves her to return to his wife Penelope. In the medieval *Telegony* Penelope is described as the epitome of virtue: 'a better wife there may be none'. She is portrayed as the perfect wife in all versions of Odysseus's story, having been pursued by many suitors for 20 years of her husband's absence, yet loyally waiting for his return. This juxtaposition between Circe and Penelope contrasts the difference between good and bad women. Circe again demonstrates the bad ways in which a woman can behave.

Here we find another case of Circe being used as a example of what not to do, particularly if you are a woman. In medieval times there was a huge fear of, and campaign against, the use of spells and witchcraft; seen as heresy against the Christian religion, it was thought to involve working with the Devil instead of with God. The medieval Church deliberately spread the fear of witches, independent women, healers, midwives etc. in order to control and manipulate women. For hundreds of years people were sent to trial as witches and murdered when they were judged to be so. This included men and children too, but the vast majority of victims were women. In reality these women were not witches; they were simply independent and lived alone, or were herbalists, or midwives; some had even simply got on the wrong side of someone who accused them. Much like Circe herself, they were misunderstood and used as examples to strike fear into other women in order to make them submissive to the will of men and the Church.

However, Circe could never give up her independence and the power she acquired through working with spells and plants. She fought back with those exact powers that the authorities around her feared would be used against them, turning those who threatened her into animals. Unfortunately this was not an option for the women murdered during the witch trials. Although some may well have stood up for themselves until the bitter end, it would have been near impossible to resist their fate.

Witches as Scapegoats

The tradition of witches in mythology spans across many cultures and countries. These women are characterized not just as scary, child-eating loners (sure, they are sometimes!), but they are also protectors, powerful and helpful too when they want to be. Circe is a large part of the tradition of witches in myth, and in Western culture she is one of the first. Throughout history, particularly in cultures where Christianity became the main religion, witches have been vilified and used as an example of all that is evil. Most, if not all, of these mythological witches are female and most, if not all, are to be feared and avoided. However, within each story you often find examples of these witches helping people – not for any reason other than to be helpful, or sometimes because they hope to get something out of it themselves. Much like humans, witches are both good and bad, selfish and selfless, mischievous and helpful. No one, including our famous mythological witch, is simply good or bad. In the ancient world, and still within native communities today, we see the telling of stories that have balance; equilibrium is important. It is our current Western culture that feels the need irrevocably to separate good and bad, heroes and villains.

During the medieval period in Britain the *Telegony* was more accessible to the public than the stories of Troy, and so more people knew about it. In this version of the story the emphasis is on the curse that Telegonus must bear, his conception having been the outcome of sorcery. This is a warning story about morals used to portray a certain message. Since Circe was a sorceress, and even though it appears to have been Odysseus's choice to lie with Circe, their union was inevitably doomed, for at the time of Homer's *Odyssey*, even in that of the medieval *Telegony,* the status quo was that women should be controlled while men could be free. The fear of witches in medieval times was exaggerated by rumours that they would change innocent people into animals, that they ate children, that they caused disease and put spells on the land and crops to bring famine. The world around these innocent people was trying to blame anything bad that could happen on 'witches' – sometimes male, but most often female.

WHY CIRCE?

Let's now consider the good traits that Circe possessed, that explain why Odysseus would have chosen her to bear his children, or at least why the writers of his story did. She was powerful and independent enough to raise children alone, yet caring and nurturing enough to make sure that they made it to adulthood. She also had divine ancestry, which was very important. Not anyone could be trusted to bear the children of Odysseus, especially one who would end up defeating him. For, although there is confusion over the precise genealogy of Odysseus, he was still a king, descended from a king, and potentially of divine ancestry through his great grandfather Autoclyus, the son of Hermes. So it was very important that the person who eventually takes the life of one of the greatest ancient Greek heroes should have the ancestry to back it up. Enter Telegonus: Odysseus's own son and that of the goddess and witch Circe, grandson of the sun god Helios.

3.

Impact and Influence: Circe's Far Reach in Cultures Through the Centuries

*'The Goddess is indignant; and since she
is not able to injure him, and as she loves him
she does not wish to do so, she is enraged against
her, who has been preferred to herself; and, offended
with these crosses in love, she immediately bruises
herbs, infamous for their horrid juices, and,
when bruised, she mingles with them the
incantations of Hecate.'*
– Ovid, *Metamorphoses*

THE LONG-LASTING INFLUENCE OF A POWERFUL GODDESS

Throughout history it has been common to have retellings of the gods and heroes of ancient myth. However, enabling the story of a secondary character to take centre stage and become the subject of an entire book is a more recent phenomenon. There have also been retellings about mythical characters such as Ariadne, Medusa and others, drawing on the common theme that women need a voice now. For a long time these characters were mere tools, playing minor roles in the stories of greater, more famous characters. To consider their own reasoning and point of view is a new trend and one that I hope continues. Unfortunately the women of ancient history in Greece did not have the autonomy that we have today, so I agree that it is an important time to delve into these stories.

There are many examples of characters called Circe in literature, film, television and video games. Often the character named Circe will be a woman who is a seductress, witch or enchantress; she is usually powerful and takes no prisoners. Turning humans into pigs is a recurring theme, among the things for which Circe is now most famous in the wider world. Universally Circe seems to be a force to be reckoned with. Her strength and power translates across all forms of media. She is not always portrayed as someone evil and unnecessarily harmful, but certainly as someone who can stand up for herself if she needs to and is powerful in nearly every story.

CIRCE AS THE ARTIST'S MUSE

Circe is often depicted in ancient art; many Greek pottery vessels portray her with various men she has transformed into beasts. One example appears on a famous krater (a vessel used for mixing wine with water, as wine wasn't drunk neat as it is now) which dates from 440 BCE. Circe is pictured on the right, being pursued by Odysseus to her left; some of her beasts follow him.

All myths are changeable and adaptable. Many are told by ancient authors or playwrights, adjusted for the sake of drama or to share a certain message. Such a practice goes back to the ancient oral tradition; before poets such as Homer wrote down the myths, they would change frequently to meet the orators' specific needs. From the *Odyssey* to the krater, we can see that the story of Circe was a popular and enduring tale. When I compare her story to that of other women in ancient Greek mythology, I am struck by her independence, freedom and power. While sometimes being labelled as 'evil', like Medea, she also manages to keep her authority and independence, not always subject to the whim of men and gods. This is what still attracts us to her and makes her story so fascinating. Labelling Circe as merely a witch or a seductress would be to flatten her as a character without exploring the epic depth available.

As is common with classical mythology, Circe is also a favoured subject of paintings – particularly those from the Pre-Raphaelite, Romantic and Classical disciplines. Often with paintings such as these, a particular climax of a character's myth will be the favoured scene for the painting. British artists of the eighteenth and nineteenth centuries chose to portray scenes from Greek and Roman mythology; familiarity with these stories was seen as a sign of intelligence, education and good breeding.

A CLEVER WAY TO SHOW BOTH SIDES
OF THE STORY

John William Waterhouse has created some of my favourite depictions of mythological women in art. His painting *Circe Offering the Cup to Ulysses* (1891) is a powerful rendition of a polarizing and powerful mythological woman. Ulysses is the Latinized version of the name Odysseus.

We already know the point in the story depicted, as the title confirms this information. Firstly we notice how Circe's fair skin stands out among the background of deeper and darker colours. She is the centre of the portrait and the first thing we notice. Her stance is solid and bold. She offers the wine to Odysseus with an air of authority and insistence, her head held high and her arms outstretched. We can see the shape of her naked body underneath the very sheer fabric of the clothes she wears. This could be seen as a deliberate attempt to gain trust and favour with Odysseus, especially as we know that after this scene she will seduce Odysseus into a romantic relationship lasting for a year.

When we begin to look at the details of the painting beyond the main character, we come into contact with the darker side of Circe's character. If we look behind Circe, we quickly see that she is seated in front of a mirror – a useful tool enabling Waterhouse to show us her point of view as well as that of Odysseus. The mirror shows Odysseus approaching Circe to the right, looking cautious and carrying a weapon in his hand. He already fears that Circe might not be trustworthy from the information he has received.

A Powerful Position

On the left side of the mirror you can see the stern of Odysseus's ship. Here Waterhouse uses the mirror as a technique to tell the story that people viewing the painting would be expected to know well; the scene is recognizable even without reading the title. Just underneath the ship, still in the reflection, we can see two wild boars. Another one comes from behind the mirror and yet another is lying on the ground next to Circe's feet; it may already be dead. We know already that the pigs are a warning to Odysseus; they don't want him to suffer the same fate, but they also need him to rescue them, which he will do.

Strewn around the floor are berries, leaves and a toad – an indication from Waterhouse that Circe is a witch and not to be trusted. The discarded berries are the ingredients she will use to mix with poison to curse the men, while the toad is a familiar, associated with witches and evil women in general. To the right we see a censor burning incense, giving the whole scene the atmosphere of a ritualistic event.

Waterhouse's Circe does not show that she will eventually become a lover and an ally of Odysseus. On the contrary, the scene, even down to the roaring lion heads on the arms of her chair, is one of profound caution and fear. We see a glimpse of the provocative and seductive nature associated with Circe from the sheer material of her dress and the way in which the material comes loose at her hip. This representation of her is in line with the seductress and sorceress stereotype that many associate with the character of Circe. Now it is time to give her more depth and understanding.

AN INTERPRETATION OF OVID

Another very famous image of Circe is again by John William Waterhouse, who painted many mythological characters. This painting, called *Circe Invidiosa*, was painted in 1892, after he completed the painting *Circe Offering the Cup to Ulysses*. It was inspired by a particular passage in Ovid's *Metamorphoses* on the myth of Circe, Glaucus and Scylla.

> *There was a cove,*
> *a little inlet shaped like a bent bow,*
> *a quiet place where Scylla, at midday,*
> *sought shelter when the sea and sky were hot;*
> *and, in midcourse, the sun scorched with full force,*
> *reducing shadows to a narrow thread.*
> *And Circe now contaminates this bay,*
> *polluting it with noxious poisons; there*
> *she scatters venom drawn from dreadful roots*
> *and, three-times-nine times, murmurs an obscure*
> *and tangled maze of words, a labyrinth –*
> *the magic chant that issues from her lips.*
> *Then Scylla comes; no sooner has she plunged*

waist-deep into the water than she sees,
around her hips, the horrid barking shapes.

Being Bad or Being Human?

This image and the passage from Ovid connected to it show Circe in a dark and dramatic light – maybe even an evil one. It reinforces the stereotype that I have been attempting to hide from so far. She is deliberately and coldly transforming someone to suit her own jealous needs. I ask myself why have I decided so far not to see her in this light. Firstly, I feel a responsibility to defend the women of history and myth who couldn't defend themselves. I believe that the women of ancient Greece, and other ancient societies, were often unfairly treated, held to standards unequal to those of a man. To see Circe as evil, when the (male) gods and heroes around her seem to behave in ways as bad or even worse, yet can still be deemed worthy of hero worship, does not seem justified. I see it as part of my mission now to give Circe the voice, autonomy and freedom that she and the women of her time were not granted.

However, I also believe that a rejection of the shadow or darkness from oneself, when it comes to Circe or anyone, shows how I feel about being seen as 'bad', 'evil' or even 'naughty'; I acknowledge through this process that this is what is happening here. As women we chronically suffer from a desire to please people and put others before ourselves, to earn continuous approval from society or others. Was Circe evil? Maybe. Do we all have moments when we have 'bad' thoughts? Absolutely. Does that mean we are evil? No; it simply means we are human. Nobody can control their thoughts 24 hours a day, seven days a week. Allowing yourself to acknowledge and question dark thoughts when they do come up will create for you a kind of peace within that cannot be achieved without acknowledging your shadow.

MAJESTIC BEAUTY

Another of my favourite painted depictions of Circe is Wright Barker's rendition from 1889. I love this painting because it shows Circe unashamedly in her power. She stands at the top of a small staircase at the entrance to what we can assume is her palace on the island of Aeaea. Her stance is defiant and bold as she lifts her head towards us as the viewer, outstretching her arm as though she is proudly showing off her home and life. She looks every bit the powerful and beautiful goddess with her flowing skirt and bare breasts.

Behind Circe billows a scarf or a piece of material. It is not totally clear where this is coming from, but it gives an air of magic and mystery; because of this, it almost looks like smoke pluming. Her hair is tied back and adorned with a crown and flowers, which shows her status as a goddess and a daughter of the sun. Her face and body are objectively beautiful and so this appears to be a woman who wants for nothing, including the attention of a man; she lives happily in her own life and world. She carries a lyre in her hand. Although I can find no examples of Circe playing the lyre in ancient texts, the instrument can symbolize wisdom and knowledge; it is also related to the god Hermes.

Showing Circe Through Symbols

It would not go unnoticed that Circe is completely surrounded by tame beasts: lions and wolves. The wolf at the very front of Wright Barker's painting looks more vicious and less tame, but it is directed at us, the intruding viewer, rather than at Circe. All of the other animals seem calm, even docile. There are versions of Circe's myth in which we know that the men she transformed into beasts have their physical forms changed but not their minds or souls; they remain human on the inside, trapped in an animal's body. I believe that Barker depicts this here as he shows the animals' tameness through their eyes and stance. The lion and lioness lie down on either side of her, while the lioness behind looks positively fearful.

The tiger skin that drapes across the stairs on which Circe is standing may serve as a warning to the other animals. Yet we must note that none of the other animals is a tiger, and we don't hear of Circe turning anyone into a tiger in the ancient myths. We must therefore assume that this is another of Barker's visual symbols. A tiger is a symbol of strength and power, so we can see that Circe has overcome the strength and power of those in authority around her, such as Zeus, her father Helios etc. She now stands tall in her own authority and power, secure in her own domain and happy with who she has had to become to get there.

The red petals and flowers scattered down the stairs look similar to flowing blood. These could be a warning to us, the approaching onlooker, but they may also represent the tamed wild within both Circe and the animals by which she is surrounded. This woman is someone able to live without fear of reproach. Surrounded by beasts of her own making, she can feel not only safe but accomplished in her own right. Circe is a powerful sorceress, clearly revealed in the space she takes up and the stance she proudly shows.

OTHER INFLUENCES ON SOCIETY

When researching more modern depictions of Circe I came across a version of her represented in the video game *Assassin's Creed Odyssey*. This game, which came out in 2018, is an open-world game based on mythology and the Polynesian War between Athens and Sparta; it thus features characters from Greek mythology. The interaction with Circe is a side quest for the main character. Having not played the game, I found a video of the part with Circe.

We find Circe on an island; her home, as expected, is surrounded by beasts. Lions and pigs are prowling around. Our first glimpse of Circe shows her bent down feasting on the carcass of a raw pig; she gets up to greet the playable character with blood still on her face and hands. It is immediately obvious that this is a complicated character; beautiful, with a warm and friendly greeting, but dripping in the fresh blood of a pig, suggesting that she is not necessarily to be trusted.

Described as a witch, she offers the character some wine for them to drink together, aligning this version of Circe with the one told in ancient times. The character then retrieves the wine and comes across some moly, an antidote for poison – again aligning the video game narrative to the ancient story of Odysseus, who then uses the antidote to Circe's potion. In the game Circe watches the character drink the wine without having any herself, but the character, who has already taken the antidote, survives. He asks Circe why she lives alone. She explains that the reason is because in the rest of the world she is misunderstood as a witch. She also says that the reason she needs to poison humans is to feed her animals; the curse then passes to them as animals and they remain in her control, and she needs them to be controlled for her own protection. The player then has the option of adding Circe to your crew, leaving her or killing her.

A Shocking Introduction

This representation of Circe shows her as someone who believes that she needs protection against humanity because of the assumption that she is a witch and can do them harm. However, she ends up fulfilling the vision that society has projected on to her by becoming a danger to humans. Circe is useful to the hero in the same way that she ends up being useful to Odysseus after they both foil her attempt to poison them. Having joined the crew of the player, she has no further role in the story.

It is shocking to see her covered in the fresh blood of a pig she is eating off the ground. Yet the makers of the game seem to have attempted to give her enough of a reason to do so. Whether you think it is a justified reason or not is open to interpretation, just as her story in Odysseus's myth is open to interpretation. Circe has her reasons for wanting to protect herself, which is often something that people can relate to. In making the decision whether to add her to your crew or kill her, you may be using your own judgement of her character to decide whether her behaviour is justified. Personally I think any version of Circe is someone I would want on my side, both for her protective skills and for her powerful sorcery.

THE FAIRYTALE WITCH

Something that really leans into the rhetoric of the evil witch is the world of children's films, for example Disney's adaptations of fairy tales and other stories. This is the image of witches with which most of us grew up. Definitely not a balance of good and bad, but just pure evil – at least up until the much more recent film *The Princess and the Frog*, in which the heroine finds herself transformed into a frog and is in need of help from a spell-casting, lonely, older woman who lives deep in the heart of the Bayou of Louisiana. She is not necessarily called a witch, rather a voodoo priestess, but I think she fits the description of any witch I have ever known. She helps Tiana, the protagonist, in the best way she can, with a song and a lesson, for no reason other than to help her. She doesn't cause any upset or evil in the story, but simply does good. One other important and impressive skill that she has in common with Circe is the ability to change animals into other animals, and potentially to change humans into animals. We don't know a reason why she might use these skills, nor are we even really left questioning what she would do with them. At 197 years old she may have been through similar experiences to Circe and used this powerful help to protect and defend herself.

Of course Disney films were not the first to dismiss witches as evil. In the time of Homer's writing the word 'witch' did not apparently even exist. Instead the word used to describe Circe in Homer's *Odyssey* is *pharmekei*a, the root of our current word for pharmacy. It means someone who uses potions and herbs to effect transformation. In modern times we would call such skills spell work or witchcraft, but such terms cannot avoid the negative connotations now associated with them. If we were to use the words 'herbalist' or 'alchemist' we may not feel they have the same negative associations; certainly we do not expect the practitioner to be necessarily 'bad' or 'evil'.

CIRCE: THE WITCHES' MUSE

In modern practices of paganism many people work with the energies of mythological characters and ancient gods and goddesses from all over the world. Circe is no exception to this, and there are examples of pagans creating rituals and forms of worship around her character. My friend Irisanya Moon is one such example. She has written a book about how to work with Circe in pagan practices and rituals.

Paganism is an umbrella term for a number of spiritual groups who see nature as divine, including Wiccans, witches, druids and more. They see the natural world around them as a manifestation of the divine and they use gods and goddesses in their practices of rituals to align themselves with what they want to achieve by performing them. For example, if they were interested in manifesting more abundance they would look to gods and goddesses of abundance in ancient religions, then connect to them through meditations, research, creating altars and giving them offerings. As Circe is known as a powerful sorceress and enchantress, she would be called upon in a pagan ritual to connect the believer with justice, magic(k) and transformation.

For Irisanya, Circe is a goddess whom she came across in her pagan group of witches in Ohio, USA – a long way from her beginnings in the ancient Greek oral tradition and then in Homer's *Odyssey*. Witches will often turn to these gods and goddesses, not just from their own native land but from all over the world, to meet their different needs. According to Irisanya's accounts, the reputation of Circe within the pagan community is that she is difficult and vengeful; she is not someone to be trifled with. However, after getting to know more about Circe she realized that this is in part a misconception – a recurring theme for Circe. She is actually an extremely powerful deity to be called upon, so strikes fear in people in the way that powerful women often do. Yet working with her allows you to step into your own power in alignment with her energy.

The First Witch?

Irisanya states that she finds it important to read a translation of the text of the *Odyssey* written by a woman. As most are written by white men, it could well be the case that whoever writes the translation has an impact upon it. As an academic, it would be important to consider these details and how someone's motives might change their interpretation of the text; there are many words that don't translate exactly, for example, while some may have variable meanings – another reason for the lack of continuity in mythological stories. What is really interesting for a pagan witch practising communication with ancient deities is that Circe may well be the first 'witch' ever. As noted, there is no specific ancient Greek word for witch and no witches feature in stories before Circe (at least none that we know of). The practices that Irisanya recommends for working with Circe, or for having Circe's assistance, revolve around herbalism. As you may recall, Circe was known for her connection to nature and plants. She also used plants to create potions to manipulate the world around her.

In her book Irisanya shares some recipes for potions using herbs that are easy to find, for example mugwort, lavender and chamomile. Her emphasis is on finding herbs in the natural world around your home, just as Circe did on the island of Aeaea. She recommends using your intuition to create herbal blends for many different purposes such as teas, incense, bath mixtures, tinctures and more. Another way in which she recommends working with Circe is to consider how you might use the power of transmutation, which she describes as the act of turning one thing into something else. To do this she suggests trying something called glamour magic, a way of using how you dress to make people see you differently – for example wearing different colours or enchanting jewellery with a certain intention and so on. Other ways to use transmutation include journalling, affirmations and therapy. Finally, Irisanya outlines how to use transmutation to purify in the same way that Circe did for Jason, Medea and Odysseus. To do this you can use baths, salt, smoke and wind. She outlines ways in which you can become a sorceress following in the footsteps of Circe.

Evil or Powerfully Angry

Irisanya also discusses necromancy, a way in which modern witches can seek to communicate with the deceased. She associates Circe with this practice because of her connections with seers and assisting Odysseus with his journey to the underworld. Circe also has connections in some sources to Hecate, the goddess of magic, sorcery and necromancy.

At the end of her book Irisanya talks about why it is important for women to step into their power in the current political climate. I agree wholeheartedly: the world right now needs strong and powerful women who are going to speak out. As she is based in the USA, Irisanya relates this need to the reversal of Roe vs. Wade and the fight for women to have the right to safe and free abortions.

Irisanya also discusses whether or not Circe is evil. As we know, Odysseus described her as such before he needed her

ANCIENT & MODERN: INTRODUCING CIRCE

assistance, which Circe then gave willingly. She debates this question wonderfully, even with what could be described as affection for the character, yet remains detached enough for a healthy outlook on both sides of the argument.

I agree with her point of view: Circe is a character who turned her righteous anger into justified action, and this is could be one powerful way in which a practising pagan could work with Circe's energy, to help women to stand up for ourselves and others in the face of injustice, even when fear threatens our resolve. Irisanya thus believes that working with Circe invites us to be active when there is perceived injustice by helping others, harnessing feelings of anger and pain instead of trying to repress them and by employ some form of activism on behalf of those who need a voice. In recent versions of Circe's myth, such as Madeline Miller's book, Circe is someone who feels the need to help those who can't help themselves – among them Ariadne, Daedalus, Prometheus and mortals who suffer at the hands of the gods and monsters of their world.

WE ARE THE WITCHES

Thank you to Irisanya Moon for sharing her book with me and allowing me to refer to her amazing work in the information that I share in this book. It provides another important perspective on how people relate to ancient myths in a modern world, with their own freedom and power at the forefront. Irisanya's book is just another way in which the amazing stories of the ancient world can be reimagined, reinterpreted and retold, giving strength and autonomy to those who may not have experienced it when the original tale was recorded by Homer – and was perhaps manipulated to serve the needs of the patriarchal society in which it was created.

Modern practitioners of witchcraft look to characters such as Circe to reclaim the craft that their ancestors would have been persecuted for. A small side note: it would be impossible to say that there is not now still judgement and persecution, especially in the growing Christian communities in the Global South. Here innocent people, including children, can sometimes still come under dangerous persecution for being accused of witchcraft, when again it is not the truth.

In Western civilizations it is easy to find many posters and t-shirts printed with the slogan 'We are the granddaughters of the witches you couldn't burn'. While this is an empowering and emboldening statement, we must remember that the women who did suffer were *not* witches, they were normal women; their gift to us is that we are able to live much more freely than they were. We are able to exist as ourselves; to own property, work, vote, live alone, choose our jobs and careers – all things that they could not do without the fear of being persecuted (again, this applies to some societies, not all). So I think it is important to look to Circe to discover how we can help other women who still suffer, and to honour our ancestors by using the power we now have to help others and live boldly.

4.
Conflicts, Controversies and Misuses

'Presently they reached the gates of the goddess's house, and as they stood there they could hear Circe within, singing most beautifully as she worked at her loom, making a web so fine, so soft, and of such dazzling colours as no one but a goddess could weave.'
– Homer, the *Odyssey*

A GODDESS WITH MANY SIDES

There are so many places an examination of the character of Circe could go. Exploring why and how relatable these different sides to her are is a fascinating subject, allowing us to connect with her on a human and personal level. Her humanity is something that we can relate to and learn from, even though she is not in fact human.

The number of facets that Circe has as a character shows that her stereotypical mischaracterization as simply a witch and seductress does her a disservice. Her roles range so greatly from friend to lover, mother, helper, feminist, witch, loner and friend – and I'm sure to many other things too. Her emotional motivation comes from a mix of anger, revenge, fear, rejection, love, hope, protection, guilt and independence, with her character spanning huge chasms of the human experience. The fact that in Miller's book Circe also ends up mortal is a great full-circle moment; her love for mortals and her affinity with them means this is likely to have always been the way her story should have ended. Circe was never meant to be a goddess or divine. She was something else entirely, dancing between the mortal and immortal as a witch, able to create and defend herself powerfully, using her power to make the most of her circumstances. Spending hundreds of years alone on an island, able to refine and hone her skills, meant that eventually she had that choice to make herself mortal.

CIRCE THE ENCHANTRESS

Circe is often considered an enchantress and a seductress. This is particularly so in Odysseus's case because he was a hero, and thus would not be seen to have chosen such a woman as a partner without her having seduced him, or even cast a spell upon him to keep him with her on her island, away from his wife and son, for a whole year. Madeline Miller's Circe deliberately chooses not to cast a spell on Odysseus, although she admits that she easily could do so, acknowledging instead that she wouldn't feel good about it. There are other reasons why Odysseus might want to stay with Circe on her island, for himself as well as for his men. Once they are returned to their human form they are looked after well – fed, bathed and served by the many nymphs who reside with Circe. Odysseus himself is enjoying the unwavering affection and attention of a woman. He may not yet know that Penelope has been waiting faithfully for him, and so is out to hedge his bets.

Whatever the case, Odysseus clearly feels affection for Circe too. He might well be using her for his own comfort and needs, but he never shows much resistance after the initial 'convincing' from Hermes to get him to go to bed with Circe. Originally he does it to save his men, but once they are safe, and even when they are recovered and well looked after, he could have left the island at any point. In Madeline Miller's book Circe does not expect Odysseus to stay with her for so long. However, she makes the most of his presence while he is there and feels deep affection, even love, for him.

CIRCE THE MISTRESS

Not only is Circe a seductress in this context, but she is also Odysseus's mistress – another female archtype that is feared and frowned upon. When we consider mistresses of the world, we immediately think of the poor lonely wives at home, left to raise the children of their unfaithful husbands. That is indeed a valid point. I doubt that many people would encourage their husbands to go out and have an affair while they labour at home over housework and children, or while they work also to bring in money for the family. In ancient Greece, however, affairs were not thought of in the same way. It was standard and expected behaviour for elite Greek males to have many lovers, both men and women. The same cannot be said for women of any class.

It is worth noting that in Greek society, a certain 'type' of woman would be a wife and another would be a mistress. Their worlds did not mix; the wife of a Greek citizen would certainly not be expected to have an affair or become the mistress of another man, although that isn't to say that this never happened. It is certainly not what a 'good' wife would do. Penelope, for example, never sought to have an affair with anyone else even though the world around her presumed Odysseus to be dead: in remaining loyal she is the archetypal example of a 'good' wife.

A Woman's Sexual Power

Circe is, and was always intended to be, the opposite of Penelope – the archetypal example of a 'bad' woman. She takes Odysseus to her bed after which, although he is free to leave, he chooses not to because he is enjoying the sexual attentions of a 'bad' woman. While he is enjoying his affair his wife is resisting suitors who pressure her to remarry. She shows no sign whatsoever of sexual desire because in a patriarchal society a good woman should not pursue or enjoy sex. It is still ingrained in many women that sex is not something that should be enjoyed. It is not unusual for women to feel a lot of shame, and receive a lot of shame from outside sources, about their own sexual desire.

The term 'slut-shaming' may be recent, but the concept is centuries old. We are taught that a woman shouldn't enjoy sex, have multiple sexual partners or pursue sex because doing so would make her a slut. Yet for a man such behaviour is still often seen as desirable, a 'natural' showcase of sexual prowess and power. Fear of the sexually liberated woman still occurs in our society today, although small improvements have been made. Yet there remain many cases (for example, the overturning of Roe vs. Wade, the right to free and safe abortions in the USA) in which women's sexual liberation is deliberately being suppressed.

LEARNING TO TRUST

Homer characterizes Circe as an evil witch and temptress, but by the end of her part in Odysseus's story we can see that she may have just been misunderstood. We never really know why she randomly turns the men into pigs. It seems by her speech and actions that she does it just because she can, indicating that she is a cruel and wicked person. By the end of their time together, however, we have a very different perception of Circe. She is extremely powerful, knows a lot about the world and can predict what is going to happen. More than just a side conquest for Odysseus or an amusing distraction, Circe is an integral part of the story. It would be a very different tale if she wasn't part of it.

The affection that Odysseus eventually has for Circe is shown by his appreciation and his description of her assistance and hospitality when he tells his story of the time he spent with her. Until he spends time with her

Odysseus fears Circe as something 'evil' and a witch; he then learns to trust her and discovers that she is an extremely powerful ally.

SURPRISINGLY NURTURING

Circe is a woman capable of deep affection and compassion, qualities that you wouldn't expect to find in one of the 'villains' of myth. The ancient mythological world was rarely ever black and white in that way. Even the famous gods and goddesses of Olympus had flaws, jealousy and insecurities; they couldn't control their issues when they needed to, which often leads to the tales we know and love, and to epic Greek poetry such as Homer's *Odyssey*. Circe is thus no exception to the rule. She is not worse or more evil than many of the gods who were known to punish people in the cruellest of ways for things completely beyond their control (see, for example, the story of Athena and Medusa).

In fact, what you might assume from much of Circe's story is that she was capable of far deeper love, compassion and affection than many of her divine relations. The way that she took care of Odysseus came from love, the way she took care of Medea and Jason derived from compassion and the way she took care of her child/children also rose from affection and maternal love. Because she was compassionate, caring, affectionate and helpful, her rationale for doing things such as turning men into beasts or Scylla into a monster were more complicated and complex than the reasons the gods did cruel things to humans – usually to make a point, or simply to express their power.

CIRCE'S ROOTS

In her book Madeline Miller goes into depth about how Circe's life began and the ways in which it affected her. Circe was one of four children born to the sun god Helios and the nymph Perse, the others being Aeetes, Pasiphae and Perses. Her relationship with her mother was complicated. Perse was disappointed with Circe from the beginning for not looking or sounding right and for not being male. She distanced herself from Circe and focused upon having more children, hoping that they would be an improvement on her first-born. This disappointment then spread to Circe's siblings. They took their tone from their mother, becoming cruel and judgemental of Circe because of how she looked and sounded.

Anyone who has had a childhood of being misunderstood, judged and made to feel like a constant disappointment will sympathize with what that can do to a person. The behaviour that such treatment inspires can be understood in a different way. It would be understandable to react in a way that defends and protects yourself, even as the child feels a lack of self-worth and self-esteem. For Circe to have those things at any time in her life, she will need to release judgement from her family and instead create it for herself. To do so involves making the most of her circumstances. I believe this is where her kindness stems from eventually.

CIRCE THE HOSTESS

When Odysseus's men first call to Circe she appears hospitable and friendly, inviting them in. All enter except the suspicious Eurylochus, who stays outside. Circe feeds the men and gives them the wine that we know is poisoned. They turn into pigs, but retain the minds of humans; however, they have no recollection of their homelands. Eurylochus goes back to inform Odysseus of the fate of his men, but upon his return his emotions get the better of him and he is unable to speak. He is emotionally on edge as Odysseus and the remaining men try to draw the story out of him. Eurylochus admits at last that he doesn't know what happened to the men; they simply didn't return.

At this point Odysseus goes to the rescue in the most heroic of fashions. On his way to Circe's house he comes across Hermes, the messenger god. Odysseus is favoured by the gods, who are often there to support and help him when there is danger ahead. Hermes warns Odysseus about Circe, explaining exactly what he should do to escape her poison and defeat her charms. The god gives Odysseus an antidote to the poison that Circe will try to use on him, then insists that he must threaten to kill Circe with his sword. When she shrinks from him she will invite him to her bed; Hermes is adamant that Odysseus must not resist her. So Circe's power of seduction here appears to be not real at all. Odysseus only acts upon Hermes' insistence in order to reverse Circe's spell on his men. However, Hermes never insists that it would be necessary for Odysseus to stay for a whole year. Perhaps that is his own choice after all.

CIRCE THE LOVER

When actually in a loving and accepting relationship Circe is wonderfully helpful, affectionate and caring. She has a deep connection with Odysseus. Although they both know that the relationship cannot be permanent, and that eventually Odysseus will need to return to his wife and child, they still manage to have wonderful times and a beautifully loving and supportive home life, albeit not a lasting one. Circe throws herself into the role of a temporary wife and does a great job. She cares for Odysseus, and his men too, in the best way she can. She feeds, bathes, clothes and houses them, and also entertains Odysseus with company and sex. The couple have a deep connection that enables them to talk and trust one another, even if the relationship started off almost as if they were tricking each other into it. At least they came together as equals. Circe is finally able to let her guard down and enjoy being with someone she knows has chosen her. The fact that he is married likely takes off a lot of pressure from her fear of rejection; she knows that it is inevitable in the end.

In her romantic connection with Telemachus Circe finally finds someone who can be a permanent presence in her life. Telemachus does not crave adventure and honour in the same way that Odysseus and Telegonus do, and consequently is a much safer person to love. He has some of Odysseus's characteristics and some of Penelope's, making him the ideal person for Circe to settle down with and experience a wholesome family life free from fear. Often in life it takes many attempts at love to figure out exactly what it is that you want and need from it. For Circe it meant years of fear, rejection, terrible coping mechanisms and potentially thousands of years of solitude – yet eventually she found what she had needed all along. Her story is ultimately a love story, one in which self-love and romantic passion can in the end find a way.

The Departure of Odysseus

The relationship between Odysseus and Circe is affectionate and caring by the end of their time together. He seems to look back on her fondly, and she expresses no desire to keep him on her island with her once he has decided it is time to leave. She likely knew from the beginning that he wouldn't be able to stay indefinitely. Her affection or even love for him sees her send him on his way with her blessing and protection in whatever way she can offer it. As Odysseus retells the story, he looks back on their time together affectionately – a clear switch from his initial descriptions of Circe as evil and the dramatic emotional scenes between him and his men. After he decides to follow Hermes' advice and enter Circe's lovely bed, everything seems to be in a good and positive spirit for him.

Obviously this book is only told from the point of view of Odysseus. He fails to consider why she may act in the way she does to large groups of strange men who land on her otherwise uninhabited island. Nor does he mention his ever-faithful and loving wife Penelope here. However, it was not unusual in ancient times for women to have to be loyal and faithful to their husbands while the men themselves are not judged for sleeping with anyone and anything.

A FEMINIST ICON?

A theme that runs throughout Madeline Miller's book is that of sexual assault and rape. When she is younger, before she is exiled, Circe is aware of what can happen to nymphs; she knows that it is not unusual for them to be raped by gods. Rather than accepting that as simply part of what she must endure because of who she is, Circe expresses fear and a desire to avoid putting herself in a position where that can happen to her. The fear of the 'male', whether mortal or not, is thus planted within early on in her life. Her relationship with her mother, who is obsessed with providing children and then handing them out as prizes to kings and gods, will also have had an effect, as she challenges the assumption that that is what women do and are there for. An exception to this of course is Athena, a goddess who has taken a vow of chastity and focuses herself on the pursuit of knowledge and the art of war.

Later in Miller's version of the story it is explained that Circe uses her sorcery, for instance turning men into beasts, to defend herself against further assault; it has happened to her once when humans visited her island and found her alone. Although she was hospitable and kind to them, they took advantage of her. This provides an explanation of why in the future, and certainly with Odysseus's party, she preempts attack, turning his men into animals before they have even the chance of assaulting her. This gives rhyme and reason to her behaviour. Such justification may not have been a consideration for the storytellers of ancient times, but mythologically nymphs were certainly often the playthings of the gods and it is a fact that women would not have been safe from assault or rape then, or indeed often now. So this gives an element of humanity to Circe's cruelty, offering a reason which, to an extent, we can all appreciate and understand.

WHY IS CIRCE SO DEFENSIVE?

Circe's assessment of Odysseus and his men is just as important. Why is she so quick to treat them badly, immediately feeling the need to act in such a brutal way? A quick internet search sees a lot of speculative theories including that she feels taken advantage of, she is fed up with the patriarchal society of ancient Greece, her own desire for power or her hatred of men for their arrogance and selfishness. In a way any and all of these reasons could be legitimate. If you are a woman reading this, you may well have also felt the difficulty of existing within a patriarchal society.

The patriarchy of ancient Greece is both different from and somehow similar to the one we live in today. Women today have the ability to reach positions of power, but their experience is not the same as it would be for a man. It is a lot more difficult and much less common for a woman to be a politician, or in a powerful position in the corporate world – or even for a woman to have complete autonomy over her life, due to circumstances that she may not have been able to control. So many women – if not all, then almost all – feel the frustration of not having the same intrinsic rights as men. Yes, Glaucus rejected Circe, but if he were female and she were male it wouldn't have mattered. The ancient myths are full of men taking exactly what they want, including whichever woman they desired, without the other's consent. So could Circe in fact be a powerful and independent ancient feminist icon?

It is unlikely that a character such as Circe would have been written as a feminist icon in the ancient Greek world. Yet that is also the beauty of myth. It is adaptable to the time and place in which we encounter it, enabling us to reimagine Circe however we wish to suit the needs of a very different modern world. When we put Circe into our modern society she is beautifully independent and fiercely protective of herself and her world; she is also a skilled sorceress.

CIRCE THE JUSTICE WARRIOR

If Circe were a character in a modern-day myth there are many causes she would rally against, involving helping communities of women around the world. Pushing for equality, safety, care, education and basic human rights for women in every corner of the globe, without prejudice. The fearlessness and passion Circe uses to help others and to stand up for herself is something that many women today in my society, and maybe also yours, are now able to do, although it is not easy. They need courage to stand up for themselves in ways they couldn't before for fear of persecution from society and in particular from the patriarchal powers that be.

Circe was persecuted because of her own power and exiled to live alone on an island with only herself and her power for company. Like many women she proved to be resourceful, drawing on her intelligence and strength to create a life that she loved. One of peace, expanding her knowledge about the things that she loved, her craft, finding peace in solitude and defending that peace at all costs. What would the world look like if more of us had the ability to retreat in this way? To follow our passions, to create a place where we could live as we wanted daily without the pressure of fulfilling the needs and wants of others first. A lot of people, including me, believe that if women were allowed more peace and joy then the ripple effect of that would bring more peace and joy to the whole societies in which we exist.

One of Circe's lessons to us is to cultivate your peace where you can as much as possible. Make it a priority. When you do, everyone around you benefits too. Follow your passions as much as you can and educate yourself about the things that can benefit your life, whether these are herbs and plants like Circe, or mythology like me, or something else entirely! When I focus on something I am passionate about it gives me purpose and focus in a way that is not simply for the benefit of those around me.

A COMPLICATED FAMILY OF ORIGIN

As humans we know how complicated and difficult our relationship with our parents can be, and how this can have such a detrimental effect on our whole lives, influencing who we are as people. Of course the divine world of the ancient immortals has these issues too, perhaps even more so. Imagine the issues you have had with your own parents, but compounded by the fact that they are a divine being, a god or goddess. Can gods ever be wrong? Of course we know that they can, if only from the stories told about them. They are flawed, selfish and jealous, while a lot of their actions seem to derive simply from a desire to amuse themselves!

In ancient Greece the gods were the authority. The disasters that occurred in the natural ebb and flow of life would be put down to the wrath of the gods. Defeat in battle, drought, famine and any natural occurrences, for instance floods and storms, would be considered the actions of the gods. This is why ancient people created practices and rituals to honour and pacify the gods. Circe's father is the sun. He arguably has one of the most important jobs in the entire pantheon of the Greek gods and Circe can never escape his watchful gaze. Every day the sun will rise, travel across the sky and then set. Even completely alone and exiled in Aeaea, she is always under her father's watchful eye.

Little is said about the effect that has on her character or behaviour, but I can imagine that it would be very overbearing. Circe releases the need to seek approval from her parents when she embraces her exile. She chooses instead to spend her time doing whatever she needs to do on her own, to make the most of a life of solitude.

Daughter of the Sun

Regardless of anything, Circe cannot escape her father; every day the sun will travel across the sky. Nor can she entirely escape her family, or their necessity in the world. Circe's father uses her to set an example of what can happen when you defy the will of the gods. In a lot of ways it is a fair punishment for the spells she cast turning people into beasts, particularly in the case of Scylla. However, it seems more likely that she is used as an example by Zeus, who requests the exile because he is fearful of her power. As king of the gods, Zeus needs to continue to demonstrate power and influence over the rest of the divine world to maintain his authority. Circe poses a risk to that because she has already shown herself to be powerful, and is starting to discover the true depth of power within her.

Daughter of the Sea

Circe's mother Perse was an oceanid, or sea nymph. She was a daughter of Oceanus, the Titan god of the sea, and Tethys, a water goddess and sister of Oceanus. In ancient interpretations of Circe's myth there is very little information about Perse apart from her lineage and her role as Circe's mother. The positive aspect of this is that it leaves modern storytellers the opportunity to create Perse's story for themselves. In so doing they can imagine what effect Perse's character would have had on Circe; an element of lovelessness and neglect goes some way to explaining some of Circe's actions in her story.

Relationships between mothers and daughters are often somewhat strained, even in the mortal and modern world. Myths are also frequently linked to psychological theories about familial relationships. The famous psychologists Sigmund Freud and Carl Jung used myths to explain many psychological theories; they claimed that myths were 'public dreams' serving to explain the collective subconscious in the way that personal dreams explain the subconscious of an individual. Famous interpretations of myth by Freud include the stories of Oedipus, Narcissus and Icarus as metaphors for real-life situations. Oedipus kills his father and (unknowingly) marries his mother; Narcissus drowns when he falls in love with his own reflection; Icarus is killed because he flies too close to the sun and his home-made wings melt and fall apart. We can imagine what warnings these stories have about the human condition. For now, however, let's return to Circe's relationship with her mother.

Perse as a Mother

Madeline Miller's Perse is a vain, selfish, narcissistic social climber, only interested in what she can get out of any other figure or situation. She is disappointed from the outset that Circe is not attractive enough to marry into the divine family, although Helios describes her as being good enough to marry a mortal prince. Perse is driven by her desire to make others jealous and to have an apparently better life than those around her. When Helios gives her necklaces strung with amber beads, she shows them off to make her sisters jealous. When he observes that Circe is not a suitable match for a divine husband, Perse immediately wants to have another child for him, hoping that this will be an improvement on the last.

Her attitude demonstrates quite a severe disregard of the child's feelings, along with a coldness that the least maternal person would be shocked by. This emotional neglect has an impact on Circe's character, explaining the emotional neediness that she feels when she comes of age to look outside her family of origin for love, and the desperation caused by indifference to her emotional needs.

Mother–Daughter Relationships

If myths are the collective subconscious, as Freud has declared, what could this possibly say about the relationship between mothers and daughters? It is likely that Circe never sought her mother's approval consciously, as she was too distant from the very beginning. However, she continues to seek approval and love subconsciously; starved of love from her family, her actions when rejected romantically later in life are out of proportion. Perhaps she is taking out the rejection from her family on Glaucus, Scylla and Picus. When someone is emotionally neglected by their parents, it is probable that they will lack the fundamental ability to cope with emotions in adulthood.

Perse's daughters are in all probability never going to be able to fulfil exactly the role that Perse wants them to; anyway they are already set up for failure by their mother's character. Not good enough would disappoint Perse and too good would spark jealousy in her. What she wants is a tool to make her life better materially and socially. Using a child to do that will never work because the characters, although divine, are always going to be fundamentally flawed in some way or other, just as humans are.

LIVING UP TO EXPECTATIONS

Helios, Circe's father, is a major Greek deity with cults dedicated to his worship. He is the personification of the sun and therefore extremely important to humans. He is the son of the Titans Hyperion and Theia, brother of the moon goddess Selene and Eos, goddess of the dawn. Having such a famous and important father will have had an effect on Circe's character in many ways. If Circe's mother had also been an important deity she would also have been important and grand. However, being half nymph meant that she could never live up to the reputation of her father.

In some versions of her myth Circe's exile on Aeaea was ultimately down to Helios. Some stories say that Zeus told Helios that he had to exile Circe because of her sorcery, afraid of the power that she could have exerted had she been able to unleash her full potential in the realm of the gods. Circe may have been a bargaining tool between Helios and Zeus. As she was seen as 'too like a mortal' or not divine enough in her family it seems possible that her parents may have favoured her siblings over her. This would not only add to Circe's desire for love and approval from the outside world and in romantic relationships, but it would also explain why she was able to flourish during her exile, no longer pressured to behave in ways that would gain her parents' approval. Sometimes it is necessary for people to disconnect from their family of origin in order to discover who they really are. It is without her family that Circe discovers she is a powerful and independent goddess.

SIBLING RIVALRIES

Circe's complicated relationship with her family certainly doesn't end with her parents. Madeline Miller's Circe in particular has a strained connection with her siblings, her brothers Aeetes and Perses and her sister Pasiphaë. Aeetes is famous in the story of Jason. He is the ruler of Colchis and the keeper of the Golden Fleece. Jason is set the task of obtaining the Golden Fleece by King Pelias, who believes it to be impossible, before Jason can claim his throne as the rightful king of Iolcus. When Jason reaches Colchis, Aeetes sets Jason many impossible tasks to complete in order to get the fleece. Perses, although less famous than his brother, also has a role to play in the ancient myth. In some versions he overthrows Aeetes after Jason has completed his quest and retrieved the fleece from Aeetes. Circe's sister Pasiphaë is also famous, perhaps as much as Circe, for being the mother of the Minotaur.

Pasiphaë and the Minotaur

Pasiphaë's story is dark, disturbing and sad. In Madeline Miller's *Circe* much is made of the relationship between the two sisters. Pasiphaë is a favourite of her parents; she looks and acts like a daughter of a sun god and therefore is a goddess herself, leaving Circe jealous. There is not much chance of them being close, loving and supportive sisters. Circe is mostly resentful and confused by Pasiphaë's lack of interest in her. It seems as though Pasiphaë subscribes to the same consensus that there is something fundamentally wrong with Circe because she is different. In due course Pasiphaë is given to King Minos of Crete as a bride. To Circe this favouritism may well seem unfair; she might have wanted that life for herself. However, it does not end well for Pasiphaë.

After refusing to sacrifice a particularly attractive bull to Poseidon, Pasiphaë becomes obsessed with the idea of mating with him. She recruits Daedalus, the famous inventor and engineer, to help her in the task. He in turn creates a fake cow in which Pasiphaë can hide so that the bull will mate with her. The ruse succeeds and she becomes pregnant with the famous mythological creature, the Minotaur. Circe is recruited and granted temporary escape from Aeaea, the home of her exile, in order to assist Pasiphaë with the delivery of her child. Those around Pasiphaë are aware that it will be a difficult, perhaps even a fatal, delivery; there is also a serious element of the unknown concerning how the creature will behave. Between them, Circe and

Daedalus manage to take the Minotaur to the labyrinth that Daedalus has created. Here he is housed for many years to come, feasting on the youths sent to pacify him, until the famous Greek hero Theseus comes to the island and defeats the Minotaur.

Circe the Big Sister

One of the first occasions when we see Circe's natural tendency to nurture and look after others is when her mother gives birth to her younger brother Aeetes. Perse rejects him and Circe takes it upon herself to look after him and to nurture him as a mother figure even though she is his sister and not much older than him herself. The reason for Perse's rejection is unclear; Madeline Miller says it is because his father speaks no prophecy of him, although we know that he will eventually become the king of Colchis and the father of the famous Medea, and therefore a crucial component in many myths. Circe's nurturing of Aeetes is an interesting foreshadowing of her own maternal relationship with Telegonus. Without this early experience of helping to raise a child and nurturing him to adulthood, she may have struggled more with Telegonus, described as being a difficult child by Miller. She had no assistance in any of his childcare, which included having to protect him from the interest of Athena.

As he grew, Aeetes became favoured by his father. Circe learned from him also, including things discussed in her father's halls that she was not supposed to know about. The connection between the two siblings is the first time that Circe will have felt real love and acceptance, particularly from a family member. This makes the intimacy even more affirming for her, offering her the love she had been craving for her whole life, and which she would continue to seek in her male/female relationships into her adulthood.

DEFIANCE

Circe changes from needing approval from her parents and the gods in general to a defiance of the gods and the desire to forge her own path in the world. Through this switch she creates a life that suits her, even though it is not what she thought she wanted. It takes an acceptance of her circumstances to be able to figure out what it is that she really desires from her life – reflection best undertaken alone, without the influence of her family. Her mother's dream for her was marriage into the divine pantheon, perhaps to one of Zeus's sons or another minor deity. Her father's only desire was to keep his wife happy and to trade off his children in suitable alliances, as was the tradition in ancient Greece.

Having grown up around these attitudes to children would give anyone a limited idea of what they could achieve in life. Yet Circe was able to transcend the limitations when she was exiled. She was then able to explore her own potential in the way that suited her. She had obviously already experimented with herbalism and sorcery, particularly when she cast the spells that changed Picus and Scylla, and she was aware of her own skill and power. Rather than run scared from what could have been a potentially dangerous path, Circe decided she had nothing left to lose, so embraced her identity as a witch and a sorceress or *'pharmekeia'*.

The opportunity to be an infamous witch may not have happened had she not been exiled. She may have just been married off to some mortal prince or king and lived her life as a traditional wife and mother. This may have brought Circe some happiness, particularly as we know that the desire for love and approval underlay a lot of her actions, but she would not have been able to hone her skills in sorcery. She probably would not have been a part of Odysseus's story or helped him and his men. She would probably not have been a mother to Telegonus or her other children, or have helped Penelope and Telemachus either. Even the parts of stories where she was a more minor character, such as that of Medea and Jason, would have been different. So Circe's determination to make the most of her unfortunate circumstances is one of the most important aspects of her character.

SINGLE MOTHERHOOD

Let's consider what life would be like for Circe as a mother. She manages to raise Telegonus to adulthood which is an achievement in itself; those of us who have had children know that it isn't easy at all, and others may have heard this too. Raising a child alone as a single mother, literally from birth, would be extremely challenging. Circe may have had her nymphs around her, as some stories suggest, but others don't mention whether they were there or not. In Madeline Miller's version of Circe's story, she suggests that Circe had sent them away. If Circe was completely alone on her island, then motherhood would be very stressful indeed. Circe is a witch, however, so could use her skills and powers to help her with motherhood if she wanted to.

Madeline Miller describes a very poignant scene in which Circe drugs Telegonus when he is a child. She is trying to cast spells to keep him safe and to keep him away from Athena who has attempted to take the child – probably because she knows him to be a threat to Odysseus, whose patron she is. As Circe is constantly trying to cast the spells to keep Telegonus safe, he becomes more and more difficult and frustrated. She therefore freezes him, whereupon she can see the terror in his eyes and how confused he is. Overwhelmed by distress, Circe releases him from this spell. She embraces him and is regretful and sorry, only hoping that he will trust her again. Mothers who have lost their temper or been driven to despair while dealing with their children will recognize this feeling. Fortunately Telegonus doesn't react in fear to her for long. He is soon back to his demanding and rambunctious ways while his mother struggles to cope.

INSPIRATION FOR MISFITS

Circe is a character often motivated by her desire for love and affection. We see this right from the beginning of her story, in her pursuit of Picus and Glaucus. Her desire for love overrides all sense of proportion when she uses that as motivation to cause such irreparable damage to her love rival in Scylla and to her unrequited love in Picus. As noted above, Circe's desperate need for love could likely stem from the rejection she felt by her parents and siblings in her home as a child. The bitterness and sadness she felt because of that have continued to grow into her adolescence, when she experienced romantic rejection for the first time.

After many, many years of solitude on her island with no one but animals for company, however, Circe begins to feel remorse and regret for the way she acted in the face of heartbreak, but her defences become stronger, so that when she then meets visitors to the island she immediately assumes the worst, making it necessary to turn them into animals anyway. This may be because she doesn't want to risk the pain of getting to know them, or because she doesn't trust any strangers, or even because she fears the emotional pain of connecting with someone and then being rejected. Rather than acting out of fear of her own power and the effect it has on others, she acts out of self-defence and the desire to avoid rejection or emotional pain.

SEEKING ACCEPTANCE

The craving that Circe has for love and acceptance begins in childhood. An outsider from the beginning because she is unusual, she is also considered 'outside' the divine circle into which she is born. Other daughters of the sun god are described as radiant and glowing, but Circe is not. As soon as she is able she seeks love from outside sources, falling so deeply for Picus and Glaucus that she feels rejection profoundly as well. Unable to cope with such intense emotion, she behaves in a reckless and dangerous manner.

I think that we all have the ability to act recklessly when we crave love and attention, particularly if we come from a neglectful or abusive childhood. Sometimes the things we do to get the attention that we desire could put ourselves or others at risk. Love, affection and attention are very powerful, even addictive, emotions. It is human (even for Circe) to want love and connection. Independence is also a quality that we value in society, and sometimes it is very necessary. Independence may be a reaction to trauma or grief, as we seek to protect ourselves from further destructive experience. We go too far in the other direction to avoid codependence, which in turn isn't good. Henceforth being human and seeking human relationships may become a total minefield.

A LOVING SOUL

This may even be the case for a half-god, half-nymph who craves the very human experience of connection and love. When Circe does have that connection, with Odysseus, she shows Odysseus lots of care, love, attention and nurturing in return. Circe is not meant to be the perfect wife or even woman, yet when she receives what she is looking for, she makes the most of it. She knows it is temporary; Odysseus is married to Penelope, and anyway he is human and cannot live forever, unlike her. Still she throws herself into her changed existence, caring for Odysseus and his men, spending time with him, indulging him and for once enjoying her endless life in the way that she has always wanted.

For Circe, living alone on her island will never be the same again after she has known the feeling of being loved in return and of having someone to shower with her love. When Odysseus and his men leave, she is left to return to her life of solitude. This changes again when Telegonus is born, whereupon she is thrust into a world of parenting alone. In this role she is also able to give and receive the love that she has been missing, but in a very different way – and again with the knowledge that it will be temporary. Even if Telegonus chooses to spend his whole life on the island of Aeaea, he still will not live for very long in Circe's life.

CIRCE THE OUTSIDER

Circe is regarded as an outsider in many ways – something a lot of people will be able to relate to. Born to a nymph and a god, she did not fully fit in with either and was destined to be a loner from conception. Her siblings may have had more of one ancestry or the other, but Circe was not pretty enough to be a nymph and not divine enough to be a god. She actually has a lot of human traits, including the way she looks and speaks, that may put her outside the circle of her divine ancestry but ultimately make her a lot more appealing to humans, including Odysseus, Penelope and Telemachus.

These three may be the first characters who connect with Circe in the ways that she needed. These ways could have helped her if she'd had these connections from the beginning, making her realize that she was whole and worthy as she was. This is another aspect of Circe's character to which we can relate. It is not uncommon for people to feel like misfits and to search for a place of belonging, even to crave being away from the world and to seek solitude.

EXILE TO AEAEA

Circe does not have a choice in her exile to Aeaea, but she does seem to thrive there. Without judgement from her family, with her own space to do as she wishes, she can develop her skills and please only herself. As lonely as we would be doing that for an immortal's lifetime, perhaps we can imagine doing it for a certain period of time. What skills would we work on? How would we dress (if at all)? What judgements could we release? I think that solitude can be extremely scary, especially when you are not used to it. However, once you allow yourself to accept the discomfort and to think about what you could do with it to benefit yourself, then it can be extremely liberating.

Circe would have to confront her solitary confinement again when Telegonus left the island. I imagine that 20 years in the life of an immortal is like the blink of an eye, but the amount of love and connection for her in that time would have far exceeded anything she had or would experience again. Having someone depending entirely on her, learning from her and being in her company in a way so different to anything she had experienced before, even in a home full of characters, would feel like a profoundly different stage in life.

In a similar way to anyone who chooses to become a parent, life before is a distant and obscure memory and life after will never be the same again. The middle parenting stage is all-consuming, but it will not last forever. We teach our children to go and be in the world in the knowledge that one day we may well be completely alone again. This is a bittersweet truth of life.

The Benefits of Exile

Upon her exile Circe was forced to be self-sufficient, with no prior instruction on how to do things such as starting fires, cooking, cleaning etc. She is forced to figure out herself how to do all those things – but is then left in the enviable position that she has literally everything she could ever need, which most of us don't have without a lot of hard work. She is given a beautiful and safe home, the tools she needs to survive and even food to eat. Her strength of character really begins to show when she has to work out for herself exactly how to use all these gifts in order to create a life for herself. Whereas most people are given some instruction, at least in order to survive and thrive in a world where they must look after themselves, Circe is left alone without a paddle; she simply has to get on with it or suffer for eternity. Being alone means more than simply having to care for oneself, of course. It also means facing up to every fear you could possibly have about being alone, facing your own mind in a way that could cause mental torment.

To me such an experience feels similar to what a lot of us faced during the lockdowns of the COVID-19 pandemic, particularly the first one in 2020. Not only were we faced with the fear of being extremely sick or potentially even dying, but also much of our life was suddenly taken away from us. I know I'm not alone in having struggled mentally with that. Our social connections with family and friends were abruptly taken from us, as were our daily routines. We faced difficulties in getting supplies and for many of us connection to a news source that accentuated the fear we felt was our only connection to the outside world. Even those of us who lived with other people were subject to a lot of these changes and upheaval. Unfortunately many people didn't make it through that time in the same state mentally as they had been before; some were even driven to take their own lives because of the strain on their emotional and mental health. I know of very few people who do not know someone affected by the epidemic of mental health issues and the loneliness caused by this lockdown.

TAKING BACK CONTROL

Circe knew that to counteract the fear she felt from living alone she needed to take control of her exile and of her life. In order to do so she forced herself to explore her island and to use it to her advantage. She had to connect herself with the reason she was exiled, namely for being a powerful witch, and make it a huge advantage to herself and her life. Without knowing why or how she would need to use *pharmekeia*, she still was drawn to explore it as much as she could. This was the only way that she could regain control of her life, at a time when her punishment had seemingly removed any control she had over events.

She thus managed to find meaning and purpose in the life she created around the nature that surrounded her on her island. She discovered techniques for using the plants of the island, exploring the different ways in which they could affect her, or those around her. At the time Circe did not know what vital importance those skills would have in shaping her future, but they did. For her interactions with Odysseus, for helping Medea, for stories seemingly so much more important in the world of ancient Greece than her own. For protecting Telegonus, the son she would bear Odysseus, destined inadvertently to cause his father's death and then become a new hero in his own right. Even for eventually, in Miller's book, getting her own freedom through becoming mortal and spending the end of her days exploring with her husband Telemachus and their daughters. In the end, *pharmekeia*, sorcery and magic may have been what caused Circe to be exiled and brought her and others suffering – but it was also the reason she gained her freedom and played an integral part in many myths of ancient Greece.

CIRCE'S HOME

Circe's home is something to reflect upon. It is her sanctuary, in much the same way as our homes can be for us. For her it represents protection from a hostile world; a safe place in which she doesn't need to worry about being misunderstood. As she is the only person on the island of Aeaea, it is likely that her home is the only building there. Described as a palace and necessarily suited to the daughter of a god, we know that it is more than a simple country cottage in the forest. Yet is extravagance necessary or suited to Circe? Probably not. Although she grew up in a palace and a home full of feasts and parties, the descriptions of her suggest that she found her home an empty and lonely place.

When alone in her own palace on the island Circe creates her own company in the animals she keeps. She would rather be around animals than the humans who happened to stray upon her island, encroaching upon her space. We know that she would have likely used a kitchen space in which to prepare potions and practise sorcery. She may have had a garden or outdoor space for growing herbs or cultivating plants in a way that meant she need not always rely on finding them in the wild. In some versions of her story Circe is given a loom by Daedalus; she would clearly need a space for this, as well as a bedroom. Several other bedrooms would also be needed, for Odysseus and his men, for Telegonus and for Penelope and Telemachus too – and of course for the nymphs who stayed with her.

Although Circe was expected to be solitary, her home is set up and more than ready for the guests who show up on the island. There is limited information regarding Circe's home in the ancient myths, but I like to think of it as an important reflection of her character as it would be for us – especially if we were forced to spend so much time alone in our homes. Such a situation is similar to that faced by many during the COVID-19 pandemic and the subsequent lockdowns.

The Isolation of Lockdown

During that unsettling time our homes became our sanctuaries and fortresses. We were forced to relate to them in a way that many of us had never had to before. Sales in DIY goods and home furnishings skyrocketed because people knew that in order to spend such a large amount of time at home happily it needed to be peaceful and a true reflection of themselves. We learned that we could, in fact, do whatever we needed to do from our homes and we took solace in the fact that there, at least, we were safe. Denied travel or even basic social interaction, we decided to make the most of the spaces around us. This is why I believe that Circe would have had an important relationship with her palace; it would have reflected exactly who she was and what she needed from her home.

Alone or Lonely?

The notion that Circe's island and home was also inhabited by helpful nymphs brings up other questions in her story. Would Circe have wanted a house full of young nymphs looking to emulate her and learn from her? Likely not – especially at first if she is used to her solitude and has developed a system and routine that she enjoys and thrives in alone. Yet as we know she is naturally quite caring and nurturing, and so may in fact have enjoyed assuming that role with the visiting nymphs. The mythological world is full of jealousy and spite. Circe may have been envious of the nymphs' freedom, including their ability to come and go to and from Aeaea, but then she knew also she was safe there, it was her home; would she have really been in need of escape? Would that be something she was dreaming of at all? However, she may well been jealous of the nymphs' ability to enter a romantic relationship and have a family if they wished: something that, exiled on her island, she couldn't do.

It is likely that Circe may have enjoyed the nymphs' assistance after decades spent alone. Maintaining her home, described as a grand dwelling or even a 'palace', may not have been a priority when she lived alone; her main focus was expanding her knowledge about the herbs and plants with which she worked. It is likely that the nymphs would be doing some sort of caretaking around the home and land of Circe as handmaidens and assistants, so as to earn their keep and education in her arts. Circe may have found this overbearing and it seems as though she didn't have a choice over whether she wanted the nymphs to be present or not. However, I like to think that her nurturing nature would take over and she would relish the chance to share her knowledge with other nymphs. Given her character, she might also hope to give them a glimpse into what life would look like if they did choose to live independently and in tune with nature, rather than becoming just another wife, mother and a plaything for a god as so many nymphs seemed to.

AN IMPORTANT CONNECTION TO NATURE

Circe is deeply connected to nature in so many ways. She is part of the sun, the daughter of the sun god Helios, a personification of the sun, although she doesn't necessarily see that in herself. Indeed she compares herself unfavourably to other members of her family, believing that she is not as pretty or as bright; nevertheless she still has that natural ancestry from her father's side. Circe's mother Perse is an oceanid, or sea nymph: nature spirits in mythology who reside in places such as forests, woods, rivers or seas. As noted above, beautiful nymphs would often find themselves to be the desired target of a god for sex, in this case with Helios, a personification of the sun, and many divine ancestral lines are through the unions of gods and nymphs.

These nature connections in her blood may be what inspires Circe to become a witch, working with nature to create her spells and craft her world in the way that she does. She lives and works in harmony with nature on her island. Before her exile Circe is experimenting with spells beyond her control; she discovers how powerful nature can be when she turns Scylla into the monster who devours men. This disastrous experiment obviously changed Circe's life forever – yet it made her into the character necessary to continue Odysseus's story. Settled on her island, Circe had free reign of whatever part of nature she wanted. She spent many of the thousands of years of her life experimenting with different plants and herbs, using her instinct in the absence of any teacher or guide; such inherent skill may have been something she inherited. Having harnessed such power, she has simply to try to discover what to do with it. She is able to pass on this important knowledge to Penelope and also, to an extent, to her son Telegonus. Circe may well have also passed it on to her daughter(s) and Telemachus.

As the first 'witch', Circe was the discoverer of the craft, then its master and teacher. If mythology is real, then the beginning of herbology, spell work and homeopathy may well have begun with her magic. Recording this may have been Homer's intention when he first wrote down the character of Circe, although it is more likely that this derived from a previous oral tradition that predates the *Odyssey* by who knows how long. It is therefore likely to be a sought-after explanation of the origin of working with plants for many different reasons including enchantment, healing and more.

Circe's Connection with Animals

Circe has a clear affinity for working with animals. For a long time she is completely alone on the island of Aeaea apart from the animals there, particularly the ones she has created. She coexists peacefully with wolves, lions and other creatures. In Miller's story she creates a lioness who becomes for a long time her closest companion. Circe frequently turns mortals into beasts, such as pigs, lions or wolves – as well, of course, as the occasional monster. In multiple versions of Circe's myth it is said that when the mortals are changed into beasts they retain their mortal minds – making the punishment, or perceived punishment, all the more cruel. If the lions and wolves of the island are indeed former humans, you could be forgiven for questioning why they do not then attack Circe in revenge. It could be, of course, that they believe she is the only person capable of changing them back to their original form, or it could simply be that they fear her power too much. She has turned them into animals, but their fate could have been worse and they know it.

Turning Men to Beasts

A powerful sorceress in ancient mythology was definitely someone to be feared – even by Zeus, the most powerful of the gods. As such, it is understandable that Circe would be feared by mere mortals also. When Circe is confronted by multiple men from Odysseus's party she is already convinced that they will judge her, perhaps even threaten her. Madeline Miller goes so far as to suggest that Circe has been sexually assaulted by previous male visitors to her island, and that is why she gives Odysseus's men no chance to act in the same way.

The other authors of Circe's story, the (presumably) male and ancient storytellers, offer her no such excuse. She acts quickly and out of self-defence, first turning the men into pigs, then rounding them up and caging them. We do not know what she plans on doing next. She may well slaughter and eat them; pigs are mostly useful as food. Or she may feed them to the other wild beasts that she has tamed, such as the lions and wolves. Whoever she turned into wolves and lions in the first place may have caused her to feel threatened, or they may not. If they were human first, she clearly prefers their company as animals. When they are animals, whether through fear or not, they are less of a concern for her; she is able to coexist with them in peace.

INSPIRING A CONNECTION WITH NATURE

Circe's connection to nature is a theme woven throughout all versions of her story. We see it in her working with plants and *pharmekeia*, in coexisting harmoniously with animals, in using the laws of nature to create her world and in employing magic to meet her own ends. It also lies in her divine ancestry, being a child of the sun and of a sea nymph.

The modern world encourages disconnection from nature. I have heard it said that today's children spend less time outdoors than some prisoners do. As I child of the 1980s, mostly growing up in the 1990s, I spent much of my time outdoors – playing with friends, exploring nature and investigating more urban environments too. The area I lived in had housing estates, shops, schools etc, but it had lots of natural space too; fields, woodland, simply overgrown bits of land that weren't specifically for anything, parks and so on. I spent a lot of my childhood deliberately creating my own space in these pockets of nature. There my friends and I would set up a whole house, a school, a dance studio and more.

These little pockets of nature were natural canvases; we could project whatever we wanted on to them. Children may have less opportunity to do this now; they may be more easily distracted by computer games or TV, both of which were certainly a factor in my childhood too, but they would probably have had a greater impact if they'd been better or if I'd had more access to them.

Working in Harmony with Nature

Circe is not *playing* in the natural landscape around her in the same way that I, and others, did as a child, yet she is coexisting with it, engaging with its variety and beauty, in a way that we all could benefit from if we disconnected from technology more. In what ways would this be beneficial to us, either as a society or as individuals? It has been proved that mental health issues are helped by fresh air, nature and exercise. When you help your own mental health, or that of an individual, you improve a lot of societal issues too; addiction, abuse, abandonment, neglect and stress are all linked to mental (and physical) wellbeing. When people feel better in themselves there is less of a strain on health services financially, leaving more money available to help elsewhere, for example in schools or in keeping the environment cleaner.

If we are to take inspiration from Circe, we would explore the nature in our immediate vicinity. Yes, it's nice to go away on holiday, but how much do you know about the nature on your doorstep? Could you walk to the canal down the road daily, or explore the park around the corner, or visit your local nature reserve? You can imagine how Circe would do this, noticing the details of the natural world around her, paying attention to subtle daily changes as one season moves into another. This is our chance to feel at one with the natural world, as she did.

RIGHTEOUS ANGER AND ITS LESSONS FOR US

Circe is of divine ancestry and therefore often classed as a goddess. She is known in mythology as the goddess of sorcery. When Odysseus overcame Circe's sorcery with the help of the messenger god Hermes, he then confronted her and she turned his men back into their human form. Circe and Odysseus enter a romantic relationship, resulting in him and his men staying with Circe and the nymphs for a year; only then does he move on and continue his journey home to Ithaca. Why did he stay for so long? They seem to have a loving connection for a year, after which Circe helps Odysseus by forewarning him of dangers ahead before he finally leaves. His departure is inevitable and they both know it. Odysseus is already married to Penelope, regarded as the ultimate ideal for a Greek wife while she waits patiently for Odysseus's return from Troy for 10 years, not even knowing whether he is still alive. She resolutely refuses to remarry, despite being pursued by many worthy suitors.

So we know that Circe and Odysseus's relationship was not meant for marriage and a family. She may have fallen for him because he seemed to be the only man who outwitted her attempt at sorcery. In many of Circe's stories we can conclude that she is lonely and desperate for love. She attempts to seduce multiple mythological characters then, when rejected, she turns them into beasts. I believe there are so many interpretations available about Circe, and basically about any mythological character. I prefer to think of Circe as an empowered woman rather than a victim of her own desperation, craving attention and love. We certainly know that she turned those who rejected her into beasts. However, we also know that they were likely coming to her for reasons of their own; Glaucus, for example, was seeking a potion to achieve his own ends in seducing Scylla. I want to think of Circe being more like someone who has had enough of trying to meet the needs of other people and not receiving the gratitude she deserves. Wounded and hurt, she reacts swiftly to the impunity of those who seek to exploit her power.

It's OK to be Angry

The image of Circe as an angry, spurned woman is one that permeates through a lot of her representations. Her wrath is definitely something that no mortal would want to face – to be turned into a beast yet retaining the heart and mind of a human, with no ability to escape or to communicate their distress. Would any of us want to do similar when we have been hurt or upset by things in life? Or even when we feel scared or threatened? We may feel the need to turn others into beasts, even if we are not able to, but I am sure at some point in life most people consider trying to exact some sort of pain or revenge – often emotional pain, but sometimes not. Some people definitely do act upon that impulse. Consider the stories of scorned women wrecking their partners' suits, cars or watches when they discover that they have been cheated on.

In Circe's case, she does not take out her anger on the man but on the other woman. Nor is she in a relationship with him; he hasn't cheated on her. Her anger, as unjustified as it is extreme, is also directed the wrong way, yet we can still relate to it. It is precisely this anger, described as it is by men, that they particularly fear. They are alarmed that women have an ability to take out their stress and frustration on men: to hurt them in ways they can't imagine, for instance by hurting those around them and by casting spells they could never understand. This is why in a patriarchal society a character such as Circe is classed as 'evil': she is a vengeful woman who is difficult to control. Men in a patriarchal society want women to be placid and controllable; they then don't have to live in fear of what a powerful woman who is angry can do. In the story of Circe that is written by men, she is clearly to be feared and needs to be isolated from the world, somewhere she can do as little damage as possible. This is where angry and powerful women belong – in contrast to those like Penelope, devoted wives and mothers who wouldn't hurt a fly.

This is why it is important for modern women to retell Circe's story. We know why she is angry, and we understand; we too are angry at treatment received at the hands of men. Educated and successful, we are ready to use the stories of mythological women to make our point about why the patriarchal society is unfair and why it is time for change.

Selfishness

As we know from other myths, it was Circe who in fact turned Scylla into a monster because she was jealous of Glaucus's interest in the nymph. To act in this way shows an extreme selfishness and a level of evil that is difficult for mortals to comprehend. In the world of gods and goddesses, however, it is a common theme of cause and effect, of emotions that lead to dire circumstances and the dangers of sulking when you don't get what you want. There are other ways to frame this, though, as we will find out later.

Circe's actions were not always selfless or well intentioned – not by a long way. This is particularly true as regards her treatment of Scylla. In Madeline Miller's version of the story Circe spends a lot of time thinking about, and deeply regretting, turning Scylla into a monster, not only because she has ruined Scylla's life, but also because she has then brought about the deaths of hundreds of mortals as a result. She transforms Scylla because she is in love with Glaucus herself, yet he desires Scylla. The rhetoric of unrequited love has clearly been going on for centuries; it is certainly something that most people can relate to, having experienced it at some point in their life. How you dealt with that at the time probably did not involve taking it out on the other person with whom your crush was involved. Heartbreak and rejection can be very difficult emotions to process and deal with, but they are a fundamental part of the human experience.

CIRCE'S LESSONS FOR US

In Ovid's *Metamorphoses* Glaucus goes to Circe for help when he is rejected by Scylla, asking the enchantress to 'make her share my hell'. At this point Circe offers herself up as a romantic partner and Glaucus rejects her; even though his love for Scylla is unrequited, he is so enamoured by her that it is Scylla or no one for him. At this point Circe directs her anger onto Scylla, likely thinking that if she became unattractive to Glaucus then he would choose Circe instead. Scylla's revenge was to kill some of Odysseus's men. Ovid describes this being how she showed her hatred for Circe, but in other versions of the story she also takes her revenge on humankind by claiming many other innocent lives.

We can't help but wonder what could have been different about Circe's story if she had simply been accepted by Glaucus instead of being rejected by him. She may well have been happy; Scylla would not have become a monster and lives could have been saved. On the flip side, she would not then have been exiled to Aeaea and would not have looked after Odysseus and his men. Nor would she have given birth to their son, Telegonus, nor would he have killed his father Odysseus. The story of Homer's *Odyssey* would have been completely different.

We have to accept the parts of us that are enraged, angry, bitter and jealous and send them love: there are reasons for what we go through. We should always remember to seek positive reasons and to believe in our ability to learn from events: 'it is happening for you, not to you' and there is a reason for it. This is a vital part of Circe's lesson for us.

Modern Short Stories of Circe

Rise of the Witches
L.D. Burke

Black clouds obscured the full moon as Circe spread enchanted herbs over the jagged boulder at the edge of the tallest cliff on her island. Thunder boomed; lightning flashed. Rain stung her face, but the Sorceress of Aeaea ignored it all as she wove her iron will beneath the spell.

"I will be left alone. No gods or men will set foot on Aeaea. Aóratos."

Aeaea trembled as the magic set.

Two rock vipers slithered from the boulder's tip, their bronze eyes illuminated in a lightning flash. Circe stumbled back, tearing her chiton. In the millennia she'd lived on Aeaea, she'd seen no snakes.

The wind screeched like a woman under attack, and human-like shadows darted between the fir trees. Unease gripped Circe as she descended the rocky trail. A wispy, gray woman stepped into Circe's path.

"He killed me." Her scratchy wail blended with the wind.

Cursing the unwelcome guest, Circe stepped around the figure. "This is Aeaea, home of the sorceress Circe. None are welcome here."

Thunder echoed through the trees, and the shadowy figure materialized before Circe again.

"My husband killed me." Circe stood with a bulging stomach before a screaming, stone-eyed man. His spittle hit her cheek. "He claimed the child I carried was not his." Hairy hands wrapped around Circe's neck. "Eleni of Athens prays for justice."

Lightning flashed, banishing the vision and the shade. Circe ran as more women's voices wailed in the wind, shouting their names and stories of deaths at a lover's hands. The cacophony pursued Circe past the empty livestock pens and through the herb garden. When she reached the safety of her kitchen and slammed the oak door, the shades rattled every shutter in her marble manor. Her lionesses looked up from their place before the hearth and growled. In the entry hall, her wolves snarled.

Huffing, Circe leaned against the door and put a hand to her throat.

"You look terrible." Medea, her niece, stared with furrowed brows from one of the two chairs before the hearth. A sack of calamint seeds, a gift from Medea's travels, sat next to a goblet of wine on the table between the chairs.

Not in the mood for Medea's taunting, Circe stomped down the hall to her bedroom for dry clothes. When she returned, Medea held two full wine goblets and a pitcher sat on the table. She handed a goblet to Circe and motioned to the other chair. "Tell me why you're shaken. You've cast spells in storms worse than this."

Circe took a long drink of bitter wine and studied Medea's face. They had the same golden eyes that glowed faintly with Titan ancestry, the same tanned skin, the same black braids. But where Medea looked young, Circe looked haggard. Like she'd given up. Perhaps she had.

RISE OF THE WITCHES

Once, she welcomed guests to Aeaea. But that was before she learned that poets' stories filled with lies and half-truths hurt worse than no stories at all. Circe only allowed Medea on Aeaea now, though her niece's concern made her question that decision at the moment.

Medea took her aunt's hand. "You may live in solitude, but you aren't alone."

Circe stiffened. She'd confided in a few gods and mortals over the centuries – even Medea, once – and each time had been scorned. But, loath as she was to admit it, the vipers scared her, and she couldn't understand why wailing shades called to her for justice. What did they expect Circe, exiled witch of Aeaea, to do?

She took a gulp of wine. "Niece. I may need your help."

When Circe finished her tale, Medea's eyes flickered with excitement. "No one has ever prayed to us." She drummed her fingers on the arm of her chair. "Eleni, the others, none sound familiar. They must be commoners."

"They should pray to Themis. Or Dike." Circe slammed her goblet on the table. "I cannot help them."

Medea crossed her arms. "Can't? Or won't?"

"Both. I cannot leave Aeaea, and I do not assist mortals."

Medea snorted. "No, not you. Never."

"Those days are long past."

"I know, I know. 'If I'm only a footnote in tales of men and gods, I'd rather not be mentioned at all.'" Medea leaned forward. "But just because a story isn't written doesn't mean it isn't told. Answering the prayers of women calling for aid against men who controlled them? That would spark stories. Ones I'd think we both would want roles in."

Circe shook her head. "Why do they not pray to you, Medea, who turned herself immortal?"

"Because they do not wish to be immortal. They wish to be avenged. So, they pray to Circe, who turns men into swine."

The storm broke overnight, and Medea sailed at dawn, promising to discover who sent snakes to Aeaea. Medea's words hung in Circe's mind long after her niece departed. She'd never considered that where men saw a seductress to be conquered, women saw a powerful ally. Perhaps she should answer the shades' prayers. After all, she knew how it felt to be ignored. She had called to her father countless times early in her exile, only for his chariot to pass without pause.

She mulled it over each time she tended the calamint. As the seeds grew, the spell became clearer. When the white flowers bloomed, the magic spoke. "*Calamint. Black roses. Fir needles.*"

Flanked by lionesses, she cast the summoning on Aeaea's peak in the shadow of the boulder anchoring the island's veil. As she worked, she wove her will with the herbs: Eleni's husband washed ashore on Aeaea. The herb's woodsy, floral scent swirled in the wind as she rolled a palm-sized stone in the paste and flung it into the sea. "*Éla edó.*"

The sea trembled as the spell took hold.

Magic beckoned Circe to Aeaea's clifftop two weeks later. There, surrounded by wolves, she watched a ship grow on the horizon. "Tonight," she said to her pack, "you eat pork."

The ingredients for the transformation potion called to her like old friends as she descended the mountain: mandrake root, alder cones, hawthorn bark. As she chopped the herbs, she pictured a slow transformation as agonizing as Eleni's death.

Darkness fell as the potion cooled in bottles on the counter. When the crescent moon rose, the wolves snarled and ran barking to the shore. Circe collected a bottle and followed her pack. Dirt turned to sand beneath her sandaled feet as she emerged from the forest. Growling, her wolves circled a dark-haired man lying on his back in the sand. Circe shooed them aside and squatted next to her guest. The man's head lolled to the side, revealing a strong jawline covered in dark stubble and faint age lines at the corners of his eyes. Clearly this man was old enough to control himself. Circe squeezed his cheeks until his mouth popped open and poured her brew down his throat.

His fingers twitched, then his eyes fluttered open. He sat up with a groan. "What…happened?" He pressed his palm to his forehead. "Could you tell me where I am Lady…?"

"Circe." His eyebrows shot up and his eyes darted between her and the snarling wolves. Circe smirked. "You are on the island of Aeaea. I summoned you after Eleni of Athens prayed to me for justice. Why would she have done that, do you suppose?"

"Lady, I–"

"Metamorfóno."

He screamed. His bones cracked, and his skin turned pink. He fell to all fours as his hands and feet reshaped into hooves. His scream morphed to a pig's squeal.

Circe tilted her head to the side with a crooked smile. She learned long ago never to doubt her power, but a spell manifesting still swelled her chest with pride.

The pig charged Circe. A wolf sprang in front of her, snapping its jaws. "Now, now," Circe said. "Share with your pack."

Terrified squeals and lupine yipping echoed through the forest as Circe climbed the path to a grove of fir trees. By the time she snapped off a branch, the squealing had silenced.

* * *

"You've been busy," Medea shouted over the squealing pigs rooting in the mud for kitchen scraps.

The women, flanked by lionesses, stood near the gate. Circe rifled through the bundle of seeds Medea brought from her travels. "My fir trees are stripped bare. My black roses are cut. My calamints are flowerless. But I answered each shade's prayer."

Smiling wickedly, Medea opened the gate halfway. The largest pig headbutted the others and shoved through. Medea slammed the gate, trapping its back leg. It squealed as it scrambled free and bolted into the forest. She clicked her tongue at the lionesses, and they bounded after it. Medea's smile widened as the squelch of ripping flesh silenced the pigs in the pen. Medea elbowed Circe in the side and wiggled her eyebrows.

Circe rolled her eyes and walked to the herb garden.

Medea heaved a sigh and followed. "Plant the roses. Those seeds came from one of Rhode's personal bushes. She said you'll need them."

Circe knelt at the garden's edge and dug holes for the seeds. "How many of my father's wives are you visiting?"

"Just Rhode. With all the visitors to her gardens, I thought she might've heard who sent the snakes."

A breath caught in Circe's throat, and she turned to Medea. "And?"

"She hasn't. No one has." Medea shrugged. "Anyway, we should brew growth potions while I'm here. Women will be calling for aid."

"Why?"

"The missing men's families are threatening the murdered women's friends and sisters. They believe the women killed their sons." Medea leaned against the fence. "I told them prayers to Circe, Protector of Women, will be answered."

Heat flared through Circe's body, and she snapped to her feet. "Are you mad? Protector of Women? I am not a goddess to pray to!" She threw the seeds at Medea. "Go back. Tell them to pray to Hera. She is the goddess of women. I am not protecting anyone." She stomped into her kitchen and slammed the oak door in Medea's face.

Medea flung the door open. "You must! Who will help these women if you do not? Most mortals barely notice them. Olympians hold them down to ensure offerings and prayers continue. Titans care for no one."

"I want to be left alone!" Circe turned on her niece ready to banish her from the island, but the tears in Medea's eyes stopped her. Medea hadn't cried since she begged Circe to aid Jason and the Argonauts. "Why does this matter to you? You are not known for softness."

"I see myself in them." Medea's voice cracked. She looked at the ground and hugged her elbows. "You aren't the only one the poets misrepresent."

For the first time, Circe understood her niece's nomadic lifestyle. The tales painted her as bloodthirsty, insane, and murderous. Not unjustly. But to only be remembered for that, without exploring why you believed such violence your best option? It was worse than being remembered as a seductive sorceress.

"I will continue–" Medea grinned and opened her mouth, but Circe held up a hand. "I will continue *if* you assist me. We must control the narrative."

Magic whispered to Circe. She beckoned Medea to follow her, and they returned to the garden. Circe snapped off stalks of mint, filling the air with a fresh scent. Circe placed the herb in Medea's hands and closed her fingers. "Spread the story that all women need do is speak my name and throw a mint sprig into the wind while picturing those who threaten them. Make it well known that Circe, Sorceress of Aeaea, is the reason the people disappear."

Medea gripped Circe's forearm and grinned. "I can hear it now. A new myth spreading on the lips of women, spoken at looms and over knitting. The rise of the witches."

* * *

The setting summer sun warmed Circe's back through her lavender chiton as she knelt in her garden rubbing a growth draught over the rosebuds that grew from Rhode's seeds. "Come on darlings."

Slowly, the buds broke and blood-red petals unfolded.

Leaving the flowers to absorb the sun, Circe picked up her rubbish basket and lugged it to the pigsty, her wolves yipping happily at her heels. She emptied the contents into the pen. The pigs squealed, headbutting each other in a fight for the scraps. A wolf whined at her side, its head tilting toward the pigs. Circe scratched it behind the ears. "If I loosed a pig every time you asked, there would be nothing left for the lionesses."

A breeze rustled the trees, carrying mint's fresh scent. Circe squared her shoulders. "*Miló.*" The pigsty and wolves disappeared as a vision captured her mind

"I am Tasoula of Athens." Circe walked through an Athenian market with her head down and a basket clutched at her chest. A gray-haired woman stuck out her cane, and Circe tripped, spilling figs, olives, and dried meat into the street. "She calls me murderer. Blames me for her savage son's fate. Says I will be next. I call to you, Circe, Protector of Women."

Circe's vision cleared, but her eyes squinted in rage. A woman threatening another woman over a violent man. She would not allow it.

The setting sun filled the kitchen with orange light, and the mortar and pestle scraped against each other as Circe ground the spell ingredients in her kitchen. While the transformation draught steeped over the hearth, Circe, flanked by her lionesses, climbed Aeaea's cliff to cast the summoning. At the base of her boulder, she rubbed the paste over a stone, weaving her will with the magic: The woman washing up on Aeaea's shore, nothing but skin and bones. Circe hurled the enchanted rock into the sea. "*Éla edó.*"

The waves trembled as the spell took hold.

Circe turned and froze. A rock viper slithered around the boulder's base and disappeared into the forest.

* * *

The magic whispered the woman's arrival days later. Circe waited on the beach with her pack. Moonlight glistened off the waves as they washed the unconscious woman to shore. Her peplos clung to the ribs jutting beneath her skin. Circe smirked with satisfaction. Clearly the journey had been as unkind as intended.

She poured the transformation draught down the woman's throat and stood back. The woman spasmed and water erupted from her mouth. When her coughs stopped, the woman wiped her mouth with the back of her hand and stared wide-eyed at Circe and her wolves. "Where...am I?"

"This is Aeaea." Circe raised her chin. "I am the sorceress Circe." The woman's eyes bulged, and she scooted away. Circe knelt next to the woman. "Do you know the kind of man you raised?"

The woman paled. "It wasn't his fault. His father—"

"*Metamorfóno.*"

The woman screamed and fell to her hands and knees. Her spine stretched. Her breasts slid toward her legs. Her cries morphed into a blood-curdling *mooooo*. Big, brown eyes darted from Circe, to the wolves, to the woods.

"I would offer you a pen with your son, but my wolves ate him." Circe turned and started up the path. "Come along."

The cow stumbled behind Circe, twigs snapping under cloven hooves. At the pen, Circe prodded the cow inside and slammed the gate. "Let it never be said Circe fails to answer a prayer."

The next morning, frankincense's musky scent coaxed Circe from sleep. In her kitchen next to her mortar and pestle, she found a bowl of calamint seeds encircled in incense smoke. The moment Circe touched the bowl, Tasoula's voice filled the room.

"Thank you."

* * *

Medea stepped from her ship onto the stone dock and thrust a bundle wrapped in damp cloth into Circe's arms. "We have a problem." She marched up the stone steps and down the path toward the manor.

"Hello to you, too." Circe followed her niece, fiddling with the strings around the bundle.

"Don't open that here." Medea's eyes bulged in fear. She grabbed Circe's wrist and dragged her up the path.

A weight enclosed Circe's chest. Medea feared very little. "What is happening?"

"Inside."

As soon as Circe stepped over the threshold into her kitchen, Medea locked the door and closed the shutters.

Circe tossed the bundle to the table. "Enough of this. Speak. Now."

"It started with the spell we taught the women. Tasoula established a cult. They call you Goddess of Witches. Olympus is angry. Zeus says you overstepped. Apollo prophesied the gods' power crumbling."

Circe's knees gave out and she fell into a chair. "Who is coming for me? When?"

Medea shook her head. "I don't know. Soon."

Fear clutched Circe's heart, and her hands shook. "I did not intend to become a goddess."

"I know. I'm sorry." Medea took her aunt's hand. "But I'm with you. What do we do?"

Circe didn't know. They could strengthen the veil, but it only kept Aeaea out of sight and out of mind. If Olympus targeted her, it would fail.

Tendrils of fog rose from the bundle between them. Circe tilted her head and unwrapped a forearm-sized mandrake root surrounded by shining silver mist. A wisp of hope rooted in Circe's chest. "Medea, where did you get this?"

"It's from Hecate's Garden."

Circe's head snapped up and her mouth fell open in surprise. "Hecate supports me?"

"Well." Medea smirked and shrugged a shoulder. "She left her garden unlocked."

Magic whispered, *"Aconite. Rhode's black roses."*

Cold calm washed over Circe as a plan formed alongside the spell. "Medea, help me cast a ward. And then take a message to my cult."

***

The divine ward manifested a silvery haze over Aeaea, but it could not dim Helios's blaze when he directed his attention to his daughter in noonday sun.

"Circe!"

Scalding wind carried his voice to Circe. She stood flanked by wolves and lionesses atop Aeaea's cliff. Next to her, the boulder anchoring Aeaea's veil and now the divine ward as well glowed silver.

Circe's stomach rolled. Last time she challenged her father, he'd nearly disintegrated her. The silver ward sparkled its reassurance. She forced her shoulders back and stood tall. "I am here, Father."

Helios's fiery steeds flew straight toward her.

Her heart pounded. "Hecate, Goddess of Witchcraft, hold our spell."

The heat from Helios's steeds flushed Circe's cheeks. Her legs twitched, begging to run. Her father came into view. She set her jaw and held firm. With thunderous neighing, the flaming steeds reared back and turned, halting the chariot beside the silver mist. Helios glared at Circe. Helios's power boiled the sea below, thickening the air with salt. Sweat beaded on her brow. Silver bubbles popped in the mist. Circe's breathing quickened. What if the ward broke?

"You little witch." Helios spoke with a wildfire's roar. "You dare to steal from Hecate? To stand against me?"

"I dare to defend myself and my island."

Helios burned with sunlight. "You forget your place."

"I have not interfered with Olympus." She measured her speech to ensure her voice did not crack.

"You became a goddess." His power sizzled against the mist.

Her wolves whimpered and stepped back. Her lions bowed their heads, lips raised in silent snarls. Circe stepped to the cliff's edge. "So you came to kill me. What do you think that will tell the mortals? They will the Olympians' weaknesses. My cult will believe their deity powerful enough to threaten Olympus and the Titans. Stories of Circe, Goddess of Witches, Protector of Women, will spread through markets and homes. It will pass through generations. The sun will never set on me."

Helios's eyes glazed with prophecy. Circe's tension eased. He would see the pieces she had lain falling into place. His eyes cleared and he glared at her, his heat burning holes in the mist.

She weaved her Titan divinity and iron will through the holes. "I offer an alternative. Continue acting as though I am nothing. The cosmos will bend to divine will, as it always does. I will fade, as I always have. Who would remember me when there is Zeus, Apollo, Cronos, Helios?"

He scoffed, the familiar hatred darkening his eyes. "No one will remember you." His blazing heat receded. Goosebumps rose on Circe's arms in the chill of its absence. "You will turn to stone here. Alone in the dark. Forgotten." He slapped his golden reins, and his steeds' fire flared. He flew over the western horizon, leaving Aeaea in midday darkness.

Circe sank to her knees, leaning on a lioness for support. So this was his retaliation for outsmarting him: eternal exile in eternal night. It would not deter her. Magic is strongest in the dark.

RISE OF THE WITCHES

* * *

Medea and Circe lounged on a woven blanket in the garden, sipping wine and eating lunch. The divine ward twinkled like stars against the endless night while sunlight shone from the roses that bloomed from Rhode's seeds.

Medea plucked a blood red bloom and tucked it behind her ear. "You know, when Rhode gave me those seeds, I never thought they carried Helios's power."

"My island would be dead without this light." Circe leaned into the flowers' warmth. "I am simply glad she supported me."

"Most goddesses and women do. Which reminds me, Tasoula showed me the household altar she built to you." Medea popped a grape into her mouth. "She included statues of pigs and cows she carved from a fir branch."

Circe chuckled. "I suppose that's fitting."

"She gives a set to everyone who joins the Cult of Circe. It's grown quite popular, you know."

In answer, a bowl of seeds materialized between the women, incense smoke hovering around it. *"Circe, Goddess of Witches, bless our work."*

Medea's face pinched. "That must get annoying."

Circe smiled at her niece's jealousy. "You are welcome to any seeds you want." Piles of bowls filled with every known seed cluttered her manor hall, and prayers whispered through Aeaea's breezes daily.

"It's not me they're offered to." Medea put her nose in the air and sipped her wine. "Your Athenian cult plans to sail here.

135

Tasoula's idea. She wants to learn witchcraft from the Goddess of Witches herself."

Circe choked on her wine. "It's not my place."

Two rock vipers slithered from beneath the rose bushes. Medea and Circe froze, their gazes following the snakes to the garden gate where a cloud of silver mist gathered. A pale, raven-haired woman holding keys in her hands stepped from the mist. The snakes slithered up her legs and coiled around her arms. She stepped from the mist, and the roses went dark, plunging the island into silvery night. "It is exactly your place, Circe, Goddess of Witches." She spoke in a deep, clear voice that sounded like midnight.

"Hecate," Circe breathed. "Y-you sent the snakes."

Hecate nodded. "And the shades. And I left my garden unlocked."

"W-why?" Medea sounded as stunned as Circe.

"To see what my original witches would do. I was not disappointed." She looked up at the ward overhead. "That is good witchcraft."

"Th-thank you," Circe and Medea said together.

Hecate fixed her gaze on Circe. "You have my blessing to teach." She turned to Medea. "You both have my blessing to practice your craft as you wish and to call on me whenever you need."

Mist formed around Hecate, and she disappeared. The roses lit up, returning the island to midday light. Mouth agape, Circe stared at the space Hecate had occupied. Even with Hecate's blessing, could she really teach? Could she open her island again? Her heart ached with longing for an end to her loneliness.

"If I teach," Circe said slowly, turning toward Medea, "will you stay?"

Medea grinned. "I suppose I could settle for a while."

"Well then," Circe stood, her lionesses and wolves running to her. "I shall need to unveil Aeaea."

Darkness

Z.D. Campbell

The sun has vanished! I don't know exactly how it happened. Complete darkness, as though a solar eclipse befell the entire earth, but so much worse. The sun disappeared in the blink of an eye, and I fear it never shall return. In the dawning of this tragedy, the world stood still. No one moved, no one made a sound, we all just stood there, in shock, trying desperately to focus on something, anything, in the darkness. The silence was all but the loudest I have ever heard. Suddenly, the animals, humans, and immortals became erratic. The collective sound of the entire world screaming was unbearable. To which, I believe my eardrums could have ruptured. The ringing didn't stop for at least a week. Prior to the sun vanishing, in times of darkness, fire was our source of light, and even the largest flames could only pierce the darkness but so far. Without the sun's light, or the burning flames of a fire, seeing your own hand could be perplexing at times. For the moment, the stars are the only light visible to me. Even now the moon has lost its glow, showing only a dark orb, blocking a few stars that would help light the surface. My thoughts and worries are growing tremendously, I've never seen this much darkness engulf the world.

After hours of searching, stubbing my toes, and falling on my face, I managed to find my flint, kindling and firepit.

I struck a fire and sat down contemplating my next move. The sun vanishing means one thing: something happened to my father. My father, every day on his chariot driven by four powerful horses carries the sun from east to west. This simple act, combined with the assistance of a few other gods, gives life and warmth to the world. Without my father, all the vegetation will dwindle, die, and cease to grow, as well as any animals and humans who rely on that vegetation to survive. So what could have happened?

The Titanomachy war ended just a short time ago. Maybe this could have something to do with it? Perhaps this has something to do with Picolous, as he fought against Zeus and the gods in the war. Zeus struck him with one bolt of lightning, in doing so Picolous cowardly turned tail and ran. Thinking to himself that he could try to scare me, possibly to exact revenge for his cowardice, he fled right to my island of Aeaea. He wanted to steal my island from me and make it his own. But I don't get scared easily. I stood my ground fighting tooth and nail using my powers of sorcery to keep him at bay and implement my own offensive. In our brutal duel we were at a deadlock until my loyal wolf and lion guards could intervene. We fought valiantly, and once again the disgusting coward ran for his life. He escaped and sailed away moments before my father could arrive.

My father made it his top mission to hunt down and kill Picolous. Helios and I didn't always see eye to eye. After all, it was he who banished me to Aeaea in the first place, all because I turned Scylla into a sea monster. Regardless, my father is a proud man and an attack on his daughter, even his least favorite, is an attack on him. Thus, the sun god pursued the demititan. This should have been an easy kill for Helios as Picolous was a nobody of a Titan. His only claim to fame was his Titan parents.

My father being a god means he is immortal. But maybe he was captured like Kronos and locked away? Or maybe something happened to the chariot? Regardless, this has never happened in history. There are times when my father is unable to, or simply doesn't want to, perform his duties as sun god, and the sky fills with clouds. However, we have never lost all light completely. This is something new.

Days pass, then weeks. The planet has grown cold, dark, and dead. The cold pierces straight through your skin deep into your bones. Darkness makes the world impossible to navigate. Death is everywhere. You hear the worst sounds in the darkness, the sounds of people and animals screaming. Sounds of flesh being ripped from bones and tendons snapping. Sounds that you cannot explain, and you couldn't have imagined before. The stench emanating from all the rotting is the worst part. I cannot even describe it. I am missing the sun.

Being banished and living on the island of Aeaea, I was completely alone with only my animal friends to keep me company. Honestly, I was content with my solitude and planned to live out my remaining time on the island alone. That was until Picolous came back. Impossibly, he managed to navigate and find my island in pitch blackness. I wouldn't have known if not for my wolves. As they started barking, howling, and snarling at him, from my sleep I was awakened instantly. I jumped up, grabbed a torch and started making my way to the other side of the island where the wolves were standing their ground.

I followed the sounds of the battle until it grew silent. Then I stumbled upon my wolves and lions, all dead, and Picolous standing there covered in blood, a massive sword in hand, and a deranged look upon his face. "Hello, Circe. Does my presence surprise you?" Unprompted, he charged at me, swinging his sword with precision and finesse, something he did not possess in the first battle we fought. Barely avoiding his swings, I cast spell after spell at him. He dodged them every time until I cast my most powerful spell directly at his head. He raised the sword in front of his face and deflected the spell back at me. I leapt out of the way just in time, but that gave him the opening he needed to strike and swiftly knock me down. Confused, I looked up as he stood over me, the tip of his sword pressing at my throat. He said, "This is Thenias, killer of the gods. I will use it to slay all you self-serving Libertines on Olympus. Just like I used it to slay your father." His words enraged me. "Look at what you've done!" I shouted back at him. "You sent this world into a darkness that cannot be lifted. If Helios truly is dead, then the world is doomed. You killed not just my father but everything!" Tears started to fill my eyes. The idea of my father dying, that the sun would never again shine, caused feelings of sorrow to rush into me like a dam bursting. But I had to remain strong. I refused to show Picolous weakness.

Seeing my resolve to be strong, Picolous smiled at me. Then he slowly forced the tip of the sword into my shoulder, pushing it deeper into me, until it pierced through my back. I had never felt such pain before. My whole body was burning. I screamed out in agony. "Yes, it hurts doesn't it?" he chortled. "Do you want me to stop? Beg me. Beg me to stop and I will end it all for you." "You're a monster!" I exclaimed. "The gods will stop you! They will restart the sun and bring this world back to its glory!"

He laughed derisively at me "This world is dead. It cannot be brought back. Regardless, it again belongs to the Titans. We have finally prevailed thanks to me! The gods and Titans have been locked in battle forever, the perpetual war of the immortals. But now, gods can be killed. By killing your father, I put the entire world on notice that a god could be killed by a Titan." He pulled the sword out of my shoulder and raised it to strike but was momentarily distracted.

When the fire started, I dropped my torch to defend myself. It caught the dead and dried out foliage on fire. It spread so fast; within moments the entire island was ablaze. As he noticed the flames spreading, that split second of distraction was just enough to allow me to hit him with a spell and send him flying into the flames. As I knew that wouldn't stop him, I sprang to my feet and bolted towards the sea. I had no plan, but where else could I go? Picolous had the power to kill a god. He killed my father and almost killed me. I could either let the sea take me and get lost in the vast depths of the ocean or let myself be impaled once again by Thenias.

DARKNESS

As I was frantically looking around to make sure Picolous hadn't recovered yet, I saw it; the ship that Picolous had used to get here. I still had no idea how he had crossed the ocean without the sun. But it didn't matter. If I could get to the ship and set sail, I could leave him stranded on the island just like I was. No plants, no shelter, no companionship, the most uncomfortable and isolated fate imaginable.

I climbed up the netting on the side of the ship and rushed to raise the anchor. The island fire was just bright enough that I could make my way around safely. I reached the aft of the ship, found the crank for the anchor, and began raising the chain. I had just locked the anchor in place when I turned to see Picolous taking a massive swing straight at my head. I ducked and rolled out of his reach just in time. I had to get Picolous up to the main deck if I had any chance of getting him off this ship, so I turned and cast a spell of thorn vine whip. It cracked him directly in the face causing a gash from forehead to cheek. This enraged him and he charged at me wildly.

I ran up the stairs as fast as I could, but Picolous was faster. He grabbed my ankle just as I turned the corner causing me to hit my face on the port side railing. I rolled onto my back and using my other foot, kicked him hard in the stomach. He doubled over for just a moment, enough for me to get my foot out of his grasp. He swung at me again, a mighty overhead strike. If I hadn't dodged out of the way it would have sliced me in twain. His blade cut straight through the railing and lodged itself into the wooden floor. I gathered all my power into one mighty blast and launched the demititan up over the blazing island and into the night. The sword dislodged from the deck and fell into the sea. He was off the ship and all I needed to do was lower the sails.

I took one step before I realized how badly the sword had damaged me. His slow push of the blade into my shoulder drained my energy and power like a leech. I tried again to step and fell to my knees. I gave everything I had left to try to stay awake, but eventually I succumbed to my wounds and blacked out…

As I came to, still weakened, I immediately started trying to hit the dark figure I saw standing over me. The figure grabbed my wrists and held me back down to the bed. Her demeanor wasn't aggressive but gentle and her touch and voice familiar. "Shhh," she whispered. "It's ok, it's me, Pasiphaë." I relaxed and she released my arms. She caressed my forehead while she kept a firm hand on my chest. "Picolous, he attacked me! He killed father! He has a sword that can kill the gods!" My words burst from me like a loose arrow. "It's ok. You're safe now. You're on Olympus. Poseidon brought you here," she assured me soothingly. "Poseidon? Why would he help me?" I questioned. "The gods have put aside their differences for the moment until they can figure out what happened and why," my sister replied. "What happened to Picolous?" I asked. "Did Poseidon strand him on Aeaea?" "Poseidon did mention that he left someone on the island. But he didn't say who." "Where is Poseidon now? I need to tell him about all this," I demanded. "He's gone," she informed me. "Zeus, Poseidon, Hermes, Athena, Artemis, Apollo, they're all looking for answers. In the meantime, they advised us to just stay here on Olympus until they return."

I just wanted to go back to my island. Go back to my life of solitude and privacy. It was perfect for me there. I don't like people; human, god, or otherwise. Being alone, no responsibilities, just me and no one else. It was bliss. Depressingly, I can't ever go back with Picolous there with Thenias. As I lay on the bed, staring into the darkness for hours, I mourned the life I once had.

Years, decades, centuries, and a millennium had passed. The sun never returned to the sky. Moreover, the gods never returned either. As we stayed in the safety of Olympus the demigods and I debated overlooking for the gods, but to no avail; a decision could not be reached. None of us wanted the responsibilities of the gods. Perseus didn't want to become the god of the seas, Hyppolyta didn't want to take over as goddess of war, and Hercules didn't want to become the god of the skies, let alone king of the gods, and I didn't want to take up my father's chariot and fly the sun across the sky day in and day out. I just couldn't bring myself to even want to do it. In avoiding our responsibilities, we just let the world die.

After two thousand years, the animals and humans either died out or evolved into mindless monstrosities that navigate through sound, touch, and smell. We call those monsters Blindeath. The Blindeath hunt anything that disturbs their overpowered senses. They don't care what they hunt as long as it means they get their next meal. Survival is all there is for them. They have evolved into the perfect hunters for a dark cold world; long claws, sharp teeth, keen senses of smell, hearing, and touch; intelligent, powerful, and fast. If a Blindeath locks onto you, either you kill them or, more likely, they kill you.

The only beings who didn't evolve like the Blindeath were the Immortals. Being immortal also meant we couldn't be killed by the Blindeath so they refrained from attacking us. We tried to protect the remaining life, but not being able to see made it impossible for us to do anything. Eventually, the Blindeath ran out of food. Our mountain side ran with their blood and entrails as they tried to come after us once again. We would slaughter them by the hundreds. Yet, no matter how many we killed, regardless that they could not kill us, they persisted. Then, one day, everything changed.

A bright light began cresting on the horizon like the beautiful sunrises I had witnessed before. It had been dark for so long that as the light began to get brighter our eyes were in pain. At first, we thought some noble god was trying to pick up where my father had left off and restart the sun.

Suddenly, we heard the sound of the Blindeath charging towards us. A sound we had heard a thousand times before. Our eyes adjusted to the light, and we all froze in place, and we could see movement sweeping across the land like waves in the ocean. The Blindeath were the source of the glow. We had no idea that with the glow, death would follow with it.

The Blindeath made their way up the mountainside as always, and we implemented our usual defenses. But this time, the Blindeath avoided our traps and volleys. Practically

DARKNESS

overnight, they seemed smarter, stronger, and faster. We managed to strike a few of them out of sheer luck. But the vast majority of them continued to rush forward. We fired everything we had at them. Closer and closer they charged until they were right up upon us. For the first time in thousands of years, we were forced to engage in hand-to-hand combat. The demigods fought valiantly. Some did quite well in the fight. Hercules, Perseus, Theseus, and Achilles killed hundreds of the monsters. Ultimately, their fight was in vain, and they were each slaughtered. The mountainside again ran red but this time, it was our blood. The Blindeath were ruthless in their hunger. We never stood a chance.

Terrified, the rest of us ran inside, up the stairs, and into Zeus's chambers. We barred the doors, and we stayed dead silent for what felt like hours in hopes the Blindeath would not pursue us. In reality, mere minutes passed before we heard BANG! SCRAPE! CRACK! The door was being destroyed from the outside. The Blindeath had our scent and there was nothing we could do to stop them. The door splintered as they continued their destruction. Quickly, a hole formed for the Blindeath to start climbing through. Our attempts to block the hole were easily thwarted and they pushed aside our makeshift blockade.

They encroached upon us, step by step, slowly, deliberately, knowing there was nothing else we could do, for they knew we were trapped. Something incredible came over me. I stood up and advanced on the Blindeath. "No," I whispered. I raised my hands towards the beasts, feeling the disturbance in the air. I focused on them one at a time. I could sense, deep inside them, what they once were. I could feel a power surging through me. Never had I felt such power; something divine. One by one the Blindeath's bodies began to morph and change. Hair sprouted, their sharp teeth retracted back into their jaws, and their long talons reverted to their original forms. Soon, every Blindeath devolved into their pre-darkness form. The process must have been daunting, as they collapsed after their conversion. I turned to the last surviving demigods. "I'm going to make my way down the mountain, turning them all back to normal. Everyone else, get the humans and predators out of here first then return for the gentler animals."

As I slowly made my way down the mountainside, I transformed each and every Blindeath I came across. Their collective glow started to fade. I reached the base of Olympus, turning the last Blindeath I could see back into a centaur. CLAP! CLAP! CLAP! CLAP! CLAP! A slow, sarcastic clapping came from my left. "Well done, Circe, well done," Picolous sneered. "I didn't think anyone was going to survive that slaughter, yet here you are, having morphed my army back into the pathetic animals they once were. Color me impressed." I could see Thenias swaying at his hip. "Come to finish the job?" I smirked. "Do you need a reminder of last time? For you are 0 for 2 against me." "This time will be different; this time you have no means of escaping me." He said patronizing me, he said, "The gods and demigods are all dead, the animals are all sleeping, so no back up. You're all alone. And you can't kill me. But I can kill you."

DARKNESS

"How are you capable of that, by the way? Clearly, *all* the power lies within that sword," I jabbed at him, "but where did that sword come from? How is it so strong?" "Kronos sacrificed himself, forcing his essence into the sword, focusing all of his power into the blade," he informed me. "Not until I saw your father's head fly across the room was I sure it was going to work." He raised the sword, showing its divine glow. He was trying to get under my skin, but I wasn't falling for it. "With that much power, I can kill anything." That was it, my way of defeating him; I needed that sword. I devised a plan. Under my breath I cast a thorn whip and concealed it behind me.

BOOM! The crash of thunder shook the land beneath us as a storm started to brew. I had to shout my next words. "What about the Blindeath, how can they now kill us?" I asked, not really caring about the answer. "Gaia, Atlas, Oceanus, Hyperion; they all followed Kronos's lead and gave their power to the Blindeath. Doing so all the Titans' power was focused on the claws and teeth of the Blindeath. Their power was all we needed to take you out." "So now, all the gods and all the Titans are dead?" I interrogated him. "Can you believe it?" The excitement radiated from him. "The gods' and Titans' offspring now rule the world! No more will they control us, no more banishment, no more cleaning up their—" His sentence was cut short when I whipped the sword from his hand. It wrapped perfectly around the hilt. I detached the thorn whip from the sword and immediately whipped back at Picolous. He was in disbelief, the thorn whip wrapped completely around his throat. I pulled him towards me hard, plunging the blade deep into his chest. I pulled the sword back out. Then with one mighty swing I separated his head from his body. His head and lifeless body lay at my feet.

As the storm grew stronger, heavy rain began pouring from the sky, washing away the blood of my fallen foe. I stared at Picolous lying there for quite some time, thinking, what could bring someone to do what he did? My triumph was abruptly ended by a sharp, shrill voice loud enough to cut through the angry sounds of the storm. "Hades requests your presence." It was a Harpy, a hound of Zeus. Startled, I asked, "Hades is still alive?" "Yes," she replied. "He requests that you bring the sword." Without another word, she disappeared into the night.

Per the request from the Harpy, I took the sword to Hades, the last living god, ruler of the underworld and now the ruler of everything. I knelt before Hades. "I present you with Thenias, my lord. A sword capable of killing a god." Hades grabbed the sword and immediately tossed it into the pit, Tartarus, where Kronos was once held. Hades turned to me. "After the death of Helios, we need a new sun god. My first thought was you, daughter of Helios, one with nature, life, and animals." Hades smiled. "I kept these safe for you." He whistled. My father's horses, Aethon, Eous, Phlegon, and Pyrois, trotted up to us, pulling behind them my father's chariot. I was dumbfounded. "My lord, why me?" "I saw what you did on Olympus." I could hear pride in Hades' voice. "How you protected everyone, transformed the Blindeath back into their animal and human forms, and how you defeated Picolous. You are very wise, powerful, and a natural leader. I can think of no one better to light up the sky."

I was conflicted. In my solitude, before the darkness, I was happy. However, witnessing what the world was like without light, no longer could I let that continue. I never wanted this major responsibility. But this responsibility was one I would no longer avoid. Without another word, I embraced Hades. Seeming reluctant at first, Hades smiled at me and let me know it was acceptable. I thanked him for his words of encouragement. I stepped onto the chariot, took up the reins and launched into the sky. For the first time in thousands of years, the sun rose in the east, and the world was once again illuminated.

A Mother's Blessing

C.B. Channell

My mother's gentle singing wove through the air currents, letting me know she was in her sanctum. I crept through the woods, my toe-steps careful and quiet, my breathing subdued. My mind, however, was very much the opposite. I couldn't hide all that red rage and black resentment from those who knew me best.

"By Artemis's bow, girl, what's wrong with you?" It was one of the monkeys.

I grunted, the abrupt question penetrating my thoughts, piercing my ugly mood.

"Don't ask," I said aloud, just in case others were nearby and not hearing the subvocal discussion. "You don't want to know," I added.

Myriad rumblings bounced around the inside of my skull leaving me not only furious and depressed but with a deafening headache. I stumbled face-first into a low branch causing me to scramble backward. I grasped a nearby sapling to stabilize myself. I gingerly touched the fresh scratches on my face and winced. It was still better than spending time with my family.

"SIT DOWN."

The basso voice permeated the mood, the headache, and the injuries. I sighed, obeyed, and waited. A moment passed, and then another, and I forced myself to slow my breathing.

A MOTHER'S BLESSING

Now wasn't the time to blow a gasket.

Wolf padded into my sight, only a few feet away. I grimaced, then smirked. I'd thought I was being so sneaky, and clearly he'd been tracking me since I stepped foot outside my mother's stone palace and into the surrounding woods. I let my head drop forward, my eyelids droop closed. I was suddenly, completely exhausted.

Wolf sat beside me and a moment later I felt the top of his head nuzzle my ear. I smiled despite myself. I looked up and met his liquid eyes. "Hello, friend."

"Hello, troublemaker."

"Don't start." I scowled. "My mother…"

"Is the reason I and the rest of your friends have such marvelous lives."

I bit back my reply. He was right of course, and while he'd often listened to me complain about her, his first devotion was to her.

And it always will be. Just like her and my brothers' devotion to our father, absentee jackass that he was. My heart darkened a little more. I almost wished I could pay undying devotion to someone, but I wasn't temperamentally built for it. My feelings turned cold. "Or it could be what saves me when all of you are blindly following Circe to your doom."

Wolf's eyes flashed deep gold, reflecting anger. I was about to say something to make the situation worse, when we both heard her:

"Cass! Cassiphone! Darling, come now!"

Mom.

My head naturally cocked in her direction; if nothing else, her voice was a sweet, lilting sound that always enticed, always fell gently on the ears. I turned once more to Wolf and saw his eyes again liquid, shining...her voice, her very existence meant everything to him. He and the rest of my friends didn't just love her; they worshipped her.

Well, she is a goddess, I reflected, and the usual sting of being only a demigod pricked me once again.

I wanted to ignore her, to delve deeper into the woods, to lose myself for awhile, but it wasn't possible. If nothing else, Wolf would rat me out, if the rats didn't first. I sighed and turned back toward her voice and home. My cold, stony home.

When I emerged from the trees I was struck, as always, by Circe's beauty. It was a cruelty of the denizens of Olympus that I looked so much like her and yet I reflected none of her more brilliant aspects. Where her ebony hair, straight and silken, practically glittered in the light of the sun, mine only frizzed and flopped untidily about my shoulders. Her eyes sparkled like the promise of a bright morning. Even her visage glowed like the midday sun. I, on the other hand, seemed to have a permanent dark scowl.

"There you are!" she cried and came forward to clasp my hands in hers. "Let's go down to the shore, shall we?"

I groaned and tried to pull away. "Why bother?" I said before thinking. I winced as a shadow passed across my mother's flawless face. "I mean, what difference does it make if I'm there?" I hastened to add. Despite everything, I hated to see her sad. Silence settled uncomfortably between us.

Every day my mother headed to the sandy beach to wait, ostensibly, for my fool of a twin, Telegonus. Telegonus convinced himself he was the heir to our father, the "great" Odysseus and went off in search of the lost king. He actually believed Odysseus would make his bastard son by an exiled goddess his heir. Then again, what would I choose if my only options were disillusionment or being the only boy on an island of women and sentient animals?

"Mom, he's not coming back," I said as gently as I could.

Her face hardened slightly but her expression never lost its underlying kindness. "Today is different, Cass. I want you there."

A tingle ran from my hairline to my toes. My feet itched and I wanted to dash back into the forest, but her voice compelled me. Literally. She used her Goddess-Voice on me and I was unable to resist. I felt tears raging for release but I held them. It was the only triumph I could accomplish in her power.

If only she loved me as much as the memory of the bastard who abandoned us.

* * *

We returned to the castle. My mother scanned me top to bottom, smiled slightly and shook her lovely head.

"You're like a magnet for every stray branch and clod of dirt in the forest," she said, not unkindly. I still grimaced. She soaked my hair and vigorously brushed out the burrs and other flora tangled in it. She applied olive oil to soothe

the frizz and wild ends, but it only made my hair clumpy. I looked into her bronze mirror and saw a dark child under a threatening cloud beside the sunlight that was my mother. I wilted beside her warmth.

"Well, there you are," she said. "Now it's time to get dressed. I've woven something lovely for you."

I trembled. Despite my frustration with my mother, she did allow me total freedom of Aeaea and the castle, with one exception: the Loom. It was in the only room above ground level. The only indication of it from outside was a round, domed tower set off-center atop our abode. Inside, a short flight of stairs led to an apparently blank wall. I trembled with anticipation, aching to know what was behind that facade. My mother's holy loom, where she sat and sang and lured tired travelers to their dreams. That room was sacred and had been off-limits my entire life, ever since Odysseus broke my mother's heart and left us. I leaned on the heavy stone door. It swung open silently, revealing Circe's hideaway. My breath caught in my throat as I absorbed the sight.

Arched windows stretched from the floor halfway up inside the dome. Above them was a ring of stone and above that the entire dome was a skylight. Helios filled the space, bathing it, soaking it in glowing warmth. Below, the floor was a turbulent mosaic of the sea in sapphires and emeralds. Ground pearls made frothy whitecaps. Shadow creatures of gray and black onyx glimmered in and out of sight in the shifting sunlight. Helios and Perse, my mother's parents. My mother's sanctuary.

A MOTHER'S BLESSING

A cloud floated over the sun, dimming the room and waking me from my stun. I didn't see her loom at all. I had assumed the Great Loom filled this tower. In my mind it commanded my mother's presence, more than I or my brother ever had. I walked tentatively to the center of the room. Under my feet was the center of a whirlpool in solid ebony, while above my head the sun's rays, as they emerged, formed a cocoon of golden light. The colors of Circe's hair.

"There." I heard her musical voice behind me. I didn't even have to look to see where she pointed; her bell-tone directed my eyes and my feet without any thought from me.

The loom was tucked into a niche that looked like a sea cave. It was no godlike tool, no trident or chariot or lightning bolt. It was a simple loom, worn from years of use, a gift from yet another who left Circe alone. At least he had the thoughtfulness to give her something to do in her exile.

Besides turning travelers into her pets or bearing their children, I mused bitterly. Even those couldn't provide the company she craved.

Those thoughts dropped away as I raised my eyes and saw the garment hanging on the wall behind the rickety thing. It was the simplest and yet most stunning of garments I'd ever seen. It glowed a brilliant, unearthly white and yet I could stare directly at it. I scarcely breathed as I approached it, wending my way carefully around the loom. The fabric was gossamer in my hands. Glints like diamonds on the waves winked at me, and hints of iridescent colors shimmered as I turned it this way then that in Circe's golden light. I felt as if I were floating free inside a ray of sunshine.

"You like it," she said behind me. She sounded relieved.

"It's beautiful," I said. I caressed it once more and saw the dirt under my fingernails. I never did seem to get them completely clean. I dropped the dress back to its hanging position. Suddenly the room dimmed again and the gown was just a white linen gown, striking in craftsmanship but nothing more.

Paranoia nibbled at my stomach. I spoke slowly and carefully. "Mother. Why do you want me to wear this to the beach?"

She let out a sigh through her nose. She always did that, thinking that somehow I wouldn't hear the frustration in her gesture, but Circe wasn't subtle. My mother, brilliant as the sun, deep as the ocean, could never keep petty feelings from me. Maybe that's why Telegonus used to tell me I was just like her.

Gods, I hope not.

"Wear it or don't," she said. I snapped from my reverie.

"I'm sorry," I said, softening my tone. I'd always been jealous of this loom. I don't know why I thought it was some golden treasure, a gift from one whom she treasured more than me, but it wasn't. It was beautiful in its simplicity and practical as a tool. And she'd used it to gift me a gown reflecting my heritage. "It's beautiful. Thank you."

She didn't answer, only left the room quietly, never looking back at me. Tears sprouted and stung my eyes. Perhaps I hadn't responded as gratefully as I should have, but she'd never gone to such trouble for me. Her lovers, my brother, and even the creatures that shared our remote island, ranked above me in her caretaking hierarchy. I tore off my grubby clothes and ran outside to the rain-pool to eliminate the worst of the grime and smell. Though the sun usually dried me quickly in our climate, I didn't wait. I took the dress and yanked it over my head, struggling to make it line up with my damp, clumsy body then hurried after her.

Outside, she strode purposefully toward The Beach. I had avoided the place since Telegonus left me standing there as he sailed off. The sharpness of that moment – his freedom versus my entrapment – stabbed me yet again. Mother was moving quickly, and disappeared behind the rocks that bordered our section of the island from the exposed shore. I narrowed my eyes as my feet found the familiar pathway. As I approached, I braced myself. I didn't understand why she wanted me there, but I knew my resentment was unfair. I constantly wanted to be important to her, and whatever I thought of the beach visits, she was finally including me. I berated myself a bit for being so cold with her.

I rounded the last large boulder blocking my view of the sea and drew up in shock. A large black ship was anchored a short distance away and a full landing boat was beached where once Odysseus's ship (the same one? I wondered) had sat. The landing party disembarked and Circe stood in the center of the sand waving them toward her.

Toward us. I forced my feet to move. The sand was heavier than water and the heat of the day began to penetrate my brain. Everything was too shiny, too blurry, too much. The wind picked up then, adding stinging sand to my vision problems. I stumbled forward, following the graceful curves of my mother's shape. I reached her before the landing party.

She glanced down, her brow furrowing. "Dear Cass, how did you manage that already?"

I blinked and glanced down. The stunning gown I'd thrown on was covered in sand and the hem was already crusted with mud. Guilty heat flushed my neck and face. Somehow, I could never do it right, whatever "it" happened to be at the time.

"Mother!"

We both turned, and the red in my face grew hotter. My brother.

"Telegonus!" Circe cried as she hurried toward him for an embrace. I squirmed, feeling grubby and sweaty. I crossed my arms and scowled.

I am what I am, I said to myself. I didn't feel better.

The others came up behind him, less ebullient: a woman and another young man. I watched Circe straighten and stiffen as the woman approached. She hooked Telegonus's arm and hurried him back toward me.

"You're not going to greet our new guests?" I asked, and by the pinched look in her eyes I realized I hadn't kept harsh sarcasm out of my voice.

"Cassiphone…"

"Circe." It was the woman.

My mother's face darkened in hurt and sadness. I wished she'd told me what this was all about before dragging me here. As it was, the only thing useful I could do was stare daggers at my brother. He ignored me.

I boiled. I'd spent my lifetime being second, or third, scarcely acknowledged. I wasn't going to have Telegonus return and treat me like one of mother's animals.

"Did you find our father?" I asked sharply. Circe glanced at me with a small frown.

"Our?" said the strange woman, glancing at the man beside her.

Circe turned back to her, and though I was behind her, the set of her shoulders told me she was smiling her special "welcome" smile.

"Yes. This is Cassiphone. Odysseus's daughter. *My* daughter. Cass, say hello to Penelope. This is your father's wife."

My heat turned to ice. Wife? "He left us to marry *her*?" I demanded.

"No," said Penelope. Her voice was gentle but her words were cold bronze. "He married me long before he found… Circe."

I glanced at my mother, but her face was frozen in that smile.

"So where is the great Odysseus?" I asked, turning to Telegonus. My emotions were still roiling, but my mind was focusing. My brother had never been at a loss for words in an argument. Yet here he was being almost humble before our father's wife, the woman who had a claim on him before our mother ever set eyes, or smile, or magic upon him.

"In the boat," Penelope answered, though she stared at Telegonus.

One more who won't see me, I thought. I looked at my mother, and to my shock, a glittering tear wended its way down her cheek. Telegonus stared at the ground; he could have been a statue.

My blood rose. All the suppressed rage and humiliation I'd lived with clouded my vision, and the heat roared through me, from the soles of my feet through the sloppy follicles of my hair. I ran.

"Cassiphone!" I heard Circe call.

"Cass, stop!" That was Telegonus. I leaned into my run; he could overtake me, and I wasn't going to let that happen.

I extended my arms, reaching for the gunwale just as Telegonus tackled me from behind. Our combined inertia pushed me onto the side of the boat, slamming the right side of my rib cage.

"Unngh," I grunted, sharp pain shooting through me.

That pain was nothing to what I saw, though. Odysseus, the great warrior, king, father, and, apparently, husband, lay still and waxen in the bottom of the boat. A black hole lay beneath his nipple, over his heart.

Dead. My father, our father, was dead. And suddenly I couldn't move.

"CASSIPHONE! TELEGONUS!" Circe was right behind us.

I wanted to ask what happened, but then Telegonus's expression when he faced Penelope floated into my vision. I knew.

"You killed our father," I said. Despite my trembling, my voice was steady, as if someone else were speaking through me.

"Cass," began Telegonus, but I shoved him off me with my whole body.

A MOTHER'S BLESSING

"DON'T say a word to me," I growled. I refused to look at him or even turn back to see Odysseus. I stomped in my now torn and dirty dress to my mother. She stood beside Penelope, the two of them still as statues.

"You wanted him back!" I shouted at Circe. "You waited and waited, you favored," I turned to point accusingly at my brother, "*him*, and look what he's brought you!" I stopped before the two of them, panting, my face hot with rage and exertion. They all stood silent. Circe looked sad, Telegonus looked ashamed.

I turned to Penelope. "Why did you even come here? Why bring him back? Why not let us live in peace?" I almost couldn't believe the words coming out of my mouth, but I realized they were true. If the world was only this, only betrayal from father to son, why even leave our gentle, feminine island?

"I had to meet my mother-in-law," said Penelope.

The words were ice, but they didn't penetrate at first. I stared dumbly at her, not understanding until Telegonus, my brother, took my father's wife's arm.

"Aaah, aaah," I croaked, screams of rage dying in my throat as the horrible truth washed over me. The great Odysseus had fathered yet another traitor.

"You...you..." I gasped, my arms waving, my hands grasping for anything: truth, honesty? They weren't to be had. I collapsed to the sand, just sitting and staring, my mouth working but nothing coming out. It was too much.

"Enough, Cassiphone." Circe's Voice, the compelling one, snapped me to attention. "Get up and brush yourself off."

163

I tried to resist, but it was impossible. I was powerless against the Voice. I obeyed.

She continued, though she softened the Voice: "It is imperative that Odysseus's family remain a unit, or Ithaca will fall to dissipated men."

I glanced at Telegonus and Penelope. They grasped each other's hands and squeezed, their expressions sad and dire.

"So you're okay with your son marrying his father's wife?" I managed to get out. I expected anger or at least the Voice again, but instead, tears started from my mother's eyes.

"Oh, Cass," she said, and in that moment I heard all the love and pain in her soul, saw it in her glowing eyes. Love and pain for *me*. Not Odysseus, not any of her former lovers, not even her precious son. "If only you could understand how we are all slaves to our natures." She knelt before me. I squirmed, uncomfortable at looking down into my mother's golden eyes. I watched the tears, salty as the ocean, flood those shining eyes, blinding her, blinding me.

"My mother cursed me. When Helios turned his face from her, she was devastated, cold and alone except for me. She blamed herself for not loving enough. And so she cursed me with love and the inability to avoid it. Every lover I've had has abandoned me yet I was unable to stop myself from continuing to give. Thanks to my mother's blessing, I've lived a life of heartbreak and loneliness. Except for you. My treasure."

Her tears continued to roll, but my eyes were bone dry. An unfamiliar feeling welled up in my gut: guilt. This was worse than the Voice.

A MOTHER'S BLESSING

"So I blessed you with clarity. You will never be blinded by love, my darling girl."

I trembled so hard I swore I felt the earth shaking beneath me. My throat felt dry and cracked. I couldn't speak, only listen.

"But you can't stay here. Any more than Telegonus could."

Prickles crawled up the back of my neck.

"This...this is my home," I whispered.

"Not any more." Her voice was the old Circe, firm and calm. She rose and waved her arm. The silent young man who had accompanied Penelope walked over. "This is Telemachus. Penelope's son, your father's eldest. You and he will wed, securing Odysseus's family claim on Ithaca for generations to come."

No! I screamed, but it was only in my mind. The words stopped up my throat.

"Perform the ceremony so we can return home," said Penelope behind me. The words were soft but harsh.

"No," I said.

Telemachus stood at my side. When had that happened?

"Mother?"

But Circe had turned away again. The love, the tears...all of it was more manipulation to get me to do her bidding. And for what? To secure Odysseus's legacy? What about my legacy? What about *me*?

I turned to Telemachus, wondering if he was suffering the same agonies. He stared at my mother, his handsome face, so like our father's, stony. His eyes were blue flint, cold, hateful, murderous. His body was taut, as if preparing for battle. He was more like Odysseus the warrior king than Telegonus had ever been.

"Perform. The. Ceremony."

I started. Penelope was directly behind the two of us. Trapped between mothers, both the spawn of a reckless fool.

Circe glanced at Telegonus, nodded to Penelope. She turned to Telemachus and the look on her face was pure longing. She couldn't stop loving, and she couldn't stop hurting. I felt my own salt tears sting. She turned to me, and, for the first time in my life, our sad eyes met in understanding.

She raised her arms, turned her face upwards, and closed her eyes. I held my breath waiting for the words to come, certain now that I would do her bidding. What else could I do?

I caught the blur out of the corner of my eye. Before I could register what was happening I saw Circe's eyes pop open, wide and stunned. A second later I saw the bloodstain over her heart, spreading. Telemachus stood there, his sword drawn and bloody.

"MOTHER!" I screamed and leapt to her side as she collapsed to the sand. Once again she stared into my eyes and a smile formed at the corners of her mouth.

"Take my blessing, child. Live your life with eyes wide open." And then hers closed. The blood stopped pumping out, and simply soaked into the sand.

"Well." Penelope. Her icy voice penetrated my shock. "I suppose we must return to Ithaca and hold the ceremony there."

The world spun. I opened my mouth, but only a thin keening came out. Circe was dead. One moment with her, one moment of understanding, and she was gone. My mother.

"No!"

I looked up. Telemachus turned to his mother, his face blotched with rage. "I will never marry the whore's whelp! I've avenged your honor, mother, and now, to hell with him as well! He's just another greedy suitor like the rest. I am king of Ithaca, and like my father, I will choose my own wife!"

My jumbled mind didn't register everything he said, but I clearly heard "whore" and "whelp."

"You," I breathed, "you came here to kill her! My mother!" I turned to Penelope. "You didn't have to come here. Why not keep your dead husband's body and his killer with you in Ithaca? Why come here...?"

"QUIET!" she screamed. "Telemachus, this was not what was discussed!"

I looked back at Circe's body. I didn't care what was discussed or planned. I staggered to my feet as Penelope and her son faced off. His sword dangled loosely from his hand. Before I could think, before I could change my mind, I grabbed it, wrested it from him before he knew what was happening. With strength only grief can bestow, I swung, slicing through his leather and cutting his stomach. Stunned, he stared down at the blood flowing out. He bent over in pain.

"Wha...?"

He never finished the thought. I raised the sword and swung down as hard as I could, severing his head from his spine. His blood flowed into the sand, mingling with Circe's.

I turned, bloody and still armed, to Telegonus and Penelope.

"Get. Off. My. Island," I said through gritted teeth. "And take that with you." I pointed to the boat carrying Odysseus's body.

Telegonus took one step forward, but Penelope placed a hand on his shoulder. He shuddered but remained by her side. I glanced down at the remains of my betrothed. "You may as well take this pile of meat, too. Or else I'll feed him to our wolves and tigers."

Penelope gasped. I was pleased to see the ice queen off balance. She needed to know she didn't have absolute control.

Clarity, indeed.

* * *

After Penelope and Telegonus left with their dead, I called to the animals to help me send Circe off to the Underworld. We lit the funeral pyre on the beach, none of us speaking until my mother, our queen, was reduced to ash. We gathered what was left of her and brought her to her favorite garden beside the palace. The room with the loom overlooked it, and after that day I spent many more sitting in that room, staring alternately at the loom and out the window.

I thought about my mother's blessing, and her mother's before her. How could it be that loving mothers could only give curses where blessings were meant?

Because they gave what they wished they had, not what their daughters needed. I needed her love, but she was afraid to give it, afraid of the heartbreak. The irony, that I saw only too late, was that she loved me more than any other in her life.

Finally, I went to the woods to visit my worried friends. I wept.

No Good Curse
Mason Graham

"There is only one drug," her mother used to say, "and it is called fear, and you will never run short of it." There are, in truth, many drugs, but Hekate's point stands firm. From which mouth had the tripartite goddess spoken those words? Which grinding jaw?

There is a city down the hill, these days, that imagines itself a Pentarchy – five great lords pretend at ruling, as though they are not themselves ruled by the specter of the dense grove above them. Those dying-folk have many epithets for Kirkê, but her favorite one is silence; those who say nothing of her, fantasizing her nonexistence, are those who bend most easily.

Her home has grown outward like a living thing, centuries of buckled keels and splintered hulls affixed in turn. Across its prosperous grounds and gardens her kindred roam – the flock of odd beasts that once lived as men and women, some of them ages ago, all blessedly forgetful of how they came to her service.

Now in her smoke-veiled living room kneel a Lord and Lady, one of those great Pentarchs and his red-haired wife. They are garbed in all those useless things they find precious, pitiful mirrors of flickering ember-light. Three foxes who used to be carpenters laze by the hearth; the woman's eyes are leaping between them, as if seeking to recognize an ancestor.

The man bows his head. "We beseech you, kind *polypharmakeia*, to aid us with your sacred craft," he says to Kirkê's ankles, nearly stumbling over the unwieldy title – *she of many drugs*, an unwitting defiance of her mother's pale axiom.

"Supplication suits you, sir, better than does that oily beard."

The man does not laugh – they never do – but his gaze lifts, his brow furrows. Kirkê is clad in a kind of green that is not of the sea nor of the trees; a dire, hymnal green that these dying-folk have not seen outside of fever dreams.

"Our daughter is not four days old and already dying," says the Pentarch. "Her illness has confounded our humble doctors, and yours are the only hands that might save her."

The Pentarch's wife, beautiful in her brooding, unveils the silent infant swaddled in her arms. Kirkê leans close to the scarcely breathing girl – that little apocalypse, awash in empire-blood yet teeming with frailties. Too sickly to be afraid, but her parents have brought fear enough for three.

"The sky is starving," Kirkê replies, smiling, "and you would deprive it of such spoils?"

The mother shrinks, the father widens his eyes and glances back toward the door. The pine-bristled lion blocks their way out, the wood-owl upon its shoulder regarding them hungrily.

"Please, Enchantress–"

"I promise you, my friends, you will find the humor in my jokes once you are back in your own beds. Lay the child upon that table."

The dying-folk do as bidden – they always do – while Kirkê gathers the leaves and roots and petals into which she might pour her ritual. It does not take long, and it is not hard labor, but when the infant inhales the spell and wakes from her torpor there is a new kind of warmth in the room.

The dying-folk look relieved, but not satisfied. The Pentarch's wife steps forward, looks down at her tranquil child upon the table and then back up to Kirkê.

"I am thankful," she lies, "but there is something else. We would ask that you do us the great honor of making our daughter into a son. I am too old to have more children. This will be my last chance to raise a king."

Kirkê meets the woman's dark gaze, intrigued by her gall. "That is not something that I have ever done."

"You can turn man into beast, but not woman into man?"

"I did not say I could not do it. But this is an infant. Is it not enough that she is healthy? Are you so ungrateful—?"

The Pentarch's wife kneels down again, this time close enough to clasp Kirkê's knees in supplication, and in so doing she pulls something sharp out of her robes.

It is not the first time that a visitor has tried such a thing, though usually Kirkê sees the blade before she feels it, and allows it into her skin regardless, knowing it can do no lasting harm. This time the weapon surprises her, piercing darkly and deeply. The flare of pain in her foot is like nothing she has felt before. It spreads swiftly up through her veins and she stumbles backward, wracked with cold.

She hears herself laugh, for some reason. "What is this?"

The spear-head clatters across the floor, pulling vines of shimmering rose-gold out through the new wound. This is

NO GOOD CURSE

what it feels like to be abandoned by one's own blood. The sensation knocks something free, some unwanted epiphany – that danger is everywhere, that nothing is safe. She is envenomed by that truth, which burrows into her mind deeper than memory and takes root.

Before she can gather herself, the blade is back in the right hand of the Pentarch's wife. Some divine curse is upon it, Kirkê knows now; not only to hide it from her prescience but to make it poisonous to her, perhaps deadly.

The Pentarch himself watches timidly from the shadows near the far wall. The daughter cries thinly from the stone table. Her mother is quick and sure-fingered, the terror that once filled her eyes replaced by ambition, resolve. She is brandishing the cursed spear-head forth, threatening Kirkê within her own walls; the familiars are snarling and gnashing, waiting for their Mistress's command. She could kill the woman now – she should – but she hesitates, for the first time in her winding lifespan.

"You lure us humans forth to your den, demoness, to make us into beasts. And now—"

"I have never once lured a single soul," Kirkê spits back. "Dying-folk come to me because they are lustful, greedy for what they imagine I can give them – my mere existence is no lure."

"I will hear no more of your guile, Enchantress. Your glamor does not work upon me, not while I wield this gift."

"Gift – a gift from whom? Which crooked deity bestowed this upon you? Why?"

"It is no matter. I can slay you, and I will, if you do not give me a son."

She is wrong. She is wrong. Kirkê knows it is not true. But against all logic, against all rational thought, she is not sure. And in this moment, she does not want to die.

So she sets to this new task, even as she wonders why she is so compelled. She smears and anoints two fire-breeding stones with earthen rudiments, aged and fermented and charred just so; cypress bark and lotus seed and yew leaves. This work is harder than healing, but still it does not take long. Within an hour she is pouring the ashes across the oblivious child's face, reciting the incantation that she has just composed especially for this occasion. The Pentarch's daughter is a son now — or looks like one, at least.

She would feel shame, perhaps, or anger, but there is no room for that. All else pales to this new and loathsome color of consciousness that the woman's blade has granted her – it is what the dying-folk call *fear*, the acrid blue fire that Kirkê's presence has long kindled within them. Those people have never seen Kirkê as she is, but as they would like her to be, unworldly and beautiful and predatory. What if their collective belief is enough to make it so? What if she does not get to decide what she is?

She is still bleeding.

* * *

Months have passed, perhaps years, and the poison has not faded. She has decided three times over that something must be done. She could, of course, call upon one of the higher deities for aid, but she does not know which of them may have been responsible for her curse; even her mother is not above suspicion.

So she throws herself into alchemy and ritual, as she always has, but now with a more difficult goal – she does not now seek to change the things around her, but the things within her. She roams farther and wider for materials, looks under rocks that she is loath to upturn, communes with spirits and phantoms that make her cringe and quake.

One day she even garbs herself as one of the dying-folk and ventures down into the city – she knows that men come and go by ship, sometimes bringing odd fruits and spices from far-off lands that she has not visited. If she flaunts her power among them there will be conflict, and she is not in the mood to kill. So she enters quietly as a brown-haired woman, small and unassuming; under this glamor the men do not see her as something to fear, but rather as something to possess. There is no winning.

Before she leaves, Kirkê finds the home of the Pentarch – the one with the oily beard and the hateful wife – and peers through its windows. For some reason her breast is aflame as she does this, and she can feel rivers of blood outgrowing their banks, flooding her insides. Yet all she sees is a small, healthy boy, laughing and playing with the housemaids while his father watches on. She asks a city-guard about the Pentarch's wife, and is told that she died by slipping on a loose paving-stone and landing badly.

She deserved a better death, Kirkê decides as she treads carefully out of that place.

It is dusk and she is nearly home, maneuvering through high thickets upon her great boar-steed, when she notices the torchlight outside of her house. Only for a brief moment does her skin crawl before she reads the forms of six Lampads, solemnly arrayed. The gaunt handmaidens of Hekate, whose torches drive men to madness, each flanked by Stygian dogs with empty eye sockets.

Kirkê rides up and dismounts, peering past the ghostly maidens to the figure standing upon her oaken porch. There is Hekate, that pallid, rotting goddess, all at once horse-headed and jackal-headed and lion-headed. She does not fit here, in this world, and even the wind will not go near her.

Kirkê approaches and briefly considers kneeling.

"I am here," the saffron-cloaked goddess creaks through all three mouths, "in answer to my most delicate daughter's suffering. Her unwitting, voiceless prayer."

It hurts, as always, to look upon her faces – not a striking nor bludgeoning pain, but a steady and torturous pressure on three acute points of the mind, unrelenting, maddening. Kirkê will not let it madden her.

"Eldest Hekate, I did not call upon you, nor am I in need of your gifts."

The horse-head brays. Serpents weave in and out of oak-branch crowns, sighing their distaste. "I have no gifts to give, save a motherly love. But your pride, sadly, does not hide the inner clamorings of your injured mind."

From under her sweeping robes there crawls a fiery-eyed polecat – Gale, who was once one of the dying-folk herself, a lustful woman punished by gods for her abnormal desires. Kirkê cannot help but stare at the luckless creature.

"I am well, Mother," she eventually replies. "You may return to the Underworld free of concern."

"Do not grant me permissions," Hekate says, her voice deepening into thunderous, unwritten calligraphy. "Fear is something for you to wield against others, and yet you are yourself stricken by it. You, *daimona*, demi-goddess, deathless."

"Deathless?" Kirkê scoffs. "So far, yes. I am not protected by the same laws that you are, Eldest. I do not wilt and spoil and break as the humans do, but I have bled – can I not then be slain?"

Hekate is a statue as she hears all of this, a monument to the moonlight.

"Are you afraid to die, daughter?"

Kirkê thinks deeply before speaking. "I do not know what I fear. If there is an object, it is nothing I can name, nor even see."

"No, indeed not. Yours is the primal, cosmic fear that is called *ekpl xis*, that panic in the face of the unknowable. I suspect that it is no fault of yours."

Gale has crept up the columns to perch in the rafters above Kirkê's head. If the beast could die, she would consider killing it. Instead she says, "The spear-head that cursed me so – which deity cast their spirit-poison into it?"

MYTHS, GODS & IMMORTALS: CIRCE

"I do not know," says Hekate, surprisingly. "Whom have you most angered?"

"For years I have meditated on that question," she replies. "I suspect Melinoë or one of her Furies, from whose grasp I have pulled more than one repentant murderer."

"I will find out," Hekate says, barbed teeth dripping oil.

Kirkê wants to tell her not to bother, but curiosity outweighs pride.

* * *

Time sprints onward and Hekate does not return. That means something, but Kirkê does not know what. In the following years she has stumbled her way to a new invention, an elixir that remedies her trembling mind for days at a time. She is now usually numb to her dread, which is nearly as good as being dreadless.

Over time her life has found its meter again. She has continued her crafting, not only of spells and tonics but of poems and hymns and ceramic amphoras. From time to time, she has even wandered down the hill in disguise, reveling with the euphoric Maenads in their warlike wine frenzy.

It has been decades since her mother left, and Kirkê is bathing in the fragrant hot-springs bordering her grove. The feathered she-wolf and the blood-red stag are keeping watch – aging philosophers who long ago chose quiet savagery over death. Her flock of beasts has not grown in some time; these days she is more likely to shield herself from wayward petitioners than take them into her care. Yet now the she-wolf's rumbling tells her that someone new is climbing toward her through the brush. One of the dying-folk, no doubt, but seemingly one touched by sorcery – cursed or blessed, it is hard to tell from this distance.

She arises from the boiling waters just as a shivering figure emerges between the trees; a bronze-clad knight with the face of a hardy young man, his lordly features darkened by slow labor.

Kirkê holds one hand out to stay the wary beasts. "Welcome, soldier. You must have struggled for some time to hallucinate your way through all of my barriers."

He retreats half a step, then grips the shaft of his gilded spear with both hands. "You are Lady Kirkê? The *simulatrix* herself?" His voice is faltering; he knows it is a foolish question.

"What brings you so very far from safety?"

"I am Myrnás," the soldier says, "heir to the Pentarch of our great city."

It all slides into place. She has seen this person before. She has worked her enchantments upon this Myrnás, has shaped the clay of that troubled visage. Even in his terror – her terror, rather – there is a grace, a dignity in her countenance.

"And what else are you?" Kirkê asks.

"Vengeful," says Myrnás, her voice hardening. "You took my mother from me, Enchantress, when I was a child. You caused her to die, quietly, unceremoniously, before her time."

Kirkê laughs deeply at this. "I wish I had done so."

The knight takes a bitter step forward. "You find comedy in my loss?"

"No," she replies. "Not in your loss. Just in the great irony of your accusation. Did your fool of a father tell you that I slew his wife?"

"He told me enough. That I was ill as a newborn, and that you did what the human priests and medics could not. But a witch does not give such gifts freely – you took my mother as payment, did you not?"

It would be a reasonable hypothesis, if Kirkê were the sort to trade lives. "Sometimes tragedy has no divine cause, child. Every now and then, things simply happen."

Myrnás braces herself, shakes her head. "Your tongue knows only deception, Enchantress."

The glimmering spear comes alive as its bearer leaps forth; Kirkê, fascinated, watches the distance between herself and Myrnás disappear all at once. She decides to shift her body just enough to let the iron graze her side, biting into her bare ribs without drawing blood – there is no unworldly power suffusing the weapon this time. Myrnás recovers her footing quickly and in less than a moment is poised for another keen strike. The Pentarch's child is a deft warrior, and has killed before. Too often.

There is a wild rush of crimson as the stag charges, colliding with Kirkê's assailant; the clashing of jagged, bone-sharp antlers against plates of polished bronze strikes the air. Myrnás lies on her back on the stony ground now, grimacing in pain, but her grip on her weapon has not loosened. The stag stands over her, awaiting the Enchantress's next silent command.

It would be pitifully easy to kill this troublesome human, to simply end the inconvenience, yet Kirkê finds herself

NO GOOD CURSE

reluctant. She cannot help but read the sorrow written so handsomely across Myrnás's spirit, spirals of disquiet that trace back to one primary, marrow-deep dissonance. One for which Kirkê is responsible.

"If you will cease your thrusting," she offers, "we can speak freely about why you are really here."

Myrnás cautiously sits up cautiously, her deep-set eyes glistening. "I told you, Lady–"

"You used vengeance as an excuse, and it was a good one. It got you here. Now tell me about that other, deeper thing – it looks almost like shame."

The spear finally falls away from its bearer's hand. Myrnás is breathing deeply, bargaining with herself for some time before she speaks. "I do not know what it is. I have never once felt right, Enchantress." There is still anger in her eyes, but it is pointing inward now. "I am not right, somehow. And I am tired of being wrong."

"Your father did not tell you everything, Myrnás. You are right to feel wrong – this is not your body. Not the one you were meant to have, anyway."

There is recognition, acceptance, even the faintest flicker of relief in her eyes. "You mean to say that I am not a man."

Kirkê nods. "It was I who put this upon you, when I healed your infirmity. Your mother demanded it of me, but I should not have bent to her threat."

Myrnás appears to be lost for a moment – dying-folk sometimes struggle with too many truths at once – before she grits her teeth and stands up, her ruined armor clinking.

"Take it away from me, Enchantress. Undo whatever you did those years ago."

"No good curse can be undone."

"So place a new curse. The mirror image of this one."

Kirkê smiles. "That is not how it works. But I believe I can give you something that will help, slowly, over time. You will have to accompany me back to my home, if you can bring yourself to trust my deceptive tongue."

The woman wavers. "Are you going to make me into one of your beasts, Enchantress?"

"That is a gift for simple folk," she replies, "and you are complicated."

* * *

Back in her kitchen Kirkê is sorting roots while Myrnás sits uneasily at the table – the same one she had once been lain upon for healing. This will be the second time that this one little human inspires the *polypharmakeia* to create an entirely new substance, a new sorcerous ritual. Is this what it feels like to have a Muse?

There is time to kill, as she must wait for the laurel leaves to dry before anything else can be done. So she finds herself talking to Myrnás, telling her things that she has not told anyone before – not because they are secrets, but simply because it has never occurred to her to speak them out loud.

"There is a dream I have had of late," she hears herself saying. "I don't often dream, since I don't often sleep – it is a great skill you dying-folk have, to retreat into the dark of your minds with no help – but when I sleep lately, I dream of being dead. Of being a still, breathless corpse, drained of blood and humor. Eroding into the soil to feed things that are not yet alive. And someone, far above me, is reading my entrails, seeking good omens."

Myrnás shifts in her dented breastplate. "Do they find them?"

"Sometimes. If they want to."

When the tonic is done, Kirkê pours it into a warded ceramic jar and performs the rites of incantation, whispering words in nobody's language. Plumes of burnt offerings assault the air in ethereal patterns, blue-violet gloom overtakes the chamber. Myrnás is afraid, but there is something about her fear that seems useful, perhaps even necessary.

"You need only drink one drop every new moon," Kirkê tells her. "Over time, I believe, it will get better, until you forget that it is not perfect."

Myrnás leaves to resume her life in the city, with all of those people who are so like her and so unlike her. In her new solitude Kirkê finds herself wondering just how Myrnás sees her; what is she, to her? Sea-weathered saint, dread sorceress, wilderness embodied? Just a woman?

* * *

The last bits of fiery sunlight are retreating westward as Kirkê stands upon the jagged beach. Patience has never been a problem for her, but she finds herself restless as

Great Hekate, clothed as ever in her fearsome multitudes, emerges slowly from the waves. The saltwater does not cling to her.

"It has been longer than you expected," Hekate's jackal-mouth rasps. "I hope you bear no grudge."

Kirkê is trying to remember what she expected. More years have passed since her last encounter with Myrnás, though she is having a harder and harder time keeping count. Her various methods of killing her fear have dulled her mind, but it is a fair trade. It must be.

"I never felt forgotten," she says simply.

Hekate moves forward, all at once drifting and staggering. "I inquired at great length to understand what happened to you, daughter. I visited upon the shade of the woman who pierced you, the Furies in their dim nightmare-halls, the gods of sleep and death and madness."

Kirkê does not care for the way this story is being told. "And what did you find, Eldest?"

There is something in Hekate's faces that is unfamiliar – her version of pity, maybe. "The weapon that poisoned you was nothing more than a simple spear-head, built by human hands, untouched by any demon or divine spirit. There was no curse upon it."

No, this is wrong.

"You are not above error, Mother."

But Hekate says nothing, not with any of her bloody mouths. Beyond the shoreline the waves grow quiet as well, the sea a serene mirror of twilight.

And then Kirkê is stricken all at once by centuries of sentiment. Unpleasant colors she chose not to see, until she could not deny them any longer. That *ekpl xis* – that fear – was always there, and some shadowed sliver of her self knew it well. She had tried to give it away, before she knew what it was, poured it into spells and curses and blessings, shaped it like clay into weapons of war and tools of surgery.

"What was it then," she asks, forcing the words through the still granite of her face, "about that day, that woman, that blade? Why did I only then open my soul to this?"

When Hekate responds, it is not in any of her own voices, but in Kirkê's voice, a cruel echo: "Every now and then, things simply happen."

Mischievous crabs sprout from the sand to bite at her feet, and all of them draw blood.

* * *

There is a woman waiting in Kirkê's living room. She is clad in graceful blue linen, and she looks like herself now – not precisely like the other women of her kind, but as beautiful as any of them. Maybe more so, in all her strange intricacy.

"Forgive me for intruding," Myrnás says, her voice nearly unrecognizable. "But the beasts seemed to welcome me in."

Kirkê glances around the chamber, locking eyes with the bull and the panther and the raven. "It is a fine surprise," she says. "You look well."

"I am," Myrnás assures her, "better than I was, at least." She pauses, gazing into Kirkê's eyes for longer than any human ever has. "You yourself have not changed at all in the past twenty-four years, Enchantress."

"That remains to be seen." Kirkê steps forward and sits across the table from her Muse, conjuring a kylix of wine for each of them. The seaside encounter with Hekate feels so far away now, so trivial. "You have not come here only to trade pleasantries, though. What is it you are seeking, Lady Myrnás?"

The woman drinks deeply of her cup without suspicion. "I am not sure, Lady Kirkê. I did not think much about where my feet were taking me," she says, casting her eyes downward. "I suppose I would not refuse some guidance, or solace, if it were offered. My life has been hard, in different ways, since I chose to return to myself. Many of those who have witnessed my slow progress have chosen not to accept it, and some have even accused me of madness."

"And yet," Kirkê responds, smothering a spark of anger, "you sit more easily within yourself. The wrongness has lessened."

Myrnás forces a smile. "It has gotten better, yes. But it is still not easy."

"You were on fire for so many years," Kirkê says. "There will always be cinders."

There is a long, comfortable quiet.

When they have both finished their wine, Kirkê continues, "You would be welcome to remain here, Myrnás, for as long as you need. If you desired it, I could teach you about my craft. Pass along my skills, if they can be passed."

NO GOOD CURSE

The woman looks confused. "Has it not taken you lifetimes to learn those arts? I am a human – dying-folk, you call us. I will be gone before–"

"You are not the same as the others," Kirkê responds. "Not after the spells that have been poured into you. Already you are aging quite well, for one of your kind. You will have much more time to become yourself."

Myrnás appears to steady herself against the table. "If you would like for me to stay with you, Lady Kirkê, I would."

The Enchantress pulls a reddish fruit from the bowl at the center of the table. "I still have that same dream," she says through the sweetness, "that I once told you of, wherein I am a dead thing – only now sometimes you are there, in the dream, too. I can feel your unfleshed ribs entangled with mine, the last remnants of our bodies mingling, and my dark nothingness is inseparable from yours."

As she says this, Kirkê feels the wretched pit in her stomach deepen again, the blue flame churning upward and outward. And she can see, for the first time, that there is something worth fearing.

The Island of Pigs
Kay Hanifen

Alex Winters reached out from inside the rowboat and skimmed the crystal water with her fingertips. She was feeling feminine that day but was still forced to wear swim trunks and a T-shirt rather than the bikini she wanted.

"We accept you for what you are, but the Glattons and the Versos are not as open-minded," her stepmother, Viv, said, looking at Alex with a disdain that said that she barely accepted Alex's existence, let alone her gender fluidity. But Alex wasn't in the mood for a fight, so she acquiesced and compromised by picking out her hot pink Barbie shirt to wear.

Not for the first time, she missed her mom. Her real mom who worked herself to death to give Alex everything she needed and still found time to read her bedtime stories – fairytales and myths and mystery novels. It was their special thing, and she knew her mom would have loved visiting Greece, the setting of all her favorite legends.

Viv's husband, Tom, might have been her biological father, but he was as much her dad as the milkman, as far as she was concerned. The only reason he took her in after her mother passed was because she threatened to go to the media and tell the world about the billionaire who abandoned his kid

THE ISLAND OF PIGS

after getting his secretary pregnant. She had hoped he would just financially support her from afar, but the PR manager decided that the family 'fostering an orphan' would make them look great to the rest of the world. Apparently, there was a massive scandal brewing about one of Tom's factories and the lack of proper safety equipment. Against her better judgement, she took the offer. A home in a bed of vipers is still better than no home at all.

Something bounced off her forehead. She turned sharply to her half-brother, Will, who sat with a shit-eating grin as he pretended to innocently nibble on the grapes they'd packed for their picnic lunch. Rolling her eyes, she returned to studying the ripples on the clear, blue water.

Out of all of them, Will was the only one who she felt bad for in this mess. Her existence blew up his life, and now he was stuck with a stranger who was now his younger sibling. So, she could take a little bit of bullying and acting out from him. It was easier than trying to get one of her parents to intervene.

"This place is just paradise, isn't it?" Viv said to Tom, who Alex knew was studying the island's natural beauty the way that a judge evaluates a prized horse, using aesthetics to come up with a worthy price tag.

"I can't believe no one owned this place before we put in the offer for it. It would make for a perfect luxury resort." He reached into the water and pulled out a shell, admiring it before throwing it back in the ocean. "It's all so pristine. Guests will think they found Eden on Earth. Hm. I like the sound of that. Eden Island Spa and Resort." He pulled out his phone and wrote it down as a memo.

"Is there anything to do here?" Will asked, studying his phone. "Because all I see is trees and water. I can't even get a signal."

Tom raised a dismissive hand. "We'll get started on that as soon as the building permits go through. In the meantime, go swim, play pirates, and climb trees. Whatever it is that boys do."

He crossed his arms. "What am I? Five?"

Well, you're certainly acting like it, Alex thought. She wisely chose not to say that out loud. It was always best to keep her head down and avoid antagonizing the people who were giving her food and shelter. They already tore her apart and reminded her of her place in the family at every given opportunity. She didn't want to give them any more excuses to take their anger out on her.

A movement caught the corner of her eye, and she looked up to the top of a nearby cliff. A woman stood at the edge watching them, her long, red hair and purple dress flowing in the wind. She was the most beautiful person Alex had ever seen. And she had been dragged to Paris Fashion Week several times since they took her in.

"Does anyone live here already?" she asked.

Her dad shot her a confused look. "There shouldn't be. I was told that this place is completely uninhabited. Why?"

"I thought I saw someone at the top of the cliff." She pointed up, and all three followed the trajectory of her hand

THE ISLAND OF PIGS

to the edge of a cliff that did not hold the beautiful woman that she was sure she had seen just moments before.

Her brother snickered and returned to fiddling with his useless brick of a cellphone. He may not have access to all its bells and whistles, but he was damned if he wasn't going to try to get at least one game to work and allay his boredom with the whole trip.

Tom shrugged. "It was probably just your imagination. Being out at sea can do that to you."

"Maybe." She sighed, not wanting to get into an argument about something she may or may not have seen.

Viv's eyes were on her like a cat tracking an insect. She had been looking for an excuse to get rid of her surprise stepdaughter permanently. Boarding school only covered the school year, not the summer. Alex wondered if Viv was mentally building a case to have her locked in a mental institution and throw away the key. Their family's version of Rosemary Kennedy.

On impulse, she dove from the boat into the cool, crystalline waters and swam to shore. Her family, and the two billionaire families vacationing with them, were close behind, but it felt good to put some distance between them, at least for the moment. She squeezed the saltwater from her shoulder-length hair and lay down on the beach, waiting for the rest to reach shore.

There was something about this place. It seemed to thrum with a strange energy. It gave her the vision of violin strings and the discordant, anticipatory hum of a concert as the musicians tuned their instruments before the music started. Tom felt the strange magic of this place and saw only dollar signs, but she knew there was something deeper to it. Something ancient and forgotten. Something she should flee but instead stood frozen like a cornered animal faced with a starving tiger.

"Was that necessary?" Viv asked. Alex cracked an eye open. Her stepmother stood over her with her hands on her hips. Her blonde curls were framed by the cloudless blue sky like a halo. If Alex didn't know better, she'd say that Viv looked like a saint or a Greek goddess. Helen of Troy turned middle aged.

She shrugged. "I just wanted to go for a swim."

Viv rolled her eyes. "Fine. Just try not to embarrass us too much on this trip."

She raised her hand to her forehead in a mock salute. "Yes ma'am."

Viv *tsk*'d and turned away to greet the Glattons and Versos with her typical gleaming white smile as they made their way on shore.

Alex closed her eyes again, but not for long. Gritty sand flew in her face, and she sat up, coughing and wiping it from her eyes. Her brother stood flanked by the Versos' son, Eric, and the Glattons' son, Mike. "What?" she snapped.

He grabbed her and dragged her to her feet. "Come on. We're gonna play a game."

"What kind of game?" Her gaze ricocheted between the three of them, struggling to assess which one was the greater threat. Her muscles tensed, ready to fight or flee.

His grin was like that of a shark's. *"Lord of the Flies*. Ready to run, Piggy?"

She didn't wait for a response, sprinting into the woods before he could even finish the sentence. The sand slipped under her feet, slowing her down, but she persisted, leaping over roots and weaving through trees, not caring where she was going, listening for the whooping of the teenage boys brought to life by the thrill of the chase.

Soon, though, she realized that she was hopelessly lost. The island had no map, no trails, and no people. No one to help her. Maybe this was the real plan. They would abandon her on the island while mourning how she was tragically lost at sea. The only thing the media loves more than orphans being adopted is their tragic deaths.

It had been a few minutes since she'd heard the boys' voices, so hoping that she'd lost them, she slowed down to a walk, taking a moment to catch her breath. Closing her eyes, she leaned against a tree and put a hand to her racing heart.

That was when she heard it. At first, she thought it was a human screaming, but she couldn't make out any words. Curious and terrified that this was another trick, she crept towards the source of the noise.

A pig floundered in a mud pit, struggling to escape and seeming to only sink further in the muck. She'd read enough fantasy and historical fiction to know how dangerous wild boars could be, but she couldn't just leave it there. It would likely die of starvation or exhaustion before it escaped.

So, against her better judgement, she slid her way down into the pit. "I want to help, so please don't hurt me," she mumbled as she looked for a way to help it get out.

The pig was remarkably calm around her. Maybe, like quokkas, they were so unused to human contact that they didn't know to fear humanity. "Okay, let me just give you a boost," she said.

And shockingly, the pig seemed to understand. It began to climb the wall of the mud pit as she braced against its rear end and pushed upwards with all her strength. The hooves scrabbled for purchase, and eventually she pulled the pig up and out of the pit.

Now, she was presented with a new problem. The pig may have been out, but she was still stuck in the mud. Climbing was about as effective for her as it was for the pig.

It made alarmed squeals, and she froze. Was there some kind of predator on the island? Was she about to be eaten?

"Elpenor, there you are," an unfamiliar voice said. Viv and Tom were going to have an aneurysm when they realized that the island was, in fact, inhabited. "I thought I told you to stay away from the mud pits."

Despite the scolding, the pig grunted cheerfully at the return of its owner.

"Hello?" Alex called out. "Is someone there?"

The beautiful woman she saw at the top of the cliff leaned on her staff, standing over the opening of the pit, her hair in a fiery ring around her ageless face. When she saw Alex, she wrinkled her nose as though her very presence offended her.

THE ISLAND OF PIGS

Alex gave her a weak smile. "Do you think you could get me out of here?"

"And why should I do that, boy?" she growled.

"I'm not a—" she began automatically before shaking her head. "Never mind."

The woman waved a hand. "No, by all means. Finish the sentence. What aren't you?"

"A boy. Most of the time, anyway. I'm kind of somewhere in between. Sometimes, I feel like a boy, sometimes a girl, and sometimes both or neither. Today, I'm a girl." The words tore from her lips of their own volition. When she had finished speaking, she covered her mouth in shock. "What was that?"

"Just a little truth spell. It's been a while since I've needed to use one. It's also been a while since I've seen a cultist of Hermaphroditus." She offered the end of her staff to Alex, who stood dumbfounded. "Well, grab on. Or would you rather die in a mud pit?"

Shaken out of her stunned reverie, Alex clung to the proffered staff and used it to help pull herself out of the pit. "Thank you," she said once she was on solid ground again.

The woman started walking without looking back, the pig oinking merrily beside her. "Come on. You can get cleaned up and have something to eat at my place."

Alex jogged to catch up. "You don't have to do that. I'm sure my brother and his friends are bored by now, so I can just head back."

"Then by all means. Leave. And never return."

195

MYTHS, GODS & IMMORTALS: CIRCE

"I don't think I can. My parents and their friends want to build a resort here."

The woman froze so abruptly that Alex nearly walked into her. "They what? No, this is my island."

Alex stepped back, putting up her hands in a placating gesture. "I mean, I can tell them that you own it, but I don't think they'll listen. They have the deed to it."

The woman shot her a glare so fierce that Alex physically recoiled. "I've had this island far longer than any deed written on mortal paper, and I won't stand for this."

Alex's mind raced as she ran through the stories her mom read her about women from Greek mythology who lived alone on islands. The first was Calypso, the nymph who held Odysseus captive, and the second was the witch, Circe. Her stomach dropped as the woman began walking again.

"You're Circe, aren't you?"

She turned around, her eyes narrowing suspiciously. "How do you know my name?"

"I've heard stories about you, though I never believed that they were true." She took a step back, her throat suddenly dry. Playing *Lord of the Flies* with her brother and his friends was now infinitely preferable to staying here, but she felt pinned like an insect on display underneath the sorceress's gaze. She bowed. "On behalf of my companions, I apologize for the intrusion to your island and wish to invoke the right of *Xenia*."

Circe raised an eyebrow. "You're well versed in the old ways."

THE ISLAND OF PIGS

"My mother used to tell me stories. About you and Odysseus, the gods and monsters." She hadn't mentioned her mother in months. It was a taboo subject in the family, and she was forced to leave all her friends behind for this nightmare of a Cinderella story. The memory summoned a boa constrictor of grief to squeeze the breath from her chest. Her mother had read to her every night before bed long after she had outgrown it. It was their evening tradition, the way they bonded after a long and busy day. And when the cancer began to take her, it was Alex's turn to complete their ritual. She had passed while Alex read *The Lion, The Witch, and The Wardrobe*.

The sorceress gave her an appraising look. "Your mother was very wise to do so. I was about to turn you and your family into pigs."

"Not that there would be much of a difference," Alex mumbled to herself.

Circe barked out a surprised laugh and started walking again. "I like you, cultist of Hermaphroditus."

"Why do you call me that?"

Circe arched an eyebrow. "Apparently not as versed as I thought. Hermaphroditus is the child of Aphrodite and Hermes, one with male and female traits. They represent the union of the sexes into one."

"I guess that does sound like me." She smiled. "I must have missed that story."

They reached a clearing and Alex gasped. The structure was simple and beautiful, the walls covered in a mosaic

MYTHS, GODS & IMMORTALS: CIRCE

of shells and sea glass. Chickens clucked about the yard while goats and sheep grazed in the grass. Elpenor the pig cheerfully trotted to his pen.

"It's beautiful here," she said.

Circe shrugged and led her inside. "I've had time. Can I offer you something to eat?"

Alex bit her lip. On the one hand, for *Xenia's* protections to be fully invoked, she would have to eat some of Circe's food. On the other, she remembered what happened when Odysseus's men ate the food Circe offered.

She forced a smile as she followed Circe inside. "I suppose it depends. Will this be normal food, or will I wind up in the pen with Elpenor?"

The sorceress threw back her head and laughed. "You're a clever one. What's your name?"

"Nobody," she replied, straight faced.

The laughter she earned was a balm to Alex's soul. If Circe found her entertaining enough, she might spare her and the others on the island. "Gods, not another one. The first was aggravating enough." She patted a wooden table. "Come and sit. I swear to Zeus that I will not violate the laws of hospitality or transform you into an animal against your will."

Zeus was the enforcer of *Xenia*, so Circe swearing to him was just about as good of a guarantee that Alex could get. She took a seat at the table. Circe gave her a plate with a slice of bread drizzled in honey and a cup of wine. Still, Alex hesitated, so the sorceress rolled her eyes and tore off a corner before popping it into her mouth.

"Happy?" she asked.

Alex let out a weak laugh and took a bite. It was delicious. The bread was soft on the inside and chewy on the outside while the honey offered the perfect hint of sweetness. The wine was cool and refreshing. She was still underage in the United States, but it hadn't stopped her from trying it from time to time. This, though, was finer than the thousand-dollar bottles Tom would occasionally let her taste.

Circe drummed on the table with her fingertips as she thought. "Tell me about your family."

The next bite went down harder than she intended, and she took a sip of the wine to keep from choking. She should have known this was coming, but she was too in awe of the fact that she was on the same island as *the* Circe from myth and legend to think beyond it.

"What do you want to know?"

"You said your brother was chasing you through the woods here. Why?"

She shrugged. "He doesn't see me as a sibling, just an intruder in his family. My father is a bit like Zeus, powerful and unable to stay faithful in his marriage. My mother is – was – someone who worked for him. When she died, I didn't have anywhere else to go, so I threatened to go to the news with the story unless he took care of me. It's not much of a home or family, but it's better than living on the streets."

"How did he find this place? For thousands of years, I've kept this island alone so that I could be left unbothered."

"That sounds lonely," Alex said without thinking.

The sorceress shot her a cold glare, the frostiness of it threatening to pierce her heart. "Trust me. It's better than the alternative. Nothing good has ever come from outsiders visiting this place."

"I'm sorry. I didn't mean to offend."

"You didn't," she said almost too quickly.

Alex was tempted to call her on it but decided that it would be foolish to do so. "My father was sailing in the area and was knocked off course by a sudden squall. When he saw this place, he made note of the coordinates in order to come back to it. That's about all I know."

"I'm assuming that killing them is out of the question."

"Preferably. Besides, it will raise too many questions from the outside." Ignoring the surprised quirk of Circe's eyebrow, she took another sip of her wine. "Is there a way to magically erase the memory of this place? Like, as soon as they leave, they would forget the coordinates or something like that?"

"I cast a memory charm every year to ward this island against interlopers like you." She paused. "Well, not necessarily you. I've found your company tolerable, but the rest sound wretched."

"You don't have to live with them." In the back of her mind, she wondered how Tom was immune. Maybe he was out of range of the spell when he saw it. She supposed that it didn't matter anyway. They were there, and now she had to stop them from building that stupid resort.

The look Circe gave her was surprisingly fond. "And would you want to go back with them?"

THE ISLAND OF PIGS

Alex looked down, studying the glimmering shine of light reflected in the wine. "Do I have a choice?"

"I suppose you could stay here. Become a servant and apprentice."

Her head shot up. "What?"

"If you do, though, you may never leave this island. For as long as I'm here, you will be bound to it and to me."

"Yes," she said without hesitation. If only her mom could see her now...

"There you are," came an unfortunate voice. Will stood in the doorway with his arms crossed, looking irritated. "*My* mom and dad have been looking all over for you."

Circe cleared her throat. "I believe you're intruding on my island."

He smirked, leaning against the wall in an approximation of a cool, flirtatious pose. "Hey, didn't see you there. Sorry about my brother. He's a bit disturbed in the head. How did you find this place?"

The sorceress grit her teeth. "I've lived here for longer than you can imagine, whelp."

"Well, we bought the place, so you can expect an eviction notice any day now." He flashed her a licentious smirk. "But I'm sure we can come to an arrangement."

Circe shot Alex a look as though requesting her permission. Alex gave a slight nod, and the sorceress's smile stretched warmly across her face. "Of course. But first, let me get you something to eat. My honey bread is perfection." Getting to her feet, she bustled about the small kitchen, slicing the bread and drizzling honey over it. Except that she wasn't using the same honey jar she used for Alex's meal. Alex fought back a giggle at the realization.

Circe handed him the bread and wine, and he ate and drank without hesitating. After a few bites, he dropped the plate, doubling over. The muscles and bones of his body shifted, his feet becoming hooves and his nose becoming a snout. Slowly, his screams became the squeals of a pig. It was horrible to watch, but it also brought with it a sense of relief. Will would never bother her again.

The animal that was once her brother fled the house. She glanced up at Circe. "I think I know how to solve both our problems."

She took the rest of the honey and returned to where they had built the bonfire. Luckily, several bottles of wine were already open and ready to pour, so all she needed was a drop or two in each. And then she waited and watched as Viv, Tom, and their friends drank in a Dionysian bacchanal.

The transformation took immediate effect, their screams becoming squeals as the swine scattered. Paying them no mind, she rowed to the three yachts. Setting them on autopilot, she sent them out to sea. Once they were a safe distance away, Circe would summon a storm to sink them into the watery depths. When people came looking, they would believe that the three families were killed tragically in a sudden squall, and Alex wouldn't correct them.

As thanks for her help and a welcome gift for the island, Circe gave her a modified shapeshifting potion, one that

THE ISLAND OF PIGS

allowed Alex to take the form of whatever gender best fit her that day.

And so the sorceress and her apprentice spent their days living alone on the island and tending their pigs.

Something New

M.J. Harris

PART I: ARRIVALS

Most ordinary people, when faced with a group of strange men on the other side of their front door, would probably choose not to answer. Especially if they were carrying swords and looked like they'd been dragged through a hedge backwards. They would probably go to the nearest window with a curtain, peel it back ever so slightly and wait for the men to leave. After that, they would probably return to whatever it was they were doing before hearing the bell and forget all about those strange men. But Circe was no ordinary person.

Firstly, she was a goddess. But so are a lot of people. And, truthfully, most goddesses wouldn't even get up to answer the door. They have more important things to do, as did Circe. But she had something else. A brooding, intense curiosity that compelled her to follow every sign towards something exciting. Something new. And so she did.

Circe called her lions to her side with a single click and approached the front door. After pausing for a moment, she threw open the doors with all the unhinged confidence of someone who had just had their third morning coffee. The men stumbled backwards, as the door's movement brought

SOMETHING NEW

a wind that boiled and spilled into the still air of the front porch. The lions sat either side of her feet, watching as the men attempted to regain their balance.

"Hello." Her piercing gaze scanned each soul and the shock that rendered each expression.

There was silence, as each man began to comprehend who was stood before them, and what stood at her feet.

"Can I help you?" she enquired, this time with a harsher tone.

One man stepped forward onto the porch.

"Uh, yes," he stuttered, and then, finding his words and his feet, straightened his shoulders and tried again with more confidence. "We are travellers who request your kind hospitality. Our food ran out three days since, and we would be grateful to be welcomed into your home."

"Hm." Her eyes narrowed at them. "I suppose I must, you being *brave* travellers and all." Her words purred across the threshold, smooth as velvet. She sighed dramatically, and, stepping aside, gestured for them to enter. They seemed to think she was just a mortal woman and were very confused as to why she was alone in the house.

All but one of the men shuffled into the entrance hall, and Circe held her lions back as they filed in. The last man maintained his position on the path outside her home, with a look on his face that resembled that of a toddler, suspicious that the food on the incoming fork was, in fact, not an aeroplane.

"My dear, will you not come in too? You look positively starving." Circe's voice rippled over the air and hung around the man's neck. He looked almost taken, but shook his head.

"Ah, no my lady, I've already eaten so I'll, uh, I'll just stay out here." And with that, he looked around and slumped himself down on a log that he was sure hadn't been there until a second ago.

"Suit yourself." Circe smiled, and shut the door behind her. Her mind was spinning like a tornado across a turbulent ocean. She stared out the window next to the doorway, out to the bay and beyond. She wanted to see their world, their lives. She wanted to know where they'd come from and where they were going. But, as certain as the sun that rises each morning, she knew she'd find out soon enough.

She turned to face the men now gathered in the entrance hall. There were twenty-three in total, minus the one who had insisted on staying outside, and they all looked thoroughly confused. Circe supposed that they weren't expecting to find a single woman and a few lions in the house up from the bay, but, of course, that was the whole point. Confusion is, and always has been, the scaffolding of the high ground.

"Now," she announced, silence filling the room as the men turned to look at her. "Please make your way into the dining hall, I must finish my weaving. Dinner will be served later this evening, you can send my lions to fetch me if you need anything in the meantime." She gestured towards an archway to the right of the front door. "Just through there." She smiled, sweetly, and walked back to her sewing room. The men grumbled slightly and started to pile into the dining hall. One of her lions followed them and took

SOMETHING NEW

his place in the centre of the doorway. The men looked uneasy, but sat down at the various sofas and discussed this strange turn of events in hushed voices.

Circe, once she was happy that they were safely contained, changed her course and hurried to the top room to the east of the house. There she stood at the window and scanned the bay for a sign of their ship. The bay was a horseshoe, filled with the glittering jewel of the Mediterranean. But today, there was a smudge on the western shore. A ship, and sitting outside, what looked to be another twenty men. How exciting, she thought, grinning to herself. More stories. Suddenly, a shout arose from the dining hall. Her head snapped away from the window. She sighed, and hurried back towards the source of the noise.

In the dining hall, it seemed that all Hades had broken loose. One of the men had found his way into the kitchen, and brought back the entire contents of Circe's pantry for him and his comrades to feast on. The lion had been no match for twenty-two hungry men, and as such had resigned himself to eating the scraps that were being tossed onto the floor. A fight had broken out over a particularly fine bottle of red wine, which had ended in its contents being spilled all over the table and the other food. The rest of the men were inhaling food like pigs at a trough, having apparently forgotten that they had asked for hospitality upon arriving. Circe cleared her throat. The men continued, apparently not hearing her. Circe frowned, and raised her voice slightly. "If I may–"

MYTHS, GODS & IMMORTALS: CIRCE

"Oh, shut up," a voice interrupted.

Circe spun around to find this voice's owner. It was one of the men who had been sitting silently in the corner, inhaling one of Circe's finest cuts of steak with impressive velocity. She pursed her lips, and stared disapprovingly at him.

"Excuse me?"

"Can't you see we're busy? Go and fetch us some more wine, be a good girl."

Circe's back straightened. Clearly, these men were not interested in hospitality.

"That's no way to address–"

He interrupted her again. "For Zeus's sake woman, go and get some more wine! What are you just stood there for?"

Circe froze. Rage boiled within her, bubbling and spilling out into her blood, pouring through every vein in her body. She had forgotten, in her years of solitude, how piggish men could be. Piggish. Such a lovely word. Really quite descriptive. Circe made a mental note to write that down.

Piggish.

Now, that's an idea.

A smile crept over her face. She turned back towards the table. The men seemed not to have noticed she was silent, and had gone back to their eating. And they never would notice. For she gave a single click, and turned on her heel, walking out the room, a gate appearing in the archway behind her. She listened with a smile to the surprised oinking that was emanating from the room previously known as her dining hall. Shame. It was such an airy room. Lovely south-facing windows.

SOMETHING NEW

PART II: THE OTHERS

Bang. Bang. Bang.

The walls shook as someone's fist met with the wood of Circe's front door. She sighed. She'd known they would come eventually, she just wished they had given her a bit more time. It was difficult enough to contain twenty hungry men, let alone forty.

Circe stood up, dusted the fibres from her skirts and made her way back towards the entrance hall and dining-hall-cum-pig-pen.

Bang. Bang. Bang.

Circe idled for a while in the doorway, keeping her new visitors waiting a little longer. She was anything but compliant with demands, especially when she really wanted to be doing something else.

A gruff voice poured through the gaps in the door frame. "I know you're in there! What have you done with my men? Open up!"

Circe sighed again. Such impatience.

She glided over to the door and unlatched the bolt, ensuring both her lions took their place at her side before she opened it fully. Once again, another twenty or so men stood on her porch, including the sulky one from earlier.

"Ah," she smiled at him. "You have returned with friends. Can I help you?" she asked, turning to the man who had been pounding on her door as if he was a very exuberant builder.

"Yes." he growled, through gritted teeth. "Eurylochus told me what you did to my men. Turn them back, or I warn you, I will have to use extreme measures."

"You must be Odysseus, I'd heard on the grapevine you were trampling your way through immortal territory." This was not strictly true. Circe's source was not so much a grapevine, but more a rather chatty rainbow goddess who seemed intent on coming to visit, no matter how many times Circe told her she had things to get on with. "I'm sure you know who I am. Please, come in, we can discuss the release of your men." She smiled, and gestured into the house, stepping backwards as she did so. As expected, Odysseus did not enter in the polite manner mortals seemed to prefer nowadays, but instead barged past her, sword drawn and hackles raised. He flung himself into the hall and began to shout.

"YOU CANNOT FOOL ME, WITCH! I HAVE DRUNK THE POTION OF HERMES, YOU CANNOT USE YOUR POWERS ON ME! I AM THE CUNNING ODYSSEUS!"

Circe stared at him blankly, and then gave a glance towards his crew, who, still stood on the porch, looked vaguely embarrassed and somewhat bemused.

"Yes, I am aware of who you are. I'm not sure what potion Hermes has given you, another one of his schemes no doubt. I'm afraid you're the one who's been fooled there." She cleared her throat. Odysseus faltered, but maintained his battle stance. "May I ask, what exactly are you trying to prevent me from doing? I turned your crew into pigs because they were acting like pigs. If you'd like the same to happen to you, please continue."

She stared at him expectantly. Odysseus gulped nervously, and sheathed his sword.

"But, Hermes, he said that you would try to turn me into a pig, and that I should rush at you with my sword after drinking this potion." He held up an empty bottle, with a white label that read 'Hermes' Extra Special Potion, No Added Sugar'. His men looked at him in disbelief. Circe narrowed her eyes. "And so what, you thought that would work? You are not as cunning as Athena makes you out to be. But then, most people aren't. She likes to have her pets."

She turned and wandered towards the gate into the pig pen. Odysseus looked confused, and then gestured for the rest of his men to follow them inside.

She gazed blankly at the pigs. "Your men were disrespectful to me. They treated me like dirt. I cannot allow you to return to mortal society if that is how you treat other mortals. You must prove to me that you can do better." Odysseus glanced worriedly at his men and then approached the gate.

"I will deal with my men. Please, just turn them back."

Circe turned to him sharply, her eyes piercing his retinas and staring into his soul. She frowned, and then waved her hand over the pig pen. Instantly, the room was transformed back into her dining hall, minus the wine stains, with the remainder of Odysseus's crew sitting around a huge table. Odysseus and the others cheered and rushed to their friends. The men who were (until recently) pigs, looked confused, both at the sight of their human forms returning and also that there was suddenly a table in the room where before there had been an arrangement of chairs and sofas. Circe, on the other hand, had already made her way back to her weaving. After all, she had a dinner party to plan.

PART III: ELPENOR

For the first time in a very long time, chatter and music echoed off the walls, falling stone to stone and landing in Circe's ear. The dining hall seemed bigger, with enough seats to fit all forty-five of Odysseus's crew and Odysseus himself. It was strange, the men had been sure it was barely big enough to fit just half of them in when they'd first arrived, but that was a secret Circe wasn't telling. They also weren't sure where all this food had come from – they'd eaten all the food in the pantry, and there certainly weren't any staff around to cook more. The only inhabitants of Circe's home seemed to be the goddess herself, her lions, and the wolves that prowled the perimeter, although now they were happily devouring scraps from underneath the table.

The men seemed to be behaving themselves, thought Circe, as she surveyed the table in front of her. No fights over wine had occurred just yet, although she had noted some loaded stares from Odysseus whenever his crew got too rowdy. She was sitting at the head of the table, as the host, and also because it was too difficult for the men to get their heads around who was the head of the household if it only consisted of Circe and

SOMETHING NEW

various wild animals. Next to her was Elpenor, the youngest of Odysseus's crew and much quieter. He had been only fourteen when he left to fight at Troy, and even now he did not look much older. War ages the old but time is paused for the young, Circe considered, as she poured another glass of wine. She felt a twinge of sympathy for the boy. To be so far away from his family, when she could see hers just by looking into the sky.

"So, what are you most looking forward to seeing when you get home again?" she asked, breaking him out of his transfixion with a small bug that was crawling around on the table.

"Oh, uh, my family, definitely. My sister had just had a baby when I left, he must be around ten now," he smiled.

"Would you like some more wine?" she asked, offering the bottle to him.

"Oh, no thank you," he said, politely, "I'm not really a big drinker."

He seemed uneasy. Circe called the nicer of her lions over and positioned him to the right of Elpenor. He smiled at its large eyes that stared inquisitively up at him.

"He won't bite you," said Circe. "He knows you are a friend."

Elpenor's eyes widened, and he reached out to touch the cat's head. It pushed into his hand, and instantly his shoulders drooped slightly. He laughed.

"I never thought I'd get to stroke a lion. Never even thought I'd get to see home again."

"Would you like to? See home, I mean."

"Well, of course. Wouldn't we all?"

"But right now. Just to see what had changed."

Elpenor stared at her.

"What do you mean?"

Circe smiled. She put down her cup, and waved a hand gently over the table. Gradually, the walls of the room became lighter, the men became chairs and the table became a hearth in a family home. Everything, from the crew, to the lion, to the food on the table, morphed into a domestic scene in the main room of a small house. A young woman with mousy brown hair sat with a little boy next to a fire, speaking to him in hushed tones. She held him close to her, and patted his leg. An elderly man sat opposite from them, dozing into the late evening. He was sat in an old wooden chair with intricate markings and was covered by a red woven blanket. An older woman bustled through and into another room. Elpenor watched each and every one of them, with wonder.

"Are– are we really there? Can they see us?" he whispered to Circe, who had placed them both on seats at a small table in the corner of the room.

"No. I can reflect what is happening there, but I cannot place us in its sight."

Elpenor watched as the young woman stared into the fire, the boy leaning into her side, his eyes fluttering closed. The man in the chair stirred.

"That's my father," he said, turning to Circe. "He was fighting abroad when I left. I guess he's home now."

His gaze lowered to the blanket over the man's lap, with its indent where the right leg would have been. A tear escaped his eye and ran down his cheek, dropping onto the hand that was propped under his chin.

"He looks like you," Circe said, gently. Elpenor raised his gaze to look at her, and then back at the sleeping form.

The older woman reappeared through a doorway on the back wall. She was carrying what looked to be a pile of clothes, and she paused to smile at the gentle snoring of her husband. Elpenor did not say anything, only staring at her face and matching her smile.

But as quickly as it appeared, the room began to fade. Elpenor spun around to look at Circe.

"What are you doing? Bring them back!"

"I can only hold the illusion for so long," she whispered, a tear falling as the dining hall reappeared.

Elpenor sat back in his chair, and the air hung heavy around them.

"You'll see them again soon, Elpenor."

His eyes widened at her. And in her heart, Circe willed for her words to ring true.

PART IV: GOODBYE

Soon enough, days stretched into weeks, with no sign of Odysseus ever planning on leaving. His men spent their days whispering to each other in groups, wondering when, if ever, they would set sail for home. In the evenings, they laughed and drank, telling stories into the early hours of the morning.

Elpenor seemed to have found his feet somewhat, and had begun to drink with them. This had led to many an encounter when Circe found him wandering around the island at dawn, trying to find his way back to the ship. She had taken to going for a morning stroll to watch the sun rise. It was the only time the island was truly quiet, and she couldn't sleep anyway with the worry that Elpenor would end up taking a stroll off one of the steeper cliffs.

This morning, like all the others, the sun had been greeted by the birds and risen from its slumber. It carved shadows into the rockface, highlighting the many deep caverns that lay within. Circe pottered slowly around the bay, her dress dragging along the sand like a stream heading for the ocean. She looked up to the sky, to the birds, and breathed out. She missed the peace that came with solitude. It had been exciting, at first anyway, with new people on the island. But now she missed the freedom and the quiet that had drawn her here in the first place. And to make matters worse, she still hadn't finished her weaving.

Circe reached the eastern shore of the beach and turned to follow the cliff-path back up to the house. As she rounded the corner, she saw Elpenor in front of her. He was a way off, and it was too early for running, so she walked slowly behind him as she pondered why he was walking in the opposite direction of the ship.

When she reached the top of the cliff and approached the house, he was nowhere to be seen. She looked around, scouring the undergrowth and bushes for a drunken sailor with a tendency to wander. Seeing nothing, she shrugged and made her way inside. However, upon reaching her quarters, she heard footsteps above, echoing from the roof like the pitter-patter of heavy rain. With an inkling of who this might be, Circe made her way up to the terrace.

Stood in the glow of the morning sun was Elpenor, facing the bay's opening to the Mediterranean.

"What are you doing here?" she asked, coming to stand next to him.

"Jus' looking at the bay."

He was slurring. She glanced down at the empty bottle in his hands.

"Don't you think you should get back to the ship?"

"Whassa point? Not goin' home any time soon."

Circe sighed. She turned to walk back inside, pulling gently on his shoulder to guide him back in.

Suddenly, he jerked his shoulder forward, out of her hand, tipping himself forward. She lunged to catch him, but her hand missed him by an inch. He toppled backwards, looking up to the sky, his eyes wide. Circe shouted, but he couldn't hear. He fell further and further toward the ground, until he lay on the dirt path, two storeys down, his eyes still staring at the sky. His chest tightened, and a small breath escaped his mouth. A bird flew overhead, reflected in the glaze of tears over his pupils. Circe stared down at him, choking on a sob.

Although it is no surprise for an immortal goddess that all mortals die, one way or another, Circe would never get used to the silence that came afterwards. The golden glow of the sun lifted off him, and sank further into the ground. She stood, frozen, on the roof, watching as his soul began its journey to Hades. Her lions nuzzled at her hand, and, tears rolling down her cheek, she motioned for them to fetch Odysseus and his men.

The next few minutes seemed to happen in slow motion. Odysseus and his men found Elpenor. The crew wailed and held each other. Odysseus stood, stony-faced, staring at his body. He looked slowly up to the roof, where Circe still stood. Making no expression, he turned and walked back down the cliff path, calling for his men to follow. They looked at each other confused, but eventually they trailed after him, a river of tears falling towards the sea.

They left that day. They never said goodbye. Circe watched as they sailed out of the bay and into the sea, still stood on the roof where Elpenor had been. So alive.

As the sun set, Circe sat on the roof, the glow of her father's light shining over her. Her lions lay next to her, their heads resting on each of her knees. So, this was how the adventure ended. With a soulless form and an empty home. She was certain that Odysseus would lie through his teeth about what had happened here. But she had expected that, and it was no bad thing. The less people knew about her, the better. Although he would be back. She could sense it. But she would not let them stay. She would not be drawn by the excitement of something new. Not this time.

This Slow Death
Elena Kotsile

The loom thumped, weaving the shreds of his skin into an unsettling yet enthralling tapestry. Not my best work, though. The raw material was harsh to handle, but the relentless thudding of the loom had an almost meditative cadence.

Almost.

Outside my window, the sun showered the meadow in a brilliant warmth. Below the hill, frothy waves sprayed golden at the mouth of the cave. Within me, however, cold violence spread its darkness over hidden places, bruising my soul. It was an irresistible sensation, like an open wound I couldn't stop scratching.

My fingers ran down Odysseus's shredded skin. A familiar pain bolted down my lower back where years ago he'd hurt me for the first time, but not the last, when he'd knocked me down upon the stone floor. The sun had been shining that day, too: the golden flare on the copper vase went back and forth, back and forth. In a sense, it had never stopped.

In spite of being years since I'd last seen him, alive at least, those embodied memories wouldn't go away. No enchantments, moonlight, or herbs could help me forget what had been done to me. Nothing could help me suffer through those sleepless bearings.

MYTHS, GODS & IMMORTALS: CIRCE

"Lady Circe." Polyksene interrupted my thoughts, unaware of her little mercy.

"What is it?" I turned my head over my shoulder while keeping on with my weaving.

Polyksene wore an old scar across her left cheek. Apollo had marked her fair face as a reminder that no one rejected a god or a man. My fate was sealed, too, by a god. I had plans for Hermes, but not yet. Not before I finished with this skin.

"Where should I leave those?" As she came closer, her timid heart fluttered. My nymphs were afraid of me, as they should be, but along with fear came respect. Those heartbeats were something different.

"Are those the last pieces?" I hovered my gaze over her scar, the honey eyes, the wheat hair. Polyksene had her mother's eyes but her father's face lines. Both had abandoned her after Apollo's violation, but it was the mother who had sent her here to serve me, to keep her away from the father who had other plans for her.

"Yes," she said, and the wrinkles around her nose betrayed her disgust.

Skinning a human hide must beat being a sex slave to the gods, I thought, but I didn't say. A woman shouldn't joke about the pain of another, especially when they share the same.

"Leave them inside that kophinos." That one was made of reeds growing upon Odysseus's companions' graves.

I'd had them killed, too, and buried them in my garden. But before putting them in the ground, I'd removed their

THIS SLOW DEATH

livers and fed them to my pigs, and so their souls were forever trapped in Hades' entrance, fading into madness. Unfortunately, I hadn't gotten to all who had sullied my home. Some had already died of old age or illness. If only it hadn't taken me so long to react.

I'd spared Odysseus's liver, though. Not out of remorse but because he was my son's father, after all.

Polyksene placed the remaining skin in the basket. The tangy odor of the drying sweat on her temples, the relief of getting the skin off her hands, got on my nerves. I turned my attention to the loom, dismissing her. It wasn't her fault for being a frightened mouse. She'd been raised that way and couldn't escape her upbringing. What was my excuse?

I was the daughter of Helios and Perse. Oceanus and Tethys were my grandparents. And yet, I couldn't bring myself to walk away from the boundaries of my home. It was as if my island had become an oddity, the beach an iron cage with bars bleeding rust, the cave's rocks sharp blades cutting through the bone.

That bleak sunny day when Odysseus's cursed ship had reached my shores, I'd welcomed him and his lot. I'd invited them into my house among my nymphs to sit by my hearth, eat my food, and drink my wine. And then, after they'd drunk and sung and danced, they'd defiled us all. My divinity and wisdom had done nothing to help me. A common man had fooled me.

Odysseus had been easy on the eyes, I ought to admit as much. I might have allowed him in my bed had I been given the right to choose. Maybe he'd seen right through me. Maybe my eyes had betrayed my desire, and he'd thought I was his for the taking without needing to ask.

Odysseus had broken the law of hospitality and, with it, had broken me into a myriad of pieces. I still collected them in the desolated scatters of my life, and what if years had passed since then. I was still reassembling my body and mind. I was still not whole.

And for this, I'd sent his son to kill him and bring me back his body to skin it.

* * *

"Mother, please stop," Telegonus said.

The day had moved on, and now twilight crept over the horizon, casting a dying glow. Below the hill, the sea was serene as the rising moon promised a stormless night. Owls hooted through the crawling dusk, their calls shadowing the airy song of the nightingales. A shiver ran through my skin when the evening jasmine breeze hit me.

"Close the window, will you?" I covered my shoulders with a weathered shawl and turned to look at him. My son. My living scar.

His name meant the one who'd been born away. Everyone, except my nymphs, assumed I'd named him as such to honour his father, who had sailed away on his way to Ithaca when his son was born. That hadn't been the reason. When Telegonus was born, my heart had already been away from him. He'd been born away from love.

THIS SLOW DEATH

Telegonus had inherited my dark, curly hair and full lips but had his father's blue piercing eyes that sent shivers down my spine every time he looked at me. As he closed the window, my gaze shifted towards the windowsill, where a moly bouquet stood inside a clay lekythos. Spring water and Odysseus's eyeballs nurtured the flowers, and Telegonus had no idea.

"This needs to stop," he said, pointing at the loom.

His eyes were two frozen flames. His trembling hands formed fists, the veins of his naked arms emerged like violet snakes. The boy who tried to become a man by issuing orders to the woman who'd birthed him.

"No," I said. "When I finish with it, it'll adorn the footrest of my throne."

He thought he could rule this house now that he had come of age. Besides the eyes, he'd also taken his father's sense of entitlement. I should have smothered him in his cradle when he'd been a baby. Now, who knew what pain he would inflict on others? How much of his father did he carry in him?

"You don't need this," he said, kneeling before me reaching for my hands. I let him touch me but didn't hold him back. His watery eyes searched for something in me that had been long dead.

"You have wonderful garments to embellish your palace," he continued. "Embroidery the gods would envy. This is an abomination. It isn't you."

For a moment, a warmth rose to my chest, and a desire to kiss his beautiful curls. He was Odysseus's son, but he was also mine. Then I remembered his father's deceit and withdrew my hands from his embrace. No matter my powers, I couldn't take Odysseus out of him. His fate was sealed, too.

"You won't tell me what I need, who I am, or what suits me."

His silence crashed on the floor and was so loud I wanted to scream. Hot tears ran down his velvet cheeks.

"Mother," he said. "You wear an armband smithed with my father's teeth and a necklace made of his clavicles. Now, you're weaving his skin, disturbing the nymphs. How does this help you?"

Did he have any specific nymph in mind?

Polyksene.

"Perhaps you're the one who's disturbed."

Telegonus stood up, wiping away the tears from his face. He wasn't ashamed to cry in front of me. There might have been some specks of hope left for him yet.

"He was my father, and I killed him. For you. I stained my hands with family blood. For you. And I would do it all over again for what he did." He opened his arms and moved a few steps away as if I threatened him. "Mother, I beg you. End this atrocity."

Telegonus spoke of atrocity, of abomination, when he'd been the product of one. I should have named him Homodeinus for all the dread he dragged behind him from the moment he'd been conceived.

"Polyksene told me you were different before—"

I stood up, my shawl dropped on the floor and slapped him hard on the face. The memory of who I'd been before

THIS SLOW DEATH

Odysseus hung between us like a dead bird, feathers dripping with bile.

"You dare speak of me with the nymphs. You insolent boy."

"Forgive me, Mother. I asked because I wanted to know about you." His voice cracked.

"Get out," I said. But Telegonus didn't move.

"I hadn't yet been born," he said, "but I know the story about Medea coming here seeking your help. And how you cleansed her and her lover of their crimes, offering them absolution in the eyes of the gods. I wonder if you found the strength to forgive her after what she'd done, how you cannot forgive me for the sins of my father?"

I'd forgiven Medea for slaughtering her brother, my sweet little nephew, because back then, I used to believe in love.

"Get out," I said, turning my back on him. "You sicken me."

Silent tears licked the edges of my eyelids, but I still couldn't cry. I bit my knuckles as the heavy door shut behind me. Telegonus was gone, and I disintegrated within the void in my heart where love for my son should have been.

The guilt of not wanting your child. The shame of showing him.

* * *

The next night, for the first time in eighteen years, I carried my steps to the beach where Odysseus had come ashore. I stood at the mouth of the cave, seeing the lights of my house up the hill. So close, and yet so far away.

The moon was full, giving me the strength to advance my plan. Fear was rooted deep into my soul, paralyzing my body that more and more felt as if it weren't my own. The previous day, my words had hurt Telegonus, and for a passing moment, I'd been justified. But an elusive sense of affection had kept me awake, questioning myself.

I am a horrible mother.

"Bring in the animals," I said to Polyksene as the troubled sea cooled my feet, and I walked inside the cave.

I didn't have to take her with me, but where I was going, I wanted her to go, too. It could be I wanted her with me out of spite, for her to see my deep revulsion for life, the lengths of my loathing.

Polyksene's scar shone silver in the moonlight. A terror ran through her jaw, but she didn't complain and took her place by my side, holding the sheep in one hand and the goat in the other.

"What's your business with Telegonus?" I asked.

"He's kind and generous," she said, her voice a whisper of rustling leaves.

"Is he now?"

Polyksene's stiff body moved next to me, her lips pressed. She heard the irony in my words and disagreed with me. She thought of him as something else, something better. How could she? Had she forgotten what his father had done to us all? How I'd failed to protect them?

"Take off your sandals," I said. "We walk barefoot from here."

THIS SLOW DEATH

"Where to, Lady?" she asked, her frail voice a fledgling crashing on the cave's walls.

"We walk towards the darkness that lies deep in the cave. The type that swallows all form, dissolving it into nothingness."

"We should have taken a torch with us, then," Polyksene said.

"We need no fire to guide us. The darkness must be absolute, pressing our bodies like a living thing." Carrying a lit torch wouldn't work. The flame would have distorted the enclosing blackness and misinformed me about the right place to perform the ritual.

As we left the shores of Aeaea behind us and descended into the earth, the animals grew agitated. I calmed them down and eased their concerns, chanting the right words close to their ears. They wouldn't feel the growing darkness anymore as it turned alive, pulsating against our necks. The sole light came from the walls, emitting a faint silvery blue. But as we walked deeper into the cave, the blue radiance faded, and the air became thicker and colder.

"Do you have plans to kill me too?" Polyksene asked.

"Don't be absurd," I said. "Nekyia doesn't require nymph blood."

"I thought Nekyia could only be performed at the land of the dead," Polyksene said, and her breath was heavier with every step.

"I can do this here just fine," I said. "All I need is deep darkness and animals to sacrifice. Death is everywhere and can function under all conditions. No need to travel as far as Kimmeria."

MYTHS, GODS & IMMORTALS: CIRCE

"Then why did Odysseus travel all the way to Acheron's estuary to talk to the oracle when he could have come here instead?"

Polyksene's naivety was a butterfly that had lost its way over the vast ocean.

"I told him so to drive him away from my island."

I brought my hand on the cold cave walls, searching for the markings that would show me the way. Hot liquid ran down my elbow from my shredded fingertips as they traced the carved symbols. My mind knew there was pain, but my body was too numb to feel it.

What do I hope to accomplish by subjecting myself to this torment?

I didn't know right from wrong anymore, but I knew this: Telegonus and I couldn't stay under the same roof until I made peace with myself. Coming here was my last resort to forgive myself for the dread that had fallen upon my house. If I couldn't do that, Telegonus had to go.

I was venom. Poisoning myself and everyone around me.

The air was wet and slippery, like the surrounding void. The blood from my shredded skin was the first offering, which meant we were close. The darkness was so thick that my mouth became one with my eyes, my breaths embedded in the bones of my chest. The primordial Womb engulfed my heartbeat, throbbing at the soles of my bare feet.

Gaia. She loved her monstrous children despite hating their father.

THIS SLOW DEATH

"We've arrived," I said.

I kneeled and dug two holes in the soft mud. I was blind, with earth between my fingers and under my nails. Then I reached my hand, searching for the sheep and the goat. Polyksene's scream upon my touch was deafening.

"Keep your voice to yourself. Or you'll face the same fate as the animals."

Hot arterial blood from the sheep and the goat filled the two holes in the earth as I chanted sacred words for my sacrifice to reach below, where no living thing could walk or breathe. Then I stood and waited, eyes wide open, staring at the darkness before me.

* * *

First came Absyrthus, Medea's brother. His small, brutalized body crawled towards me. In Nekyia's invoking darkness, the dead emitted a grey light with moving shadows carrying thunderstorms within. His hunger petrified me.

"This blood isn't for you," I said, betraying him once again.

Repentance brought me to my knees, facing his amorphous, gaping mouth. My brother hadn't talked to me since he'd heard I offered haven to Medea after her crime instead of delivering her to him.

I am sorry I chose love over justice for your death. Please forgive me.

Then Asterius came, my sister's son. Pasiphae had called for me after his birth, but none of our combined sorcery had made him right. He'd been the product of my sister's forced mating with a beast, yet she'd loved him and had done all she could to ease his life. She'd even breastfed him, bleeding over his horns.

Telegonus was beautiful, and all he sought was my affection.

Asterius stood before me, half human, half beast, growling. He would have torn me into pieces if he could. And I might have welcomed it.

"This blood isn't for you," I said, and for a moment, I saw my sister's ghost in the hordes of the dead who had smelled the blood and were closing in.

I am sorry the world wronged you so. Please forgive me, for I wasn't strong enough to help you.

Third came Asterius's sister, Ariadne. Her ghost illuminated the darkness of the cave with its blinding bolts, blood running in between her naked legs. I'd received word of her fate when Theseus had sold her to Dionysus, and I'd done nothing to save her. I hadn't even tried.

Ariadne hovered over the sacrificial blood, her eyes lost in the lands of the afterlife.

"This blood isn't for you," I said, and my heart sank, refusing her.

I am sorry I didn't come for you. I am sorry for the pain you endured. Please forgive me.

And then, I saw him. His hunger was the greatest, and his arrogance and superiority shone brighter than any other ghost through the mist.

A sharp pain in my belly and a shortness of breath.

Gaia, please give me the strength to carry on.

"You," I said, pointing a trembling hand at him. "This sacrifice is for you. Come and drink, Odysseus, and talk to me."

One minute, he was there, and then, in the blink of an eye, he stood before me, grinning. His face sank into the blood I'd prepared for him, and he drank and drank, and for a moment, I was worried the blood wasn't enough to satisfy his hunger and that he wouldn't be strong enough to talk. And all this revisiting pain would have been in vain.

Not in vain. I've understood something. But I can't shape it yet and dress it with words.

He rose, and Polyksene, behind me, gasped. His body wasn't a shadow anymore but solid, keeping its grey light, thunder in his eyes, and blood running down his jaw. A real, strong body.

I stepped back, holding my hands in front of me. The world spun, and my spine tingled with a familiar fear.

"You wanted to talk," he said, his smirk gleaming brilliant red.

The screams inside my head consumed my words. My mouth opened and closed as if I were a fish outside water.

I refuse to be afraid again.

"Why did you do it?" I asked, and it wasn't what I wanted to say. I didn't care for his reasons for hurting me. But I couldn't find any other words to utter. I needed time I couldn't have to spare to gather my thoughts. I'd played this exchange in my mind countless times, and I'd always been brave and articulate.

Now, I was, too, a ghost of myself.

"I did plenty of things. Be specific, woman, before my hunger consumes me."

"This slow death I'm living. I don't deserve it. You took away my trust and love for the world and left me an empty shell. You robbed me of my agency, and I've no means to fix myself, to be the one I was before I met you."

"Have you lost your wits? I gifted you a son. A boy strong enough to overcome me and kill me for you. What more would a woman want?"

"Telegonus wasn't yours to give." Or mine to refuse. Telegonus belonged to himself and hadn't asked to be born, as I hadn't asked to mother him. And despite all, my child loved me.

Self, forgive me for blaming you. Son, forgive me for not loving you, for not knowing how.

What more would a woman want? I wanted everything life had to offer, but first, I had to live again like a person and not like a shadow. I took off the armband made of his teeth and the necklace made of his clavicles and dropped them on his feet. Odysseus's mouth twisted, seeing his remains spoiled.

He couldn't offer me absolution. Only I had the power to do that.

"I don't forgive you for hurting me," I said, and with my feet, I covered the pools of blood with mud.

The grey light of the ghosts disappeared, and the darkness became complete again. Polyksene cried behind me. I turned and searched for her body and felt her sweaty palm as she held me tight.

THIS SLOW DEATH

I knew now why I'd brought her with me. It hadn't been out of spite but of fear for facing Odysseus alone. Of fear for her being away from me. I wasn't afraid anymore. The darkness around us was as thick as butter, but in some deep valley of my mind, warm light emerged.

I existed whole.

Shifting Destinies

Claire L. Marsh

Curved like a giant wave exploding from the sea, the coastline intensified her descent. An echo of its dramatic angles; she swooped past the sand-coloured rock bleeding copper and levelled out moments before turquoise waters could take her. Mist cooled her underside as speed forced air against her face. Her outspread wings loomed, a dark shadow skimming the waves; signalling to lesser creatures she was the predator. The beast to be feared.

A shimmer of pink and purple with gossamer wings propelled her instincts. Soaring upward, she snapped her beak shut around the fluttering dragonfly. In this form, it was as tasty as the sugar-dusted cubes of rose and pistachio Turkish delight she bought from the market and hid in her dressing table. The body she was born in felt like masquerading in an actor's garb; ill-fitting, scratchy and awkward. But as this, she was unstoppable.

Circe coasted on momentum, basked in the fast-moving colours and shapes washing together. It didn't matter she'd transition with insects on her breath, arms weighted to her sides by an ache that called for attention and nail-less toes where talons had pushed through. It was worth it for every second of her raptor form.

Her thoughts and emotions streamlined. She heard and understood the calls of her kind, warning of humans ahead. They recognized her as one of them, part of their community; a respect and loyalty not offered in her other form, even from kin. Her mother's face flashed to mind, a contradiction of beauty and spite that stretched her hatred to the tip of every feather. It made her ravenous.

Gorgias would be there, working the land with his brothers. This dictated her flight path home. Her silhouette, the majesty of her movement or the way prey scattered and fled, often drew his attention. It was admiration, she thought, but hoped for more. Perhaps he also felt trapped in his given form, no matter how strong his muscles were, how the afternoon sun made perspiration tumbling down his chest glisten like a prism, refracting the plainest light into rainbows. An emptiness pulled at her falcon stomach whenever she got close.

Flight slowing, she recognized his shoulder-length, wavy dark hair, the olive tones of his skin. Settling her yellow feet on a preferred boulder, Circe angled her head for a better view. She could perch for hours, watching him lift, carry, laugh, stretch his toned, gleaming body. Until the hunger became unbearable.

A smudge partially within her forty degrees of vision moved.

Recognizing the smudge from temple, she took flight, her perch already several hundred yards behind her tail feathers. *She's a peasant, a nobody, luring him with loose robes and cardamom scents. Well, curves can no more hide a feeble mind than aromatics can obscure her family's goat stench.*

Circe targeted Euthalia, swooping in circles like a feathered tornado, sinking her beak into the older girl's scalp. Ascending and descending, over and over, clumps of hair flying; she screeched at her enemy.

The brothers, including her beloved Gorgias, lifted and swung mattocks in the air, protecting Euthalia. Circe smelled her blood. She dived through two brothers' shoulders, but they almost caught her wing. Filthy peasant needs to learn her place and stay among the tenant farmers. Not Circe, the daughter of a god, she should have her pick of suitors... no matter what rebuke passed her mother's lips.

* * *

An ocean breeze chased her through the window, lifting the drapes like folds on a dress. Landing on her bed, Circe thought about her natural body. The intention was all her magic required, her shape fluid and realigning, flowing as water. As her feet contacted stone, talons shifted to toes.

The single mottled brown feather was the only trace of her falcon remaining. Circe collected it from the floor; it smelled of cliffs and waves. Pulling her hair into a chignon, she slid the feather into it, the rich bronze drawing out similar tones from her curls. Lighter colours in her hair showed she'd been 'kissed by the sun'; her father's words when she was small, balanced on his knee. It made her feel closer to him and his purpose, as if she, too, could be destined for greatness. But even at fifteen repeating his words, her mother's voice was louder – 'copper in your hair marks malleability, the gods know your temperament changes with the winds.'

You're far from perfect, nymph. The thought spurred her; she dressed in a sunlit bronze gown to emphasize those tones in her hair. Adding jewellery to her arm and a silk scarf around her waist, she headed to the main tower.

It was her favourite part of their estate and its scent filled the hallway all the way to her father's library. The room opened to the inside and out; every inch filled with plants, herbs and flowers. When her mother, Perse, was first pregnant, this was her father's gift. As soon as they understood language, all her children were taught about the religious uses of plants and herbs. But Circe was alone in her innate affinity, matched by a curiosity she couldn't quench. When she was younger, she'd tried to impress Perse with her knowledge but, at most, her mother seemed dismissive. Still, she remained thankful she wasn't prevented from cultivating her talents.

During the late afternoon, until the family was beckoned to dinner, Circe had the garden room to herself. There she would not be disapproved of by her mother or ridiculed by her siblings. Hours with books, plants, and the support of her tutor, Sofia, calmed her more than temple could. It was like swimming underwater. Her darker thoughts and strongest emotions became the world above the surface – distant, blurry, and less salient than immediate senses.

"Come, gently touch these leaves. Tell me what they feel." Sofia sat on the floor, bony fingers immersed in the soil of a long narrow planter.

In the decade she'd known Sofia, Circe couldn't recall one occasion she had raised her voice, despite several incidents when her behaviour warranted it. She sat opposite her, the planter between them. A dark green shrub, teardrop leaves with tiny white berries and almost no scent.

"*Laurus nobilis*," Circe said.

"Young lady, you are as intelligent as your father is hardworking. I know you can identify bay laurel. Close those beautiful eyes, stretch out your hand and tell me how this plant feels."

Sofia guided her fingers to the leaves. There was some similarity in the texture of her mentor's sun-aged skin and the undulations of the leaf. *That is touch, not perception,* she scolded herself, saving Sofia the task.

"It has sun. It has room to grow; organic matter to assist. The soil could be drained further, it fears stagnant water. It fears stagnation, it's resilient and hardy. She can withstand challenge if she's growing, fed."

Daring to open an eyelid, Circe held her breath as Sofia delayed judgement. The old tutor increasingly tested her this way. She smiled, exposing teeth as white as pearls as she clapped.

"I can feel from the soil this plant requires assistance, but that's from here," she reached across, touching Circe's head, "but you can know from your heart. You have a true gift, and you nurture it with a sincerity that no one can teach."

Circe kissed the top of Sofia's head and couldn't suppress her buoyancy as she whispered a 'thank you' to the plant. "Does she bring victory?"

Sofia's hand clutched the locket on her necklace, her lips moving without a voice. The older woman's expression wiped the pride from Circe's body. Had she said something incorrect? Part of her tutor's smile returned, but didn't commit.

"Have you read about this, little bird?"

"I don't think so. It's something I know with my heart, intuited from her." She was hesitant, desperate not to disappoint again.

"You know of magic, were born of it. There's also sorcery, witchcraft. These women use spells to make things happen outside what is destined. They can draw power from nature. It's part gift, part training. *Laurus nobilis* brings wisdom. This can make one victorious in battle or guide away from failure. Is this mysticism something you wish to learn more of?"

The feeling of soaring above water swept through Circe. "Yes, absolutely."

* * *

Circe had tried staying out of it, continued eating, but her face performed rogue soliloquies. *And Phaethon's an insufferable idiot.* By far, the worst of all her father's children. Mortal with an ego and sense of entitlement equalling any of the greatest gods.

"You don't think I can do it. I'll prove it. What's that face for, Circe? Are you challenging me?" Phaethon jumped to his feet, cheeks pomegranate red.

"I said no–"

"That's simply her face. Hideously plain, mortal even. No offence," said her sister Heliades, interrupting.

Circe stuffed her mouth with grapes. She glanced at her mother, a smile dawning on her face. A face that reversed the ritual masks worn by peasant children. Hideous creatures with fangs, red eyes and dangerous intent covering their cherubic heads.

"Phaethon, I promised any gift you wished for. This would curse you with death." Helios, her father, shone golden. Handsome, strong, with vast knowledge of mortals and the heavens; yet quick to react to his sons and the many who shared his bed. At least, when they were in favour.

"This is my wish. To ride your chariot across the skies. You promised."

"The sun's path takes formidable skill to navigate. An error and the world could freeze or burn, a fate you would share. We have just met my son. Must I lose you so soon?"

"If I'm descended from the great sun god Helios, I should be able to command the reins. I am Phaethon, the strongest son of the beauty Clymene. It is my right." He stood close to her father's chair, a proximity lacking respect.

Circe thought it for a moment. It barely flirted with her consciousness. *Pig-headed boy.*

A gasp.

Heliades was on her feet, pointing with one hand, giggling behind the other.

Snout investigating the ceramic tiles, Phaethon's long black body had a razor line of thick, black hair from head to

SHIFTING DESTINIES

mid-back and a stubby, curled tail. Even as swine, his breed was uncertain. And aggressive, he darted beneath the table, coming for her feet.

"I'm sorry, I didn't mean to. I swear." The minute she said it, intention clear, the pig turned back into a snuffling mortal, hunched by her sandals.

The apology made no difference, neither did reversing it. Her mother, who was open about her despise for Phaethon, was incensed, screaming at her. Phaethon himself seemed bemused, a little winded, and skulked away on two feet. Yet her mother still decreed she was banished to her chambers for a week.

Circe bowed her head to her father and left the dining hall. Halfway down the long hall, she felt tears moisten her cheeks. She focused on her sister and mother revelling in her mistake; the anger pushed aside weakness. A pang of self-pity returned as she passed Sofia's concerned eyes and, forbidden from speaking, couldn't explain.

* * *

For the thirty-seventh hour of her confinement, she reread her favourite book on herbs and healing. Circe spotted the spindly shadows creeping under the door before gentle tapping arrived. She threw open the door to what, she hoped, was early release. Sofia smiled, raising a finger to her lips, and passed Circe a linen-wrapped package.

A book; bound in dark, leathery material and musty like her horse's stable on a damp day. She lifted the cover; the first

MYTHS, GODS & IMMORTALS: CIRCE

three pages were mottled, aged and stained, but she placed her palm over them anyway, tracing handwritten names with her finger. At the top of the fourth page, written in black ink, was '*Sofia Stivaros*'.

One third of the pages were blank. Completed pages showed collaboration and editing, '*four*' bay leaves crossed out, '*six*' etched next to it. Each followed the same format – an intention, a list of ingredients, a recipe, an incantation. Its owners had coloured outside these lines; notes scribbled and forced into margins. '*I repeated the words three times. The bird flew, so I didn't speak the fourth. It dropped from the sky, unable to breathe. This spell demands a payment. Be warned, it takes fingers.*'

* * *

Circe savoured each page. By the end of day five, she was spinning and clashing against her cage. Her falcon demanded flight. The book made promises, showed her what she could be, what was within grasp. Dozens of sisters had nurtured these spells. These were women who wouldn't suffer injustice. Sofia believed in her; she had gifted her the grimoire to use it. The thoughts wouldn't let go.

Small knocks on her balcony door broke their pattern. Peering down, her sister, Heliades, was throwing pebbles at the glass. *If you think I'm to be tricked, you're dumber than you appear,* Circe thought, giving Heliades a wave through the closed door.

A freckled veneer of sweetness, Heliades ushered her to come out. *Opening a door is not stepping through it.*

"Heliades, you have come to visit me, how sisterly."

"I miss you; hate the thought of you suffering and alone. How much time you're sacrificing with Father and, of course, your precious garden room. Sofia is forlorn."

"That's considerate. What, specifically, do you miss about me?" The small, upturned quiver of Heliades' top lip almost cracked Circe's sing-song tone with laughter. *Who would've thought the darkest cloud has brought sunlight to my day?*

"Dearest Circe, your frivolity of heart. After temple, we passed this joyous young couple – embracing, faces flushed. I commented to Mother, 'Circe would appreciate the beauty in this moment.' A simple boy, one of several born of farmers, and his curvaceous beauty, with parents so lowly they're tenant goat keepers. Penniless, yet rich in passion."

Her feet were on the balcony, yet she couldn't remember moving. She gripped the edge; the stone grated against her palms but release and she would fall or fly. "Gorgias with Euthalia, you swear it on your life?"

"Does this upset you? I hoped to bring comfort. Perhaps I was mistaken. He has many brothers. Although he is the only one standing six feet, with those muscles you admire. Do you have affection for him?"

"You swear it or I'll turn you into a dung beetle."

They both knew her threat was unmatched by her powers. From eight years old, Circe's abilities developed with the predictability of the seas; the only constant being at every brisk turn, she'd tried rendering her sister's form as wretched as her character. And failed. But now Circe had her book. *Revenge is coming, even if it takes me a year and costs me a finger. Or three.*

"I swear. A handsome pairing they make too," said Heliades, strolling away.

Circe shoved the nearest pot off the balcony ledge. Its body shattered, splinters of terracotta marking where her sister had stood. One day or one year left didn't matter. *This ends.*

* * *

The grimoire was on her bed, where she'd left it, but with one difference. It was open on a spell. Circe read *'an illusion to appear where you are not.'* Everything she needed for it was close; her escape predetermined.

From balcony pots she fetched thyme leaves for apparition, fennel to keep out meddlers and from her drawer, a silk parcel of vanilla beans, extracting three for compulsion. And popped a square of Turkish delight in her mouth, for luck.

Following the instructions, she ground the items in a bronze bowl with her fingers until none was independent of the other. She yanked a hair from her head, adding it to the bowl. Passing olive oil around her cheeks until her tongue felt coated, she spat. Lighting a white candle, she tipped it; wax coated the surface of the mixture and she set it on fire.

"They who hide their forms with double faces and double voices, let them see. Mother of all nature, I burn these for you. You rule, I hail. Come make them see."

Orange flames crackled and stretched to her words. As her confidence grew, they surged higher, the candle snuffed, and the fire became silver. Freeing itself from the bowl, snaking in the air, taking her image. A shimmering, vitreous version of her, hovering. Circe gawped while it mimicked her in colour and form. As its likeness increased, it became weightier, lowering to the floor. Stood motionless, its eyes hollow, painted glass. She completed the ritual by kissing its lips. They kissed back.

A shadow self, to be seen and heard, but never touched.

* * *

She waited until the food tray arrived outside her door, took it in and watched her other self, miming her routine. While everyone feasted, her falcon soared from the turret stairwell, diving under the stars and inside the garden room. Shifting her shape, the ingredients were at her fingertips. Breath quickening, she prepared the tincture. A glass beaker on the side was the right size to grind and mix; she added spit; with Sofia's scissors she slashed across her left palm and watched blood pour into it.

The blood bubbled like lava, pulling the saliva, herbs, plants and soil into itself. It rolled in the beaker, spurts of air bursting the surface. The glass burned, but she couldn't, wouldn't let go. Her eyes swirled, tied to the substance that was coagulating, thickening; smoke smelling of liquorice root rushed inside her nostrils. It coursed down the back of her throat like strong liquor and pushed words from her mouth. They came from her thoughts and her voice, and yet so much more: like each woman who had performed the spell was speaking it through her. All demanding vengeance, their intentions were clear.

"Come to our sacrifices. One for you, one for us. Take blood, take bone."

Circe extracted the small, smooth, black pebble from the scorched, ashy base of the beaker, placing it onto her tongue. The pebble would be safe within her beak.

* * *

Heliades was cruel and cunning, but she hadn't lied. Her Gorgias's mouth pressed to Euthalia's breast like a suckling infant, his strong hands greedily widening her thighs and eyes meant to worship hers, mesmerized with non-goddessly orbs. *She's stolen his affection with common biology, offered readily. Dropped her robes as the sum of her worth.*

Tears blurred her vision, sorrow clogged her throat, but the pebble in her beak vibrated to a more familiar rhythm, called it from dormancy. It pushed her into her true form; unbound itself from her stomach, rising and capturing the space between her organs like diffused oxygen. Stronger than tears, more instinctual than sorrow. Fury and hatred as energizing as any fuel; Circe's intent was clear; their voices unified.

* * *

Euthalia was bathing under the moon. *Some sins cannot be washed away*, Circe thought as she waited for the girl's

SHIFTING DESTINIES

turned back. She scooped Euthalia's robes under her arm and awaited her prey. Power leaked from her body in tiny bursts, sparking from fingertips, biting for satiation.

The older girl left the water. Approaching Circe, her features expressed confusion. *She doesn't heed who I am, what I am, the gravity of her treachery.*

"Give back what is mine." Euthalia spoke as staccato as a crime of passion; forty stab wounds in an adulterer's chest before realizing there's a knife.

"You have stolen from me. And that can never be returned, Euthalia."

"I took nothing from you. Why would I? You're no one to me, a stranger touched by the moon. Surrender them or I'll take them from you."

Circe's mouth curved.

The girl charged, hands pulling at the robes clamped against Circe's body. With the celerity of a mantis, Circe dropped the robes and gripped Euthalia's hand in her own. Palm to palm, the black pebble between them.

"Goddess Nemesis, come to your gift, take what's owed. For what Euthalia stole, leave her bereaved of his memory." The pebble burned. Circe watched the girl's eyes widening. "I ask worms and maggots to infest her skull, marrows, flesh, reshaping her weapons against men until they're blind to her wiles."

Circe witnessed the bones in Euthalia's face moving and twisting, her lips parted by screams. Both their hands and forearms birthed rippling flames; Circe's were blue, painless, rising higher, lunging and striking at Euthalia's orange ones.

A circle of flames rose from the earth, each a translucent, chanting woman. Circe chanted with them; intentions married. She observed the skin blistering, melting, dissolving on the girl's hand and arm. Her eye sockets narrowed and sank deeper, her nose flattened, her chin retreated into a stubbier neck. Circe saw her clavicle lift, a snapping noise followed by a cry that reverberated through her own body. Euthalia fell; her arm, the only part not contorting was more flame and charred bone than flesh.

The circle kept chanting; but Circe's lips dried, her throat emptied; perceiving the suffering for the first time. *This is wrong, no one deserves this.* As she released Euthalia's hand, the flames extinguished, the pebble dropped, but the screams continued.

"By the Gods, I repent." Circe dropped to her knees. Seizing a sharp rock, she slit her arm, elbow to wrist. Blood poured over the girl's trembling, furled body. "This gift completes the debt." She wrapped the robes around Euthalia, blood soaked through into crimson wings on their surface.

Smashing the pebble between rocks, she gathered the shards, willed them to flame, tipped them to the back of her throat and gulped. Smoke on her breath; chanting in reverse, she pictured Euthalia's body repairing.

When she was still, Circe relied on her strongest magic with a thought. She cradled the little black kitten in her arms. It didn't know it was human. Kitten Euthalia couldn't be carried in a beak, so she walked the two hours home. She would find

SHIFTING DESTINIES

somewhere to hide her until healed, then return her home with only segments of her memory astray.

I'm not a wicked person. She armoured her thoughts with the phrase, but her flashbacks showed her the opposite.

* * *

The sun would be on the horizon within an hour. Her legs felt as heavy as her eyelids as she climbed the turret's stone stairs. A gentle, barely audible murmur that could grow into a snore emanated from the warmth sleeping against her chest. On tiptoes she crossed the hall, opening her door a slither to slip inside. She nestled the kitten between cushions on her bed.

A figure shifted inside the darkness, *my shadow self*. Approaching the soft old chair, Circe bent to kiss it.

"What have you done?"

Circe gasped at her sister, who was uncrumpling her body. As if the shock had returned her wits, she noticed the heap of ash in the centre of her floor. "Why are you in my room?"

"I was sent to fetch you. Then commanded to wait. Mother is furious, she fled to temple. Father is uncharacteristically despondent and crossed realms. It is Sofia," said Heliades.

"Has she taken ill?"

* * *

Circe couldn't understand or accept what Heliades told her. *How could it be true?* She ran to her mentor's chamber, knocking on the door.

"Come in." Sofia's voice had wilted.

Circe approached the candles' glow near her bed, stepping inside the wavering amber half-moon. Air slammed her lungs, contracting her stomach. Her hand clamped bile inside her mouth until her sobs choked her throat with it.

"Forgive me Circe, I cannot take your hand to comfort you."

A rim of each iris remained, filled with yellow like the yoke of a hen's egg, bathed in red lightning; there were weeping lesions where Sofia must have clawed her own eyes. Circe struggled to redirect her stare lower to the wadded bandages. *How did this happen?*

As if reading her thoughts, Sofia answered, "I woke holding a blackened beaker that smelled of putrefaction; called by the grimoire. It had both my hands; dissolved my skin. My screaming brought your parents, others. Before taking my eyesight, I watched my bones desiccate, stumps haemorrhaging."

"You gave me the book, I don—"

"To soar as a falcon, strengthen your bond with nature. I never imagined death magic would call you, little bird; the spells name gods and goddesses but they draw from death. You are a necromancer now, forever walking with a foot in the underworld, and the dead will know you."

"I didn't mean to. I reversed it."

"I know, but you cast it. You have its mark; when you act on impulse or anger, it will rise. I cannot tend the garden and am being moved elsewhere; your mother's promised I'll be looked after."

"No, you have to stay, mentor me, help me control this."

"Circe, I was blind to your darkness; I've made this mistake twice. There will not be a third." Her stump lifted to her neck, a phantom hand reaching for a locket she'd held every time she felt afraid. "Cleanse the grimoire with sage, to only open with beneficence. Then bury it. If you're deserving, it will find you."

* * *

Circe returned to her chambers, soil clinging to her arms, embedded under her nails like she'd crawled from a grave. She was too numb to cry any more. Not even the purring of the soft, black kitten in her arms soothed her. Its white whiskers fluttered as it nuzzled her. "This is partly your fault, beastly siren."

Pork

Erin Murphy

She couldn't stand the sight of it, anymore.

There was a time when pork had been a delicacy. When Circe's island had been so quiet; so secluded and calm that pork had not been a necessity. A time when she and the nymphs, the oceanids, had made their meals with the bounties of the earth. The squealing of swine was nothing but a distant and unpleasant memory, for most.

How she wishes now that she'd never seen the first man. That she'd never invited them to her home. But she'd already been picturing the meals that could be made in gluttony, with forty men appearing on her doorstep. She wishes she had been blinded by the promise of a belly filled and an island safe. Besides, she'd rationalized at the time, if they'd made it so far to stumble upon her dwelling, the one place of sanctuary for herself and the other nymphs, she couldn't allow them to simply leave! Not with that knowledge. And they did seem so much like pork stock...

Color her unsurprised when each of them, without fail, were reduced to squealing pigs.

Circe could not make anyone into anything, you see. Oh, no. No, she merely pulled what lurked beneath to the surface. The fact that not a single one of those beasts presented themselves as a lion, wolf, a beast of claws and anger…It told her all that she needed to know. They were swine. All of them. Each of them. And she'd watched as the nymphs herded them to the pigsties, ready to be culled a bit at a time to feed the island for weeks. Weeks! Weeks that they need not forage. Weeks that their meals were fresh and prepared from the pens behind her home. Security can be so intoxicating for the fleeting moments that one has it.

Perhaps if she'd not been so blinded by that excitement, that intoxication, she would have noticed the straggler.

She would have seen the last man, Eurylochus, who lingered in the brush. She would have noticed him, aghast at how his brethren were being herded like the livestock they acted no better than. She could have stopped him before he fled. It wouldn't have taken much of anything. A word. A phrase. A wave of her hand. All it really took was attention. That, she did not have. To this day she curses every ounce of naivete she'd thought stamped out long, long before they ever set foot on her island. Security *is* the most intoxicating folly, after all. She'd been too eager to think them safe.

Curse the gods for meddling, as they always did; always do. Curse Poseidon for chasing the man here. Curse Athena for giving him the courage to ever leave that boat. Curse Hermes most of all.

Curse Hermes for drawing his eye where it did not belong. Curse Hermes for offering him moly, bane to the only thing she had to defend herself with. Curse Hermes for every

MYTHS, GODS & IMMORTALS: CIRCE

baneful day she'd been forced to spend in *his* presence. Odysseus's presence.

She can still see that moment, in her mind's eye. The moment when Odysseus presented himself at her door, looking every bit the role of the world-wearied hero. How mournfully he'd recounted his tale to her; ten years from his home, and the god of the seas enraged with him. And now, could you scarcely imagine it? His entire fleet, missing. Forty men in total.

Circe's eyes dropped as a squealing pig ran through her conservatory at that very moment, chased by one of the younger girls. She couldn't have been more than eleven, then. Bare feet padding along the tile as she ran with her arms outstretched after the runt of the litter. A fond smile dared to crack her lips. But when her eyes rose from the girl's image, she found his eyes following her. Following that little girl in ways not fit for a girl. Not fit for a *child*. She attempted and failed to disguise her anger, her disgust.

"Drink," she'd said, "we can speak after. I'm…afraid I would know if there were suddenly forty men hiding in my home, wouldn't I?" She'd smiled as she said it. Her father's smile. Every bit as bright as the sun he guided through the sky. It split her rosy cheeks, creased the corners of her eyes where the barest signs of age were beginning to claw at sun-ruddied skin. And yet there was no sign of that same light to be found in her eyes when she handed him the cup. A cup filled with muddled wine, and honey, and herbs from her very own garden. Ones she'd cultivated magically for their poisons. A pig was too good for him, she thought. Much too good. And she did not doubt that his meat would be rancid, unfit even for Scylla, where she guarded their island from the waters.

"That you would, I imagine." Odysseus had met her eye; locked her gaze as he took gulp after gulp. Even knowing what she'd done, he was still avaricious for every drop of wine, every bit of honey that covered the taste.

It was only when he'd thrown the cup to the ground and risen to stand over her that she realized —

There would be no effect.

Only an hour earlier, Hermes had given him the bane to her magic. The only thing that would ever give him a chance against her. And Circe was not so foolish as to think that in a battle of nothing but strength, she would be victorious. The King of Ithaca had spent his summers hunting. The last several years on ships. He'd seen constant battle...and Circe knew only her magics.

To call it a battle would have been all too generous. Before Circe could even attempt to call for aid, he'd slammed her to the earth, pressing his blade to her throat with the intention to swing —

"Please–!" she'd begged. On palms, she'd crawled backwards. And the beast advanced towards her with a sadistic slowness. That of something playing with its meal. Pressed against the marble of a column, Odysseus's steel nicked her throat. A bead of mottled gold trailed down her neck to pool against her collarbone. Even half-gods bled gold, it seemed. "Anything. Everything—"

Everything.

Everything.

Everything to protect her island. That is what she promised him. That is what she offered, when she was against the tiles. Everything. She could return his men. She could sponsor their journey, so they might never go hungry on their travels. She could even get him to the underworld to speak with a prophet! One that could guide him. Anything, truly, he need only ask —!

She was foolish to think that 'everything' would not include her too. That it would not include her, and her freedom. That it would not result in his men running rampant through her island, destroying wildlife, ruining groves. That it would not mean Odysseus taking her as his bride.

She'd agreed on the terms that neither he, nor any of his men, lay a hand on the nymphs and oceanids of her island. They'd all suffered enough. Found their way here in hopes of protection, and yet, here they were, suffering at the hands of others who saw them as sub-human. She could bear that weight for them. Consider it a duty, if it kept their filthy hooves from them. And in turn, he'd made her swear on the Olympians above, the Chthonic below, that she would not raise a hand against him or his men.

And swearing on the gods was not so simple a promise to be broken. It was not a matter that could be lied out of; a mild transgression if broken. Refusing to do so, or worse, acting in defiance, would bring her into the view of every god and goddess whom she'd sworn by. It would put her beneath the keenest eyes Gaia had ever seen, throw up a flare to her very location. And regardless of what her relationship to them might have been before that moment, that second of defiance, all she would ever know after was a slow, cold, cruel death for herself and her family.

So swear she did.

And a year she waited.

A year.

A year she laid with him.

A year she'd spent beside him. In one year, bore him three sons. Until finally, it seems the men had grown sick of this game. Perhaps their appetites were ruined, when one of them fell from the roof of her home. They'd blamed her for that. Said that her witchcraft made him fall. That it had turned his wine to something stronger, something that made him believe he would be unharmed if he leapt from the tallest point in her home. And if she had, well...they had no proof of that, did they?

They begged Odysseus to leave. They begged, pleaded that they continue their mission back to Ithaca. Because while Odysseus had found comfort away from his wife in Circe, the rest of his men hid their longing for home in the destruction of her own. Finally, something they were uncannily good at.

Did you know that pigs will devour anything? Yes, anything. So long as it is made small enough. Made within reach. And these swine were no different. Odysseus had to be all but wrenched from her bed on the day that they left. In the end, it was not her power that made them leave. No god intervened on her behalf. It was mere boredom; simple longing on the part of the men who did this that ended the whole ordeal.

The last of her promises had been to offer them *safe* passage to the underworld. Would that she could have slammed the gates to Hades behind them. She wished she could have set them adrift forever on the River Styx. Woe that Hermes would do his duty as psychopomp and retrieve them from her home. But it seemed that she had wronged him somehow. For the life of her, she could not ever recall how. Could not conceive of what she might have done to anger him. She'd never once crossed his path, prior. Never snubbed her offerings to him. Never spoke ill of his gifts.

She was a woman. And she was not in need of him. Perhaps that was all the reason he needed to take a knife to the tapestry that was her carefully woven life.

But even with Odysseus no longer in her home, his presence still haunted her. Haunted her, in the smashed amphora that lined the halls. In the ruined art. In the ways that their granaries risked running empty. Odysseus had left them in peace, yes, if peace could be reconciled with starvation. But at last, for the first time in a year, her magics were her own, again. A year out of practice, certainly, but her own, nonetheless. Which is what found her with a child on one hip and two more in her belly, wading through their freshly planted fields and flicking potion from her fingers in the hopes of having something grown before winter came.

Let it never be said that Circe was not resourceful. In fact, it might be said that was all she had. A handful of herbs to make a powerful potion, a mouthful of words to make a curse. She had taken an island, abandoned by man and hidden from divinities, and she'd made it a paradise for herself. Herself, and the nymphs who found refuge here. She'd made a home from nothing for those with nothing, and she was not going to let one arrogant man with more aid than he knew how to parse ruin that for her.

Poor Odysseus.

Woe upon Odysseus, running from the god of tides.

He was a fool to confide in her, as though she were really his bride. One night during his occupation, and after a night of drinking, he'd confessed to her that there was a prophecy. A prophecy that his death would come at the hands of the ocean. It made sense to him, it seemed, that Poseidon would be after him. Never mind that the God of the Seas was demanding recompense for his injured child. No, woe is him, running back to his kingdom and throne while a parent chases him in earnest. All he'd done was make the beast blind! Surely that was not deserving of such anger.

Circe had only listened silently. Prayed that the child she'd just had was not a beast in his eyes, like Polyphemus had been.

And once he'd finally fallen to rest for the evening, she realized —

There is more than one way to drown.

From the moment her son was old enough, she'd knelt before him. She'd held his tiny, chubby hands in her own, and spoke unto him a new prophecy:

"You will kill the king you come from."

He'd still been just a babe. Unsteady on his little legs just as a deer was, wobbling with the weight of his own body. He'd smiled at her, unknowing of the words she said, only that his mother was speaking to him. How she hated to weigh such tiny shoulders down before they'd ever even stand upright, but she could not leave this island. She could not crash this wave. She could not end this cycle. He would.

Little Telegonus.

Telegonus did not understand the prophecy. How could he? A sweet babe, who'd known nothing of violence. Who hid in his mother's skirts when addressed. Who had to stand on the very tips of his toes to look into the cribs of his sleeping brothers. And Circe would pet a hand over his head. Catch curls between her fingers and gaze at her other two sons with him.

"Your duty," she would say, "is to keep them safe, Telegonus."

And Telegonus seemed to understand that.

She hated that features she found repulsive in his father, she adored in him. These big, beautiful brown eyes, ringlets of curls to match. Circe hated Odysseus. She did. She hated his image, his voice, his laugh, his everything. Her body ached with the burn of hatred, and it was an ache she was prepared to feel every moment, every second, every iota of time for the rest of her life, until at last she was delivered to the underworld. It was an ache she was shameful to admit she was prepared to pass on to her son. The ache of what his father had done, not only to her and her island, but the wake of destruction he'd left behind him for gods and men alike.

Her son would end it. He would end this curse upon them both. He would set them free of his father's presence, and he would do it with all the cunning of his mother and the ruthlessness of his father.

And so, they trained.

They trained from the time he was old enough to hold a spear. From the moment he could grasp this thing he held in his hand that was meant to find a target in the straw dolls set up for him at the end of the practice field. Oh, how he would laugh, and leap, and celebrate as his spear found its home in the eye of the doll, knowing only that he'd succeeded. He had won this little game. And Circe would sweep him up into her arms and spin him, announce his victories to the other nymphs.

When her son was ten, there were newcomers to the island, in fewer numbers than Odysseus and his men. Far less wary of the world around them.

He need not know where the sudden infestation of boar came from. But proudly he chased them through the woods with nymphs and oceanids on his heels. He cheered with each tipped spear that resulted in the wailing squeal of one of these beasts. And Circe, for her part, had waited on the steps of their home. She'd waited with hands clasped in front of her, until finally her son came into view, carrying a particularly large beast on his shoulder, the rest carried by his hunting party. He'd beamed up at her, face streaked with mud and pride. Pride for having done well. Pride for having succeeded. Pride for having won. And there was meat enough for everyone that night. She took extreme delight in stabbing through it to bring it to her lips.

And when her son was seventeen, at last it was time for him to leave.

"Find him," Circe had whispered, in what she worried might be their last embrace. She'd cradled her son, running a hand over the back of his head, just how she had soothed him as a baby. There, on the beaches of Aeaea, with a ship large enough for just himself and one other to help man the sails, Circe would say goodbye to her son.

And turning from him, she would clasp the hands of her most trusted oceanid. She'd known her since Circe was but a child herself. She had been her mother's closest friend. And now, she was sending her to watch over Telegonus. In silence, they touched their foreheads to one another. Tears ran down Circe's cheeks. There were no words for the grief between them; for the pain and suffering and agony shared through a lifetime. "Care for him," was her only order, before she stepped back. Telegonus helped the oceanid into the boat, waved goodbye to his mother, and ran the ship out into open waters.

Circe raised the tides for him.

She sent a gust of wind to herald him.

She looked up towards the sky where her own father was pulling his chariot, and silently willed that chariot to take its dear, sweet time crossing the horizon.

May this come to a swift end.

When Telegonus finally arrived in Ithaca, he'd seen his father. Old, and wizened...something like regret in his eyes.

Regret and guilt that had come far too late to do anyone any good. He had a wife in Ithaca. A son, Telemachus, perhaps a decade older than him. For a number of days, Telegonus had just...watched.

Watched this strange inversion of his own life. The son with his father. His mother. Their home. And he'd watched the father leave that home each morning. He watched the son practice shooting, and hunting. Telegonus was not a fool. He would not survive breaking through doors, sending a spear through his father's chest.

Which is why a terrible accident had to occur.

Telegonus waited. Watched the routes that his father would take. He lay in wait for him to cross paths...before emerging from the underbrush, spear in hand.

And in the end, Circe did not see Odysseus's final gasps. She did not see him as he was dying, begging for her forgiveness, before he was dragged away by Thanatos. Perhaps even by Hermes, the one who set their paths to cross in the first place. But she had been right, there was more than one way to drown. More than one way to find death from the ocean.

Her son was half mortal, yes. A quarter godly. And a quarter of the sea. A quarter the oceanid, the sea nymph, that Circe's mother had been.

Telegonus and Odysseus had stared at each other for a long and quiet moment. He recognized his father. He knew his father recognized him. Perhaps it was the glassiness of Telegonus's skin, something nearly like scales. Maybe it was the way his eyes glinted like that of a beast. He didn't need to speak when he raised his spear tipped with the tail of a stingray.

He almost found it disappointing. At least the boar he'd hunted had run.

After that, it was a matter of painting the scene. Telegonus had thrown himself over his father's body. "It was an accident!" he cried. "An accident, I was looking for my father, Odysseus!" He'd sobbed to the heavens and screamed for forgiveness. He'd cradled the head of this man he'd known only as the reason his mother jumped at loud noises. The reason his mother locked their wine stores. Kept their weapons sharp, since she could no longer rely only on her magic.

And people came.

They came and comforted Telegonus, upon learning who he was. Told him he could never have known this man was his father. He was cradled by his father's widow, as she sobbed that he couldn't have realized until it was too late. He was embraced by his father's son, who told him his father would have loved him. Would have loved to meet him. Would have never raised a hand against him for something he could not have known. Through it all, Telegonus played the part of the grieving son. The guilty child. The boy who'd only been looking for his father.

In the ultimate irony, they'd brought Odysseus's body back to Aeaea. Brought him to the place he'd ruined, to the women he'd terrorized, because, as his wife recounted, "they had cared for him when she could not."

Circe had been waiting to greet them. She stood on the shores in her mourning robes and ran to her son as he disembarked. "It is not you they bring me, thank goodness it is not you I—" She kissed his head. Held him, her little boy, as she sobbed. Others might see that sobbing as something of grief. He knew better. It was relief. For the first moment in eighteen years, the fire of anger had left her. Extinguished by her son.

She welcomed Telemachus and Penelope into her home. Arranged a meal for them. Wine. Pork. She comforted the grieving widow, the lost son —

When a suggestion was made.

Telemachus would stay on the island with Circe. He would take up the roles his father had left behind. And in turn, Telegonus would return to Ithaca, where he would become king. He was younger. Sharper than Telemachus. Better suited for the position of a royal at his age. And Telemachus, bless him, just wanted to be where his father had been happiest.

Through sobs, Circe agreed. Whatever Odysseus's final wishes would be, she said. Though as she locked eyes with her eldest son across the table, they both understood what this meant.

He would leave her.

He would become king.

He would inherit possibly the only thing of worth that his father had left behind.

The flames of her rage had been extinguished, but not her son's. She'd merely passed him her torch. Handed him off.

Loved him with everything that she possessed and poisoned him all the same.

And Telemachus...

Telemachus made a good pig.

A shame he went to waste, now Circe no longer had the stomach for pork.

A Friend Made of Clay
Lourdes Ureña Pérez

One day, the poets would compose entire sagas about it. Not about her specifically, of course. Poets only sang of women to condemn them. Praise was reserved for the men around them. Still, she was a fierce figure, a sorceress capable of transforming the flesh and enchanting the mind, of taming beasts and bending the world itself to her will. Daughter of the sun and the sea, it was easy to think of her as infinite, but even the great witch of Aeaea had to get started somehow. Of all the spells, there had to be a first.

The ageing of gods was a strange thing, so that sometimes they'd spend centuries unchanged, then age a decade in an instant. Circe had been slower than most. From the moment her golden eyes opened she was not a baby for long, but rather than reach teenagehood within a few months like her sister Pasiphaë before her, she had dwelled in the sweet years of childhood for a long while.

It was a happy childhood, in as much as children are happy because they haven't yet learned of concepts such as loneliness and neglect. Her mother Perse spent her days lost in her own reflection within the lovely puddles she created, as much as her father Helios was unable to see further than his own shine. They had no time for infants. Still, Circe was content. She wandered the endless halls of the house of the sun, buried deep beneath the earth, and found a wonder in each brick and tile. Then she ran out of corners to discover, so she discovered boredom.

From the moment her father rode his chariot into the dawn till he came back at twilight, the house was plunged into darkness, her and her siblings' eyes the only source of light. Perse, a creature made of the free-flowing water of the ocean, disliked being confined to the earth and, without the attention of her husband to draw, she left to waste the day away with the other nymphs. For a while, Circe chased after her older siblings, but she soon found that her childhood innocence only made her prey. She might have wanted to grow then, but still she remained the same.

Loneliness crept, slow and steady, like the tide that came in at night and made the sand of the shore forget it'd even been above water. Circe walked the halls. She moved deeper into the earth until marble became rock under her feet, became soft compressed dirt. It was cool there. Dark in a way that seemed different than the absence of her father's light. Under the torches of her golden irises, she looked around and found she had stumbled into a treasure of clay. Rich and red and moist, she held it in her hands and delighted in the pleasure of its tact, its malleability.

It was her first taste of creation and, as many gods and Titans had before her, she became addicted to it.

From sunrise to sunset, she worked at her clay, making all sorts of things. At first they were merely shapes: a long twisted rope, a perfect sphere. It filled her with satisfaction when the

A FRIEND MADE OF CLAY

image in her head came to be under her hands. Then she began to copy the objects that surrounded her. She made a slightly wonky apple and painted it gold. Made a shell like the ones her mother kept her paints in. Made a lovely pendant of flowers and corals and gave it to her to wear around her neck. This Perse found immensely amusing. She laughed about it all throughout dinner that evening.

"Can you believe it? As if I'd ever wear anything as unrefined." She showed Pasiphaë and Aëtes as Helios watched from the head of the table and they all snickered at the absurdity. "Imagine how it would look next to my amber beads!"

Circe never tried it again. Instead, she kept creating her silly little things for herself. Soon she graduated to more intricate designs. She made a replica of her father's chariot and thought of giving it to him. She destroyed it instead, echoes of laughter in her ears, and repurposed the clay for something else.

Although lonely, Circe didn't much enjoy the company that could often be found in her father's house. When their halls were full of nymphs, naiads, gods and goddesses, she would often hide away in the nooks and crannies to avoid being seen. From there, she could listen in on their conversations. Most of what they talked about seemed inconsequential to her but sometimes, if she listened for long enough, she would hear tales of the mortal world.

These stories fascinated Circe. They were often related to the actions of this god or that, for deities rarely speak of anything that does not involve them, but it was the rest that Circe craved to hear, the parts when they would speak of mountains and rivers that held great cities and strange animals she'd never seen. What did a mortal look like? What sound did a bird make? What did it feel like to see the sun shine up in the sky instead of in your own living room?

These questions permeated her mind and found their way to her hands so that soon she was creating small figurines of the creatures in the stories. She made the swan Zeus had turned into to impregnate a mortal woman. She coaxed a small fawn out of clay and imagined it growing up to run at Artemis's side. She sculpted the snakes that adorned that poor priestess's head after the great Athenea cursed her for soiling her temple. She made insects and fishes and little by little her room turned into its own clay ecosystem. Each figure was perfect in her eyes, as nature dictates children should be in the eyes of their parents. She named them, cleaned them even though dust never settled in the houses of gods, touched them softly as she passed them on her way.

After her mother and siblings had made fun of her for the pendant, she'd taken to working solely in her own room or in the deep tunnel where she found her clay, but theirs was a big house. It was stifling in its darkness, yes, but certainly more spacious than her small quarters and sometimes the craving for space clawed at her insides until she had no option but to attempt escape. She was in one of the many empty rooms, carving lines into the trunk of a laurel tree that was still partly a fleeing naiad, when Pasiphaë came in. She was accompanied by her entire cohort and had moved on from adolescence a while ago so that she now appeared as a gorgeous, golden-skinned young woman of blushed cheeks and lips. They were clearly talking about her upcoming wedding to King Minos, her sister's distaste and sulkiness at having to marry a mortal – albeit a royal one – clear in her voice. Then she saw Circe and a cold, sharp smile spread over her face. She felt a shiver run down her spine.

"What is this?" she said, and Circe thought of stories of terrible beasts toying with their prey before the slaughter.

"It is nothing." She rushed to hide the sculpture behind her back, but there was no point. A shark can always smell blood in the water.

Pasiphaë didn't pounce. She moved in slowly and with every step she took, she backed Circe up further into the room.

"Are you making another ugly little trinket for mom to mock?" One more step with each word. "How considerate of you! Dinners had been getting rather dull."

Scylla's feet were so light on the marble that Circe hadn't heard her circle the room until her hands were on her, twisting her wrist so hard she had no option but to let go of the half-sculpted figurine. She heard the wet noise it made when it hit the floor, then the squashing of it under Scylla's foot, her work destroyed. Somehow that hurt more than the shooting pain in her wrist.

"Oh, no!" a lovely voice crooned in her ear. "That's a shame." There was a deep satisfaction in her tone, but when Circe looked at her sister, she did not see the same reflected in her face. Pasiphaë's expression was still hungry.

"I wonder…" she began, the rounded sound of her vowels like glacial water.

They all took off with Pasiphaë leading the way and Scylla guiding Circe by pressure on her wrists. She didn't fight it. It didn't even occur to her to try. She wasn't sure where they were taking her and could only hope that they'd grow tired of this game soon enough. They walked by their mother's open door and Perse took the time to look away from her reflection long enough to say:

"What are you doing?"

"Playing," Pasiphaë said.

Perse looked at her, then at Circe with her arms twisted behind her back.

"Well, don't make a mess," she said and turned back to her mirror.

They walked away. Circe did not call for help. What would have been the point?

She was scared, in a way. Her sister's torture had been only as frequent as her indifference for as long as she could remember. It was always somewhere between unpleasant and unbearable, but it always ended and then she'd usually leave her alone for a while. She knew she couldn't do any permanent harm – Helios did not take kindly to his things being broken – but there was plenty she could do that did not leave a mark.

It was only when she saw they were heading to her own rooms that Circe started to panic. She twisted her wrists, testing Scylla's hold, and was rewarded with a cracking of bones and a sharp stab of pain for her troubles. There was no escape. Her door opened under her sister's hand, unaware of its betrayal of its duty to keep her home safe.

A FRIEND MADE OF CLAY

"Ooohh, look at this!" Pasiphaë sounded delighted and her choir cheered right on cue. "Turns out we have a little Daedalus living among us." She praised her, the name of the mortal craftsman quick on her tongue. She used to listen to the same stories as Circe, but Pasiphaë held nothing but disdain for them. "It's such a pity." She held a sculpture of a cicada Circe had named Tithonus after the mortal her Aunt Eos had loved. "That you are unable to stop your hideousness from impregnating everything you touch." She let the cicada fall from her hand, the dry clay exploding into a thousand shards.

Circe heard herself gasp, felt the pain shoot up her arm. She was fighting now, twisting and clawing, but Scylla's hold was unbreakable. Her bones weren't.

As she struggled, Pasiphaë picked another figurine from a shelf.

"Ugly Circe." She let it fall. *Crash.* She picked up one more. "With her ugly hands." *Crash.* "Making ugly things." *Crash.*

Circe was screaming now. *No* and *stop* and then:

"Please!" she cried. And Pasiphaë stopped. She looked at her with a wicked glint in her eye, and smiled.

"Ah, how delightful," she said. "Aren't you full of surprises today? Although I suspect you will be better at this than at your crappy artwork." She held the swan in her hand now as she walked up to her. "Go on, then, Circe. *Beg.*"

And Circe did. She begged and cried and watched as Pasiphaë crushed each one of her creations into dust. Even when it was clear her desperation was just egging her on, she couldn't stop.

273

Soon, there was nothing left to destroy. Scylla, Pasiphaë and their friends enjoyed her suffering a bit longer but in the end they grew bored of her tears and left her there in pursuit of something new that could hold their interest. Circe remained, rubbing her broken wrists as they healed themselves slowly until she was able to move enough to search among the remains. Nothing had survived. She found a wing here, a foot there, something that could have been a long neck further down the pile. She gathered every shard slowly, letting them cut her fingers as she did so. Bleeding seemed like a small punishment for having been unable to protect them.

Then she found it. It must have fallen down from its shelf among the chaos – the noise drowned out by crying and laughter – and remained hidden between her bed and her nightstand. The fawn, a little clumsy like some of her first creations, had broken one of its fine legs on impact, but was otherwise intact. Circe dragged herself towards it and cradled it in her arms with soothing noises meant more for herself than the creature.

How lovely it was, its smooth spotted fur, its vigilant ears raised as if it had heard a noise among the bushes. Even in its imperfections – the too-long neck, the rounded body – it looked so lifelike it was easy to imagine it leaping through the forest, running side by side with Artemis and her huntresses.

She touched the place where its leg had broken off then. It was a clean break and she had found the leg lying right beside it. With careful hands she brought both pieces together and saw that they fitted perfectly. A strange feeling flapped its wings inside her chest. Maybe she could fix it.

A FRIEND MADE OF CLAY

With the wings of hope on her back, she flew down the halls of the dark house until she reached the tunnel where she usually collected her clay. She wasn't sure it would work, but thought that she better find some that matched the color of her fawn just in case. She examined different areas under the golden light of her eyes until she found the perfect one. As she took what she needed, her fingers touched something new. It wasn't clay, although it was equally soft under her hands. When she looked, she was surprised to find green instead of the reddish brown she was used to. It was a plant. Some sort of herb she'd never seen before. Suddenly, she thought of the stories of heroes injured in battle, of wise men able to cure and alleviate suffering with their ointments and concoctions. She took the clay. She took the plant. She went back to her room.

The fawn was waiting for her, comfortable but still hurt among the silk pillows of her bed. Circe got to work. She made a slip with the clay and water, then used a small piece to stick the fawn's leg back in its place. She hadn't inherited much of her father's power, but her gaze and touch were enough to cook the clay until it became solid. Then, she smashed the plant into a paste. She didn't realize she was crying until tears wet her fingers, mixing with the green and the red of her blood. It was such a silly thing. Her creatures had never been alive, but she felt their loss with an intensity only children are capable of. What did a goddess know of death? Gods didn't die, that was a thing of mortals. Gods just lived and lived and lived and everyone they knew lived on with them. Circe didn't have anyone else. So she cried for her made up children as she healed the only one she had left. She tore a strip off her bedding, spread the paste on the fawn's wound and wrapped it up tight.

"If only you were real," whispered Circe, ashamed of her weakness even in the emptiness of her room. "I could really use a friend right now."

With the bandage firmly in place, she lay on the bed next to it and, with tears still in her eyes, she fell asleep.

It was an indefinite amount of time later that she awoke. Time was an elusive thing there, but she could tell by the hue of the darkness that her father was home, so it must be night. Dinner had probably come and gone without anyone coming to get her. Was that what had woken her up? She felt no hunger, but there was something licking her face. She saw it then, the fawn, still lying among the pillows of her bed, except now the brown of the clay was spotted with white specks. Except it wasn't clay at all. It was fur, soft and delicate. Moistness gathered at the tip of its snout, shiny under the light of her eyes and as she watched it the little creature stuck its tongue out and licked it.

The fawn was alive. Undeniably. Unmistakably. Circe watched its small chest move with every breath and marveled at the sight. Slowly, she reached out a hand to touch it. She expected it to shy away from her, as famously skittish animals tended to do. Instead, the fawn stretched its head forward to push it into her palm. Through the fur and skin, she could feel the delicateness of its bones, the sweetness of its heartbeat. It licked her hand, its tongue rough and cold.

A strange sound rumbled deep within her lungs. It bubbled up through her throat and stumbled out of her mouth. High

A FRIEND MADE OF CLAY

and clear and graceless. She was laughing. Pure, unadulterated laughter. Shaking her shoulders and bringing tears to her eyes. She had never laughed before. The fawn seemed startled at the sound, but it didn't retreat in fear. It seemed to know instinctively that she wouldn't hurt it.

Remembering its injury, she reached out and took the fawn carefully into her lap. The bandage was still firmly in place, but underneath there was no wound nor scar. It made something stir within her, the thought that, despite Pasiphaë's violence, this creature remained unharmed. Fear followed relief in an instant. Fear at the fragility of the life that she held between her hands. At what her sister would do with a creature of flesh and bone. The memory of the clay shards cutting into her skin made her shiver.

She wouldn't allow it.

Her body was faster than her mind. Before she could even make a decision she was grabbing a bag to gather her belongings. She did not have much, but it would have to be enough. Her hands worked and her head reeled trying to come up with a plan. She could take the ways of the water her mother used to escape the palace, but would the fawn survive the trip? She could ask her father to take her for an excursion in his chariot then disappear into the mortal world. She was confident he would not look for her.

She found herself putting increasingly useless things into her bag. A shell comb. A summer dress. Where was she meant to go when all she had ever known were these halls? It didn't matter. She needed to go where her sister couldn't find her, where she

277

could experience the path of her father's chariot instead of only his absence.

At last, she deemed she was done, so she took the fawn into her arms and cradled it close. The animal, sweet and innocent as only new things could be, licked her nose. Despite the trepidation strangling her heart, Circe smiled and kissed its head.

"Don't worry, my friend. I will get us out of here," she said against its fur.

On her way to the door, she happened to walk by a mirror and what she saw made her do a double-take. There was no child there. In her place, a woman stood, shiny eyes and hair streaked with gold. She was older now, at least as old as Pasiphaë. Her legs were long and her body was full of curves, but it was her eyes that caught her attention the most. Not the color, or the luminosity, those hadn't changed. It was the strength, like melted gold had turned solid overnight. She nodded to her reflection.

Circe walked out of her room, and left her childhood behind.

Prove Them All Right
Elizabeth Roberts

She stood on the cliffs of her island, scowling as she looked out to sea. Her thoughts dragged back with the tide: further back than the day she had been caught up in the currents of Odysseus, before her island was full of beautiful creatures, to when she was a young goddess and had fallen deeply in love for the first time.

The breaking of a heart could change someone forever. Circe feared that moment had set her down the path she was now on. That crucial moment that all the stories had gotten wrong about her. She had accepted it, there was no point in denying what they all wanted to believe she was, she'd proven them right in the end. But back then, Circe had been a naive girl.

* * *

Scylla had been a devastatingly beautiful nymph. She would swim in the fair currents of the sea each day, playing and laughing with the others. She would drift on her own, on days when she wished for peace, letting the sea decide her destination. Her sisters had chided her for this, telling her tales of what lurked around them. There was a particular emphasis on the lonely witch who lived on one of the islands, claiming her to be evil, deadly, and dangerous.

Of course, this only made Scylla more curious about the island, and the witch who occupied it. She went there, filled with the purpose of catching a glimpse of this witch. She slipped away from her sisters and swam to the tree-lined shore. The island was lined with bluffs that overlooked the water, but made it difficult for Scylla to see, no matter the angle at which she craned her neck. There was no path forward but to go look between the trees.

She climbed out of the water and up the sloping grassy knoll onto the island. It was even more wondrous than she had imagined from the water. There was a sense of peace that hung in the air, she could hear the birdsong carried on the thin breeze, the notes seemed perfectly formed to her ear.

Scylla wandered in the groves of trees, having forgotten her main intention was to track the legendary witch of the island. She marveled at the light spilling through the leaves and the warmth of the afternoon sun, her thoughts floating effortlessly away. She walked along the high shoreline, watching the dazzling patterns dance across the water's surface.

That was, until a voice spoke behind her. It was as crafted and lovely as the birdsong. "What are you doing on my island, little nereid?"

Scylla spun to face her, finding herself inches from the other girl's face. She was as beautiful as her voice was melodic, her eyes keenly searching her, though they betrayed a certain mirth at her presence. They were a warm honey color, as the light cut through them just so. Her hair seemingly moved like rays of sun, a fiery color that Scylla thought might actually burn her skin if she touched it.

PROVE THEM ALL RIGHT

"Are you afraid the evil witch will curse you if you speak?" she said, impatiently. "I don't know what sorts of stories they are spinning about me these days, but I could curse you without a word out of your mouth."

"No, I am sorry. I was just surprised, that is all."

"Surprised I live here? On my island?" she chirped back, indignant.

"I was lost in the beauty of things here, that's all."

She didn't look around, as if she already knew what Scylla was talking about, "Why have you come here? I don't have time today to deal with silly sibling squabbles."

"I came to meet the witch, it's true. But only because I was told of your great powers."

She scoffed. "My great powers? I know what kind of gossip spreads like wildfire amongst you nymphs, and it isn't tales of greatness." She feigned thinking deeply. "Did they tell you I was mysterious, maybe deadly, a lonely spinster on this island? I can hear them now, giggling as they tell each other of the curses and spells I have cast."

Scylla did not know what to say. She swallowed hard; all that would come to her mouth was the truth itself. She couldn't lie with those golden eyes seeking so deeply into hers. "I wouldn't say you're wrong, but I came to see for myself."

"To go back and spill more of your tales into the sea?"

"No, no. I rarely listen to my sisters. Their stories entertain me but nothing more, I want to see things for myself. I trust not the eyes of others to tell me the truth."

The witch cocked her head at that, considering for a moment. "You seem different, but it could all be a farce. I want to trust you not to run back to your sisters and tell more stories."

"I would never. They will never even know I am here."

She cocked her head to the side and looked her up and down once more. Finally, she sighed and said, "I have been rather lonely these months."

So, Scylla stayed on the island following the young witch across the island, through the sunlit trees and to a wide meadow where a small hut stood merrily by a cooking fire. It was nothing exciting, but the scene was surprisingly homey and inviting. Scylla had expected much different things from the infamous witch.

There was nothing else in the clearing but a lounging jaguar, which shocked Scylla. Fearing the big cat would notice them, she stopped dead in her tracks, frozen, trying not to breathe.

The witch turned quizzically, seeing that Scylla had halted, and followed her trembling finger to the place where it pointed. She let out a laugh, and sauntered over to the jaguar, who opened one eye and let out a large purr at the sight of Circe. It rolled over, showing its belly, and let Circe scratch it.

"This is Atticus, he's my only friend on the island. I charmed him, he is quite harmless, as long as he senses you have nothing to hide." She looked up, her eyes piercing Scylla. "Do you have nothing to hide, little nymph?"

The jaguar rolled over and began to stalk towards her. Scylla wanted to turn and run, but instead she stretched out her hand, her eyes shut tight.

PROVE THEM ALL RIGHT

She felt the large gust of air from the cat's nostrils as it sniffed her, then a strange wet sensation, which Scylla thought must be the end – the cat was about to bite down and she would lose a hand. But it continued, and finally she cautiously opened her eyes, to see the big animal licking her.

Circe laughed again, gleefully and merrily this time, which warmed Scylla deep into her bones. She felt as if she had stood under the most perfect ray of sun which had reached inside of her. "He likes you!" She grinned at Scylla, which didn't help the feeling. She might as well have drunk the vast swaths of wine from the parties her sisters dragged her to, the way her limbs felt numb and heavy at the same time, and her head spun.

"Good thing he didn't eat me," she said, petting him before walking to join Circe by the fire pit.

"He has been known to," Circe said, tone serious.

"Really?"

Circe only quirked her eyebrow and smiled more, leaving the question unanswered. Scylla felt happy to be in her, and the jaguar's, good graces. Circe built them a small but bright fire, which she started with some sort of whispered incantation. This awed Scylla as she watched the flames dance and cook the fish that Circe had strung over them.

Circe only grew more and more interesting as the night wore on and the darkness crept over the island. She was witty, keeping Scylla on her toes, but never unkind to her. They talked of all things, and ate together, smiling in the waning light of the fire.

The warm dizzy feeling lit the pit of Scylla's stomach whenever Circe looked at her with those piercing honey-colored eyes. She felt like she was spinning amid the stars, freed from the Earth.

Scylla woke up in a soft bed she didn't know. She startled out of it, walking from the room into a warm grove of trees. She was confused until she saw the figure stooped over the fire, her fiery locks of hair.

"You're finally up," Circe said, smiling as she looked up from the fire. "You fell asleep here by the fire and I managed to cajole you to bed very late at night."

"I can't even remember that, I am sorry if I took your bed."

"Don't even think about it, I like sleeping under the stars with Atticus every now and then." She smiled. "Do you want some food?"

Scylla was hungry, now that she thought of it. There was a small table spread with all types of luscious fruits, which would have taken hours to prepare, if not for Circe's skills in magic. "It looks wonderful," she replied, sitting next to the other girl.

They talked of meaningless things over breakfast: the sounds of the birds, the juiciness of the fruit, and the way Atticus was jumping about, trying to catch bugs. Then Circe's glowing aura seemed to dim, and she turned quiet.

"What's wrong?" Scylla asked, as Circe began to clear the small table quite abruptly.

"You are going to leave me aren't you? You must be getting back to your sisters soon." Her words were biting, cold. Gone were the warm rays of sun that spilled from her.

PROVE THEM ALL RIGHT

"I get lost for days, they're used to it. If you don't mind me staying, I will stay for a little while longer." Scylla wanted her to feel better, but she also wanted to stay more than anything. Nothing had felt as real as this in a long time, locked in her little world with her gossipy sisters.

Circe smiled, sheepish at her behavior and quick judgement. They fell into a quiet rhythm, Scylla watching and helping as Circe went about her daily chores. She enjoyed her company immensely, happy being in her presence all day. As the sun waned in the day and Scylla took in her surroundings, she felt the deep want to stay forever.

They lay together that night, looking at the sprawling sky, littered with stars. Circe talked about her father, the Titan of the sun, Helios, and how the absence of him at night had scared her when she was young, as children are afraid of all that they don't know.

Scylla realized, looking at her in the dark, this was why, even in the darkness, she emitted a glow, like a living sun ray. The reason her eyes had that unique honeyed color, she was indeed a piece of the sun itself. She was lost in thought, staring at the girl beside her, absorbed in her presence rather than her words, when those honey eyes locked on hers.

Circe's words pierced her distant thoughts. "What?" she asked. "Why are you looking at me like that?"

Scylla couldn't account for what caused her to do what she did next – she acted on pure impulse, not a single rational thought prompted her – she leaned in and kissed Circe's warm lips.

Neither of them pulled away, the kiss growing deeper, until finally Circe pushed against her.

She looked deeply into Scylla's eyes, searching there for something. "Are you sure?" she said quietly.

Scylla was caught off-guard by the question. She realized, seeing the fear that lingered in Circe, the effect that others had on this girl. She was not allowed to be just a girl, but she was labeled a witch, banished and lonely, with vicious rumors that circulated even to Scylla's own ears about her.

"Of course, I am," Scylla offered, trying to reassure her and chase away the fear. "Are you?"

Circe smiled, not answering with words, but with another kiss.

Scylla slept in her bed again that night, but this time it was on purpose, and she was not alone.

The next fortnight fell like warm rain, slipping between the cracks in Scylla's fingers. Each moment was lovelier than the last. Circe excitedly showed her each and every crack and crevice of the island, pointing excitedly like a child at her favorite trees and rocks. They ate lunch in the meadow and on the shoreline, Circe performing illusionary magic for Scylla, making beautiful flowers appear, and the water sparkled like diamonds. They bathed in a clear spring that ran among the rocks, they spent every night in each other's embrace, and spent multiple days not even leaving the bed.

One night, as Scylla was drifting to sleep, Circe curled against her back, she heard Circe whisper, "I wish you had found me sooner."

Scylla had squeezed her hand tighter at that, to say what she didn't think she could put into words, that she had found her now and she did not intend to leave.

PROVE THEM ALL RIGHT

But such perfect spells are always broken and illusions cannot last. The enchantment that had been cast over them both broke when one of Scylla's sisters found them.

They had been lounging along the shoreline after a swim in a small inlet of the island. The currents and waves didn't reach there and the water sat perfectly still. Not that such things bothered Scylla, being a nymph of the sea, but Circe was wildly untrusting of the beings that controlled the movements of the sea.

Circe lay against Atticus's flank, who was sunning on the rocks, and Scylla had her head in her lap. Her eyes were closed, and she was drifting between sleep and wakefulness when someone shouting bolted her upright.

"SCYY-LAHHH!" came the shout from far out in the water. She knew the voice of her sister before she even saw her. Themisto, her sister, bobbed amongst the waves, waving hard at her, she was approaching, getting closer by the second.

Scylla scrambled to her feet, yelling back, "Just a minute!" before turning to Circe. She hoped that would stave Themisto off a little longer.

Circe's expression was a mixture of things, but Scylla didn't have much time to dissect it all. Blocking the line of sight of her sister, she took Circe's hand and kissed the back of it. She looked deeply into her honey eyes. "I will be back, I just have to talk to my sisters, explain. I'll be back, I promise."

Circe said, "Okay," before Scylla turned and started towards the sea, but what she didn't hear was Circe asking, "When? When will you be back?" It was caught by the wind as Scylla went to join her sister.

Circe became embittered as the days passed and Scylla did not reappear. She had been gone months now, without so much as a kind word to her. Circe had moped around the island following her departure, staring out at the glistening water that revealed nothing.

She had left her, the loneliness seeping in faster than it ever had before. She felt the emptiness of the island and the confines of it acutely as she wandered aimlessly about it. Atticus had to nudge her about to get her started on her normal activities.

When Scylla finally did crawl back to Circe's shores, she offered a thrilled smile, as if no time had passed and she had just been out for a swim. Circe glared at her, unwilling to shed the annoyance and anger that hung heavily on her.

Scylla realized she was not happy to see her, and asked, "Circe? What is wrong, darling?"

"You left." That was all Circe could say.

"And I am back." Scylla seemed shocked. "I promised you I would be back."

"It's been months! I have been alone here for weeks and weeks!" she shouted, not meaning to raise her voice; but she was desperate.

"What am I, your prisoner? Do you not think I had things to attend to at home, Circe?" Scylla shot back.

"You didn't so much as send word, you could have told me you would be away so long."

"I have a whole life that is not on this island. I have a family, I had to attend to suitors…"

"Attend to suitors?" Circe asked incredulously.

Scylla waved her hand, seemingly trying to wave away her words. "There was a suitor that was determined to have my hand. He would not leave me alone, but I turned him down. He was just an ugly, old fish."

"Who?" Circe asked, her rage brimming within her, uncontrollably so. She wasn't sure who it was aimed at, Scylla, or this suitor who pursued her beloved.

"Glaucus. Don't you see, I would have never considered it, least of all now, when I have you." Scylla tried to reach for her, but Circe was glowing hot with rage and Scylla couldn't touch her skin.

"You should have told me something, anything." Circe wiped away tears that had angrily sprung to her eyes.

"I needed to get rid of him and he wouldn't leave me alone. You don't understand the hell I have been through trying to get back to you," Scylla said.

"I don't understand? You left me here with no word about when you would be back. I've been waiting since, alone. I worried you had died."

"Don't be silly, please. I am here now," Scylla pleaded.

The damage had been done already. Circe felt jealousy bubble from her every pore. Not only did Scylla have another life, where she could come and go as she pleased, unlike Circe who had been banished to this godforsaken rock, but she also had this other suitor pining for her, desperate to steal her attention and affections from Circe.

Circe wanted to punish Scylla right then and there. She wanted to turn her sweet beauty to something that no one would ever want, not even Circe herself. Most of all, she herself didn't want to feel this gaping want in her chest anymore for another, one who could leave her at will.

When she struck out at Scylla, magic passing through her, she hadn't even formed what she wanted it to do. Circe had no clear thoughts in her mind as she lashed out at Scylla.

As soon as it was done, she wanted nothing more than to take it back. Scylla's beauty left her the cruelest way Circe could have imagined: her summer tanned skin greying into scales like a reptile's; her face becoming multiple on long, arching necks, she was taller now than the trees; her teeth became fangs and gnashing in multiple rows; her words became nothing more than the braying barks of dogs; and her legs grew into twelve.

As she stopped changing and was stuck in all her horror, Circe could only stare upon what she had done. Her jealous rage had fueled such a fire in her that she had destroyed the one she loved. The monster before her stared back, confronting her with all twelve of its unnatural eyes. The creature let out a pitiful bark.

Then, before Circe could speak a word, the monster scuttled back into the water. She was too stunned at her own power to stop it, or try to change Scylla back to her beautiful form. The monster disappeared into the waves and Circe never saw her again.

* * *

PROVE THEM ALL RIGHT

The tales of Scylla traveled across the waters to Circe's shores. She guarded the entrance to the sea on the strait with Charybdis, terrifying sailors and destroying ships. She was feared and barely spoken about above a whisper for her terror struck deep in their hearts.

The story of Scylla and Circe had never been told with any accuracy. Jealousy, though it had caused Circe to do it, was misattributed to Circe being jealous of Scylla because Glaucus loved her. They said that Circe had loved Glaucus and wanted him to love her instead of Scylla. Only Circe, and her poor victim, knew the truth.

Circe had never been able to atone for what she had done, but she believed her fate was sealed. She was to be, as all the rumors said, the evil, jealous witch. So she began to be that witch.

But now, as she stood looking over the rocks where she had changed Scylla forever into a monster, Circe felt immense regret. She wished she could tell her so, but she was still locked on this island, just as Scylla was now locked away in her cave above the sea.

Circe cursed the Fates, as she often did. Those deities who spun each thread of one's lives which they were all doomed to follow had never been kind to her. But as the eyes of the monster she had made flashed in her mind, she thought for a moment; maybe it was what Circe deserved. She had proved them all right, after all, in the end.

From Darkness, Awake
Zach Shephard

I can smell the predator's pheromones as I deliver drinks to his corner booth. It's like walking into a cloud of sweat and arrogance, chemicals and lechery. Overlaying the stink is a pine aroma, intended to conceal what's really going on. Nice touch, Drew.

I've followed this guy long enough to know his trick works on pretty much every woman he encounters. Not me, though. I've been mixing herbs into magic for millennia – I can spot a love potion when I smell it.

There are three others in the booth with Drew. The two men look just like him: bleached-white smiles, obsessively manicured hair, expensive clubbing clothes, steroid-stuffed bodies. The woman on his arm is the oddball in the group. She's a university student, Asian, maybe ten years Drew's junior, wearing a slim red dress and diamond jewelry anywhere Drew could stick it. Her name is Allie Chia, and she's under a powerful spell.

But not for long.

I arrange the drinks on the table, making sure everyone gets the right one. Drew looks me over, a smug smile curling up one side of his face.

"Haven't seen you here before," he says. "You new?"

FROM DARKNESS, AWAKE

I smile sweetly. "First day. Can I get you anything else?"

"You sure could," he says, and winks.

Allie's observing our whole exchange, but seems blissfully undisturbed by her date's flirting. She's just smiling and existing, and little else. I wish I could have helped her a week ago, but I had to stick to the plan. I didn't live this long by taking chances.

"My shift ends in an hour," I say, knowing Drew's concept of time is about to go right out the window. "Enjoy the drinks."

I head back to the bar of The Woodpecker Club, with its clientele that's just like Drew. Men with too much confidence and not enough charm slither between the red booths, faces illuminated by golden floor lighting. They zero in on the club's women and shout tired pickup lines over the thumping music. A few of the guys accept their rejections and move on, but most are oblivious to how poorly they're doing. If Drew strikes a deal with his buddies at the table, this whole game will change. I'm worried for the women of Miami.

From across the floor I see a change in Allie's expression. Awareness blooms in her eyes like poppies opening in the spring. She looks around, as if trying to figure out where she is without loudly advertising her confusion. She's waking up.

She excuses herself from the table, but the guys don't notice. They're too busy laughing and slapping each other on the shoulders. If they keep drinking what I served them, they should be distracted for a while. I follow Allie to the restroom.

There's only one stall-door closed. I hear stifled sobs from the other side.

MYTHS, GODS & IMMORTALS: CIRCE

"It's going to be okay," I say.

A sob catches. She's listening.

"I'm here to help you, Allie. But time's a factor. Drew won't be distracted forever."

There's a quiet moment where all I hear is the club's muffled music. I can't risk waiting much longer. The concoction I slipped into Drew's drink is potent, but who knows how much he'll chug down? If Allie won't trust me, I'll have to —

The stall's latch clicks.

The door cracks open. One dark-brown eye, hovering above a streak of smeared makeup like a balloon on a string, peers out at me.

"Who are you?" Allie asks.

"The person who's getting you out of here."

"What did Drew do to me?"

"Something awful. And if we don't leave now, he'll do even worse. Come on – I'll explain on the way."

We slip out the back of the club, me pulling Allie by the hand. She's still a little disoriented. I can't leave her alone just yet, which is why she'll be joining me as I break into Drew's house.

* * *

We drive through downtown Miami, all concrete and glass. It's a quiet night. Wherever the street lights don't shine, palm trees stand like blackened fireworks, frozen in place. I pass Allie a bottle of water. She cracks the seal and takes a long drink.

294

"Thanks," she says, wiping her mouth. "Now can you please tell me what the fuck is going on?"

"Short version, or long?"

"Let's start short and go from there."

"Drew works for a criminal drug operation. They've developed a new product that's bad news for women. And if his deal with the guys from the club goes through, he'll sell it all over Miami."

Allie's quiet. In the lights of the dashboard, I see realization dawn on her face.

"Holy shit," she says. "How long was I with him?"

"About a week, I think. Long enough for his drug to have a lasting effect."

"So he was poisoning me?"

"Sort of. He doesn't slip his drug to victims – he takes it himself, and it makes his body produce a pheromone that's tough for women to resist. Normally the spell wears off once you get away from the stink-cloud, but your case is a little different. I think prolonged exposure to the drug turns victims into infatuated zombies."

I realize too late I could have worded that last part better. The poor woman has spent the last week as Drew's arm candy, being carted around as an example of what his drug can do. She deserves some compassion.

"Sorry," I say, "I didn't mean—"

"It's fine. You didn't do this to me. Hell, you're the one who got me out. I should be thanking you.

"Oh my god," she says, and brings her hands to her head. "I'm sorry. I don't even know your name."

MYTHS, GODS & IMMORTALS: CIRCE

"Helena," I say, but not quite quickly enough. Allie picks up on it. She lets me get away with the fake name anyway.

"Helena," she says. "I don't know how you saved me, but – thanks."

I decide now's not the time to tell her about the potion I slipped her, even though I took the same one myself to protect against Drew's pheromones. She might not feel great about someone messing with her drink.

"Heads up," I say. "We're almost there."

I turn onto a bridge spanning a narrow band of water. On the other side, the homes are big and expensive-looking, with plenty of greenery to keep nosy neighbors at bay.

"Oh god," Allie says. "Why are we going to Drew's place?"

"If I'm going to take his operation down, I need more information about it. This is my next place to check. You don't have to come in."

"No, I should – he has dogs. They're mean, but they like me."

"You remember his dogs?"

"Sort of. Things are starting to come back. It's all just so fuzzy."

I park the car down the street. I grab my satchel from the back seat and sling it over my shoulder, the sound of glass jangling within.

We head up Drew's stone walkway, fake grass to either side. The home is modern and luxurious, with a flat roof and lots of right angles. A pair of wooden doors stand at twice my height.

"I don't suppose Drew gave you a key?" I say.

Allie looks down at her slender red dress, arms spread. "He didn't even give me pockets."

"Maybe he's got a spare under a rock or something."

As Allie turns to search, I pull a glass vial from my satchel. I remove the stopper and down the juice. Power rushes into me, like waves assaulting the shore.

I take the door's handle and yank hard enough to break it open.

"What was that?" Allie asks, returning.

"Just some creative lock-picking. Let's move."

We step inside. No alarms going off, but I didn't expect any – Drew doesn't strike me as the type who'd want police showing up at his house. Which explains why his home security is entirely canine-based.

Three dark shapes rush at us down the unlit hall, snarling. I know Allie said she could handle them, but I'm not taking chances.

"Stop," I say. The dogs hit the brakes, skidding across the hardwood floor and tumbling to a halt at my feet. German Shepherds, all of them. Any menace they may have had in their eyes has drained away by the time they sit and look up at me. They pin their ears back submissively, as if awaiting instruction.

"Okay," Allie says, kicking her high heels off. "You're teaching me how to do that later. Come on, boys." She leads the dogs through the dark, and I hear her close a door.

"Dogs are handled," she says, returning. "What're we looking for?"

"Something Drew would keep private and secure. Maybe a laptop, some documents, anything like that."

Allie snaps her fingers. "The safe. In his bedroom."

"Beautiful. Lead the way."

We feel our way up the stairs and into Drew's room. I risk hitting the lights to speed things along. The room looks about how I expected: black-and-white color palette, very tidy, abstract painting hanging over the bed. Allie shows me to a sizable closet, where a safe sits on the hardwood floor. I crouch before it.

"Got any more creative lock-picking tricks?" she asks, like she knows I wasn't entirely honest about the front door. I test the waters for forcing the safe, but my strength has already diminished significantly, and I don't have another of those potions handy. Some improvisation is in order.

I set down my satchel and sift through its vials. I find a purple one that swirls with golden glitter like a snow globe, and another that could pass for liquid mercury. I pour them both onto the safe's hinges, and as they mix, they start bubbling.

Allie watches with raised eyebrows. "I'm gonna want some explanations once we're out of here, 'Helena.'"

The chemical reaction is taking a while. Allie sits on the bed, her eyelids looking heavy. The potion that broke Drew's spell is catching up to her.

As the mixture eats halfway through the safe's hinges, I hear a car door shut.

Allie snaps alert. We rush to the window and peek through the blinds.

Drew's Lamborghini is in the drive. He's approaching the house, and he does not look happy.

"Oh fuck," Allie says. "Fuck fuck *fuck*. What do we do?"

"Closet. Go." She rushes inside. I hit the bedroom's lights and join her. We close the door and hold our breaths.

I hear Drew step into the house. Something gets thrown or kicked down the front hall, tumbling across the hardwood.

"Oh no," Allie says. "My shoes. I left them by the door."

"Allie!" Drew shouts. "Where the fuck are you?"

Heavy footsteps climb the stairs.

"He knows I'm here," she whispers, "but he doesn't know about you."

"Allie, don't—"

She's already through the closet door, closing it behind her. A moment later, I see light bleed across the floor.

Drew's yelling at her. I can't see what's going on, but Allie's just letting him unload. I'm worried about what might happen next.

Every instinct in my body is telling me to run. That's how I've survived this long, despite always having a target on my back. But I can't do that now, because there's an innocent woman involved. Allie needs to get out too.

Drew's a big guy, and I don't know how much of the strength-potion's juice is left in me. I'll have to take him by surprise. It's a matter of patience: if I listen closely, I can wait for the perfect moment to —

The safe's door falls off with a clang.

Okay. New plan.

I burst from the closet and slam into Drew. He twists as we entangle each other, sending my momentum around him instead of through. Neither of us goes down, but we're off balance. I can't tell where Allie's ended up in all this. I swipe my fingernails at Drew's face, but he throws a heavy knee into my gut and I buckle. Before he can strike again, I wrap both arms around his legs, lift with all the strength I've got left, and dump the gorilla on his head.

Drew lands hard, but I'm not far behind. Panting, I spot Allie. "Run!" I yell.

Her eyes go wide. She points past me. "Gun!"

I turn to see Drew drawing the pistol from his waistband. I grab his wrist and divert the gun's barrel. A shot goes off. Allie screams.

Drew and I roll, fighting for the gun. We're each trying to control it with one hand, while clawing and punching with the others. He's too damned strong, and the potion's wearing off. I can't hold him any longer.

Drew gets me onto my back and straddles me. He grabs my throat with his free hand. I'm still holding the gun-wrist, but he's gradually turning the barrel toward my head, our arms trembling against each other.

I didn't want to do this. I *never* want to do this. But I'm out of options.

I throw my free arm up and touch my fingertips to his forehead. I utter a word that was old even before the Greeks, and the change begins immediately.

Drew's eyes go wide. The neatly trimmed stubble on his face is overtaken by white bristle, which emerges all across his body. His lips become thick and fleshy, the bottom one so heavy it droops. His nose widens, tilts upward, flattens. Giant pink ears stretch from each side of his head.

Most important of all is the change to Drew's hands: his fingers curl inward, twisting and fusing until they resemble cloven hooves. The gun drops.

A red streak shoots overhead, as both of Allie's bare feet slam into the pig-man's chest. He tumbles over backwards.

Allie rises, picking me up with her. There's a line of blood on her arm where the bullet grazed her.

"Helena, what the f—"

"No time," I say, as Drew rolls onto his hooves and knees, shaking the cobwebs out. "Go!"

I snag my satchel from the closet and run, Allie leading the way. We get to my car and disappear into the muggy Miami night.

* * *

The first few minutes of the drive are quiet, as we let the adrenaline fade. I pull some napkins from the glove box and hand them to Allie.

"Thanks for bailing me out," I say. "Nice kick."

She wipes the blood off her arm. "My parents made me take taekwondo as a kid. Which that wasn't. Now tell me why Drew turned into a Ninja Turtles villain."

Not a conversation I'm keen on having, but I owe her this much.

MYTHS, GODS & IMMORTALS: CIRCE

"Okay," I say. "You've already figured out my name isn't Helena."

"Duh. So what is it?"

"Circe."

"Circe. As in, Greek-Myth Circe. As in, Actual-Goddess-Sitting-Next-To-Me-In-A-2024-Toyota-Camry Circe."

"You've heard of me?"

"We read Ovid in my lit class last semester. You didn't come off great."

"Believe me, I'm aware."

I can feel Allie's eyes on me. I glance over. She's staring hard, and not being shy about it.

"For the record," she says, "there's no way I'd believe this if I hadn't just watched you turn a man into a pig. So you're a sorceress? Just like in the books?"

"Sorceress, yes. Just like the books, no."

"What parts are different?"

"The ones that made me look like a lovesick psychopath."

I make a turn, heading for a motel I've got in mind. Allie's still staring. I don't have to look to know that.

"Yeah," she says. "I'm not getting stalker vibes. So what's the deal? Why'd they write you that way?"

"All those times guys rejected me in the stories? It was the other way around. But they couldn't handle being shot down, so they started a 'We Hate Circe' club and spread a bunch of false stories about me."

"So you don't actually go around ruining guys' relationships?"

"No, that part's true. I've been breaking couples up for

FROM DARKNESS, AWAKE

millennia. But I do it to get trapped women away from abusive partners – not to claim their men for myself."

Allie looks to her lap, where she picks at a fingernail. "Thanks again," she says. "For getting me away from Drew."

"Of course. I just wish I could have done more for the rest of Miami."

"What do you mean?"

"Drew's drug operation. I can't pursue it anymore."

Allie leaps forward, the seatbelt snagging her. "*What?*" she asks. "Why not?"

"Remember Glaucus, from the stories?"

"Vaguely. Something about a fish-tailed guy who wouldn't love you back."

"Again: other way around. Glaucus wanted me. And when I turned him down, he swore to get revenge. He's been chasing me ever since. He wants me dead. And now he knows where I am."

I park in the motel's lot, half-lit by a neon red sign overhead. Allie's clearly struggling to piece everything together.

"I don't get it. How does Glaucus know where you are?"

"It's the sorcery. Any time I cast a spell, Glaucus shows up within a few days. Potions?" I ask, poking a thumb at the satchel in the back seat. "Potions are fine. That's just mixing herbs together. But sorcery is a much more overt thing. He senses it somehow, and I'm sure turning Drew into a pig sent up a flare. Glaucus is on his way."

I exit the car. Allie follows me toward the motel's booking window, where a bored-looking woman scrolls her phone.

"So?" Allie asks. "What's Glaucus gonna do? You're a goddess. You're immortal!"

"That's another thing the books got wrong. Deities may have infinite longevity, but we can still be killed." I address the woman at the window: "One room, please." She lazily gets things together, showing zero interest in the immortality conversation. I accept the key and thank her.

We go to the room, with its bed that smells like an old record shop I visited once. Allie collapses face-first onto the fuzzy orange comforter.

"This is wild," she says, voice muffled by the fuzz. "Just one-hundred-percent insane. What do we do now?"

"*You* rest. You're still recovering from your Drew-cleanse. I'm going to take care of some things. I'll be back in the morning, okay?"

"Okay," Allie mumbles, half awake. "Watch out for angry mermen, Circe."

I head out for a drive, my skin prickling anytime I glance toward the coast.

* * *

I visit some of my stashes, collecting clothes and cash for Allie. She'll have to leave Miami and start a new life somewhere else, which she won't be happy about. But this is the existence of a woman on the run. You get used to it.

I gather some things for my own escape, then head to the beach. The sky is lightening – just a touch of pink on the horizon. I sit on the sand and listen to the waves sigh against the beach. It sounds like a brush drawing through my hair.

I'm going to miss the sea.

I'll have to head inland. That's what I do whenever I know Glaucus is coming. But I won't be able to stay there long – the pull of the salty air always draws me back, like a lost dog sniffing its way home. And besides, avoiding the coast isn't enough to save me from the merman. There's also the matter of Glaucus's followers: he was the first real woman-hater, and misogyny as we know it has descended from the examples he set all those years ago. His men are everywhere, just waiting to become the next Drew.

The sun rises. I say a brief hello to Dad, and head back to the motel.

* * *

I give Allie the fresh clothes and some food. As she's changing, I explain that we're both getting as far away from Miami as possible.

Her head pops out the top of the sea-blue t-shirt. "Nope."

"Allie, I—"

"You can leave if you want, but I'm staying. Drew's drug could hurt a lot of women. I'm not letting that happen."

I sigh. Her heart's in the right place, but she just doesn't get it.

"Believe me," I say, "I don't like this either. But if Drew catches up to you – or if Glaucus finds me – we won't be helping *anyone* anymore. It's a crummy world, Allie. You've got to be safe if you want to make a difference."

She scoffs through a mouthful of blueberry muffin. "That's some high-level bullshit, Circe. 'Staying safe' is exactly what *keeps* people from making a difference. 'Staying safe' is what the world wants from us. I mean, come on – you porkified Drew with just a flick of your fingers. And I bet you could do a lot more than that. But you're letting the threat of some *man* keep you from reaching your full potential. You may be a literal goddess, but you're buckling to the patriarchy just like everyone else."

I turn away and busy myself with the bag I packed her. I can't tell what makes me angrier: Allie's stubbornness, or the possibility that she has a point.

"Even if I wanted to help, I can't. We didn't get any information from Drew's house. And I'm sure the moment he stopped being a pig, he called some goons over to guard the place. That was my last lead."

I turn to pass the bag to Allie. She dusts muffin crumbs from her hands and chokes down the last bite without enough chewing.

"No need for leads – we've got everything we need right here." She taps her temple. "Drew carted me around for a week, remember? And now I'm remembering a lot of how that went. I think I know where his boss lives. I've been there. And I'm going back. You're welcome to come."

She accepts the bag and heads out the door.

Damn it, Allie. I'd better not regret this.

FROM DARKNESS, AWAKE

* * *

Allie gives directions as we go, pointing us toward the coast. The city's just waking up. I roll my window down to listen to the gulls and feel the sea breeze on my face. It's a beautiful day – one I could normally enjoy, if the threat of my nemesis weren't lurking beneath the waves.

"One ground rule," I say. "If things get dicey, we bail. Got it?"

"Sure."

"Also: no sorcery. I already drew Glaucus's attention with the metamorphosis. I don't want to give him any more beacons."

Allie looks up from my phone, which she's been scrolling. "Are you kidding me? You've got a magical 'I-win' button in your pocket, and you're not going to use it because you're worried about how some guy will react? Don't let a man hold you back, Circe."

"Sorry. It's just not worth the risk."

"Ugh. Whatever."

She resumes scrolling. I thought she was looking up directions, but I see a lot of text.

"What're you reading?"

"*The Odyssey*. Did you really turn the whole crew into pigs when they popped by your house?"

"They didn't 'pop by.' They broke in looking for food, and… more."

"Shit, Circe. I'm sorry. What'd you do?"

I shrug. "I turned them into pigs."

Allie directs us to an isolated part of Miami, right near the coast. We park at the end of a long brick driveway.

MYTHS, GODS & IMMORTALS: CIRCE

Somewhere beyond the limestone gateway is a beachside mansion, inhabited by the drug lord responsible for our current problem. It looks like no one's around, but I roll up the windows anyway.

"So," Allie says, "what's the plan?"

"You tell me. I normally take a lot more time to prepare than this." We both look through her window, up the drive. The palm trees flanking the gateway sway in a light breeze. I shake my head. "This doesn't feel great. We don't have enough information."

"The boss's name is Gregor. I remember that now. He's Drew's dad."

Nepotism. Sounds about right.

"And he's got a weakness for gorgeous women," Allie says. "He'll lose his shit when he sees you."

"That still doesn't tell me how we approach the place. What if--?"

There's a knock on my window. I turn to see a man in a breezy tropical shirt and khaki shorts. His sunglasses partially cover a scar running down one side of his face. He's smiling, in the way men do when they don't realize just how charming they aren't. I roll down my window.

"You're Drew's girl," he says, pointing at Allie. "He's not here."

Allie just grins widely, like she's panic-frozen. I cut in.

"He wanted us to meet him here," I say, "but we're early. Think we could go on ahead?" I touch my hair without making it too obvious: a move I've had a few millennia to perfect.

308

FROM DARKNESS, AWAKE

The man's sleazy smile spreads. "You pretty ladies head on up. I'll let Mr. Vardanyan know you're coming." He pulls out a radio. "And stop by to see me on your way out, okay?"

I smile. "Can't wait."

The iron gate swings open. I pull up the drive.

"Sorry I wasn't more help," Allie says. "The last time they saw me I was zombified, so I figured I'd keep up the act."

"Smart move. Now we just need to figure out what we're doing next."

We pull up to the vast yellow mansion, with its arched windows and barrel-tile roof. A man like the one from the gate greets us.

"I'll take your car around to the garage," he says. "Mr. Vardanyan's waiting for you."

I can't come up with an excuse to lug my satchel with me, so it stays in the car. I already don't like how this is going.

We step into a big, luxurious foyer. I don't get a chance to take it in before something hits the back of my head.

Lying on the floor, the last thing I see is Drew and his men rushing Allie. They swarm her as everything goes black.

* * *

A familiar scent wakes me up: the odor of sweat and arrogance, chemicals and lechery. The same pheromones I smelled on Drew at The Woodpecker Club.

I open my eyes, but it's not Drew standing before me. It's an older version of him in white beach attire, with thick silver-black hair combed to one side. He's leaning over, hands on his knees, to be eye-level with me in the chair I'm strapped to. We're in a wide dining room with a glass wall that looks out on the beach and waves below.

"So," Gregor Vardanyan says, "you're the little lady who broke into my son's house. He was just telling me about you."

Allie's off to the side, held by a couple of brutes. Drew stands near her, but his eyes are fixed on me. He looks uneasy, like he's afraid I might break free and lunge at him.

"Drew tells me you did something to him," Gregor says. "Changed him. Care to explain what that's about?"

I look past Gregor to the tumbling surf, wondering where Glaucus might be. I can't afford to be tied up here. There's got to be a way out.

A palm strikes my face, jarring me to the side.

"I asked you a question," Gregor says. "If I have to ask again, your friend gets the next shot. And it won't be so gentle."

Despite everything, there's ferocity and fearlessness on Allie's face. Like she could take anything Gregor's got without flinching. But I'm not letting that happen.

"I turned your son into a pig," I say.

"That's what he said. I didn't believe it then, either."

"I could prove it, if you like."

Concern widens Drew's eyes. "Dad, don't –"

"Shut the fuck up." Gregor looks at me, smiles genially. "Okay, pretty lady. Let's see it. Go ahead and work your magic."

I raise my fingers, my wrists zip-tied to the chair. "I need my hands."

FROM DARKNESS, AWAKE

Gregor laughs. "Sure, sure. Of course you do." He signals one of the brutes. "Cut her loose."

Drew tries to protest again, but Daddy shuts him down. The brute draws a knife and cuts my ties.

In a flash I snag the gun from his hip and get behind him, holding the barrel to his temple.

"Drop the knife."

He does. Gregor's still smiling, unamused.

"You have no idea what you're getting yourself into, girlie," he says. "You pull that trigger, you're as good as dead. Your friend, too. So go ahead and drop the gun. If you don't make me ask again, I'll forget this little outburst."

I scan for escape routes, but it's useless. There's no way out of this mess without risking my life and Allie's.

This is exactly why I've played it safe over the years. It's why I never act without a plan. Because the world's full of dangerous men who will do anything to get what they want.

I look at Allie, who didn't deserve any of this. She knew what it was like to be a victim, and didn't want anyone else to feel that way. So she decided to become a hero, despite the risks.

She's staring me straight in the eye, like she's trying to convey a message. I hear her past words in my head: *Don't let a man hold you back, Circe.* I think about how I've spent my entire life doing exactly that, and realize just how disappointed I am.

"Fuck this," Gregor says, drawing a gun. "I'm out of patience."

You and me both, big guy.

I reach out to powers I haven't touched in far too long. This is more than simple metamorphosis – this is a muscle I've been afraid to flex ever since Glaucus started hunting me, all those centuries ago.

A distant rumble makes its way in from the sea, intensifying as it nears. The glass wall shakes. Shadows dim the room, like storm clouds overtaking a ship. The men look around in fear and confusion. Even Allie seems worried. My will stretches beyond the borders of my body, rattling the entire mansion. Whatever the consequences, I've committed to this path. I summon Night, and the powers of Darkness and Chaos.

The windows smash inward, letting in a roaring wind. Everyone but me hunches, taking cover. I release my hostage and drop his gun. I lift my arms to the sides and rise into the air, hair whipping in the breeze. Black bolts of lightning snap from my body, ravaging Gregor's home. I direct the winds in such a way that Allie and Allie alone is nudged past the broken windows, toward the beach. She takes the hint, and escapes down the deck stairs.

One of the men aims his gun at me. I snap my gaze to him. The gun splits and shifts into a dozen mismatched pieces, like a cubist painting. The man drops the metal mess and tries to run. I strike him down with a thought, darkness oozing from his vacant eyes.

Gregor and Drew have huddled together in a corner, staring up at me in terrified awe. I float over to them.

With a gesture of my hand, the mansion crumbles.

FROM DARKNESS, AWAKE

* * *

I hover above the collapsed wreckage, where the mansion's second-story dining room once stood. Allie's on the storm-darkened beach, standing in a bubble of calm I've allowed within the chaos-winds. I descend toward her, shredding the shoes from my feet along the way. I want to feel the sand on my toes.

I land gently. Allie stares in shock. It occurs to me that my eyes might be unsettling, filled with marbled darkness as they are.

"Ho. Lee. Shit," Allie says.

"Are you all right?"

"All right? I just watched an *actual goddess* obliterate an evil drug lord in his own house. I'm better than all right. I'm fucking ecstatic!"

She embraces me. I hug her back. We hold each other a moment before she backs away, grinning.

"I knew you could do it, Circe. How's it feel?"

"Good," I admit, looking at my hands. "Really good." I flex my fingers in and out, feeling the world contract and expand with them.

"Oh no. Oh, that can't be good."

I follow Allie's gaze to the sea.

There in the distance is a bare-chested man with hair like seaweed, half-risen from the waves, balanced on his merman's tail. We eye each other from afar.

"That's him, isn't it?" Allie asks. "Circe, I'm so sorry. I shouldn't have gotten you into this. What do we do? Do we run?"

Gaze still fixed on Glaucus, I shake my head.

"You were right, Allie. I've spent too long holding myself back, all because I was afraid of a man. I won't do it any longer." I smile at her and squeeze her hand. "Thanks for waking me up."

I move seaward, striding atop the surf. Glaucus comes forward. I drop a bolt of black lightning beside him, just to test the waters.

A sudden fear rushes into his eyes, replacing the anger and determination he's held onto for millennia. I can't help but smile.

I rise into the air and advance through the storm, a sea-god shrinking before me.

The Circead

Jamie Simpher

"I'm considering smiting you," said a disembodied and disdainful voice.

I could hear the sneer on her face even though she had yet to appear corporeally in the garden beside me, and I knew who it was even though she hadn't spoken to me in three years.

"Let me explain," I said.

"Explain like your life depends on it," she said. In another moment, a body had materialized. Artemis was all hardness and angles. Her bare brown shoulders were sharp, her pelvis was pointy through her white gown, her knees and elbows were corners. She strode towards me so gracefully that my breath caught in my throat, and her face was the moon. She had high cheekbones, eyes like obsidian, and perfect bow-shaped lips that only smiled when she mocked you.

As she mocked me now.

"Men," she said. "They'll fuck you every chance they get."

"Believe it or not, Art, that was one of the things I loved about him."

"Any pig or dog would have done the same. That's why we call them pigs and dogs."

"He was different."

"He wasn't."

I sighed. "If you only came to say I told you so, then mission accomplished."

"I did more than tell you so. I *showed* you his true nature. You chose to ignore me." Her gaze was chilly, her face stormy. I had never seen her like this.

"That *man*" she spat the word "had an overblown sense of his own intellect, a self-important illusion of himself as some kind of epic hero, and a streak of cruelty."

"We don't love people for being perfect. We love them for their imperfections. The way he snores. His failure to read anything I recommend to him. His shitty cooking. How much he drinks. How he only ever wanted sex on his own schedule."

"You liked those things?"

"No, they drove me crazy," I said. "But they're part of who he is."

"He was just another fucking pig. Like this one," she said, kicking a small brown boar. It squealed and scampered off, casting a wary glance at her once it had reached a safe distance.

"He wasn't like that."

"The fact that you deny it means that you didn't love his true self – the pig – you just loved your idea of him. If you think about it, you never even knew him at all."

"Does that matter?"

Artemis started, but I cut her off.

"Does anyone ever really know anyone else, or do they just love the idea of them?"

"You're philosophizing to the wrong entity," said Artemis. "I don't even believe in love. It's just two people who both want sex at the same time."

"He stopped wanting that weeks ago." I sighed. "That's what hurts the most. I could understand if it was just that he wanted to go home. But how could he fall so far out of love with me that he didn't even want to sleep with me?"

* * *

He and I used to sit on the beach together in the warm evenings and look out at the stars and the ocean. He would tell me about all the places he had seen, and all the places he'd like to see. "Let's go on an adventure," he said. "We'll discover new lands, engage in epic battles, win glory, make names for ourselves." I laughed and told him our names were both rather famous already. "We'll pick new names," he said. "Create new lives, new legends."

"We're already living a legend. The greatest love story ever told," I said.

I didn't realize I was only one short chapter of his epic.

* * *

"Beats me," said Artemis. "Men are changeable. And like I've said, he was a pig."

"But he wasn't."

"But he was."

"But he was *mine,*" I cried. "He was mine. And he's just moved on so fast. For three years I was the love of his life, his dream girl, his best friend. Now all he can talk about is *her.*"

"You mean his wife. Don't act like you didn't see it coming."

"I didn't. I mean, I knew he wanted to go home, but—"

"You thought he would take you with him." She cackled.

I shrugged. "He loved me."

I suspected he only wanted to go home because that's what he was supposed to want. He had to be able to see himself as a clever adventurer waylaid by bad luck, bent on returning home no matter how long it took.

I had noticed, over the last year, that he talked more and more often of what he had left behind. That he used the same words to describe his home that he once used to describe his life with me. That more and more he was gloomy and missed his family. But not until a few weeks ago had he suddenly refused to touch me. He accused me of bewitching him. Finally, I couldn't stand his constant rejection, his casual indifference any longer, so I asked if he was going to leave me. Then I asked him to hold me while he broke my heart.

"Are you going to miss me?" I asked him.

* * *

"Art…I can't. I just…" I closed my eyes. Artemis had no patience for tears, and she was still considering smiting me.

She was right about him, of course – by definition, she always was – but she was also wrong. Yes, I had seen instantly that he was just another dog, but before I could do anything about it, he had knocked his goblet of wine to the floor, his bronze arms bulging, his eyes flashing. As his "men" squealed and trembled,

THE CIRCEAD

he stood over me. No man had ever come so close to me, and he was intoxicating – the smell of him, the power of his body, his broad shoulders. Before I knew it, he had one hand around my neck, and his other arm around my waist. I looked up at him and was lost. He could have crushed my throat, but he was gentle.

"I fell in love," I said.

"It hardly matters anymore, does it?" said Artemis, with another haughty toss of her hair. "By now the sirens will have got him. No one leaves this island alive."

I sighed. "I don't know if that's true."

She stared at me. "You didn't."

"I'm afraid I did."

Her eyes flashed. "Give me one good reason why I shouldn't smite you. Why should *you* escape unscathed when all other women who fall in love fall to their own destruction?"

"Believe me, I'm not unscathed."

"You're still human, you're still standing, you're not enslaved – not even married."

"But I feel like my guts have been ripped out and I'm rotting away inside."

"Who could ever have predicted this? *Oh, wait.*" Artemis rolled her eyes.

"But here's the thing," I said. "I think maybe…it was worth it. The pain I feel now doesn't outweigh all the happiness he gave me."

"Do you even hear yourself? You haven't talked about anything except a *man* since I got here. We don't even pass the Bechdel test," said Artemis.

319

"You're the one who wanted to talk about him," I said.

"You used to be so much more interesting. Now look at you: a puddle of tears and self-involved heartbreak." She shook her head. "I thought maybe if I could give a woman the ability to see what I see in men – pigs, dogs, asses – that maybe she wouldn't lust after them."

"You tried to make me immune to love."

"The only thing falling in love ever did for a woman is make her a slave."

"No. Love sets you free."

Artemis snapped her fingers, and in the space above her shoulder, an image appeared of a pair of lions pulling a chariot. "Do you recognize these lions?"

I sighed. "No."

"This is Atalanta. Her father wanted a son, so he left her to die."

I had heard Art's rant on the custom of abandoning baby princesses a million times – the inherent Oedipal risks of abandoning any child (though the gods knew we could do with a few less men); the notion that leaving a child on a hillside wasn't murder (not that she disapproved of murder, but it's the *hypocrisy* of the practice – if you want someone dead, just kill them); and the implication that women could not make good heirs – or whatever else they wanted to be, like hunters or warriors, for that matter. I prayed silently that she would spare me the spiel.

Artemis glared at me. "I heard that," she said. Looking as prim as someone like Artemis could ever look, she continued. "I sent her a mother – a bear – to raise her and make her strong. I kept watch over her until some hunters found her a few years later. She was wild and as strong as any man. She pledged her virginity to me in exchange for the chance to prove her strength. When she was fifteen, I sent her a gift: the Great Boar. Someone stole the kill from her, but she had the world's attention. That's when a *man* interfered. Her father reclaimed her, and he wanted her married. Because of her pledge, she told him she would only marry a man who could defeat her in a footrace; anyone who tried and failed, she would kill." Artemis smiled. "A clever bargain. Many men thought to be great lost their lives because they wanted to own her."

"Isn't that sort of cruel?"

Artemis looked incredulously around at the pigs and dogs who sniffed around our feet. "They deserved it. All they wanted was to make her a slave. And eventually, one of them managed it. He cheated, of course – no one could have beat my Atalanta in a fair race – but what can you expect from a man whose masculinity is at stake?"

"What happened?"

"She fell in love with him. He was an idiot. Long story short, she's going to spend an eternity by his side – as a literal slave to Love."

"At least she's with the one she loves," I offered.

"Good for her, they can roar sweet nothings to each other while they're yoked together doing slave labor," said Artemis. She sighed. "Then there was Hippolyta. I made her a queen and gave her a magic girdle, for strength. She went from an Amazonian Queen to a slave in a matter of moments, all over a few muscles." She snorted. "At least he was strong. Still, I had higher hopes for her." Then she turned her hard black eyes to me. "And for you."

"Come on, Art, I'm not a slave. In fact, I think I'm better for having known him, even if it didn't last forever."

She snorted. "Could you please, just for like one second, get angry? You were just abandoned by an ass who claimed to care about you."

"He was an ass at the end. That doesn't outweigh all the happiness he gave me."

"Tell that to Medea."

Medea I knew well. She was my niece, and as a young girl, she had lived on my island so I could teach her. A colorful child with golden eyes, she had amazing talent – until her father decided she had had enough education and sent for her. The next time I saw her, I have to admit she frightened me. Always intense and passionate, she had grown into a ruthless young woman. She asked me to perform a cleansing ritual to forgive her for a crime she would not confess to me. At first, I refused, but she told me her father was after her, he wanted to kill her. So I relented. When I was finished, she kissed me and ran off with her new husband.

I didn't get much news on my lonely island. But even I heard of Medea's crimes.

"Art, Medea killed her own babies."

"She gave up *everything* for that man. Her family, her innocence, her virginity. She betrayed everyone she knew for love," Artemis roared. "And he threw her away like a piece of

THE CIRCEAD

garbage for a lesser woman with lesser fire. Medea did the only thing she could do to hurt him as badly as he hurt her."

"Those kids…"

"I'm just saying, at least she got *angry*. She got *even*. You're just sitting here moping. *This isn't you.*"

"Well, I've changed! He changed me."

"Yeah, I can see that. You used to be extraordinary, and he made you ordinary." She shook her head. "You're not the first one to disappoint me." She got to her feet. "I guess I just need to get used to the fact that there really is no one out there like me, and there never will be. I guess girls will always fall in love." Her eyes flashed and she clenched her hands into fists. "Your weakness will not go unpunished."

She pointed the long, sharp blade of her finger at me, and I closed my eyes and held my breath, waiting for her to strike me dead.

When I opened my eyes, she was gone.

No longer frozen in fear, the beasts of my menagerie peered up at me with sad eyes, the dogs clamoring to sniff between my legs and the pigs rolling about in their own filth.

"Great," I said, reaching down to pat a little retriever dog by my feet. "Now I have no boyfriend, and no friends."

The little dog rested his head on my knee. It occurred to me that this pup – all these dogs – were men once. Sure, their true forms were unattractive. But if I turned them back to the way they looked when they came to this island – the bodies of men – well, they'd still be dogs and pigs but at least I'd have a warm body, someone to crawl into bed with, someone to hold me.

323

Ever since he had left, taking the best of the wine, I'd been wandering around my lonely island palace, marveling at the way it changed when I was alone. With him here, it felt bigger, the stones of the walls glimmering with the echoes of our laughter. Now, the walls were pale and forlorn, and they closed in on me. It was unbearable. I needed a man, no matter how boorish, to break the awful silence and fill the lonely space.

I pressed a hand against the little dog's forehead and said the charm that should have turned him into a man. But it didn't work. I tried it again and again, but all I got for my efforts was a lick to my hand. Panic overcame me. Why wasn't my magic working?

Then I caught sight of the full moon, clearly visible in the daytime.

Artemis. Of course. I had not been smitten, but neither could she let me go unpunished for my crime of loving a man.

"It's just as well," I murmured to myself. "It wouldn't be the same."

Evening found me alone again, sitting at my usual place at the head of the table. In the three years he had spent on my island, he never once tried to take my place. At the time, I thought it was sweet, a sign of respect for my independence. In retrospect, I couldn't help but wonder if he never tried to sit at the head of the table because he knew he wasn't staying.

I couldn't bring myself to eat anything. Even food made me think of him. We had learned to cook together – nothing too fancy or difficult. We baked fish with oregano and overcooked the rice. He was a terrible cook, but I loved watching the gentle way his shoulders curved as he hunched over the garlic he was

THE CIRCEAD

chopping (he would lift the knife and bring it down with each chop, which took twice as long and made for uneven slices, but I never told him how sloppy and inefficient he was). I loved how he would come up behind me while I sautéed vegetables and wrap his arms around my middle and rest his head against my shoulder.

So now he had ruined food for me, too. I couldn't eat, and I couldn't sleep, all alone in the big bed. *This is the bed where I lost my virginity,* I thought to myself. *This is the bed we shared.* It still smelled like him. I buried my face in his pillow, smelled his sweat and morning breath on it. His scent comforted me, but it also hurt.

In the past three years, I had fallen into the habit of sleeping naked. Now, as I rose from the bed, I put on a nightgown for the first time in ages. I slipped on my sandals, descended the stairs, and wandered out the back door of the palace.

There was a tall hill with a lookout point, where I used to watch for approaching ships. I had always meant to take him up there. I even thought maybe we could sleep out there one night. We talked about it, but it never quite happened. Now, in the middle of the night, I began to climb.

It wasn't the easiest climb in the dark, and there was no moonlight for me. By the time I reached the top, I was breathless, and a little scratched up and bruised from tripping and banging my shins against the rocks. But finally, I made it.

I stood alone in the dark, at the edge of the point. The sea was below, glittering and black. Oblivion. I could smell the ocean. I could see the stars. I could feel the air.

This island, with its white sand beaches and rocky cliffs, used to be a paradise, a refuge from the patriarchal structure of the outside world, my own domain. Artemis had brought me here as a child, and I used to fill my hours exploring its beauty. But by the time I reached adolescence, I was restless. The only visitors I had were the men – who didn't last long – and occasionally the sirens. The island no longer felt like a place to explore; it wasn't big enough.

He promised we would have adventures, but said for now, he was enjoying staying put, having a home with me. But he said someday he'd take me off the island and we'd see the world together. I'd believed him. Now I didn't know if he had ever meant it at all.

Once my kingdom, the island was now my prison. Now that I had been kissed and held and opened like a diary, could I spend a lifetime here, alone, with no one to love me – not even Artemis and her sharp, angular affection?

Maybe I could. I had lived a whole lifetime before I met him. I had never imagined, before he came to my island, that I would fall so helplessly in love that I'd feel like a limp and smiling ragdoll in his arms.

But could I live without my magic?

Magic was more than a gift bestowed upon me. It was a craft I had developed, a talent I had nurtured, my heart light burning bright summer after endless summer on my timeless island. It was the color I used to paint my world. Without it – and without him – I was a half-person, all hollowed out, with an empty hole where my heart should be.

Who would I be now?

I picked up a smooth black stone and hurled it over the edge of the cliff. It disappeared into the night before it disappeared into the dark water. I couldn't even hear a splash over the sound of the crashing waves.

They say if you jump from high enough, it's not the impact that kills you. One step over the edge and I would be free.

For the last three years, I had been his lover.

Who am I now? If I am not his, who am I?

One moment of freefall, my stomach dropping with sickening relief.

One splash in the wine-dark sea and the woman he had once loved was swallowed up. The panic that had seized my heart since he told me he was leaving – like a knife crushing my lungs over and over – finally released me.

From the edge of the cliff, I watched myself disappear into the endless black sea. The wind whistled through the hole he had left in me, leaving me cold in my bones. I had rearranged my life to make room for him, had reshaped myself to be his ideal woman, jettisoned parts of me to fit around him. Some parts – like my magic – I might never get back.

I was still hollow. But the empty space in my heart now belonged to me more than he ever had.

Who would I become?

The Perfect Distance

Theresa Tyree

My name was never Circe. Like all the myths you know, it's what the victors of history chose to write down. They knew the word "sorcery" and bent the stalwart Ks of my name into supple curving Cs to match it; seductive, sensuous sounds, perfect for a witch they could ridicule and rape.

My name is Kírke and this is the story they won't tell you. A story of love blooming beneath the sea, a thief, a father doing his best (but falling short), and the finest friend I ever had.

* * *

Skylla had seaweed eyes; green, gorgeous in the broken light of the sun falling through the waves, easy to get lost in. She was a nymph in my father's palace under the waters of Okeanos, but even in the court of the sun god, she outshone everyone else.

At least for me.

Her seaweed eyes glinted with fish scales whenever she got me talking about magic and reagents. It made me blush. I'd never felt attracted to anyone before. The other nymphs' descriptions of ikor pounding through their veins at the sight of an attractive god never made sense. But when Skylla sang and held me in her gaze, I felt safe.

Her songs made me feel daring enough that, sometimes, I even joined in.

This wasn't how Odysseus described her when he arrived on my island.

He was a surprise, he and his crew. My father told me that the only way to keep my magic from harming others like it'd harmed Skylla was to stay on my island – but he'd never said anything about having others visit me there.

Odysseus and his crew were simply the first to manage it.

We tested out my proposed loophole together – because they needed safe harbor, and because I was lonely.

The goats and pigs I kept weren't skilled conversationalists.

Odysseus was. He was also completely devoted to his wife, which put me at ease with him. He was nothing like the monsters of my past, just a man who wanted to throw off a curse and get home.

"Even without Poseidon throwing me off course, I'm not surprised you don't get many visitors here," he told me as his crew cleaned the dishes we'd used for our meal and tidied the extra tables and chairs I'd grown with an incantation to accommodate the size of the group. "You've got two horrifying monsters guarding the strait that brought us here."

This was the first I'd heard of my isle being guarded. My father hadn't said anything of it when he'd settled me here.

"What kind of monsters could keep ships away from my island?"

He scoffed – the sound of a man who'd encountered many monsters since the Trojan War took him from his home nearly twenty years ago. "What *isn't* keeping ships away from your island, enchantress?"

"There are really so many?"

"Mayhap it's simply I've been put on the worst path, but I feel I've encountered most of the mortal-eating beings in the ocean's grasp." He pursed his lips gently to the side. "Though, there was one that seemed particularly determined, now that I think of it."

I smiled, amused that my father had thought to keep both my new friend and me from exploiting our loophole by stationing me a guard. "Tell of this particularly determined monster, tactician."

"If you take pity on my dry throat, goddess, I will spin as many tales as you like."

It'd been so long since I'd had someone make me smile.

Cups filled, a toast to new friends and old stories made, and drunk, I leaned close across the table as Odysseus told me of the two horrors that guarded the strait of my island. Kharybdis was familiar enough to me, but her new neighbor...

My eyes grew wider as he described her.

A woman from the waist up, but attached to long tentacles that harried ship and sailors like a pack of hunting dogs. Teeth like knives, coral-sharp talons, and the speed and reach of a riptide.

"Skylla," I breathed, tears flooding my eyes.

Just as I remembered her all those years ago when the pool we bathed in was poisoned with my magic.

THE PERFECT DISTANCE

"Yes! She—" Odysseus frowned. "Wait, how did you know?"

I looked at him, let him see the tears in my eyes. This wound went deep, and much as I liked him and his stories of his adventures and brilliant wife, he deserved to know what he was getting into.

"Are you strong enough, great tactician, to carry the tale of my broken heart?"

Odysseus's face changed then. He placed his hand on the table, open; an invitation. I took it, gripping his fingers tightly, and let my tears fall.

"Skylla didn't always look like that," I told him, wiping water from my face. "Once, she was everything to me." I took a shaky breath and, gods bless him, he waited for me to take three more. "Until now, I'd thought her dead."

Odysseus squeezed my hand and searched my eyes. "So these are happy tears, then."

I smiled as more spilled down my face. "I'm sorry. It's callous to be happy when she killed a half dozen of your crew."

He offered me a sad smile. His eyes were that of an old man's when he spoke. "I've come to see the beauty in even the worst times over the last decade or two, my lady." He squeezed my hand again. "It's good your love still lives. I know that no matter what form Penelope took – be it wyrm or harpy – I would sail another ten years to be at her side once more."

I nodded and dabbed at my eyes.

"Can what was done to her be undone?"

My clever friend.

"I don't know," I confessed.

331

* * *

Before, Skylla and I would often bathe in a secluded pool on the surface. It was a nice stop on the way back to my father's undersea palace, and afforded us a place of relative privacy to enjoy a well-earned soak after hunting down spell ingredients and excitement all day. People of Father's court knew where the pool was, could approach it if they wanted, but understood it was mine and Skylla's.

Then Glaukos came.

There are many words I could use for him, but the best is "entitled."

He was a human fisherman who came upon a magic herb quite by accident – though he'd tell you Apollo gifted him prophetic visions, which he suspiciously couldn't use on demand – and, upon eating it, gained immortality instead of perishing. Many of the nymphs in my father's court fawned over him as a novelty.

It made him think he was entitled to our attention.

"Pay him no mind," Skylla told me one night as we disrobed for our bath. "Helios might be a bit of a distant father, but he made it clear he'll not stand for his golden-eyed brood being harassed in his home." She brushed my cheek with her thumb, making me raise the eyes she was talking about. "Besides, I'll knock Glaukos's teeth in if he bothers you. See how much the nymphs like him then."

"Careful," I said. "He might like that."

Skylla laughed, throwing her head back, her long hair falling over her shoulders. I fished the hydrating potion I'd crafted to defend her kinky curls from saltwater damage out of my gathering pouch and placed it by the edge of the pool.

Something about the water seemed silkier than usual, as if the warm currents that pushed it from the bowels of the earth were even more fluid and wet than water itself. Perhaps it was the full moon's light that made it look like liquid silver.

"Well, if he does, I know you'll brew a potion to mend my knuckles and his attitude." Skylla folded the green chiton she'd worn to go hunting for herbs with me that day over the bough of an olive tree then turned to wink at me.

I blushed and leaned towards her, the perfect distance to let her steal a kiss.

She dipped her head and met my lips with hers. "Your magic's always been more use than my fists anyway."

I leaned into the comfort of those words and the warmth of her hand on my face. "If you didn't use those fists to scale cliffs for my reagents, I wouldn't have any magic at all."

Skylla laughed again, a chortle instead of a shout. Gods, I loved the dynamics of her voice, how it could rise and fall like a wave, catch you in currents, lull you with susurration. "I suppose we're well matched, then, aren't we?" She drew me to her, and I went willingly, pressing my body against hers and stealing another searing kiss.

Little did I know it would be my last before I lost her.

"Go on," I said, nudging her towards the water, my peplos still over my arm. "Get comfy. I'll hang up my dress and then wash your hair."

She squeezed my arm and headed for the water.

I heard a splash, a hum, and then a scream.

I whirled from the tree in time to see Skylla's change.

Scales erupted from her skin. Her fingernails became clawed talons. A set of eight monstrous tentacles split from the water like spears, the tips of them spreading into three fingers that opened and closed like the maws of ferocious hounds.

Alarm nearly spurred me to dive in after her, but she reached out a hand and looked at me with panic in her seaweed eyes, stopping me in my tracks, saving me, even as she changed.

In the moment that I hesitated, I was grabbed from behind and pulled away from the pool.

"What's happening to her?" Glaukos yelled as he pulled.

"How should I know?" I looked around me, trying to hear the power in the world around me.

There had to be something I could do.

"It's *your* magic!" Glaukos grabbed my arm as I struggled to get away from him. "Your notes said this concoction could create bonds between creatures! That's a love potion, isn't it?"

My mind came to a standstill.

He'd been in my room.

Going over my notes.

He'd used my magic to try to woo us, and he'd hurt Skylla.

I wanted to curse him, turn him to dust right then and there – but he was more valuable to me as a source of information.

I needed to save Skylla.

"Do you have the potion?" I asked.

"No. I poured it all into the pool."

⊠ 334 ⊠

Without the potion, I'd never know what he'd put in it. Who knew if he'd even done it right? The next best thing I could do was get a sample of the water.

"Skylla!" I screamed.

She looked up, clawing at her skin – her seaweed eyes gone black like a shark's.

Seeing Glaukos, she opened her mouth and screamed.

Her teeth were like knives, her voice a discordant choir, baleful like a wolf's howl.

She threw herself towards the edge of the pool, crawling her way out of the water, her tentacles limp and useless behind her.

She didn't know how to use this new body.

And I didn't need her with me. I needed her to take the water while whatever poison Glaukos had spilled in it was still fresh.

"No, please, the bottle!" I threw my head towards the potion I used for her hair. "Get the water! I need the water!"

She stopped, changed course, snapped the bottle up in her claws and unstoppered it.

"Oh no," Glaukos said, throwing me aside. "I'll not have you doing any more magic tonight."

I wasn't strong like Skylla. I couldn't topple this man with my hands.

I raised my arms towards the sky and screamed for help, and my father, the sun, arrived. I pointed, and he smote Glaukos down, away from Skylla, who also fell from the power of the blow.

Immortal or not, he wouldn't rise from a blow like that again.

One threat dealt with, I lunged for Skylla, but my father caught me instead, pulling his golden cloak around me.

"Tell me what's happening, child."

"Skylla," I babbled, still reaching for her. "Papa, he hurt Skylla."

My father looked at Skylla, his arms tightening around me protectively as she shrieked the direction Glaukos had fallen, as if her voice alone could continue to pummel him with blows.

"I will deal with her."

Before I could reply, I was flying through the air, and landed softly on the stand of my father's chariot. The impact startled the shining golden steeds, and they set off again, continuing through the last colors of sunset and back to their stable.

As they flew me back to safety, I kept my eyes on Skylla, and wondered what my father would do.

I went to my notes and tried to discern what Glaukos had done, which recipe he'd mistaken for a love spell (I had none, what useless drivel when I could provide food, water, life to those who needed shelter). I hoped Skylla had bottled the water, but when my father arrived, it was only to tell me that Skylla was dead, and I must pack my things.

"The Isle of Aiaia will keep your magic from harming anyone ever again," he told me as he showed me around my new home. "It's a magical place, and it's yours. But you must never go to other lands, Kírke, or your magic may bring about further ruin."

I took his words to heart.

How could I not?

My love was gone because of me.

***

Odysseus's expression hardened as I finished my story.

"I'm sure your father thought he was doing you a favor, telling you she was dead," he said, his face telling me exactly what he thought of that. "Lucky for you, you've a friend with a ship cursed to run into every sea monster from here to Itháki."

"I couldn't ask for you to go back towards her."

He shook his head. "Curse'll just put another like her in my path. I'd rather see someone get their happy ending before one of these monsters gets lucky trying to kill me and robs me and Penelope of ours."

My heart hurt for him, for me, for Skylla, but he didn't give me time to dwell on my grief.

"Besides, you've been practicing your craft here for years. You've probably got a clue or two about how to cure her that you didn't before." He gave me a smile; a trusting, confident smile. The kind that said anything was possible. "Right?"

I'd learned to do much on the Isle of Aiaia, but to reverse a change I didn't know the catalyst of...

I held myself and shook my head. "You're kind to put your faith in me, my friend. But if I leave this isle, my magic could hurt everyone around me. Even you." I swallowed, tried to regulate my breathing. "Even her."

His face hardened. "Kírke of Aiaia, are you telling me that you're going to let the love of your life languish at sea because you think your magic will make her lot worse?"

His words pulled air fully into my lungs, let me gust it back out smoothly and pull in another.

"Do you even hear yourself? You, great sorceress, whose island is guarded savagely by a woman who must love you as much as you love her to fight so hard to keep any from approaching. You, who grew furniture from seeds and summoned a feast for strangers – none of whom are ill or ailing after sitting on and consuming items born of your magic, I might add."

I took another steady breath, but shook my head again. "It's only because we're on my island. If I leave—"

Odysseus cut me off with a hand waved through the air, like he was performing magic himself. "No, I'll not let you use your father's words to bind yourself. The Gods know much, but it's clear that your father lied to you, Kírke. He told you Skylla was dead. Who knows what he told her to make her guard you so fiercely? Doesn't she deserve to know the truth? Like you do?"

Another breath, strength flowing through my veins, my thoughts falling into order.

He was right.

Skylla needed saving, even if I could nothing for her body.

Odysseus took my hand in his, his eyes softer now, sympathy and comfort radiating from them like the warmth of the sun. "The work of men violated your privacy, stole from you, and lied to both you and your love. Let this man help you throw off those bonds and set it right."

I pulled him into a hug and let my tears fall on his shoulder. "Thank you, my friend."

THE PERFECT DISTANCE

He rubbed my back and squeezed me just the right amount to feel contained and safe.

It made me long for Skylla's seaweed eyes.

I wiped my own and then set them flashing on his. "Make ready to sail."

* * *

Odysseus was right: I was so much more powerful than when Skylla first transformed.

"So you don't need the water she was bathed in now, eh, enchantress?" Odysseus leaned against the ship's mast, watching me as I worked over my cauldron in the middle of his deck.

I shook my head. "No. Not to save her, anyway."

"Ooh. That sounds ominous. What have you in mind? Shrink her to the size of a fish, bring her home with you in that bowl?" He gestured to my pot.

I laughed. "Don't be ridiculous."

He shrugged. "Tell me your plan, oh great Kírke. I am uneducated in the ways of magic."

His mirth pierced through my nerves. How grateful I was to have his support.

"Alright, cursed wanderer." I gave my pot another stir, transforming the seafoam brew to the bright azure I was looking for. "Transformation magic is tricky. I'd need to know what was done to her to undo it, but if I wanted to transform her again…" I used a water nymph trick Skylla had taught me long before our first kiss and coaxed my potion from my pot as a seamless ribbon of water directly into a flask. The fluid remembered how to move through the air like the crest of a wave, even if the arrangement was of my own devising. "I can at least bind her into a form similar to what she once had."

Odysseus hummed low in his throat – like a man who understood change. There was no going back, only forward. "The same, but different."

Talking with him was easy. He understood without explanation.

"Precisely." I hung the flask from my belt, then leaned back against the mast with him. "All I need now is to get close enough to get her to listen to me."

Odysseus grinned. "Leave that to us, goddess. No harm will come to you if my crew and I can help it."

Rallying cries came from the crew as they extended their oars into the water, and the warmth of their voices overwhelmed me.

Never had I thought to find sunlight in sound. Not since Skylla was lost to me.

I leaned my shoulder companionably against Odysseus's and he returned the pressure.

"I'll do the same," I murmured.

His grin widened.

The drummer beat out a rhythm that sang through my chest as the ship approached the strait. On one side, Kharybdis with her insatiable appetite. On the other, Skylla.

THE PERFECT DISTANCE

Odysseus had told me how, even while maintaining the perfect distance from both on the last voyage through, he'd lost friends.

But both he and his crew were fearless now, heading straight for Skylla's cliffs.

We heard her before we saw her. Her beautiful singing voice might have changed to shrieks and roars, but even with that I could tell she was crying, harmonizing horribly with herself in her multi-voiced agony.

I hadn't known there was more of my heart left to break.

"What did your father tell her to cause her such grief?" Odysseus asked.

"Your guess is as good as mine." I reached out to the kritamo plants growing on the rocks, using their network to help me navigate, needing to find her.

The moment my magic touched her, she felt me.

Her keening stopped and she roared. The sound echoed off the rocks, assailing us from all sides. Tentacles slithered for the boat like hunting dogs, their length and girth, and the spikes between the three-pronged fingers at the ends all larger, longer, and deadlier than when last I saw them.

"How dare you return with such tricks?" she bellowed in her tritone voice. "You think to disarm me? To clear the way for your brethren so you can steal miracles from her? She wants to be alone! She would never leave her island. Your illusion will not keep me from my task. I will guard her until my last breath, and crush you between my teeth."

Skylla's tentacles lunged, and I threw a hand towards Odysseus's sails. Calling to the fibers, I spun threads out like new linen stalks.

341

Flowers sprouted between the crew and Skylla's grasping claws. She shrieked with new fury when the threads snared her.

Odysseus grabbed an oar and struck one of the tentacle heads into my snare, then spun on his heel, tied one of my threads to an arrow, and fired it towards the cliffs. The arrow buried itself in the stone, such was the strength of his bow.

"Go, goddess," he called to me. "We'll handle things here." He caught another tentacle with his bow, used the curve of it to throw it into more of my threads, then jerked his head towards the rocks where Skylla's voice came loudest. "She needs you."

I didn't need more urging.

The feather charms on my sandal lacings threw me into the air where I caught my gossamer line and slid down it to the cliffs.

The potion I'd brewed jostled on my belt as I collided with solid stone, but the tie holding it there held. I scrambled to the top of the cliff and jumped from ledge to ledge, letting my charms carry me further with each leap.

I was being reckless. I knew it in the back of my mind, but refused to slow my pace.

Tentacles broke free of my traps and pursued me – seemingly more infuriated by the illusion she thought me to be than the ship that'd already escaped her once.

I kicked off harder, flew faster, following the pull of familiar magic – my magic – that seemed centered on Skylla's voice.

She was much as I remembered her from the pool. Her scales had grown to armor, her claws into talons. The black of her eyes was all-consuming.

Her hair was matted and tangled, damaged by salt and lack of love.

But it was her, alive.

Our story didn't have to end in tragedy.

"Skylla!"

I took the flask from my belt and leapt for her.

The loop of a tentacle slammed me against the rocks. The flask with my potion flew out of my hands and was lost beneath the churning water.

Using the fingers of her tentacles, she advanced on me, holding herself suspended between rocks, and leaned close. Her teeth glittered sharp in the Mediterranean sun.

Even baring them at me, she was beautiful.

"To think the captain had enough sense to give you her voice," Skylla said, caressing my cheek with a claw. "You're a fair facsimile, at least."

I shook my head, my breath caught in my throat.

Every inch of her was brimming with magic.

Whatever Glaukos had done, Skylla had magnified the effects. The water she bathed in, the plants around her, even her skin stood out like they were the burning colors of a sunset.

Another mage might hunt her.

I only saw opportunity.

"It's me," I told her, grasping her hand, holding the sharp-tipped webbed fingers closer to my skin. "Father told me you were dead, Skylla. If I'd known you were here…"

Skylla's scale-plated brow furrowed. Even with the fury with which she'd pursued me, I could tell that having me before her was the best source of comfort she'd had since we parted.

"Helios tasked me with guarding his daughter, so none would ever abuse her magic again." She wrapped her other hand around my throat, a claw pressed gently to the dip between my collar bones. "Kírke is the only one who could unburden me of this task. And if you're a trick…"

She trailed off, her unspoken words clear in my mind; she would never forgive herself if harm befell me because she'd been tricked by a ghost that looked like me.

If I could just convince her I was truly myself, I could use the power within her to transform her.

"A ghost couldn't kiss you like I used to," I told her.

Even if I was false, Skylla couldn't resist one last kiss.

She leaned in, the perfect distance for me to catch her lips with mine. She was cold and tasted of salt, but that could have easily been the taste of my tears.

Kissing her felt more like home than my isle had ever been.

I'd thought our kiss would help me put her back together, but it was me who was transformed: my heart was whole again.

I felt her heart swell in answer, the sweet relief as she finally believed me to be myself. She kissed me again, and the magic within her yielded, letting me spin it around us like a warm cocoon.

I held her close and fell into the water with her as her form shrank to once again fit perfectly against mine.

* * *

Odysseus fished us out of the sea himself. He helped Skylla stand on wobbling legs that were now two instead of many, and wrapped his cloak around both of us to keep us warm on the voyage home, hushing her when she started to apologize for the damage to his ship (and previously his crew).

"We all knew the risks when we went to war," he told her. The kindness of his smile touched his eyes, setting her at ease. I felt her relax against me under the weight of his cloak. "It's enough to see your story end happily."

I thought about those words as I tended to Skylla's hair and summoned her clothing from threads of my own.

I had received my happy ending.

What about his?

"Who is your friend?" Skylla asked me as I pulled her hair back from her scale-pebbled temples into a plait. "He seems too good to be true."

"He is," I told her. "He's the first man I've met detached from his loins. Who cares more for kindness than beauty or power."

Skylla's eyes gleamed. They were still black, but twin pinpoints of seaweed green lit up the abyss. "He sounds like you."

I kissed her and thought of how I could give Odysseus what he'd given me.

It was clear when we docked that Odysseus's pentikóntoros ship needed mending. Enough that he stayed with me and Skylla another year on Aiaia.

I couldn't undo Poseidon's curse, but with so much time and assistance, the scope of my magic grew.

We spent the days foraging for spell components we could use in repairs: olive wood for wisdom and a peaceful journey, pine sap for perseverance and sealing, minerals and herbs to paint the bow with auspicious mati eye symbols. In the evenings, I carved charms for swiftness and directness into the finished pieces while Odysseus told stories and Skylla learned to laugh again.

It was bliss; my old loneliness nowhere to be found.

Even my goats and pigs seemed happier.

When it was finally time to send Odysseus off, his ship was more beautiful than my father's chariot, and Skylla's hair was long and shining again.

As he and his crew pushed off the beach with farewells full of sunshine, Skylla raised her voice in song.

I joined in.

And together, we sang a blessing to speed him on his way.

Blood Stains the Golden Fleece

Mathieu W.R. Wallis

My brother is dead and it was my fault. In my grief, I couldn't decide whether to array myself with the Golden Fleece or to shove it so far down my throat that I would choke to death upon the hardwood flooring of my lover's quarters. The sudden sway of the Argo followed by the ecstatic shouts of its crew urged me to pick the former. Wrapped in sparkling gold I stepped out onto the main deck and was immediately greeted by a bitter gale. My shoulders hunched and my eyes narrowed against the wind. Through my obscured vision I spotted a small shock of lush verdure peeking out through the wild tempest. "Within Aeaea," the wooden oracle creaked for the entire crew to hear, "Circe will free us from the winds of Zeus."

The sister of my father, King Aeëtes, Circe was a sorceress like myself. Exiled by her father Helios to this island, this verdant prison was a far cry from the stagnant streets of Colchis. What will she think of me when she hears that her brother intends to kill me? As if digging a grave, that question began to shovel a deep pit within my stomach. Impulsively I scanned the ship for Jason. With him, I would feel safe. He wasn't difficult to spot; his powerful yells directing the fifty or so oarsmen manning the ship could be heard even through the deafening storm. His hair, brown as bear fur, danced with the rain. I could tell from his unbreakable stance, holding onto naught but wind for balance, that he was prepared for chaos to rain upon him and his crew.

Jason anchored the Argo on the western shore of Aeaea. I wondered if Circe had lost her sanity living in such isolation, noticing the broken ancient structures peaking above the trees. Along the beach, I spotted a form standing in solitude dressed in plain silk which I assumed to be her. Circe was striking, tall and slim, her skin an unblemished golden beige. Her unconfined dark hair highlighted her azure eyes which pierced through the downpour, examining the crew. As they met mine, I unwittingly glanced at my feet. The aura she bore was undoubtedly divine. Grasping the fleece, I followed Jason into a rowboat with four other Argonauts and we made our way to her shores. With a suppressed *chink* of metal, Jason subtly placed his hand on the hilt of his sword as we got closer to the shoreline. Confused, I followed his gaze. Barely noticeable movements scurried across the greenwood.

"Medea, my brother's fleece fits you well. It seems the chambers of Colchis were never truly its home." Circe's voice was smooth, yet rich like aged wine. Bewildered by her recognition of me, I smiled nervously. Jason stepped onto the wet sand, paying Circe little attention as he offered his hand to me. I accepted and joined him by his side.

"Forgive the intrusion," Jason said. "Pleasure to meet —"

"There is no pleasure being drenched under this curse," Circe interrupted, swaying her hand to indicate her wet clothes clinging to her body. "I do not remember sending you an invitation."

"I am Jason of the Argonauts," he said haughtily, allowing an annoyed glare to escape his eyes.

"Am I supposed to know who that is?" she retorted mockingly.

I stepped back towards the water, startled as a pride of lions slowly emerged from the greenery, steadily encircling our group, their movement tactical and their eyes hungry. With a loud *shing*, Jason unsheathed his steel sword. Circe's eyebrows narrowed and she glanced back at the lions, unfazed by their approach. My eyes widened in awe as, with a simple snap of Circe's fingers, all the lions fell limp onto the sand as if their souls had been plucked from their bodies. Circe's eyes met mine and anxiety flooded my lungs.

"The Golden Fleece must be brought to Iolcus," I said. "After taking it from your brother, I was cursed by Zeus. Bless us and we shall repay you for your kindness. I implore you."

"*Implore?*" Circe highlighted with a smile. She could tell we were desperate. "I need nothing. I will bless you and you all will leave me in peace." I was taken aback.

"But Zeus would not curse the daughter of a king for simply *stealing*," she continued, staring me down as if omniscient of my sin. She's bluffing, she must be. Unflinching, I glared back.

"Zeus has done worse for less," Jason interjected, attempting to shift her focus off me. Her eyebrows raised in morbid curiosity; eyes still locked with mine. "Zeus *has* done worse," she agreed.

Jason lifted his blade towards Circe as she started to make her way towards me. "*Let's both keep our animals under control*" is what her stare told me. I calmly touched Jason's shoulder and with hesitation, he lowered his blade. Circe smirked at Jason as she passed him. An overripe scent churned my stomach as she pulled out a vial of dark green viscous liquid. Eyes shut, she drank the putrid concoction and suddenly gripped my forehead with one hand. I felt a second heart hidden deep within me die. Breath escaped the Argonauts as the storm above our heads was cut perfectly in half like a knife through butter, rays of sunset violets illuminating Aeaea.

My eyes followed Circe's and saw she was observing patterns in the shifting clouds. There was a fantastical element to them I was unfamiliar with. "This spell is complex. I cannot in good conscience recommend sailing immediately. If the storm doesn't return by morning, you are safe." Astonished but still troubled, Jason sheathed his sword. With a wave of her finger, Circe resurrected the lions from death. She turned and started to make her way into the forest, the lions following her. "I have enough wine to satisfy your crew if that's what you're so worried about," she called out without looking back.

A group of the Argonauts were assigned to look after the ship while the rest dined with Circe. She had a seemingly endless supply of wine along with platters of dried meats and rich breads. Due to my unease at the removal of the curse, I wasn't inclined to drink that night. I did, however, build up the confidence to walk over to where Circe sat on a broken throne, flanked by a myriad of animals. Her eyes flicked up when I approached and she gave me a soft smile.

BLOOD STAINS THE GOLDEN FLEECE

"I never knew potions could dispel such curses," I said. Invested, she leaned forward on her throne.

"You seem to be knowledgeable of pharmakeia." I nodded quickly.

"Is my niece a witch?" Circe exclaimed with a grin on her face. "It's a shame you have to leave so soon."

It was a shame.

"Circe, how did you recognize me at the beach?" I found the courage to ask. "I don't remember meeting you before."

"You sail on a talking ship, my dear. That is much stranger than knowing what my niece looks like."

Circe could see I was dissatisfied with her answer. "I have visions," she sighed. "I believe my father taunts me by showing me Colchis. I wish not to speak of it."

"Of course." With a nod, I left. Imagining her hurt filled my heart with pity. Outside, I found where the guests had set up their camp and I lay next to Jason, already asleep under the stars. I matched my breath with his and I let myself sink into an abyss. Within the currents of my mind, I felt a strong pressure against my ribs as if a large animal had stepped on me. I was helpless in this darkness. Something sharp and warm pierced my skull and tore my head from my neck.

* * *

I wish I could've gifted a dream eternal to Medea, then she wouldn't have to face the suffering that awaited her. A suffering I knew too well. The Argo had left my shores while Medea slept. Fleeceless and recently stirred, the fledgling sorceress emerged from the forest. One of her fists was clenched in front of her chest as if she was keeping her heart steady, expecting it to fall out at any moment. Eyes wide and unbelieving she joined my side staring blankly at the empty horizon. Her jaw clenched and her face tightened. Medea failed to hide that she was flooded with sorrowful confusion. Not wasting any time, she turned back towards the forest screaming for her lover. "You promised to take my hand!" she cried. "You promised to find me a new home!" Her vulnerable screams echoed across the island, heard only by my animals and me.

She was a fool to fall for a man like Jason. 'Heroes' tend to be avaricious. On the other hand, however, I felt a deep sense of pity for Medea. Whatever she had done to help Jason escape with the fleece must have caused her great suffering. I found Medea collapsed atop a patch of grass, curled up like a child. The lions had already found her and were gently nudging their noses against her back. She clawed at the dirt, hiding her face.

With a quick wave, I made the lions back off, giving her some space. I planted myself at the base of a tree close to her. "Many years ago, I fell deeply in love with a sea-god," I said. Medea stayed silent and unmoving. "He was named Glaucus. Similarly to you, he was enraptured. Fallen for a nymph named Scylla. He came to me asking for a potion to trick this nymph into falling in love with him."

"He *knew* I loved him," I continued. "I said to him, '*Chase after someone who shares the same purposes and wishes as yours, and who was captured by equal passion. Though I am a demi-goddess, daughter of Helios, though I possess such powers of herbs and charms, I promise to be yours.'* And as if he wanted to see me hurt, cutting as deep as he could go, he then said to me, *'Leaves will grow on the waters, and seaweed will grow on the hills, long before I will stop loving Scylla.'* I was naive when I was younger. I didn't understand that people would use me for the miracles I could offer them. He *broke* me, so I ruined him." A resentful fury escaped me as I retold my story.

I looked back up in surprise as Medea rolled across the grass, revealing her face. Her eyes were red from crying; she stared up at the sky. "What did you do?" she whispered.

A part of me was glad she took an interest. "In reality, Scylla was afraid of Glaucus, terrified of his appearance," I explained. "I made Glaucus experience that same fear. Late at night, I poured poison into the pool where she bathed. I transformed her into a hideous creature."

For the first time that day, Medea looked me in the eyes. "Why go so far?" she asked. I wasn't sure of the answer myself.

Shrugging, I said, "Love is violent, Medea."

Medea sighed deeply. Her eyes glazed, lost in her thoughts.

"Why does love turn one into a conduit of evil?" she finally said in a remorseful tone.

"What do you mean?"

"I killed my brother for him, Circe." A wave of nausea hit me. *Stupid girl*, to murder your brother in the name of love?

"A vision came to me before you arrived on this island," I said. "During my morning routine, the weather darkened to an unnatural hue. I went to the beach to get a better look at the incoming clouds. The sea was red with blood." My eyes grew wide recalling the vision. The details were vivid in my mind. "Pieces of a dismembered corpse washed up onto my shores." Circe's face paled. "Was it my nephew, Medea? Is he truly…" Circe nodded.

"He cornered us on the Brygean Islands," she said in barely a whisper. "Apsyrtus promised us that if we handed him the Golden Fleece and returned with him, he would resolve the issue with my father. He was my brother. I had known him since the day I was born but yet for some reason, I couldn't bring myself to believe him. Aeëtes was convinced that Jason was conspiring to take his kingdom away, he would have surely killed him if he'd had the chance. Fearing so strongly for Jason's life I let myself be blinded by love. I remember luring Apsyrtus onto the Argo, poisoning him, and then dismembering his body and throwing each piece into the ocean. I planned it all quickly, desperately, as he followed me to the Argo. I knew what had to be done. My father wouldn't follow us until he had picked up all the pieces. We had many ships on our tail. We would all have been killed if I hadn't done what needed to be done."

"Circe, love does not act that fatally, that swiftly. Does it?" I shook my head. Again, she was lost in her thoughts. I waited patiently for her to gather them.

After a few minutes of silence, she spoke. "Jason once told me that the gods assisted him at every step of his journey. It was why he was always so confident. The Argo acted as an

BLOOD STAINS THE GOLDEN FLEECE

oracle of Hera, guiding them. He ran into me before he met my father. The king's daughter, the witch with the power to steal the Golden Fleece that night. Did he mean to meet me there on that staircase? And was I meant to--?"

"Fall in love the moment you set eyes on him," I finished. It was quite the theory. Tragic if true. She fell dead silent. Poor girl. I knew what it felt like for the gods to manipulate your life.

I softly touched her face. "They used you, my dear. I'm sorry," I said simply. The well of emotion that built up within Medea throughout the day seemed to flood over her. There was no more need to share words. I held her tightly, shielding her like a loving mother would. She wasn't able to breathe with how heavily she sobbed. With me, she was going to be alright. I would protect her.

"I'm so sorry, Medea," I whispered.

"I can't go back home," she stuttered, "not after what I've done."

"It's okay, I can make room for you here." She hugged me back, her face was warm. "No one can find you here."

"He will suffer for what he's done. Hera cannot stop me," she spat.

"I would prefer you to stay," I said softly, allowing a small smile to paint my face. "But if you ever leave this island to go searching for Jason and everything you said is proven to be true, do what I should have done to Glaucus: *kill him*. Make him suffer for what he has done to you."

Circe stared blankly past my shoulder for a moment before nodding.

❈ 355 ❈

"While you are here with me," I held her hands tight, "you have the precious opportunity to become whomever you wish to be. Don't waste it."

She nodded again.

* * *

I was detached from my sense of reality, like a dissociated spirit watching my body from above. Did the gods truly trick me into falling deep within a pit of my obsession to the point that I lost everything? Was Jason feigning love to get the Golden Fleece? How did I not see this? Circe genuinely cared for my well-being, for better or for worse. She knew about my disgusting sin yet she didn't send me away, instead she wanted to help me. Was she so isolated that even the company of a murderer would satisfy her loneliness? In truth, we were both abandoned and together we were suffering for it. Was I right about Jason, truly? Was there a layer to this story I had no control over? If so then I could not dream to match the cruelty of the gods.

Weeks passed. Circe told me that she redirected the passing fleets to follow the Argo, they had no idea I was left behind. Over the past few days, I had become enchanted by the beauty of Aeaea. It helped me to forget about the lands over the waters if I simply let the island take me. The Argonauts had left but the pain hadn't. I felt my chest tear at every dawn, the rising sun cruelly reminding me of the morning I could never forget. In a kind attempt to distract me from my depression, Circe spent all of her time with me. She showed me the beautiful hidden nature of the island. In the evenings she taught me the depths of witchcraft and shared old tales. The eagerly playful animals under her protection distracted me whenever I was lost in my thoughts.

One evening in the middle of a stroll across one of the many trails, the skies turned an ashen black. "Circe will free us…" the skies roared. I recognized the creaking of wood within its voice. The Argo was speaking to me. Was I witnessing a vision? Swirling with a violent motion, the clouds formed a figure covered in shadows throwing a locked chest off a cliff into the raging waters beneath. I snapped out of the vision, stunned. The sky turned back to its normal evening hue as if nothing had changed. Hurriedly, I sprinted down the side of the island trying not to trip on any rocks, arriving at the location the vision had shown. A shimmering golden glow passed through the thick waters crashing against the jagged rocks of the shoreline. Without thinking, I entered the harsh currents. Was it Circe I had seen in my vision? What was she trying to discard? I dove beneath the tide, my body thrown side to side with magnificent force. Sharp rocks cut my skin as I descended deeper. The chest was wedged between two rocks and the top was broken from the drop, its contents barely visible. I opened the chest, and my heart sank as my eyes adjusted to the glow under the water. The Golden Fleece lay at the bottom of the chest. The Argo, reduced to the size of a skull, weighing it down. "Circe will free us…" the Argo spoke once again, its voice reverberating the water around it.

I gasped loudly as I broke the water's surface, Fleece and miniature ship in hand. Exhausted, I crawled onto the shore, my body cut and bloodied. I lifted the drenched Fleece in front of me; it gleamed against the setting sun. The Golden Fleece, that Jason would have never left without. The Argonauts, Jason, did they ever leave Aeaea? My head spun. Circe tried to hide this from me. I heard the shuffling of leaves behind me. Quickly spinning around, I was just able to spot a brown bear disappearing into the forest. I adorned the Fleece once again, picking up a hefty rock from the shoreline as I entered the foliage.

I doggedly pursued the bear through the forest, blood dripping from the numerous cuts across my body staining the Golden Fleece with a deep crimson. My mind felt narrow-sighted, fury driving my intent to get to Circe. She had lied to me, now she was forcing my hand like my brother had. Maybe she'd suffer the same fate once I was done with her. Hera hadn't been the one manipulating me, it was her, it was always her. The bear disappeared behind the main ruins, past where the Argonauts had dined a few months before. Hopping over rubble I saw her. Circe, wearing an expression of curiosity as the bear approached her. She glanced upwards and saw me. I lifted the stained Golden Fleece in front of me and dropped it on the floor. Eyes wide, she stood her ground as I walked towards her. I tightly gripped the rock in my right hand. "Medea," she stammered. Hearing the fear escape her voice emboldened me. "How did--?"

I struck her across the jaw and with a shriek she fell to the floor holding her face, blood dripping from her mouth. I stepped forcefully onto her chest so she couldn't move. Tears escaped from her eyes as she reached her hand up towards me. I swatted it away. The trees rustled behind me as Circe's animals emerged from their hiding places. The bear's deep growls cut as Circe snapped her fingers. It writhed with pain on the floor.

"Did you kill Jason?" I snapped.

"Medea," Circe whispered. "I would never--"

"Show me where he is."

"Hera has taken your mind."

I stepped off Circe. She desperately tried to catch her breath and get to her feet. With a loud crack I slammed the rock into her cheek and she fell once again. She was barely conscious as I crawled on top of her, pinning her down.

"Your loneliness eats your heart, doesn't it, Circe?" I said softly, raising the rock one final time.

"Is this what your brother saw before he died?" she spat through her broken teeth. I froze in place. Pain coursed through my body as a force bludgeoned me to the ground beside Circe. The bear tackled me, biting my arm and forcing me to drop the rock I wielded. I screamed in agony as it started to claw into my back.

"Stop!" Circe commanded. The bear immediately let go of my marred arm. She wobbled to her feet and stood over me. Sorrow painted her face. With a simple lift of her hand, a multitude of the surrounding animals transformed into soldiers. The bear changed to Jason, beaten and bloodied. "Just leave," she said, defeated.

Jason was shaken. He stumbled to his feet clutching the hilt of his sword. "You're mad!" he yelled. One glare from Circe was all it took for Jason to fall on his back in fear. "The gods are mad!" she bellowed.

"Is killing me the only way to satisfy you? Isn't *this* enough?"

"My hands are not worthy of killing you. They are not cruel enough," I said weakly, turning towards the beach. Circe's face paled with guilt.

"He's going to betray you, Medea."

Without another word, the Argonauts grabbed their belongings, placed the Argo back onto the shore where it expanded into its original size and we sailed away from Aeaea. Looking back to the shore I saw a form fall to her knees in despair.

* * *

Nightmares come in strange forms, Medea. We were lost deep in a wood I didn't recognize. The sun was setting. When I reminisced about Aeaea, a voice whispered to me that we would die in that forest. I tried to warn you, drag you to make our way out but you didn't budge. Eyes glazed over; you were not in your mind. Then I saw death. A giant brown bear prowling the woods, a monster not under my control. Immediately, I dropped to the floor. You stood unfazed, starting to walk out in the open as if you were trying to be spotted. It reared its massive head towards you, jaw slack and drooling. Moments later I watched in horror as it charged, you simply stood your ground. Maybe you imagined it would be intimidated by your presence, but I believe you had just accepted your fate. The unstoppable force toppled you, pinning you to the floor only a few feet away from me. I watched as its paws crushed your chest and began to wrap its jaw around your head. Some part of me, despite all my fear, let out a yelp to attempt to grab its attention. It ignored me and tore your head from your neck. Only a second later it responded to my rebellious cry. Right before it overpowered me, I woke up nauseous. My heart beating rapidly. Although I wasn't dreaming anymore, I could hear what my last whimper sounded like. It was pitiful.

Years have passed since I last saw you. But when I stood among the ocean which imprisoned me, I realized the truth: that a witch's true purpose is to burn the ocean for the one she loves. But whether it was born out of love or pity, *you* didn't kill me. When I woke this morning to more bodies on my shore, they were those of Jason and his children.

Poor Medea. You broke just like me, didn't you?

Biographies

L.D. Burke

Rise of the Witches

(First Publication)

L.D. Burke is an award-winning journalist and speculative fiction writer. She fell in love with fantasy stories as a child while sitting on her grandfather's lap for story time and again as a teen reading fantasy romance novels with her grandmother. She is a member of Wulf Moon's Wulf Pack Writers and David Farland's Apex-Writers. Find her at ldburke.com

Z.D. Campbell

Darkness

(First Publication)

'Darkness' is Z.D. Campbell's first publication. He is excited and honored to join the prestigious world of published authors. The majority of Campbell's life has been in academia. He obtained a Masters of Fine Arts in Theater in 2017 and a Bachelor of Science in Psychology in 2015. He would like to thank his friends, family, and partner for all the love and support.

C.B. Channell

A Mother's Blessing

(First Publication)

C.B. Channell is a Chicago-based author who spends part of each year in Los Angeles. She has a B.A. in Anthropology and has always had a passion for mythology and folklore. She has previously published an assortment of short fantasy, horror, and mystery. This is her second appearance with Flame Tree Publishing.

Imogen Dalton

Ancient & Modern: Introducing Circe

Imogen Dalton is an academic of classical studies, specializing in mythology.

BIOGRAPHIES

As a freelance writer she has worked on articles and magazines on the subjects of mythology, spirituality and theology. Her interests also cover mythology from other ancient societies such as Norse, Celtic and Egyptian. Her background as an artist and a holistic therapist gives her a unique perspective on the energetics and rituals associated with ancient religions. She also has a YouTube channel where she discusses myth, religion and rituals.

Mason Graham
No Good Curse
(First Publication)
Mason Graham is a writer, researcher and musician currently based in Los Angeles, California. He is new to short fiction, but has long been experimenting with narrative and emotionally evocative imagery in his songwriting. He studied Ancient and Medieval History in graduate school, and has brought his fascination with mythology, religion and linguistics into all of his creative pursuits. He is committed to exploring the rich and varied perspectives of modern humanity through the scope of classical myth and traditional fantasy.

Kay Hanifen
The Island of Pigs
(First Publication)
Kay Hanifen was born on Friday the 13th and once lived for three months in a haunted castle. So, obviously, she had to become a horror writer. Her work has appeared in over fifty anthologies and magazines. When she's not consuming pop culture with the voraciousness of a vampire at a 24-hour blood bank, you can usually find her with her black cats or at kayhanifenauthor.wordpress.com.

M.J. Harris
Something New
(First Publication)
M.J. Harris is a writer and illustrator from England. Their interests are in religion and the impact of illness and disability on ancient societies, aiming to highlight diverse narratives, especially in classical literature where often only a singular perspective is considered. They previously won the

363

St. John's College Oxford Classics and Ancient History Essay competition with their discussion of community in ancient Greek, Roman, Mayan and Mesopotamian civilizations, before exploring wider narratives in classical reception.

Elena Kotsile
This Slow Death
(First Publication)
Elena Kotsile (pen name) is a science editor and a neurodivergent ESL writer based in Berlin, Germany. Her creative works are forthcoming or have appeared in various international and Greek journals and anthologies (e.g. *Baubles From Bones, If There's Anyone Left, The Future Fire, Air & Nothingness Press, Acropolis Journal*). Besides scientific articles, she writes poetry and fiction in English and Greek. Nominated for the Rhysling Award and Best of Net.

Elizabeth Roberts
Prove Them All Right
(First Publication)
Elizabeth graduated from the University of Oregon but attended the University of East Anglia during a study abroad and would love to live in the United Kingdom again someday. After graduating, she started a teaching program and is currently studying to be a teacher. She loves literature, especially Greek myths, and has always had stories and ideas in her head about writing, but this will be her first publication.

Dr Ellie Mackin Roberts
Foreword
Ellie Mackin Roberts is a Material Religion Research and Engagement Fellow, and Research Fellow at the University of Bristol. Ellie's main research interests involve the material culture and art of ancient Greece, particularly archaic and classical Greek religion, including the role of women in the religious landscape of the ancient Greek city. Her popular history books include *Heroines of Olympus: The Women of Greek Mythology* and *Brief Histories: Ancient Greece*. She makes Greek mythology and history videos for a general audience on TikTok.

BIOGRAPHIES

Claire L. Marsh
Shifting Destinies
(First Publication)
Claire writes fantasy and horror stories generally, from flash fiction to short stories. Her background in lecturing forensic psychology often reveals itself in complex, challenging characters with figurative or literal demons. When she's not writing, Claire works as a civil servant, helping to create evidence-based standards for policing practice throughout the UK. She's a Globe Soup member and micro competition winner, and has stories shortlisted on Reedsy, on MockingOwl Roost, Literally Stories, Spillwords, 101 words and elsewhere.

Erin Murphy
Pork
(First Publication)
Erin Murphy is a young author, originally from the US, now living and attending graduate school in Tokyo, Japan. She hopes to study myth and folklore from around the world but has a special place in her heart for the myths of ancient Greece. In her free time away from the keyboard and classes, she loves to sew, play video and tabletop games, and study myth for her own hopeful book in the future!

Lourdes Ureña Pérez
A Friend Made of Clay
(First Publication)
Lourdes was born in 1997 in Spain. She developed a love for stories early on and found a way to stick to that passion in every area of her life as an avid reader, tireless writer, and professional literary translator. As an English teacher, she also brings her love for literature into the classroom. A jack-of-all-trades, her hobbies are numerous and diverse, but always moved by the same impulse to create something new.

Zach Shephard
From Darkness, Awake
(First Publication)
Zach Shephard lives in Enumclaw, Washington, where he dreams up fantasy, science fiction and horror stories. He frequently uses mythology in his writing, because it's a lot easier to explain bizarre plot choices

when capricious deities are at work. His fiction has appeared in *Fantasy & Science Fiction*, the *Unidentified Funny Objects* anthology series, and several of Flame Tree Publishing's books – including *Medusa*, where he got to reimagine another misunderstood mythological character. For more of Zach's work, check out www.zachshephard.com.

Jamie Simpher

The Circead
(First Publication)
Jamie Simpher graduated from the University of Iowa in 2014. She spent nearly a decade writing ads, but recently left that world to pursue an MFA in creative writing at the University of Alaska Fairbanks. One day she aspires to be a swashbuckling pirate captain sailing the high seas. Her poetry has been published in *Small Wonders Magazine* and nominated for a Rhysling Award, and she has been named a finalist in several short fiction contests.

Theresa Tyree

The Perfect Distance
(First Publication)
Theresa (they/she) is a queer nonbinary Greek woman who grew up dreaming of magic amongst the trees in the American Pacific Northwest. She makes her home near Portland, Oregon with their platonic life partner and cat, and spends their days coming up with new stories of queer perseverance and hope. She has particular interest in writing the 'missing scenes' of Greek mythology that empower marginalized people and add to her own heritage.

Mathieu W.R. Wallis

Blood Stains the Golden Fleece
(First Publication)
Ever since he crawled out of the Canadian snowfall, as all Canadians are born, Mathieu has strived to write stories that inspire others in the same way that books and film continuously fuel his creativity. From silly stories in elementary to the sweeping arcs in tabletop games with his friends, he always writes. At 23 years old, this is his first published story. Inspirations for this retelling include Robert Eggers' *The Lighthouse* and Madeline Miller's *Circe*.

Myths, Gods & Immortals

Discover the mythology of humankind through its heroes, characters, gods and immortal figures. **Myths, Gods and Immortals** brings together the new and the ancient, familiar stories with a fresh and imaginative twist. Each book brings back to life a legendary, mythological or folkloric figure, with completely new stories alongside the original tales and a comprehensive introduction which emphasizes ancient and modern connections, tracing history and stories across continents, cultures and peoples.

Flame Tree Fiction

A wide range of new and classic fiction, from myth to modern stories, with tales from the distant past to the far future, including short story anthologies, **Beyond & Within**, **Collector's Editions**, **Collectable Classics**, **Gothic Fantasy collections** and **Epic Tales** of mythology and folklore.

Available at all good bookstores, and online at flametreepublishing.com

Myths, Gods & Immortals
Circe
New & Ancient Greek Tales

This is a FLAME TREE Book

Publisher & Creative Director: Nick Wells
Editorial Director: Catherine Taylor
Editorial Board: Gillian Whitaker, Catherine Taylor, Jocelyn Pontes, Simran Aulakh, Jemma North and Beatrix Ambery

FLAME TREE PUBLISHING
6 Melbray Mews, Fulham,
London SW6 3NS, United Kingdom
www.flametreepublishing.com

First published 2025

Copyright in each story is held by the individual authors
Introduction and Volume copyright © 2025 Flame Tree Publishing Ltd

Quotations from Homer's *Odyssey* are from Samuel Butler's 1900
translation (second edition, 1921), and those from Ovid's *Metamorphoses*
are from Henry T. Riley's 1851 translation (Books VIII–XV, George Bell &
Sons, 1893).

25 27 29 30 28 26
1 3 5 7 9 10 8 6 4 2

ISBN: 978-1-80417-933-5

All rights reserved. No part of this publication may be reproduced, stored in a retrieval system, or transmitted in any form or by any means, electronic, mechanical, photocopying, recording or otherwise, without the prior written permission of the publisher.

Publisher's Note: The stories within this book are works of fiction. Names, characters, places, and incidents are products of the authors' imaginations. Locales and public names are sometimes used for atmospheric purposes. Any resemblance to actual people, living or dead, or to businesses, companies, events, institutions, or locales is completely coincidental.

Content Note: The stories in this book may contain descriptions of, or references to, difficult subjects such as violence, death and rape, but always contextualized within the setting of mythic narrative, archetype and metaphor. Similarly, language can sometimes be strong but is at the artistic discretion of the authors.

Cover art by Flame Tree Studio based on elements from Shutterstock.com: Kiselev Andrey Valerevich, Kozlik, Olek Lu, Tiny Art, WinWin artlab

A copy of the CIP data for this book is available from the British Library.

Printed and bound in China